Cross My Heart
A Philosophical Romance
By
Emma Browne

Dedication

To all you women who want to change the world: go for it!

Chapter 1

Julia

When I came home to my cosy flat in Edinburgh after spending a year in Kenya, the last person I expected to see sitting on my living room couch was Nick.

But there he was.

He wore a grey T-shirt with a tight pair of jeans, looking as though he didn't have a care in the world. His long dark hair was tied up in a man bun, and there was a small pencil behind his ear. His short, scruffy beard just added to his relaxed appearance.

Startled, I shook my head and decided it couldn't be him. Maybe I was just imagining Nick sitting in my living room. Maybe I was so tired, I was seeing things.

One could only hope.

Then he looked up from his laptop, his eyes twinkled when he saw me. 'Hi.'

Nope. I wasn't making it up. Somehow Nick was sitting in my living room.

I shrieked. Or, maybe it was more like a yelp.

Nick scrunched his eyebrows and tilted his head to one side, biting his lip as if to hide a smile.

Nick was not my favourite person. I would say I *never* had liked him, but that wouldn't be strictly true, as I did go through a phase of fancying myself quite in love with him. Still, that passed, and soon we'd developed a rather more hostile relationship. And though I was surprised and decidedly unhappy to see him on my couch, he was one of my brother's best friends, so not exactly a threat.

To anything but my sanity.

I took a deep breath as warring emotions washed through me. Surprise was swallowed by attraction, which was (quickly) pushed aside by irritation. Why was he there? Why did he seem so comfortable on my couch? Why was he there? How did he get access to my flat? *Why was he there?*

Deciding I was too tired to deal with the questions now, I pushed the emotions aside, set down my backpack, and got my frozen pizza out of the carrier bag so I could go put it in the oven.

'Huh, you look like you've seen better days.' His American accent had softened somewhat over the almost ten years he'd spent in Scotland, but it was still distinctly there.

I guessed my tired, frazzled look wasn't a hit.

'Yes. In fact, I consider most days where I don't come home after travelling for thirty-six hours to find you on my couch 'better days."' I sneered. Whilst I was a mess – I had a coffee stain on my shirt, my curly, red hair had given up on the braid a long time ago, and I'm pretty sure my mascara was smeared around my eyes – Nick was…not.

Of course he wasn't. Nick was never a mess.

No matter how hard he worked on the football pitch, or how dirty he was from being on his job site where he worked as site manager or something on construction projects, he was never a mess. Dirt and sweat just added to his physical appeal. And, let's be real: despite being over my crush for a long time, I was still a little (a lot) attracted to his looks.

'Wow, I missed you too.' Nick grinned and rubbed his hand over his chest as though his heart hurt.

'Uh-huh, sure.' I rolled my eyes at him. I was hungry and sweaty, my hair was a mess, and I was tired enough to fall asleep standing up. All I'd been able to think of for the past hour was how I would put the pizza in the oven, have a quick shower, eat dinner, and go to bed. I might even skip the shower. I didn't have the patience to play nice with the guy who had done everything possible to be a thorn in my side for the last nine years.

I stepped over his laptop cord and walked toward the kitchen to put the pizza in the oven. I stopped in the door and took in the mess. The cupboards and counters had been ripped out and were partway through being replaced. It was a construction site. It looked like there were new tiles on the wall, and the sink was definitely new.

'About the kitchen,' Nick said, coming up behind me as I took in the destruction formerly known as my kitchen.

'Wow…' I cleared my throat and looked around with wide eyes as I grasped for words. 'Where are my hard hat and steel-toe boots?'

'It's not that bad.' Nick looked at me cautiously. 'Really, it's just a few hours off being finished.'

'Uh-huh, or a few days. You know, either or,' I said wryly. 'Does the oven even work?' I unwrapped the pizza and went about trying to find a baking sheet to put it into the oven on. 'Gosh, I should have gotten takeout…' I muttered under my breath.

'Yeah, it works.' Nick put the oven on and took the pizza out of my hands. 'Hey, why don't you go sit down or have a shower or something? I'll sort your dinner out.'

I looked at him sceptically, but I decided I was not about to battle through a construction site in order to eat. 'I'm not sharing the pizza.'

'Mmm-hmm, Jewel, off you go.' He pointed to the bathroom with his chin. 'You'll feel better after a shower.'

Julia. My name is *Julia*.

Not Jewel.

Nobody else called me Jewel, and it drove me crazy that Nick would. I'd thought ignoring it would make him stop, but after nine years, it was still what he called me. Probably because he knew it drove me up the wall. I rolled my eyes but didn't have the energy to set him straight. 'I'm going to need coffee with it, black, no sugar. I bought some.' I handed it to him. 'Dare I ask what the state of the bathroom is?'

'Sure, thing. Yeah, no worries about the bathroom. I even cleaned it the other day.'

***

As it turned out, the bathroom was clean and tidy. I found an old bottle of bubble bath in a box labelled 'Bathroom' in my bedroom and had a nice soak for about twenty minutes until Nick knocked on the door to say the pizza would be ready in ten minutes. I quickly washed my hair, using some of Nick's shampoo, which smelled a bit too much like him to be comfortable. I pulled on a pair of leggings and a loose long-sleeved shirt and wrapped my hair in a towel.

'Your pizza's just here on the table when you're ready, Jewel.' Nick pointed to the coffee table in the living room. 'Do you want a beer or anything?'

'I think a beer would put me to sleep. I'll just have a glass of water with my coffee, please. Where have all the glasses gone?' Just thinking about the mess in the kitchen made me want to give up and start crying. Nothing was where it belonged.

I must have looked a bit frazzled since Nick said, 'Calm down, Jewel.' He stroked a hand down my arm. His touch made me feel... *things*. Unable to deal with more emotions, particularly emotions I was sure weren't meant to be there, I moved away from his hand.

'The kitchen should be a quick enough job to finish.' Nick found me a glass and handed it to me with a shrug. 'Your system wasn't working for me, so I decided to rearrange things, and while I was at it, I figured I might as well upgrade the kitchen. So right now, things like plates, glasses, and stuff are in the bookshelf in the living room. I packed the rest away in those boxes until I'm done.' He pointed to the boxes lining the living room wall.

My earlier resolution not to deal with things tonight flew out the window as my warring emotions burst through. 'Right. Well, two things. One, I'm not paying for all this.' I held up a finger. 'And two, could you not have finished it before I got home? How long have you been living here? *Why* are you living here? And why wait until you were just about to move out to renovate the kitchen?' I shook my head and went to fill my glass with water. I sat down on the couch. I felt a headache coming on.

'Yeah, of course, I'm not expecting you to pay. Why would I?' Nick frowned and shook his head as though I was being stupid.

I took a bite of pizza to stop my tummy from grumbling. It was just a simple ham and pineapple pizza, but it tasted so good after having airplane food and snacking on cashews for too long. 'I assume you cleared this with my parents, in any case.' My parents did technically own the flat and had been taking care of it when I was away.

Or so they'd said.

7

Turns out their taking care of the flat meant letting Nick move in and renovate it.

'And to be fair, we weren't expecting you until tomorrow.' He went on as though I hadn't spoken. 'I'm sure that's what your mum said.'

'Yeah. Mum got it wrong.' My mum never had been great with details.

I looked around at the mess. There were boxes with food and kitchenware all over the lounge, and the kitchen had one cupboard in place and sawdust on the floor. 'In any case, there is no way you would have had that sorted by tomorrow.' I waved one hand at the mess and used my other hand to stuff my mouth with pizza. 'Just look at it!'

'It'll look great when it's done, though. You'll see.' He smiled confidently.

'Uh-huh…' I groaned around the pizza and reached for another slice. Nick reached for one too, and I slapped his hands away. 'Not sharing.'

'Oh, come on, seriously?' He raised his eyebrows and sat back with his beer. 'Scrooge.'

'Get your own.' I sighed. 'When are you moving out?'

He looked at me with a funny expression. 'We'll see, I guess.'

I returned his funny look with one of my own. 'Right, because I want my flat back. So, no rush, but as soon as possible would be good.' I longed to have the flat to myself and not have to deal with the pesky butterflies his cheeky grin conjured up in my stomach.

He took the last sip of his beer and raised his eyebrow. 'Do you want me to finish the kitchen first, though?'

'Ha-ha, very funny.'

He smiled as he unfolded himself from the armchair and stretched his tall, lean body. I looked away, refusing to be drawn in by his muscles, and tried to focus on the pizza.

Nick reached for his empty beer bottle and went into the kitchen. He put some old Jack Johnson music on and got to work. I finished eating and tried to ignore him altogether— something I found was easier said than done. After not being around him for a year, one might have thought some of my annoyance with him might have shifted. But, no. Somehow, I hadn't been back for two hours, and the insufferable guy was already back up my nose.

Chapter 2

Nick

I used to think there were two kinds of people in this world: the kind-hearted and the mean. I found both difficult, but perhaps the mean ones were easier. If you knew someone was mean you could cut them out emotionally, something I was an expert at, having grown up with a mean dad.

The kind ones were more difficult. Their kindness could trick you to believing you could trust them, but for reasons outside of their control you could still end up hurt if you weren't careful. Mom had been like that. Her heart was kind and I remember feeling safe with her. Then she died and left me alone with Dad.

If I knew whether a person was good or bad, though, I knew how to relate to them. As that made life easier, I stuck with it.

Then I met Julia.

To begin with, I wouldn't have noticed her had it not been for her crazy red hair. Her hair was wild and no matter what she did to it, it didn't seem to comply but had its own life. Otherwise though, Julia seemed like any other sixteen-year-old girl. She was shy around me at first; she'd blush whenever I spoke to her, but she was always kind. And, since her brother Jack, our friend Michael, and I would hang out at Jack's parents' house quite a bit – we were growing men after all, and Mrs Reid's food was to die for – I saw Julia a lot.

I wasn't sure what to think when, seemingly out of nowhere, Julia started giving me cutting remarks. I'd known her as the meek girl who treated everyone kindly, and suddenly she'd say things like, 'What are *you* doing here? Did someone leave your cage open?' Or, 'Nick, as an outsider, what do *you* think of the human race?' She treated everyone else like they were her BFF, but me like I was… *an enemy?* I wondered if she was joking or if I'd done something wrong. Playing dumb, 1 laughed off her comments, but they kept on coming, so I started responding with remarks of my own.

11

As she no longer fit the box of being the kind girl I had neatly put her in, I found that maybe my black and white thinking around people being good or bad was a little too simplistic.

It wasn't long before I realised that maybe Julia didn't hate me as much as her comments would have me believe. In fact, I started suspecting that the opposite might be true. And, being honest here, I started *liking* the way her mean comments were only directed toward me. I felt singled out by her. In a good way.

I know. Crazy.

But as I got to know her more, I started seeing her differently. Her wild hair matched the passionate, strong woman she was. She was adventurous and daring, but, more than that, her passion seemed to be contagious. She had a knack for finding causes and then fighting for them with everything she had – sometimes to her own detriment. She would talk so engagingly about whatever cause she was working for that people couldn't help but get involved.

I loved her passion and zeal, even though I sometimes questioned her motives. I wasn't sure she was as good as she wanted people to think.

People said she would be a politician or a preacher, but I think she cared too much about the individual to be so focussed on the masses. When she went to university to be a high school teacher – or, like they say in Scotland, a secondary school teacher – it seemed right. And I knew the teenagers she taught loved her.

Most people did.

As Jack and Michael became the first true friends I'd ever had, I started feeling like I had family for the first time in my life. Up until then, the friends I'd had were guys who were more interested in what gadgets I could buy them than they were in me. Coming from a dysfunctional family, I had few people who seemed to care about me as a person. But somehow Jack's parents, Mr and Mrs Reid, became John and Karen to me and they treated me much like I was their own son.

Still, Julia would never be like a sister to me.

Maybe our cutting comments were easier than dealing with actual real feelings, particularly as nothing would ever go anywhere.

So we kept on fighting, both of us trying to best each other and coming up with practical jokes for each other. And while it might not have been the most mature approach – and by now we were 28 and 26 years old and should probably start thinking about growing up a little – it was the safer option. I wasn't about to change the way we interacted. She was the kind of girl a guy keeps hold of, and a long term relationship just wasn't in my future.

Julia being back a day early was a surprise, but a welcome one. In fact, the way the mess in the kitchen annoyed her told me we were already back on our safe, wrong foot with each other. Now I would just have to walk the line of keeping her close enough, yet far enough away.

Piece of cake.

Yeah, ok. Maybe not.

Her rumpled appearance, messy hair and exasperated eyes as she'd looked around the kitchen had made me feel like pulling her in for a hug and stroking her hair instead of pushing her away. Then, after her shower, hair tamed and in relaxed clothes, I'd had the urge to smell her neck. Still, I was stronger than unhelpful urges like that and busied myself with the kitchen instead.

She spent the afternoon in her bedroom, presumably unpacking and it was a couple of hours later when I hollered from the kitchen, 'Jewel!'

I smiled to myself. She hated when I called her that.

'Yes, my gemstone,' came her reply in a syrupy tone as she entered the kitchen. 'Did you need me?'

I hid my smile and looked up at her from where I was working on hanging a cupboard door. 'I was just going to see if you wanted anything to eat? I'm going to cook up some pasta, and I can make enough for you if you want.'

'Yeah, okay. Sure, thanks.' She sighed and put a hand to her stomach as if to stave off hunger. 'Do you need help?' She tapped the side of her head with a meaningful look, 'I mean, I know you do need help, mentally—but I'm offering help to cook or chop or something now, not the kind of help you really need. Sorry about that.'

'You're too kind.' Turning to the fridge, I started pulling out some mince and vegetables. I passed her some vegetables, a sharp knife, and a chopping board. 'Not sure if it's safe to give you a knife, but you can chop these. Just small pieces will be fine. Onion first, please.'

Smirking, she took the chopping board and brought it into the living room, as there was no counter in the kitchen. I changed the music to some instrumental swing jazz that reminded me of eating in street cafes in Paris, and started frying the mince.

'So…anything new happen here?' She asked as if to fill the silence between us.

'Nothing much.' I shook my head. 'What was Kenya like?'

'Oh, you know… hot, beautiful, and intense.' She shrugged, trying to pass it off as though it was nothing. I lifted an eyebrow and waited for her to continue. 'Fine! It was amazing. I don't have words. My life has changed, and I already miss it. Happy?'

'A little testy, are we?' I looked at her sideways. 'Is that onion ready yet?'

'Yeah.' She passed me the chopping board, and I dumped the onion into the pan and gave her back the board. 'Actually, I've missed having pasta. I didn't have it at all in Kenya.'

Her admission felt like an invitation. 'Oh yeah? What did you have there?'

She was quiet for a while, as though debating whether to keep talking. I waited her out.

'Mostly a lot of maize porridge and beans. Some rice.' She sighed. 'Whenever I had time to go into town, I would sneak in to the restaurant next door to the supermarket and order fries and steak. The steak would be hammered into a thin strip and still managed to be as rubbery as a shoe sole, but it was the most 'western' thing on the menu and made me feel a little closer to home. But I haven't had pasta since leaving Scotland a year ago.' She kept chopping and was too lost in her memories to worry about any awkwardness between the two of us.

'It seems your mom missed you,' I said when she came into the kitchen with the chopped mushrooms a while later. 'But don't worry: Michael, Miranda, Sophia, and I have been going over for family dinners. In fact, last time, she mentioned something about how she likes us better than she likes you and Jack anyway.' I smirked at her as she rolled her eyes at me.

'Ah, it's so cute how you think she was serious. Clearly, she didn't want to hurt your feelings by being too excited about me coming home.' She patted me awkwardly on the back, but quickly pulled her hand away, as though she'd been burned. 'Anyway, Jack is talking about coming home soon too, so get ready to be thought of as the annoying, lesser accessory again.'

I snorted. 'Whatever you need to tell yourself to sleep at night, Jewel. It's got to be hard when your own mom doesn't even like you and your brother as much as the random stray people she's taken in.'

'Whatever. Are you ready for the water for the spaghetti yet?'

'Sure, just pour it when it's boiled.' I added a tin of chopped tomatoes and some spices to the bolognese sauce.

Julia looked out the window and toward the big-top tent pitched in the Meadows. There was a soft rain, so people weren't having picnics, but there were still plenty of park-goers about. 'I miss the sun already,' she sighed.

'Yeah. I don't know what happened to summer, but it's actually been sunny and nice here up until yesterday.'

She turned to face me again, a resigned look on her face. 'Show me where you've put my plates so I can get some out.'

I pointed to a box, and she set the table and went to sit down as we waited for the pasta to finish cooking.

15

Chapter 3

Julia

I shook myself awake when Nick said, 'Jewel, it's time to eat.'

'Stop calling me that.' Even in my exhaustion I couldn't let his nickname for me slide.

Nick snickered. 'I almost called you Drool, cause—'

'I do not drool! That's ridiculous.' I wiped my hand across my mouth just to make sure. I rubbed my neck and made a mental note to take pills before going to bed to get rid of the budding headache.

Nick set down our plates of spaghetti bolognese on the coffee table. He'd placed a salad, the garlic bread, and two glasses of water on the table already.

As I looked at the food, I started feeling quite overwhelmed. I hadn't realised how much the bolognese sauce gave a sense of home. With that realisation, part of me felt thankful to be back and to get to eat the types of food again that I had grown up with. Another part of me, though, was suddenly overwhelmed with a deep sense of loss. After eating ugali, a maize porridge, with every meal for a year, I never would have expected to miss it. But somehow, I already did.

Not wanting to let on to Nick the feelings warring inside me, I smirked and said, 'Going all out, are we? You didn't have to kill the fattened calf, you know. It's not like we like each other.'

'I've only cooked you dinner tonight so I can tell your mum I took care of you when you got home.' He winked at me.

'Suck-up.' I rolled my eyes at him. 'Are you going to eat? Actually, let's swap plates. I need to make sure you're not poisoning me here.' Considering how we had gone through a phase of playing practical jokes on each other a few years back, this wasn't as strange as it sounded. 'Take a bite, and then pass me your plate.'

He rolled his eyes back at me, but he did as I asked. The food was amazing—not that I was about to tell Nick, he already struggled to get his head through the door. I tried to pace myself,

17

but I was soon using garlic bread to mop up the last juices from the sauce on my plate. I looked up, and I saw Nick watching me with a curious look. I stopped chewing and raised my eyebrow at him. 'What?'

'You look like you haven't eaten for months.' He pointed at my almost empty plate. 'You like?'

I sighed. 'It's been a while since I've had meat, I guess. I wouldn't read into it if I were you.'

'Are you going to church tomorrow?'

I shook my head. 'No, I'm going to try to catch up on sleep, and then I'm out in the afternoon. Also, I take it you won't be going to church either, considering the mess in the kitchen.' I gave him a pointed look. 'It's a shame, though. Somebody ought to go offer prayers for your soul.'

Nick laughed. 'Yeah, I'm sure your mum will cover that. God and I are on hiatus, so he won't be getting any prayers from me.'

I looked at him in surprise and searched his face to see if he was being serious. When his eyes met mine, I decided he was. 'How long has this hiatus been going for?'

'A while. I realised that I don't think I like God much, so I decided to quit the act and stop doing all the Christian things.'

'Huh…'

Nick shrugged like it wasn't a big deal, but I could see it wasn't something he took lightly. 'Yeah, it got too much to stand in church with people and sing about how great God is, or about how much I love him, when I actually think he's a callous, evil sadist.' Nick gestured with his hands and wore a look of disdain.

I cleared my throat to give myself a chance to recover from the surprise. 'Evil sadist sounds pretty intense. Not sure I'm quite there, but I know what you mean about it all seeming a bit much.' I was surprised to be able to relate to Nick on anything, never mind on our view of God.

'What? No trying to convince me to come back from the dark side?' He shook his head and gave me a crooked smile. 'You surprise me Jewel. Where's your soapbox? After being in Africa for a year, surely you ought to take the opportunity to preach at me?'

'Yeah well, I'm not sure there's much to say,' I took some more garlic bread. 'I don't know how to make sense of the poverty and suffering I saw every day in Kenya. God seems to me to be unjust and uncaring, and I don't think I like him much right now either. I thought 'the Gospel' is meant to be good news, but it doesn't seem very good to me, you know?'

Nick laughed, 'Better not tell your mum or she'll start giving you little tracts. Last time I was there she snuck a little tract with a picture of Jesus carrying a lamb across his shoulder into my jacket pocket when I wasn't looking.'

'For real?' I snorted even as I knew Mum would definitely do something like that.

'Oh yes,' Nick nodded slowly and raised his eyebrow. 'A few weeks ago she gave me one with a white dove on it. She's pretty intent on getting me back to church.'

'Did you tell her you're not feeling it with God? Or why is she doing this?' I shook my head, feeling a little embarrassed at mum's behaviour. It wasn't the first time; my mum had always been the kind of mum to go that extra mile too far.

'No, but a couple of weeks ago she asked if I had been away or why I wasn't coming to church.' He shrugged. 'I told her I hadn't been away, I was just being a heathen. So she patted my shoulder with a sympathetic look and told me we all go through ups and downs, but the Lord remained the same.'

I laughed as I rolled my head from side to side to stretch my stiff neck muscles. 'How helpful of her.'

'Yes, I thought so.' He shook his head and smiled. 'Still, I can't fault her for caring.'

'I suppose not.'

Finding out that Nick was reconsidering his beliefs about God made me feel happy and annoyed and confused all at once. Happy, because we had never agreed on much when it came to our understandings of who God was. His saying he was reconsidering his stance made me feel like I might have a chance of having a real conversation with him rather than just another argument. Annoyed, because his sudden willingness to reconsider his ideas made me feel like I ought to revisit my own opinions with a more open mind as well, else he would have the moral high-ground yet again. And confused, because I shouldn't want to want to engage with him in any kinds of discussions, never mind in discussions about God. That felt too much like relating with him and, knowing how charming everybody else found him, I figured it might be a slippery slope. The last thing I wanted to do was to start liking him.

I took the last sip of my water, thinking I had to get rid of this unsettled feeling I had when I was around Nick, and work out a strategy for dealing with him whilst he was living in the flat before continuing a conversation like this. I rose and gathered up the dishes to take into the kitchen.

'It's ok, I'll do the dishes tonight,' Nick said leaning back in his chair.

'But you cooked. If you cook, you don't have to do the dishes. That's like the law.'

'Yeah, you can have the law tomorrow, but tonight you can leave them. Just go to bed, you look like you're about to collapse.'

'Ok.' I did feel exhausted and couldn't be bothered to argue. 'Thanks for dinner. It didn't suck.'

Nick grinned at me as I left the room. 'Yeah, yeah, I saw you inhale it, but whatever.'

'Oh get over yourself.' I yawned, but despite feeling tired, it was a long time before I fell asleep that night.

Chapter 4

Julia

The following day I slept in until noon. Rolling out of bed, I went to have my first non-bucket shower in a year. It was wonderful to be able to just stand there and let the water run over me, without having to think of how to make one bucket of cold water last me through washing my hair and body. My body was sore from travelling and I almost cried with relief as the water pounded my tense muscles.

Feeling like a person again, I got dressed in a pair of shorts and loose white tank top I found in my wardrobe. I never would have dreamed of wearing such short shorts in Kenya, but in Edinburgh I would fit right in with the tourists and shoppers on Princes Street. I added a denim jacket and a pair of wedges and went out to meet up with my friends, Miranda and Sophia, at a coffee shop on Princes Street. It was a nice day, with the sun shining and not a cloud in the sky. It wasn't Kenya, but for Edinburgh, this was the best kind of day.

Miranda and Sophia were both waiting outside when I showed up a few minutes late. Maybe I was still on African time. Miranda had her shoulder length dark brown hair in a bun and wore a white tank top with a pair of skinny dark green trousers and a pair of black flats. Her green eyes shone when she saw me approaching, and she started skipping towards me. She caught me in a big hug.

'You're baaack!' She squealed and we rocked from side to side as we hugged. Ever since she moved in next door to me when we were five, we had been inseparable, and this was the first time we had seen each other for a year.

'Yay!' We smiled at each other like lunatics and I went on to hug Sophia.

Sophia had become our friend during fresher's week at uni and had stuck with us since then. She was wearing her long, light brown hair down, and a pair of flowery silk trousers with a sleeveless, white top. A big satchel-style leather bag hung across her chest and a pair of leather sandals on her feet. Sophia had never been much of a hugger, and after a while of me squeezing the air out of her lungs, she gave a little cough to say she'd had enough. She smiled at me as I laughed a loud, happy laugh.

We talked over each other as we went up the stairs to get our drinks to go, and took them out into Princes Gardens. Sitting on the grass with a coffee in the familiar park with Sophia and Miranda made me feel as though my year away had just been a vague, but nice, dream.

'How is it that just a couple of days ago I was in Kenya by the sea and now here I am with my to-go cup, sitting in the park, looking at Edinburgh castle with you girls again, as if this last year never even happened?'

Miranda smiled as she leant back in the grass, pushing her shades onto the top of her head and angling her face toward the sun. 'What was Kenya *really* like?'

I sighed. 'It was *really* good.' I got my phone out and quickly scanned through the photos of the last few days before handing it to Miranda. I showed her a picture of the Indian Ocean. 'That's the view from my classroom window.' I looked at the photo and felt my heart sting in sadness to have left. There were too many people and places I missed.

'I know! From looking at your Instagram account, it looks like you've spent the year in paradise.'

'Yes, in some ways it was like a paradise.' I thought of the massive contrasts between rich and poor, beauty and ugliness, joy and hopelessness. 'But keep going through the pictures on the phone and you'll see it wasn't all roses and sunshine.'

'What's this?' Miranda held the phone so I could see the picture.

'That's the area of town that most of my students live in. There are massive class divides in Kenya, with the wealthy living in mansions with big walls, and the poor living next door in a tin roof shack,' I said as Miranda swiped to the next picture. 'And that is the Likoni ferry, which connects Likoni to Mombasa. They pack as many people they can onto it and cars, buses and trucks. It's crazy.'

'Huh, it doesn't look very safe.'

23

I snorted. 'No, safe isn't a word I'd use to describe the ferry. But anyway, how are you guys?'

Sophia sipped her drink before saying, 'Fine. Nothing much has changed in the time you've been gone.'

I gave her a look as if to say *yeah right* and she went on, 'I'm still bored at work, still sharing a flat with Michael, still putting up with my parents' dysfunction whenever I go home.' She shrugged. 'See, you've missed nothing.'

Miranda handed me the phone back. 'What's it like to be home again?'

'I'm still tired from all the travelling, and I miss Kenya already, but it is nice to be home.' It was nice to be home. If only my home hadn't housed Nick The Squatter, everything would have been lovely. 'But when I got home to the flat, exhausted from travelling for two long days, not getting any sleep on the airplane cause snory Thailand tourist man was sitting next to me trying to rest his head on my shoulder all the way from Doha-'

'Ew!' Sophia cringed.

'Yeah, well, I finally get home and all I want to do is have a hot bath, eat the pizza I bought at the corner shop and go to bed. So I go in and who should I see sitting on my sofa having a beer?' I looked at the others, my eyebrows raised in expectation.

Miranda glanced at Sophia who was trying to look innocent. 'Nick?'

'*Yes*, Nick! I got the fright of my life!' Frowning I turned to Sophia. 'Wait. How did you know?'

She bit her lips and looked like she was unsure as to what to say. 'I didn't realise you didn't know. He's been there the whole time you've been away.'

'What?' I waved my hands in the air as my voice rose. 'Could you have sent me an email to let me know?'

'I thought you knew! Besides, you were away-'

'I was in Kenya, not on the moon!' My belly still fluttered just thinking about his stupid grin as I walked in the door. 'You could have told me when we Skyped.'

'I thought you knew. It is your flat.' Sophia held her hands up and raised her own eyebrows. 'But I was surprised to hear he's living there, considering how you spent so much time avoiding him in uni.'

'It's not *my* flat,' I muttered.

'What?' Sophia and Miranda both turned inquiring looks my way.

I cleared my throat and said, 'Mum and Dad own it, and they've always liked Nick - heaven knows why.'

'So what happened?' Miranda asked. 'Is he still there?'

'He made some comment about me looking like I could use a bath, cooked me dinner and continued remodelling the kitchen.'

'Aw, that's sweet.' Miranda said before catching my glare. 'What do you mean, he 'continued remodelling the kitchen'?'

'I mean he's ripped out the old kitchen and is in the process of putting a new one in. I came in and there was a sink, one cupboard and the cooker in the kitchen. Everything was packed away in boxes in the living room.' Just thinking about it got me riled up again. 'He never misses an opportunity to make my life harder. I didn't realise he's been there the whole year, but I believe it. He's definitely made himself at home. His stuff is everywhere and he's showing no signs of moving. Still, he waits until days before I get home to start renovating the kitchen.'

'So he's still there?'

I nodded. 'Yes. I've been pretty rude to him, hoping he'll take the hint, but that doesn't seem to be working.' I looked away when I saw Miranda smirking at Sophia as though they were sharing a joke.

'Yeah, Nick's never been someone to be told what to do.'

I grimaced. 'Well if he doesn't take the hint, I might have to step things up.' I too could play his game.

'Uh huh... yeah, or you could act like an adult and ask him straight out.' Sophia smiled and held her hands out, doing the Italian innocent shrug thing when I frowned at her. 'Just a suggestion.'

'I did ask him, but he didn't give me a straight answer.' I sipped my drink. 'I'm sure I'll find a way to get him to leave soon enough.'

'Anyway, back to Kenya,' Miranda said, keen to change the topic. 'How did you leave things with the school's Women's Issues group?'

I also was relieved to talk about something different, and smiled as I thought about the girls at the high school I had taught at in Kenya. Early on, the head teacher, Mrs Mwangi, had recruited me to be part of a Women's Issues working group at the school. The group included both school staff and pupils, and aimed to tackle issues facing our high school girls, such as the girls dropping out prematurely because they were absent so much they couldn't keep up with their course work. There were several reasons for why the girls were absent so much, but a big reason was that they generally couldn't afford sanitary products for their periods, so stayed home to avoid the embarrassment of leakage.

It felt like the greatest injustice that these young girls didn't just have to suffer PMS and periods like the rest of us, but they had to do it without access to sanitary products in a culture where the evidence thereof was considered shameful. And when they couldn't handle the shame and stayed home, they inevitably fell behind more and more at school, to the point where it became a better investment for them to get jobs rather than attend school. Not that there were many above-board jobs available to teenage girls without an education.

As a group, we tried to tackle this issue, and at one point Mrs Mwangi had tried giving out pads and tampons to the girls. That seemed to help, and more girls had stayed in school, but the money was running out, so we were back at square one. Grace, one of the other teachers at the school, and I were talking late one night and I mentioned to her that I didn't use tampons or pads any longer. She asked what I used instead, and I told her about my period cup.

Period cups were first introduced to me by Sophia, when I was maybe twenty. When she'd first explained that they were reusable silicone cups you put up your vagina to collect your period blood, I was grossed out because: period blood. But she kept going on about them and soon enough, she'd convinced Miranda and I to try them, and I found it really wasn't so bad. In fact, since then I haven't gone back to tampons and pads, preferring the more sustainable and cheaper-in-the-long-run option of my period cup. And the blood? I got used to it pretty quickly.

When I told Grace about it, she had the idea of giving every girl in the school a period cup each, instead of having to give out an endless supply of pads and tampons. When we brought her idea up in the group, they all seemed to think it would be worth trying, as it would be more sustainable option.

Grace and I spent weeks researching, and I spoke to Sophia and Miranda on Skype about it. They got on board too, and gave towards the initial cost of rolling the scheme out for two classes at the school.

'Yeah, I want to know how the girls got on with the period cups.' Sophia nodded. 'Did it work?'

'Well, I haven't gotten the stats yet. I'm still waiting to hear from Mrs Mwangi about how many of the girls in that class drop out of school before the start of this term. But so far it has been a success, and my guess is that all the girls will be back in school when the term starts. I mean, in the last few months, the girls that were given period cups were absent much less than before.'

'That's great, Jules!' Miranda said.

Sophia put her hand up and I gave her a high five.

'I know. Where are we at with our plans to roll this out on a bigger scale?' Since Sophia and Miranda had first heard about the initiative, we had decided we wanted to get behind this project more long term. The idea was that we would start a social enterprise – a business where our profits were donated to help projects working for women's health issues. We had talked about the idea over Skype once a month for the last six months, and each of us had long list of things to look into. Miranda's degree and experience was in business, so she had taken on the business management side of things. Sophia had taken on the strategy, networking and PR, as her experience was in marketing and design. This left me to work on the connections in Kenya and researching how we could best contribute to similar projects.

'I think we need to schedule a morning to talk about it all properly,' Miranda said. 'I have lists that I'm working off that we should talk about.'

27

Sophia smiled and lay herself back to rest on the grassy slope, angling her face toward the sun. 'Of course you do.'

'Great,' I said and leaned back with a satisfied smile. Business could wait for another day.

Miranda started fiddling with the straw of her frozen coffee.

'I missed you guys so much this year.'

Miranda snorted. 'Yeah right! I know you; you didn't have time to miss us. You will have been busy making best friends with all your students, the teachers, the close by NGOs, the shop keepers and any other random people you could find around.'

Sophia nodded. 'No kidding! I am always astonished at how many people think they're your best friend.'

I smiled and shook my head, saying, 'Yeah, well, I still missed the two of you.'

Chapter 5

Julia

The next few days passed in a blur. I was nervous about school starting again, and knew there would never be enough coffee to cope with the feeling of not being prepared enough. I spent the week wishing that I would learn to be a little less optimistic when it came to time management. Still, thankfully my students didn't seem to notice. By the end of the week, I felt I had gotten off to a good start, and already had stacks of assignments to mark.

That Friday night, I opened a nice bottle of red wine and set it to breathe on the kitchen counter. The kitchen was still a mess, as Nick hadn't done much to it during the week, and the boxes of kitchenware were still standing partly unpacked along the wall in the living room.

Nick had been working long hours, and when we were both home I tried to avoid him as much as possible. A couple of times, he had cooked me dinner, which I mostly ate at my desk whilst marking assignments and planning lessons, so we didn't end up talking much.

When the doorbell rang, I answered the door wearing a pair of leggings and a lumberjack shirt over a black tank top. As I passed the hallway mirror I noticed how my hair had come out of the bun I'd put it up in that morning, and now stood on end. Pulling at my hair tie, I opened the door as Sophia and Miranda stepped in.

'We brought food,' Miranda said and handed me a takeout bag from my favourite Indian restaurant. She wore a patterned blue dress that looked like a second-hand-shop bargain over leggings.

'Great!' I inhaled the smell of curry and sighed. 'I have wine, but we could probably steal a couple of Nick's beers.'

'Sure.' Sophia's face looked a lot more stressed. She was wearing her hair down and a loose pair of flowery trousers with a tight black top. 'Is he around?'

'No, he's out with Michael tonight.' I took out a few plates and we dished up our curries, rice and naan bread.

'Where are your wine glasses?' Sophia asked.

'Your guess is as good as mine.' I frowned. 'Nick said he would finish up the kitchen this weekend. I can't stand this mess everywhere.' Gesturing towards the boxes in the living room, I said, 'Try one of those boxes.'

Sophia looked for the glasses, but couldn't find them.

'Don't worry about it, Soph.' I smirked. 'Let's just drink Nick's beer instead. Serves him right.'

Sophia laughed. 'Still trying to get him to move out?'

'Of course.' I nodded. 'I think I'm going to have to step up my game, though. I've been knocking on the bathroom door when he's in there every morning, interfering with his shower, and I put salt in his coffee this morning, but he's not taking the hint.'

Sophia sighed. 'I think some people are just oblivious to hints.'

'No kidding.' I shook my head. 'He just smiles and says thank you when I hand him his coffee in the morning, even though we both know I put salt in it instead of sugar.'

Miranda rolled her eyes. 'That's awful, Jules! You should be kinder to him!'

'Yeah, sometimes I do feel a little twinge of guilt. He does cook for me. A lot.' I shrugged. 'But then I think he's just trying to kill me with kindness, so we're even.'

I pulled some chairs up to the balcony doors, and we sat down and basked in the sun as we enjoyed our food and stolen beer. Nothing tastes as good as stolen beer with a good curry.

'Do you feel like you've landed back here yet?' Sophia asked.

'I think so. Starting work and getting back into a routine has really helped, but it still feels pretty surreal.'

'What's work been like?' Miranda asked.

'It's been pretty intense. I probably needed more time to prepare, and I already have assignments to mark, but it's been great to be back in the classroom. And it's been great to be back in the English department with the other teachers.' I looked at her. 'How's your week been?'

Miranda scrunched her nose. 'Yeah, it's been ok. Same old thing. Sometimes I feel so old! Do you ever feel old? I'm only twenty-six, but I have a stable life with clear career goals which I know how to reach. There's this lady in the office… she's in her early sixties and she's been there for her whole career. I imagine doing the same thing every week for my whole career and it just feels… stale.' She peeled the label off her beer bottle. 'I don't want to get married or have children, and I wonder why the heck I'm in this rat race that never seems to go anywhere.'

Sophia nodded. 'I know what you mean. I'm so tired of trying to market people useless things that just contribute to the world being an unfair place.'

'I know! I'm secure and stable,' Miranda went on. 'I've got my flat and a decent mortgage, and I should be happy. But thinking I'm now meant to spend the rest of my life working at a job I hate in order to pay my mortgage just makes me feel sad.' She gave a short laugh. 'Besides, there are only so many handbags and shoes a person needs!'

'It sounds like we either need more alcohol or we need to look at what progress we're making with the period cup project.'

'I vote for both.' Sophia smiled. 'Do you have any mugs? We don't need wineglasses, but I think some of that wine would be nice.'

'Yes, look in that box over there.' I pointed her in the right direction. 'I'm starting to feel cold, though. Can we sit inside?'

We cleared the table as the sun was setting across the Meadows, creating long shadows. Sophia was pouring the wine into some teacups, and Miranda had found some tea lights and lit them. Miranda took her tablet out of her handbag and sat down, taking a sip of wine.

'This is looking nice and cosy.' I got my phone out and took a photo to post to Instagram.

Sophia sat down and took a sip of her wine. Putting her head back, she closed her eyes and sighed. 'This is nice wine, Jules.'

'Good. Nick bought it.' I winked and she shook her head at me. 'So Miranda, do you have an agenda for us?'

Miranda was swiping away on her tablet and pulled up a spreadsheet. 'I've got some notes we need to go over.' She smiled and rolled her eyes. 'This is kind of becoming an obsession.'

'I know, for me too.' Sophia nodded.

I smiled. 'I know you guys got involved with this to begin with because I asked, but it's nice to hear you're in it now because you care.'

Sophia gave me a funny look. 'Of course. If we can make a difference, then we must.'

'Yes.' Miranda nodded and put her wine down. 'Let me pull up our list of what needs to happen next.' She glanced at it and continued, 'I got some quotes from a couple of companies in China that should be able to supply the cups for us.'

'Really? How did you find companies in China that quick?' I frowned. I wouldn't have known the first thing about getting a Chinese company to supply us with any product, never mind period cups.

Miranda looked up from her notes. 'That was easy. There are lots of companies that make silicone products in China. Of course, we need medical grade silicone, so that made it a little trickier, but I did some research and found that silicone kitchen products have similar standards. Remember how I did that internship with the kitchen warehouse company when I was in uni?'

I didn't remember, but nodded anyway.

'Well, I contacted them and asked about who supplies them with their silicone products, and got a couple of suggestions from them. So I contacted them a few months ago, and now they've come up with a couple of quotes.'

Sophia looked at me and gave a sarcastic shrug. 'Simple.'

I snorted. 'So simple. Why didn't I think of that?'

Sophia laughed. 'Yeah I know.' She turned to Miranda and said, 'You're pretty amazing. You know that, right?'

Miranda rolled her eyes. 'Sure. I would still like to go out to China to meet with them and make sure they are ethical in how they operate and everything-'

'Great idea!'

'I know it's a lot of money, but I think it's worth doing our research properly on things like this. We don't want to fix a problem in Kenya by making another in China.'

'Right.' I nodded. 'We should talk about how we're going to fund all this at some point.'

'Yes, definitely.' Miranda sipped her drink and said, 'I've got all the papers ready to get us registered as a social enterprise. That is what we decided, right?'

'Yes.' Sophia nodded. 'If we're a social enterprise, it makes it clear that our business, ie: selling period cups, spends its profits on charity, ie: giving period cups to women who can't afford them in places like Kenya.'

'Right.' I wasn't as concerned with the legal details of it as Miranda was, but I knew she would keep us right, and was happy to defer to her on things like that.

'Right. So in order to register, now all we have to do is come up with a name for the social enterprise, read through the forms again, sign them, and I'll send them in. Then, a couple weeks later, we should be in business!'

'Great!'

'I'll start a list. Throw out all your ideas and thoughts and maybe we can come up with something.' Miranda took out a notepad and pens and sat back with her wine. I waved my hands at her, and she sighed and gave me a pen and some paper.

'I have been thinking about this a bit, and I've done some research. There are an awful lot of good names that have been taken already,' I said as I started to doodle on the paper.

'I know!' Sophia bit the inside of her lip and said, 'So we're about providing good, healthy and sustainable menstrual solutions for women everywhere. And our hope is that by doing that, we can be part of giving young women a better chance in life. Right?'

'Right.'

Sophia smirked. 'So let's think of some of the benefits of the cup, and mind map some of those. I'm thinking freedom, liberty, green-'

'Or we could go with more empowered woman type words like queen, vixen, foxy. Or something like chick or-'

'I like vixen; it's a bit edgy, but also because obviously the colour of foxes is red and so is blood,' Miranda stopped writing and rubbed her lips with her finger as she thought. 'What about crimson or scarlet, or rose, or some other shade of red that sounds a bit glamorous?'

'I hear what you're saying hon, but I'm not sure the blood side of it is the actual selling point,' Sophia swirled her wine before taking a long sip.

It was harder than I'd expected to come up with the right name. Miranda bit her lips as she thought about it, then sat up straighter with a smile. 'What about *I'll be dammed*?'

I laughed and Sophia looked at her and smiled. 'Very punny. It's too long and I'm not sure it gives the right idea…'

'What about the shape of the cup? What are words other than cup for that shape?' I asked.

'Bell, flower, or…' Miranda scribbled away.

'Or what about something to do with the cycle of the period?'

'Like *Cycle Cup*?' Miranda looked at me.

'Yes, or *Aunt Flo's Cup* or something.' I laughed.

Sophia smiled but shook her head. 'Again, the blood or the cup aren't the selling points here. I think we should be looking for words to do with being free or healthy or sustainable.'

'Hmm…' I let my head fall back to rest on the sofa. '*Freedom cup* sounds a bit cheesy though, don't you think?'

Miranda smirked. 'It could be red, white and blue and have a picture of the statue of liberty on the packaging.'

Sophia rolled her eyes at us. 'Duh. Yes, I'm not suggesting that we call it *Freedom cup*. But there needs to be something about empowerment, or something about the benefit of it in the name.'

Miranda sighed. 'I think we need to think some more about this. Maybe we can talk about it again next time.'

I nodded. 'Yes, I'd rather take a little more time over this and get it right, rather than just come up with something that we'll need to change later.'

Sophia agreed and snuggled in with the blanket. Yawning, she said, 'So, if you're serious about kicking Nick out of here, what are you going to do with the extra space?'

'I haven't decided yet. I was going to just keep the flat to myself, but if I'm focussing on this social enterprise and not working more than a few days a week at school, then I'm probably going to need to take in a lodger.' Nick was a pain to have around, mainly because I was becoming more and more certain that I was still attracted to him. I knew he wasn't

35

interested in me that way, and it irked me that my feelings hadn't gone away after so many years. On the other hand, it was nice not to have to think about having a stranger in my space whilst he was living in the flat.

Miranda smiled. 'Might be worth keeping him around for a while.'

I lifted my eyebrows at her. 'I don't think so. Did you see my kitchen?'

'Aye, that's inconvenient, but when it's done, it will be beautiful.' Her smile grew wider.

'That may well be, but who's to say it will stop there?' I ran my fingers through my tangly hair. 'The other day I found his measuring tape in the bathroom.'

'Do you think he's thinking of doing the bathroom next?' Miranda seemed excited at the thought, but held her hands up as she saw my frown. 'Just saying, your bathroom could really do with being done again.'

'That may be.' She had a point. The bathroom didn't seem to fit with the rest of the flat, and could use an upgrade. 'I've never liked the sink in there. Why do they even make sinks with one hot and one cold tap? You scald yourself on one, but the other is too cold.' Shaking my head, I came back to reality. 'But if he stays and does the bathroom, I have to live with him for longer, and I'm not sure I can take much more. And I can't afford a new bathroom right now. Besides, what would I do without a shower whilst he's doing the renovations?'

'Oh, come on, Jules, you know you could shower at mine,' Sophia lived just a couple of blocks away.

'Yes, well, it's not just the inconvenience of living on a job site, it's also the fact that we don't get along,' I said.

Sophia looked at me. 'Have you seen what he looks like, though? And he's like, the nicest guy ever. How can anyone not get on with him?'

The door in the hallway opened, and in came Nick and Michael. Nick wore his hair pulled back in a low bun. His dark green shirt was nicely fitted, and matched his eyes. Rolled up to his elbows, it showed off his veiny forearms. Michael, too, wore a shirt, but I didn't notice what colour it was, or if it matched his eyes. Sophia and Miranda looked at each other and laughed as I rolled my eyes at them. 'Seriously?'

Michael stopped beside the sofa and smiled. He wore his brown hair short, and his green eyes sparkled. 'My favourite girls.'

'Ah, Michael.' I jumped up and gave him a big hug as Nick walked past, giving a quick 'hi' and grin to the girls.

'I missed you, Jules.' Michael hugged me back before giving the top of my head a peck and releasing me.

'I missed you too, hon.' I smiled. Michael had always seemed to be there when I needed him, and had a way of reading situations without me having to explain them to him. 'You grew a beard!'

He rubbed his hand over his chin. 'You like it?' He lifted his eyebrow.

I nodded, and looked at him properly. He had always been self-conscious about his appearance. 'Yeah, it looks good.' I raised my eyebrows. 'And I like the shirt too.'

'Michael, are you having a beer?' Nick called on his way to the kitchen.

I looked at Sophia and Miranda and smiled. There were no more beers in the fridge.

Michael looked at Miranda and Sophia, noting how Sophia looked like she was ready to fall asleep. 'No, that's ok. It looks like Sophia needs to go home now anyway, so I'll just go with her.'

'Aw, my knight in shining armour.' Sophia rolled her eyes at him, but got up off the couch.

Michael and Sophia had lived together since just after the guys finished university. Michael wanted to stay in the UK, but with his visa no longer valid, his best option had been to marry a UK citizen. Sophia had agreed to marry him on paper, and to live in his flat for the sake of appearances so he could prove to the government they were married. But, since they both valued their friendship, and Sophia didn't ever want to be married to anyone for real, they were careful not to cross any lines. Apart from when dealing with the government, their marriage wasn't something they told people about. As far as most people knew, they were just roommates, and I knew Sophia hadn't even told her parents she was married.

'I think I'm going to go, too.' Miranda stretched out and yawned. 'There's a bus in ten minutes.' Miranda lived in Duddingston, on the east side of the city. She stayed in what had been her mum's house, next door to my parents.

'We'll have to catch up properly some other time, Jules,' Michael said, as Miranda and Sophia got ready to go.

'Sounds good. I think mum is planning a family dinner next Sunday,' I said.

'I'll be there.' He nodded to Nick. 'Are you going too?'

He nodded, his eyes twinkling. 'Wouldn't miss it.'

I rolled my eyes and sighed. Of course he wouldn't. There was no escaping him anywhere.

***

'You drank my beers?' Nick said, his eyebrow raised in question at me, as the door shut and we were alone in the flat again.

I shrugged and tried to appear casual, though the look in his eyes didn't make me feel casual.

At all.

His eyes made me feel like I was in way over my head, and like it was only a matter of time before my attraction to him would explode into an irreversible head-over-heels-in-love feeling. And that would *not* be good news for my heart.

'Ale would've been nicer, but we needed *something* to go with our curries.'

'Uh-huh,' His eyes smiled but he kept his face straight. 'I'll draw you a map, so next time you can go to the corner store when you need beer instead of taking mine.'

'I know where the corner store is, so no need to get your crayons out,' I said and gave him a teasing look back. 'Are you homesick or something?'

'No, why?'

My phone beeped and I took it out of my back pocket as I said, 'Why else would you buy Budweiser?'

'What?' He looked offended. 'Budweiser is good beer.'

I laughed mockingly as I pulled up the text. It was from Mum.

'And if you don't like it, why would you steal it? Unless…' He paused and narrowed his eyes. 'It's your favourite, isn't it? Come on, you can admit it.'

'Yeah right,' I said, distracted as I read the text.

Mum: Hey, will I see you at church on Sunday? Missing you. Also, will I put your name down to teach Sunday school this term? We're REALLY short on Sunday school teachers. x

I sighed and put my phone back in my pocket. I didn't want to go to church and I definitely didn't want to teach Sunday school.

I knew I'd end up doing both.

Nick frowned. 'Something wrong?' I got the feeling that he was happy to make me miserable, but he didn't want anyone else making me miserable.

'Mum wants to see me in church on Sunday, and wants me to sign up to teach Sunday school.' I scrunched my nose. 'I don't want to.'

He shrugged. 'So say no.'

I gave a startled laugh. 'That's ridiculous. I can't say no!'

'Why not?'

I gave him an exasperated look and huffed, 'If *I* don't do it, there won't be anyone to do it.'

'So let the kids be in the main service.' He rolled his eyes. 'I don't understand why you think Sunday school has to be your responsibility.'

I rolled my eyes back at him and said slowly, 'I can explain it to you, but I can't understand it for you.'

'Whatever.' He reached for my hair, and I ducked as he rubbed my head in a way he knew would annoy me.

'Not the hair, Nick,' I groaned. Rubbing someone's hair was something brothers did to sisters. Not something a guy would do to a girl if they had any kind of romantic interest.

'Oh, but your hair is dying for someone to come and mess it up.' He chuckled as I ducked under his arm and out of the hallway, escaping to my bedroom. I would always be in the little sister category for him. It would not be a good idea to start crushing on him again.

Unfortunately, my heart hadn't seemed to get the memo.

***

I skipped church on Sunday and went to Zumba instead. The steps were still in me, despite a year of being away, and, whilst I did feel guilty for not being in church, it was good to sweat again. When I checked my phone, I had three texts from Mum.

Mum: Are you here yet?

Mum: Where are you? I've saved you a seat

Mum: Signed you up for Sunday school. Hope that's ok. Will call later x

I put the phone away and went to shower. I didn't want to let Mum or the kids at church down, but I felt so confused about God that I wasn't sure I'd be a good person to teach Sunday school. The kids would end up more confused than they were to begin with.

Clean and dressed again, I put the assignments I was meant to be marking to one side and spent the day putting together the information for a seminar leaflet. Grace and I had been working on how to introduce the high school girls in Kenya to the period cups, and decided we needed to give them a short seminar alongside giving the cups out. We had the outline ready, but needed some materials to hand out.

Whilst that was interesting, I found it hard to concentrate, as I could hear Nick fitting cabinets in the kitchen. Having seen him on the floor with a screwdriver, attaching and levelling the cabinets when going to grab a coffee, I was very aware that his body was a little too attractive for comfort. His hair was tied back in a man bun — his usual when he was working— and his face was scruffy from letting his beard grow a couple of days. He wore a grey t-shirt, which hugged his strong arms, at times riding up to reveal his washboard abs, and a pair of holey jeans that fit just right.

I struggled to keep my distance from him, but he had made himself abundantly clear last time I had a crush on him, and I wasn't about to have a repeat of that most humiliating time.

Chapter 6

Eight years ago

Julia

'I was going to hang out with Michael tonight. He's meeting me here in five minutes and then we're walking over to Nick's together. Do you guys want to come?' I said to Sophia and Miranda. We were sitting in a coffee shop in town after spending the afternoon shopping.

'Really? Is there something wrong with Nick that he's not out hooking up with someone on a Saturday night?' Sophia snorted.

'No, I think they are going to hang out with some people later. I probably won't stay long, but I've hardly seen Michael since I got back from seeing Jack in Hong Kong, so...'

Miranda giggled. 'I don't know why you pretend you want to hang out with Michael when we all know you're really just hoping to see Nick.'

I felt my cheeks getting warm as I shot Miranda a scowl. 'Well if he happens to be around, I won't mind seeing him.'

'Sure, just as a bonus.' Miranda shook her head, still smiling. 'Anyway Miss Denial, have a good night. I'm going home to have a nice hot bath, and then I've got to keep working on my assignment.'

'Yes.' Sophia yawned. 'I have an assignment due on Monday, so I'd better go home too.'

'Ok, see you later then.' The girls headed off to the bus and I waited for Michael to show up. It was starting to get cold and windy, even though the sun was out, so I snuggled into my scarf, stuffing my hands in my pockets and leaning against the wall trying to catch a few rays of sun on my face. Knowing I was going to see Nick today, I had spent an hour straightening my hair that morning before dressing in my best pair of skinny jeans and a blazer over a loose low-cut blue shirt. I also wore a pair of gorgeous black heels that I struggled to walk in but made my legs look amazing.

'Hey, are you coming or what?' Michael startled me out of my sun worship.

'What – yes, sorry of course.' I pushed away from the wall. 'So how far is it?'

'Ah, not far. Like 10 minutes.' He glanced at my feet. 'Maybe 15 in those shoes. They're worth it, though.'

'Of course they are.' I smiled and passed him some of my shopping bags. 'Here, hold these.'

He took them with a sigh. 'Story of my life: carrying things around for women...'

We walked as quickly as my shoes allowed, and soon we stood in front of Nick's building, my feet aching. Nick buzzed us in, and we walked up the stairs to his flat. He'd left the door unlocked for us.

'Hey,' Michael said, pushing the door open.

'Yeah, come on in,' Nick called from the kitchen. 'Want anything to drink?'

'Sure, what you got?'

'I don't know, check the fridge.' Nick pointed to the kitchen as he set down a tray of crackers and cheese on the coffee table in the lounge. 'I'll have a beer.'

'Jules, you want a beer? There's wine here as well. Or I can make you a cuppa if you'd rather.'

'No, a beer's fine.'

Sitting down on the old couches, I looked around. The TV was showing a game of football. The tray on the coffee table held a wedge of brie cheese, corn crisps, some different kinds of crackers and a bunch of grapes. Fancy.

Nick himself, however, wasn't so fancy. He wore a baseball cap over his long hair, a white Henley and sweatpants. The scruff on his cheeks and messy hair made him look like he'd just rolled out of bed – a stark contrast to the otherwise neat and tidy flat.

'So...' he said and gestured toward the cheese and crackers on the table. 'Have some grapes.'

'Yeah Jules, have some grapes,' Michael said with a smirk.

'I'm fine just now, thanks,' I said, my awkwardness knowing no bounds.

Nick looked out the window. 'Been up to much lately?'

'Just uni. I went to Hong Kong in the summer to see Jack, though.'

'Oh yeah? How's he doing?' Nick said with a bored look, taking a sip of his beer.

'He's doing ok. He was there to look at a couple of projects for the finance company he works for. But there was time to do a bunch of fun stuff as well. We went up Victoria Peak and stuff. Hong Kong was just beautiful-' I stopped my babbling, feeling more awkward than ever, and knowing he didn't care what tourist attractions I saw in Hong Kong. I needed to reign in the awkward and find some form of cool. Maybe I could buy some, I thought frantically, as I realised I was forever going to be Jack's little sister in Nick's eyes otherwise.

'Cool. So,' Nick glanced at Michael. 'You guys want to play some video games?'

Video games? No, I don't want to play video games! Michael gave Nick a funny look and I felt my face grow hot as I struggled to contain my feelings of embarrassment. Nick ignored us both and put a game on. He gave Michael one of the controllers and I spent the rest of the night watching them play games.

And that is when I finally understood what Nick had been trying to subtly tell me for months. He wasn't even remotely interested in ever having a relationship with me. It wouldn't matter what I wore or how much I tried to be what he wanted, I would never have a chance to be with him.

When we finally left, Michael did his best to pretend everything was alright. After walking a few blocks with me insisting my eyes were just leaking because it was windy and cold, he stopped and put his arm around me, folding me into his chest.

'I'm ok,' I said in a brittle voice as he stroked my back and tears raced down my cheeks. He didn't say anything, but I knew he knew, and that was enough.

I soaked my pillow that night as I struggled to sleep. The next morning I had a cry hangover, my face blotchy and head sore. The weeks that followed were a blur as I went through the week on autopilot, doing my best to avoid my friends and family, especially Michael, who kept giving me sympathetic looks. I spent a lot of time taking body combat fitness classes, which left me exhausted, but helped get all the feelings out. About a month later, I went out to the seaside one Sunday afternoon. I took a long walk along the beach with my parents' black Labrador dog, Becky. That's when I decided that I was done.

I made up my mind to let go of the idea of Nick, and to look at what else there was to life. But I knew I would have to protect myself against falling for him again, so I would try to avoid him as much as possible. When avoidance wasn't possible, I would push him away as much as I could.

And that is how our war began.

Nick had been a little stunned the first time I gave him back as good as he gave, when he teased me when Jack was around. He soon caught on though, and things soon escalated. We did our best to outdo each other at putting the other in embarrassing situations. Whilst I will concede that he came up with some fairly imaginative pranks, he never did anything unkind. Unlike me. I had never been particularly unkind to anyone before, but now there was a seemingly infinite well of spitefulness that welled out of me, and I saw no reason to hold it back.

Chapter 7

Present time
Julia

It took everything in me to ignore his body on the floor and turn to the fridge to get my eggs out.

'Are you expecting to be finished with this little project of yours any time soon?' I said with my head in the fridge. 'I want my kitchen back.'

'Mmm...' Nick straightened and shot me a distracted look. 'You hungry?'

'Not at all. I'm getting these eggs out to throw at you if you don't work faster.' His smile sent my stomach in a tailspin, and I rolled my eyes at him as I fought to keep my cheeks from going red. 'Of course I'm hungry. It's dinner time.'

'You can help me cook then.' He nodded toward the fridge. 'There's stuff in there to make chicken in a sauce with potatoes.'

That did sound nicer than the fried eggs on toast I had planned, so I reluctantly agreed and started getting things out of the fridge.

'You girls seemed to have a good time last night.' He interrupted the silence.

'Yes.' I smiled as I started chopping vegetables for his chicken dish. 'Your beer was very nice.'

'I'm sure it was.' He nodded, lifting his eyebrows as he bit his lip. 'So tell me about this social enterprise you guys are starting?'

I almost cut my finger off as I stiffened in surprise. 'What social enterprise?' I decided playing dumb was my best bet at not having to explain it to him.

He laughed. 'The one you girls were discussing last night before leaving your notes lying all over the living room.' He raised an eyebrow. 'Ring any bells?'

'Yes, well it's early days yet.' I shrugged and went back to chopping the broccoli whilst searching for a way to change the subject. 'So, we've had some lovely weather this week,' I resorted to.

'Right.' He ignored my attempt to talk about something, anything, else. 'So do you have a business plan?'

I put my knife down and turned to look at him. 'Maybe that was my way of saying that you should mind your own business.'

He smiled whilst putting the chicken in the frying pan. 'Nah. If you wanted me to mind my own business you wouldn't have left the papers lying around for anyone to see.' He looked up and sent me a grin that made my pulse speed up.

Taking a deep breath, I reminded myself of what it felt like to live in a tear-fogged headache of heartbrokenness. 'Fine. We're starting a social enterprise selling period cups so we can use our profits to support women's health projects in places like Kenya, which distribute period cups to teenage girls to help them stay in school.'

He nodded and said, 'I don't want to know what a period cup is, do I?'

'Probably not, but seeing as you asked, I'll tell you.' I smirked. 'It's a little silicone cup which you stick up your vagina when you have your period. It gathers the blood-'

'Ok ok, I get it.' Nick raised his hands to stop me talking. I went back to peeling the potatoes, thankful that he'd decided to drop the subject.

When I was finished with the potatoes, I turned to put them on the stove and saw his face all deep in thought.

'So this period cup thingy...' He shot me a sceptical smile. 'It's a thing for real?'

'I don't know. You tell me.' I gave him a quick shrug and reached for the kettle on the other side of the stove. In doing so, I reached across his space just as he leaned in to stir the chicken. My hand grazed his arm which caused me to jump back to step around him instead. I felt my cheeks grow hot, and I reminded myself that – as much as I might have wanted to – feeling his arms would help in no way to keep me from lowering my guard.

His eyes sparkled and he raised one of his eyebrows at me. 'Huh.'

I quickly looked away and focused on pouring the hot water over the potatoes.

'Anyway, so what are you doing with these cups?' he said, going back to stirring the chicken.

'The plan is to sell them here as a great healthy and sustainable sanitary product, in order to fund projects giving them out to teenage schoolgirls in Kenya and other places where they are needed.'

Nick threw his head back and laughed. 'Oh Jewel, I knew you couldn't help going around saving people. You might not be trying to convert anyone like your mother, but you carry around enough guilt to be trying to solve the world's problems.'

I avoided his eyes. His words were a little too close to the truth. I did carry around a lot of guilt. And probably a little bit of my motivation behind starting the social enterprise was to do with trying to get rid of some of it. Still, how could I do nothing when I knew how to work towards solving this problem? I felt as though it was up to me to work out how to get the girls to stay in school, since nobody else was doing enough to help.

'Yeah well, obviously some of us have hearts in our chests, and some of us... don't.' I sneered at him and put the cutlery down on the counter with a loud bang.

He caught my arm as I tried to leave the kitchen. 'Hey!' He had stopped laughing and pulled me closer to him. Too close. It was hard to breathe. He looked down at my face and I couldn't help but look back. 'Don't take offence, Jewel. We all have issues, and at least yours are coming out in a way that helps people.' He searched my face. 'Still, if you keep letting the guilt win, it'll keep eating away at you until there's nothing left of you in there.' He bit the inside of his cheek as he thought about it. 'Even so, I think it's a great idea. In fact, I want in. You'll be looking for investors, right? I'll be one of them.' He nodded in decision.

I found it hard to think straight, and as his gaze sharpened I wondered if he would kiss me. 'Why...' I shook my head and tried to free myself from his hold on my arms. He didn't let go and my skin tingled. I felt my cheeks go red as his eyes roamed my face. I cleared my throat. 'Why would you want to invest in a social enterprise? There's nothing in it for you.' All these feelings and the way he was acting confused me. A lot. Frustration warred with the attraction that just seemed to grow stronger and stronger.

'I don't need the money. I have enough.' He let me go and looked away as he ran his hands over his hair. 'Besides, it would drive my dad crazy to know I spent the money on a social enterprise.' He gave a dry laugh and rubbed his hands over his face as if to clear his head. 'Anyway, let me know once you need investors.'

I nodded.

'Let's eat.' He turned to grab a plate and dished up some potatoes and chicken in vegetable and cream sauce. It looked lovely, and I almost felt bad when I said, 'I'm going to go eat this at my desk. I have about three hundred assignments left to mark.'

He rolled his eyes at me and I knew he saw through my excuse to leave. 'Sure thing.' His smile did nothing to settle my pulse down. I took my plate, murmured a quick thank you and escaped.

As I ate my food, I thought about what he'd said about the guilt taking over. Sometimes I felt like the world was closing in on me. It was only when I was working towards a cause that I felt like things fit. Did I have a Messiah complex? Maybe. Maybe I *did* need to be somebody's saviour. I shook my head to try to clear it. All I knew was that I hadn't been able to save Josie.

***

That week things at school got busy. Though I was only contracted to do the three days of teaching, I spent the rest of the week doing supply teaching. I wasn't a very nice person in the mornings before having coffee, and Nick soon caught on. We fell into a routine where he would make us coffee in the morning, whilst I tried to wake up and get ready. And whilst I was grudgingly thankful for the coffee, he also had a habit of hogging the bathroom, which was most annoying. I felt like I spent most of the mornings knocking on the bathroom door trying to get him to hurry himself up.

I kept making hints about him moving out, but kept getting no response. On the Thursday afternoon on my way home from work, I saw a bunch of cardboard boxes outside a corner shop. I felt giddy as I carried them home and left them on his bed, thinking surely he would take notice this time. Unfortunately, he was away with Michael for a couple of days of camping, so I didn't see him until Sunday lunch at my parents'.

***

I spent Saturday with Mum and Dad and their Labrador dog, Becky, at the beach in Portobello. It was the last weekend of the Edinburgh festival, and the annual busking festival was taking place along the promenade. The sun was shining, which was lovely as we walked up and down the prom listening to the different buskers. The performers ranged from out-of -sync, tone deaf kids with a karaoke machine, to a couple of super talented guitarists and an opera singer.

Dad could have stayed all day just listening to the buskers, and if somebody had handed him a guitar, he would have gladly joined in. Instead he sat in the sand, his foot tapping to the beat. The faint lines in his face and the greying hair on the sides of his otherwise full head of dark hair were the only signs of him being in his mid fifties. If anyone asked him, he would say the secret to looking young was loving his wife. And the secret to loving his wife was going for regular long runs on his own.

Mum, on the other hand, was more interested in getting the last rays of sun and sitting with her feet in the sand. It was a rare thing to see mum sit still for long; she always seemed to be busy running around with lots of projects going on. On the beach, though, she could spend the whole day tanning and reading a book. This day, she'd left the book at home, and burrowed her feet into the sand. Her never-tamed, above the shoulder, greying, red hair was flying in the breeze as she faced the sun.

'How are you finding it? Being back?' Mum asked.

I stroked Becky as she lay beside me in the sand and sighed. 'It's been ok. I miss a lot of things about Kenya, but it's nice to be home, too. Soph and Mir came over last weekend and brought over a curry. I've missed having them close by a lot. And I've missed you guys, and having food I'm used to.'

'Oh, yeah? But you told me you made friends out there too, right?'

'Sure, and now I miss *them*.' I smiled. 'It's different with them, though. Everything about Kenya was so intense, I feel like I got to know people really well. In some ways it was just the same as here, you know. Teenagers are teenagers wherever they are, and still it was so different.' I thought about the heat, and of having significantly less technology to deal with. 'It was a great year and I learnt so much, but now that I'm home I feel a bit like it was all a dream.'

'Well, did you see my text? I signed you up to help with Sunday school.' Mum looked so happy, I swallowed my sigh and gave her a weak smile back. 'And when Rachel found out you're back, she asked if you might be interested in helping with some other things at church.'

My heart sank, but I couldn't bear to say no. 'I'll speak to her and see what I can do.'

'So, do you have any more pictures of the animals you saw?' Dad asked.

I looked at him, thankful to change topics in conversation, and got my phone out. 'Yeah, you would have loved it. There were a couple of rats that liked to sit under the wardrobe in my room, so I would bring a big stick with me to knock on the wardrobe with. That would get them scurrying away and out the window, for long enough that I could zip myself into my mosquito net.'

He laughed. 'Didn't you say you'd seen some big, exotic animals though? I mean, rats are interesting too, I guess.'

'Sure, spiders and snails and bats and snakes and that type of thing are big and exotic, right?' I said and he rolled his eyes at me. 'I saw some interesting birds too, but I never saw any of the Big Five, as I mostly stuck to the city.'

It was nice to be able to talk about my time in Kenya. Most of the people I'd seen since coming back hadn't seemed very interested beyond a few minutes of catching up, so I was lapping up the attention. Mum and I chatted for a long time, our feet digging into the sand and our faces turned to the sun. Dad got bored after a while and took Becky for a walk along the shore on the beach.

He didn't come back, so after a couple of hours we went in search of him and found him picking some Beatles tunes out of a guitar, together with a guy in his twenties, with Becky sleeping on the pavement beside him. When he saw us, he gave the guitar back to the guy and slapped his back as he thanked him. Becky scrambled to sit up and came over to be stroked.

'There you are!' Mum said.

As we left I asked, 'Do you know that guy from before? What's his name?' Dad always seemed to find new people to make friends with.

'No. I don't know what he's called. Nice guy, though.' Dad smiled and looked around. 'There's ice cream up there.'

I shook my head at him with a smile. 'Then what are we waiting for?'

Chapter 8

Julia

That evening, I received an email from Mrs Mwangi. She told me that only one girl from the class we had given period cups to had not returned to school after the holidays, and that was because she had moved away. Mrs Mwangi went on to say how unusual this was, as there normally would be at least a couple that would drop out between terms, and how she hoped we could use her statistics in our plans for our social enterprise. This encouraged me, and I replied to say that everything was going according to plan, and I would start looking at tickets to visit Kenya again in January.

On Sunday morning I avoided church and went to Zumba again, before heading over to Mum and Dad's in Duddingston. I knocked on the front door before opening it and going on in.

It was my childhood home, and whilst it definitely felt like coming home, I knew very little would be familiar. Every time I came home the house had changed. This time, furniture had moved around, rooms had been painted and the bathroom had been redecorated. The only thing that stayed the same was the homey fragrance of cooking. Mum had always loved to cook and bake, not so much because of the actual work involved, but because she loved to have people over. There had always been room for another person to sit around the table.

'Here, chop these and I'll make a crumble for dessert,' Mum said by way of greeting as I came into the kitchen, and handed me a bunch of apples and brambles.

I smirked and said, 'Oh it's good to see you Julia, how have you been? Ah, it's nice to see you too, Mum. Yes, I'm ok, thanks.' I went in search for a chopping board and a knife.

Mum rolled her eyes at me and smiled as she pointed me in the right direction. 'I just saw you yesterday, so no need to be snarky with me.'

We worked in silence for a while. Mum was preoccupied with getting the vegetables ready for the roast chicken dinner she was cooking, whilst I debated whether to bring up the issue of Nick living in my flat. If I'd known she had been thinking of subletting the flat to him, I would have said no to begin with. But when she just took care of it and never told me who she'd let it to, I hadn't even thought to ask questions. Now, though, I wasn't sure how to bring it up without getting her to start going on about how wonderful Nick was and about how it would be time to bury the hatchet and make friends with him.

'Oh,' Dad said as he came in the kitchen. 'Nice to see you, Julia love.' He looked at me over his reading glasses, and set down the paper he'd been reading on the kitchen table.

'Oh good, you're just in time to set the table.' Mum looked up.

'Mhm,' Dad rolled his eyes and went in search of plates. 'I do seem to have the gift of coming just when the table needs setting.'

'I'll help you. I'm finished with these apples now, anyway,' I said just as the bell rang.

'In here!' Mum called, and Sophia and Miranda came in. Sophia was looking very put together, wearing a white and black mesh dress, a bright red handbag and a pair of sunglasses, which she slid on top of her head as she entered the kitchen. Miranda looked less summery and more as though she'd pulled on an old pair of leggings and a wrinkly, old, burnt orange t-shirt. Her hair was a mess and she wasn't wearing makeup.

'It smells lovely in here. What are you cooking?' Sophia asked as she took her black flats off.

'It's nice to see you girls.' Mum gave them a big hug each. 'We're having chicken. And there's lots of veg, so you won't go hungry, Miranda darling.'

'Thank you.' Miranda smiled. She'd swung between being vegan and vegetarian for the last five years.

Becky came into the kitchen to say hi, and Miranda sat down to give her a long hug, her face snuggling in with the dog's ear. 'Oh, Becky.' She sighed.

'Everything ok, Mir?' I asked.

She looked sleepy as she said, 'Yes, I'm ok.'

'You look like you've lost weight, darling,' Mum said to Mir. 'You've got to be careful, we don't want any more of those dizzy spells you used to have when Lisa died.' Lisa, Mir's mum, had died from cancer when we were in uni and, as Lisa and Mir had lived next door to my parents for as long as we could remember, her passing had affected us all.

Mir shrugged. 'I don't think I've lost much weight. Julia has, though.' She was right. I had lost about ten kilos in Kenya, and I felt better for it.

'Yes, you look great, hon,' Sophia said.

'Thank you.' I used to struggle with my weight a lot, so I was determined to keep the kilos off now.

Mum smiled. 'Let's serve up, and by the time we're sitting down, I'm sure the boys will be here.'

We got our dinner, and, just as predicted, the guys walked through the door just as Mum said, 'Let's pray.'

'Hello!' Nick and Michael hollered, laughing as they came into the dining room with a familiar blonde coming up behind them.

'Hey guys,' my brother Jack said as he entered the dining room. I glanced round the room and saw Miranda's face freeze as she looked up from her conversation with Dad to see Jack.

We weren't expecting Jack home for another month, so him being there came as quite the surprise for all of us, but perhaps particularly for Miranda, as they used to be engaged. I wasn't entirely sure what had happened to them; Miranda never wanted to talk about it. All I knew was that Jack left the country when he finished university, and Miranda hadn't seen him since then. That was six years ago. Miranda knew he was coming home for good, but she hadn't wanted to talk about it, appearing unaffected by it. She wasn't unaffected now, though. She went pale as a sheet as she stared at him.

'Whaaat?' I said to try to cover for her and got up to give him a hug, but had to step out of the way to let Mum pass me.

'There's my boy!' she said as she pulled him in for a big hug. 'We weren't expecting you for a few weeks yet. How come you're home already?'

'The project I was working on finished up early, so I decided to come home. I need to go back out there for a few meetings in about a month, but until then I might as well be here,' he said through Mum's hair as she continued to hug him.

Dad stood up more slowly and went over to slap his back. 'Welcome home, son,' he said with a satisfied smile.

Then it was my turn, and Jack rubbed my head as he hugged me.

'You stink.' I pulled back as the smell of campfire and sweat enveloped me.

'Camping.' He shrugged and smiled, his eyes twinkling. Michael and Nick were already getting their food. 'It's good to see you, too. I may have missed you. A little.'

'Yeah, I missed you too.' I grinned back at him.

'Mum, this all smells amazing.' He took a plate and started loading food onto it.

'I bet you guys are starving after camping these days.'

'Nothing beats your Sunday dinners, Karen.' I heard Nick say and I felt my annoyance rise at how he was trying to be charming to my Mum. He needn't have bothered, she already could've been the president of his fan club.

Mum turned to Jack. 'When did you arrive?'

'Nick and Michael picked me up at the airport on Thursday and then we went straight up north. I'm pretty jetlagged still, but I couldn't miss going camping.'

Michael slapped his back and smiled, whilst Mum shook her head. 'Boys,' she said, rolling her eyes.

I sat down to eat and looked at Miranda and Sophia, who were still sitting at the table. Miranda looked at me. 'Did you know he was going to be here?' she mouthed.

I shook my head. I was thankful I hadn't known, as I wouldn't have known whether to tell Miranda or not. Judging from the pained look in her eyes though, the right thing would have been to tell her. Definitely.

'You ok?' I mouthed back and she nodded sharply, looking away. My eyes found Sophia's, and I recognised the worry in her eyes.

'How wonderful to finally have all of you together around the table here again,' Mum said as the guys sat down with their food. If she'd been a cat she would have been purring, she looked so delighted.

'Wouldn't miss it.' Nick smiled and winked to Mum.

'Yeah, it's good to be home,' Jack said as his eyes sought Miranda's, who seemed to be looking anywhere except at Jack.

'How was camping?' Sophia asked, trying to divert his attention.

'It was great! Although Jack here slept for most of the time,' Nick said.

Jack rolled his eyes. 'Yeah yeah, you try going camping after travelling for 24 hours.'

'Did you catch any fish?' Sophia asked.

Michael nodded, 'Yes, we did some fishing off the Isle of Mull yesterday and caught a couple of sea bass. Nick cooked them up for dinner last night.'

'Best sea bass you'll have ever eaten,' Nick said with a cocky grin.

Michael snorted. 'Might have been the only sea bass I've ever eaten, but sure.'

'You've never had sea bass before?!' Sophia put her hand on her chest and raised her eyebrows like she couldn't believe it.

'Oh come on, we're not all pescatarians, or whatever you call it when you eat a lot of fish,' Michael rolled his eyes.

'Pescatarians?' Sophia snorted. 'You're making up words now. Besides, fish is good for you.'

'What was China like, Jack?' I asked, trying to get the conversation away from the fish versus mac and cheese debate I knew was about to break out.

'Good.' Jack smiled. 'I missed you guys of course, but I loved China and the Chinese people.'

'Well, it's good to have you back now.' Mum reached out and stroked his arm. 'How long do you have to go back for?'

'It'll just be maybe a week or so, in about six weeks. I've got a few meetings to do, but otherwise I'm home now,' Jack said. 'I've got a couple of weeks off now, and then I start work here.'

'Good to have you back, son,' Dad said, looking content and happy to have his family back in the same country.

It was nice to catch up with everyone over dinner, and afterwards we helped Mum clear the table before going to our favourite pub in Duddingston for drinks. I could tell Miranda wasn't excited about going. She'd been very quiet during the meal, but she came with us anyway.

Chapter 9

Nick

At over six hundred years old, The Sheep Heid Inn was the oldest pub in Edinburgh. The first few times I'd been there, my American self had been amazed, as I was with most of the beautiful, old buildings in Edinburgh. Full of character and with lots of old fireplaces, it was more of a cosy place to relax than a trendy place to hang out. And, whilst there were plenty of trendy places to go in Edinburgh, it was tradition to have a pint at The Sheep Heid Inn after a family meal at the Reid's house, so there we were.

As it was still nice and warm, we took our drinks out into the beer garden. I ended up sitting next to Julia, who, upon noticing, quickly turned away from me and toward Michael, asking him about his part-time job at the university teaching statistics. I grinned and put my arm around her chair, knowing it would annoy her.

I'd just taken a sip of my lager when Jack said, 'So what's this I hear about you girls starting a social ent-'

Julia coughed and I raised my eyebrows as she turned to point at me. 'You told him?'

I shrugged. 'Why not? It's a great idea.'

'Yeah, it sounds cool.' Michael nodded. 'Sophia told me all about it the other day.'

'We're only just getting things going,' Miranda said. 'But I think this is one of Julia's better ideas.'

'So what's the plan? And how far along are you?' Jack asked.

Julia held her hands up. 'It's early days still…'

'Oh come on,' Sophia said. 'It's just the guys. We can tell them.'

Miranda nodded and Julia rolled her eyes but said, 'Fine. We're working on getting the social enterprise registered so we can start operating properly.' She told us all about the idea, and apart from being slightly grossed out at the thought of menstrual blood, I was sold. The passion I saw in her eyes when she talked about the plan for the business they were setting up was inspiring. Her whole body was lit up and alive, and I pitied any obstacle daft enough to stand in her way.

'I love it,' Jack said.

'You do? You don't think it's just another of my terrible ideas?' Julia asked with a smile.

Jack laughed, 'You *have* had some terrible ideas. Remember that time when you wanted to set up a "sponsor a child" account when Molly and Richard, the couple leading the youth group we went to in high school, had a baby.' The glee on Jack's face as he thought of what he was about to say made Julia sigh.

'They could have used the help!' She pointed out weakly. 'They were young and shared one measly church salary. Besides, getting people to give them things they *needed*, rather than an endless amount of onesies all in the same size, seemed a good idea.'

Jack was giggling now but got hold of himself to nod patronisingly and say, 'Your heart was in the right place, but when you went to take photographs of the crying baby, wrote up a sob story and wrote down different categories of things people could give to – like contribute towards this baby's school uniform costs or buy nappies for a year – and wanted to present it to the church, all without telling Molly and Richard-'

We all laughed and Julia rolled her eyes as she said, 'Yeah yeah. Anyway, you were saying about how you think the social enterprise idea is *not* another of my terrible ideas.'

'Aye,' Jack said as our laughter settled down. 'What are the next steps?'

'We're working on a name for it,' Sophia said.

Jack and Michael looked at me and nodded, with big smiles. We had spent several hours talking about the social enterprise when camping, all of us in agreement that it was a good idea. We had wondered if the girls had a name for the enterprise yet, and had spent hours besting each other at coming up with possible names. 'I think we can help with that,' I said.

'Really? You guys spent your camping weekend talking about our social enterprise?' Julia shook her head and her hair grazed my arm.

I shrugged. 'Well, yeah.' I caught some of her curls and tugged gently at them. She had beautiful hair. Julia pulled away and gave me a glare, but soon leaned back again, and my fingers found their way to her hair again. The next time she glared at me I sent her a grin and kept playing with her hair. It was too easy to rile her up.

'Ok, so what are your suggestions for a name?' Miranda asked, getting her phone out to take notes.

Jack smiled at her and said, 'We were thinking that as the cup provides a solution for the vagina, one suggestion could be *Vagilutions*.'

Sophia, Miranda and Julia looked at each other and burst out laughing. 'That's terrible!'

'Oh come on! It's not bad at all. We also thought *Practivag* would be a good name. Because it's a practical solution for your vagina.'

Julia snorted. 'You guys have a thing for melding two names together, or something?'

I shook my head and gave them a look to say I was disappointed in them. 'Our genius is clearly wasted on you girls.'

'Hmm, yes. We're not selling vaginas though, are we? Did you come up with any names that didn't have vagina in it?' Miranda asked and Jack, Michael and I looked at each other.

'Oh go on, don't leave us hanging here,' Sophia said. 'We won't laugh again. I promise.'

Michael shrugged and said, 'Well you know how *Hakuna Matata* is the Swahili way of saying no worries?'

'Sure, like the Lion King song?' Miranda asked.

'Right. So you could call it,' Michael gestured with his arm across the wall. '*Hakuna Matwata*.'

Julia couldn't contain her laughter and neither could Miranda or Sophia. 'And then we'd have a theme song for our adverts too, right?'

'Yeah! You could be all like Hakuna Matwata, you'll have no worries because your twat will be taken care of.'

'The funniest part of this is that I can't tell if you're joking or if you for real think that's a good suggestion?' Miranda said through her laughter.

Sophia shook her head. 'No, he's being serious. Believe me.' She sighed. 'Michael you know here in the UK, *twat* is a derogative word, right?'

'Well yeah, but surely it isn't *only* used as a derogative word?' He mock frowned. 'And you said you wouldn't laugh.'

'Yeah, well we didn't expect it to be quite so bad.' She smirked.

'Even in the way you're using it, it's not exactly a word we want our social enterprise to be branded as,' Julia said. 'Good effort though.'

'So what suggestions have you guys talked about?' Jack asked.

Sophia gestured towards Miranda's phone. 'We've talked about concepts more than names really. You know, what kinds of things we want the cups to be associated with. Like freedom, being empowered, sustainability and that type of thing.'

Jack nodded. 'Sure, that makes sense.'

'Yes, so we're thinking names like *Freedom Cup*, *Vixen Cup*, *Scarlet Cup-*'

'Really? I wouldn't use scarlet if I were you. Seriously, I'm trying my hardest to not think about the blood here, and that's not helping.' Jack made a grossed out face.

'Ah, it's just a natural body function,' Sophia said with a roll of her eyes.

'Yeah, yeah, and hell is just a sauna,' he muttered.

'Honestly though, I wonder if it needs to be very complicated?' Miranda asked. 'Maybe we should just call it *Project Cup*?'

'Huh,' Julia said, chewing it over. 'I kind of like that. *Project Cup*.'

'Yes, the only thing with that is it kind of makes it more of a project that people are engaging with, and less of an everyday solution,' Sophia said.

'That might be ok, though,' Miranda said. 'Don't you think?'

'I like it.' I nodded, still playing with Julia's hair.

'Me, too,' said Michael.

'Yeah Mir, I think you're on to something there,' Jack agreed, an intense look on his face as he watched Miranda. She refused to meet his gaze and raised her eyebrow at me instead, as if she was waiting for my opinion.

'I think it's great,' Julia said. 'We should just go for it.'

'Yeah, I guess it beats *Hakuna Matwata*, in any case.' Sophia smiled.

'So it does.' Julia snorted and I bit my lip, trying not to smile.

'Have you guys decided if you're going to go with an already existing product, or do you want to produce your own cups?' Jack asked.

'I've got a couple of companies that have given me quotes,' Miranda said. 'They're both in China, and I'm going to go out and check them out and see what works best.'

'That's great. Let me know if I can help with anything on that front. I have a few contacts in China and Hong Kong that might come in handy,' Jack offered.

Miranda stiffened and said in a clipped tone, 'I think we'll be fine, thanks.'

Jack smiled at her. 'Well, the offer's there.' He held up his empty pint glass. 'I'm thinking I've got to get home and have a shower.'

'I think you guys all need a shower,' Julia said. 'I bet you've washed by swimming in a loch this weekend.'

I shrugged. 'It's not camping otherwise.'

As we left the pub I looked at Julia and said, 'You're going home now, right?'

She nodded. 'I'll come in your car if that's ok.'

'Sure. Miranda and Jack, if you want we can take you guys home before we head home,' I offered. Miranda still lived in the house next to Jack and Julia's parents', and Jack was going to be staying there until he found a place of his own. Miranda's face said she would have rather been anywhere other than in a car with Jack, but as she thought about the other option, which was walking home with him alone, she nodded. Julia took pity on her and told her to sit in the front, and Julia got in the back to catch up with Jack. Miranda spent the short ride in her own world, so I put some music on and let her have the time to think. I could use some time to think too.

Living with Julia had been more intense than I had expected. I'd expected to be kept on my toes with her constant bickering, but I hadn't expected the way I was aware of her.

All the time.

Even when she wasn't home, there was the scent of her body wash in the bathroom, or one of her candles on the coffee table. Or the way her things ended up scattered all over the apartment, making the place feel lived in and homey in a way it hadn't when I lived there on my own.

And watching her talk about the social enterprise tonight, something had stirred in me. The wild in her seemed to call out to me in a way I found hard to resist.

***

When we'd dropped Jack and Miranda off, Julia got into the front seat of the car.

'How's that for tension?' I said as I pulled away from the curb.

Julia looked out the window as if to avoid looking at me. 'Yes, if it's any indication as to what it's going to be like, we might have to send Jack back to Hong Kong.'

'Sending Jack back would solve nothing. I reckon him being back is the only way this is ever going to get fixed.' I shook his head. 'Not everything can be solved by avoidance, you know.'

'What's that supposed to mean?' Julia narrowed her eyes at me and I shrugged.

'Nothing,' I said with an innocent smile.

Julia turned away and changed the subject. 'How was camping?'

I snorted. 'You're doing it now!'

'No,' she said, working hard to remain calm. 'You didn't want to tell me, so I decided to let it go. That's not avoidance, that's common courtesy. Not that you would know anything about that.'

I rolled my eyes at her, but decided not to push it, and we sat in silence for a while as we drove the long way round Arthur's Seat – the big hill in the centre of Edinburgh – as the park was closed on Sundays.

'I'm finishing the kitchen next weekend. We should have a party to celebrate.'

Julia raised an eyebrow, the scepticism radiating off of her. 'I'm not sure I believe that. This kitchen renovation has already gone on for several weeks longer than you said it would.'

'It'll be done.' I nodded and shot her a look as I drove through a roundabout. 'So do you want to do a big party, or just the six of us?'

'Just the six…' Julia turned toward me. 'Hey, I didn't agree to a party!'

I grinned and she looked away as though looking at me made her nervous. 'I'll ring Michael and Jack, you talk to the girls.'

'Fine.' She sighed. 'I won't do all the cooking though.'

'Gosh no!' I shook my head and smiled as I glanced at her. 'We don't want to poison the others.'

'My cooking isn't that bad.' She rolled her eyes, but we both knew that, while she was fantastic at baking, she was severely lacking in skills when it came to cooking.

'Sure, sure.' I cleared my throat and made sure not to look at her. 'Not sure how none of Karen's skills in the kitchen were passed on,' I muttered under my breath, then turned and smiled. 'You can make the salad and brownie for dessert. I'll take care of the rest.'

When we got home Julia had papers to mark and I spent the evening sorting out my camping gear, showering, and doing laundry.

I couldn't help smiling as I saw the moving boxes on my bed. Julia was still doing her best to try to get me to move out. I wondered how long she would keep it up.

I had decided I liked living with Julia.

I liked that I could be who I was, and I knew Julia didn't feel she needed to put on a face with me. She was never as honest as she was when alone with me. And, while I enjoyed fighting with her, I wondered if perhaps we were at a point where we might be able to be friends. I had a feeling we'd be good friends if we tried.

So, no, I wouldn't be moving out any time soon.

I couldn't imagine living anywhere else.

Chapter 10

Julia

A few days later, autumn arrived, with temperatures dropping to ten degrees, and the wind and rain doing their best to wash summer away from memory. I came home after work, my hair plastered to my face, as I'd been caught in the rain on the walk home. Coming up the steps of the building, I heard U2's 'I still haven't found what I'm looking for' echo through the hallway, getting louder and louder as I came closer to my flat. I dropped my school bags on the floor, the door slamming behind me, as I rushed into the flat to find the source of the music to turn it down.

Coming into the living room, I stopped. The couches were turned over, blankets and cardboard boxes were held together with duct tape to shape the biggest and, I'll be honest, coolest living room fort I had ever seen.

I shook my surprise at the state of the room off, and quickly climbed over a bunch of pillows and reached for the speakers, turning the music down. 'For goodness' sake Nick, you'll get me evicted! You can't play music so loudly; what will the neighbours say?'

Nick's head came up from under the couch. His hair was ruffled and he ran his fingers through it, tucking it behind his ears, then scratched his cheek absentmindedly. He looked at me with a twinkle in his eye and a smirk on his face, as though he was enjoying a private joke. 'Nah, it would take more than some U2 to get evicted from here. I'm pretty sure.'

The gray t-shirt he was wearing hugged his upper arms and showed off the definition of his muscles as he sat himself up and leant against a heap of pillows. I ignored the fluttery feeling in my stomach at the way he was smiling at me, and might have turned my nose up as I said, 'Well, can we try not putting your theory to the test please?'

He coughed to cover a laugh and shook his head, causing his hair to fall forward to hide his face. 'Whatever you say, Jewel.'

'Don't call me that,' I muttered grumpily and gestured to the upturned room. 'What happened here?'

He leaned his head back against the sofa, entirely relaxed, and looked me up and down, considering. His gaze making me feel self-conscious, I wiped at my face to get the rain off. I was sure I must have resembled a drenched cat, so started combing my fingers through my hair to fix it. Raising his eyebrow, he said, 'I built you a fort.'

I wasn't sure how I was meant to respond to that. We were hardly friendly enough to be building forts in the living room. We were also adults, and I had no other friends I would build forts with. I took a deep breath, asking for patience as I said, 'Yes, I can see that. Why?'

'I thought you might need to relax after spending the day with all those teenagers. Besides, what else was I supposed to do with all those boxes you left on my bed?' he gave me his best innocent look.

'Did using the boxes to pack your stuff in not even cross your mind?' I gave him a weak smile and shook my head at him.

He shrugged. 'I've got popcorn and beer, and I'm going to put on an old movie. Want to help me pick?'

I thought of all the assignments I'd brought home to mark that evening and decided to steal the night off. 'Okay, but-'

'Also, I finished the kitchen.'

'For real?' I could feel my face light up at the thought of a functioning kitchen.

He nodded. 'I even put all your things away.'

I climbed across the fort and into the kitchen to have a look. All new and clean and welcoming, it looked better than I could have hoped for. He'd hung a hand towel on the oven door and, apart from the kettle, the counters were clear. Part of me admired his work and felt a tug of longing to have a handyman partner that would do things like renovate my kitchen or fix broken things.

It was a weak moment, but I did imagine what it would be like, if he was mine, and he really had renovated my kitchen because he cared about me. I quickly reminded myself *that* wasn't

71

about to happen. The longing for more with Nick should have been my first clue I was in way over my head.

Again.

Feeling all kinds of vulnerable I felt, more than heard, Nick come up behind me.

'What do you think?'

I took a steadying breath and turned towards him. Studying him I said in a measured voice, 'I think that I don't know what to think, Nick.'

He flinched and raised his eyebrows. 'You don't like it?'

'Of course I like it, you idiot.' I gestured towards the kitchen counter, my voice rising in frustration. 'What's not to like about it? It's beautiful.'

'Why am I sensing that's not a good thing?' he said carefully.

'I don't know, Nick?' I waved my hands at him. 'I don't know what to think about the fact that you just spent loads of money and time renovating my kitchen, when I've been pretty clear that you need to find somewhere else to live. And I'm confused that you would take the boxes I left on your bed as anything other than a nudge towards getting packed up and out of here. What am I supposed to think?'

He gave me a smug smile. 'Huh...'

'What do you mean 'huh'?'

'I think you're confused because you like me living here, and you love the kitchen and the living room fort, but you think I'm moving out. And seriously, where did you ever get that idea from?' He looked at me, as though he was expecting an answer, but then shrugged and said, 'I like living here.'

'That may be, but you can't stay.' I folded my arms across my chest, feeling vulnerable and insecure. I felt like he thought he knew me, and I was starting to think he was right. Maybe he did have me all figured out. That made me feel all kinds of uncomfortable.

'Sure I can. Why do you want me to move out?'

'Gah!' I said exasperatedly, my voice rising in pitch. 'Why would you want to stay? We don't even *like* each other!'

He bit his lower lip as he studied me for a moment. It felt like his brown eyes saw a little too much, and I struggled to not let his gaze affect me. 'Maybe we should change that. I'm a pretty nice guy and, all evidence to the contrary, the rest of our friends seem to think you're decent enough. Maybe it's time we try to be friends.' He lifted his eyebrow. 'Roomie.'

I made a face. 'Not sure that's a good idea at all.'

'Course it's a good idea. You're just chicken.'

I knew he was goading me, but was unable to let it drop. Part of me wanted nothing more than to be his friend. But the other, bigger, part was sure this was going to lead to me having my heart broken.

Again.

And I wasn't sure my heart would ever be able to recover from being broken by him a second time. Still, maybe it was time to act like an adult and be friendly. I could be his friend without wanting more. Right?

Right?

I took a deep breath. 'Okay. Let's be friends.'

Nick smirked. 'I thought you might say that.'

I rolled my eyes at him. 'As your first friendly gesture, you get to share your dinner with me. And I get to pick the movie.'

'Mhm... I thought you might say that, too. I've got pizza in the oven and beer in the fridge and you can pick from one of the movies I've got out.'

I wasn't sure how to interpret how prepared he was. He'd said he wanted to be friends... I'd be his friend.

***

I followed him into the living room and into the fort. He'd laid down the couch cushions on the floor to make a comfortable foundation to lie on. The couches were turned over and he'd used the boxes and blankets to form the walls and ceiling of the fort. The coffee table was set up like a tray table for a bed, ready for us to lie under and have our dinner on. He'd even hung some fairy lights on the edges of the fort so we could see what we were doing.

It all looked very cosy and made me think this might not be the best of ways to start our 'friendship'. I wouldn't want to get any ideas. I reminded myself he was only interested in friendship – nothing more.

As long as I remembered that, I'd be fine.

I looked at the films he'd taken out. They were all heist films of different kinds: *The Italian Job, The Thomas Crown Affair, Now You See Me*, and so on. I picked *The Saint*, as I hadn't seen it.

'I'm just going to go change out of my school clothes.'

He gave my wet black jacket over the white shirt tucked into the pencil skirt a quick glance and nodded. When I came back wearing a more comfortable big jumper over a pair of leggings, he had dished the pizza up. He passed me a beer as I sat down, the film ready and waiting to be put on.

'Thanks,' I said awkwardly, as I sat down next to him and reached for the pizza. Nick turned the film on, and we sat in silence as we enjoyed our pizza and beers.

It didn't take long for the film to get corny enough that it warranted commentary, and soon enough we were making sarcastic comments about what we expected would happen next, copying the accents, of course. It struck me that whenever I would watch a film with the girls and I would start commenting on the film, they would get annoyed and tell me to be quiet. But Nick seemed happy enough for us to comment our way through the film.

By the time the film was over, I was relaxed and dozy. I put my hands above my head and stretched. 'Aw, that was great. I love corny old films like that. The last film I watched was in Kenya. It was this old film about a bunch of people that were climbing some high mountain in Nepal, and I had nightmares for weeks afterwards.'

'Somehow I'm not surprised that you like corny movies, Jewel.' Nick teased, his grin setting off the butterflies in my stomach. He pulled his hand through his long hair and started playing with it, brushing it through with his fingers and massaging his scalp. My fingers itched to reach out and touch his hair, too.

I threw a pillow at him instead, but smiled. 'Life's too short to watch scary films.'

'Speaking of saints, how is your latest plan to 'save the world' coming along?'

I stilled. 'Why do you think of it as my plan to 'save the world'?'

He lay on his side, facing me now. His left hand tucked under his head, he leaned against a pillow and sighed. 'I don't mean any offence when I say that. It's just that you always seem to have some project going on to make the world a better place for people.' He smirked. 'I don't really get why, but you seem to think God cares about people and that he wants you to save them.'

I frowned. 'Oh, are we back to not being friends so quickly?'

'Come on. Can't we have a discussion about life and still be friends?'

'Yes, well, it seems like it's less of a discussion and more of a 'let's criticise Julia' conversation. But if it really *is* a friendly discussion...' I raised my eyebrow at him. 'Why don't you think God cares about people? Do you not think he cares about you... or anyone at all?'

'Of course God doesn't care. If there is a god, he's an ass. Why else would he have his own son killed with the most painful of deaths, just to satisfy his own anger? That is child abuse of the worst kind.' He shrugged. 'Then he makes people live in poverty, and sends people to hell if they don't do as he says.'

'I know what you mean, and I did see some horrendous poverty in Kenya,' I said slowly. 'But the Bible says he does care enough to die for us. And I think if he cares so much, then so must we. To follow him must mean that we work as hard as is possible to show people that he cares about them.'

His eyes scanned my face, seemingly searching for something. Then, abruptly, he asked, 'What about that is the worst bit for you? That they suffer or that you have something they don't?'

'Both,' I said without thinking. 'They don't deserve to suffer, and I don't deserve to have all this privilege.'

'Why do you think you don't deserve what you have?'

'What have we done to deserve it?'

'So if everyone in the world had the amount of privilege you enjoy, would you feel you deserved it then?'

I frowned. 'I don't think so. Because the privilege we have is at the expense of something, whether it's the environment or other people. And I don't think it's right that we should have anything that costs something that we ourselves aren't paying for.'

'Gah, you confuse me!' He looked at me with a bewildered expression. 'So do you or do you not want people to suffer?'

'Of course I don't want people to suffer.' I frowned at him. 'What do you think I'm starting a social enterprise for?'

'I don't know, Jewel, it looks like a noble initiative from the outside. It seems to me, though, you're starting it because you feel guilty, and this is a way of appeasing your guilt.'

I gave a startled laugh. 'You haven't got a clue what you're talking about.'

'Well, why work so hard to please God? If he's so good, then why can't he sort out the poverty issue without your help?'

Finally a question I could answer, I thought and smiled. 'Of course he could. He could solve poverty right now; he's powerful enough. But if he did, he would override man's free will, and in doing so, we become robots which have no choice as to whether we worship him or not.' I shrugged. 'God isn't interested in robots. He wants relationship with people that choose to follow him because they want to, rather than because they have to.'

The left side of his lip pulling up, he waited for me to finish talking, a single eyebrow lifted. 'I call bullshit,' he said. 'That sounds like a regurgitated Sunday school answer and doesn't at all match up with how you live your life.'

I gave him a sheepish grin and tried to stave off my cheeks going red. 'Yeah, you might be a bit right about that.' I sighed. 'I know what you're saying, but I do think he is a good God, and I think that it is our job to worship him and to work to make him happy.'

'Do you even know what makes him happy?' Nick shook his head at me. 'Gosh Julia, I think the social enterprise is a great idea, I do. But will it make God happy? And if it doesn't, then what?'

I shrugged. 'Then we work harder.'

He looked at me for a long while, carefully scanning my face. I felt my heart start beating faster and my hands go clammy. When I couldn't stand his gaze any longer, I said, 'What?'

He shook his head, as if to clear it, and said, 'Ah, Jewel, what have you done that you need to work so hard to make God happy with you?'

I laughed nervously and rolled my eyes, deciding to deflect rather than answer his question. I brought out my worst American accent as I drawled, 'Ah, Nick, what has God done to make you think he's a sadist?'

Nick gave a startled laugh, the serious look in his eyes replaced by a twinkle as he looked at me. 'That's a terrible accent. Say something else.'

'Life is like a box of chocolates,' I said in my best Forrest Gump accent, but couldn't keep a straight face as Nick laughed at me. I threw a handful of popcorn at him to get him to stop. 'Oh come on, it's not that bad, surely.' Shaking my head I said, 'What's your Scottish accent like?'

He snorted and said, 'Ach m'lass, it's awfy dreich outside the day, so I built you a wee fort.'

'Aw, and that was terribly sweet of you.' I smiled and shook my head. 'Your accent is awful though. How long have you lived here? You'd have thought you would have picked it up better by now.'

He was giggling by now, the sound of his laughter warming my belly and making me feel all fluttery inside. 'Ma Scottish isnae that bad, ma hen,' he said through his laughter, his hand on to my shoulder as he tried to make himself understood. My whole arm tingled and I was very aware of how close he was.

'Oh yes, it is. That's okay though.' I smiled, struggling between feeling happy that we were able to hang out and have fun together, and feeling like I was on dangerous ground. I reminded myself that this was only a friendship, and not to be getting any ideas.

'I probably ought to go do some lesson plans before it gets too late.'

Reluctantly breaking the connection, I stood up. Nick's gaze scanned my face and I felt my cheeks grow warm. I told myself not to make things awkward, but didn't know how to not be awkward.

'I'm going to leave the fort up for a couple of days. That okay with you?' Nick asked as he pulled back.

'Yes, that's fine.' I drew a deep breath. 'I'll help you tidy it on Saturday.'

The fort stayed in the living room for the rest of the week, and was a nice reminder of the evening we'd spent together hanging out as friends— for the first time since that time in Nick's flat in uni.

Chapter 11

Julia

'Would you please turn your damn alarm off and get yourself out of bed?' Nick's frustration came through the door loud and clear. He liked his weekend sleep-ins after getting up early for work through the week, and seemed decidedly unhappy to be woken before ten on a Saturday.

'I'm up. Sorry!' I guiltily wished it was a few weeks ago and we weren't friends yet. Waking him early on a Saturday morning back then would have filled me with glee – I might even have done it as a prank rather than as an accident. Now I felt guilty instead.

I checked my phone and quickly ran my hands through the tangly mess that was my hair. There was no time for coffee if I wanted to be at Miranda's by nine. I got ready as quickly as I could and ran to catch the bus to Duddingston. I missed it, which left me waiting for the next bus in the pouring rain for twenty minutes.

While I was waiting, mum rang to ask if I could come to church 'not tomorrow, but next week'. She went on about how people had been asking after me, and told me she needed my help with serving teas and coffees after church, so I agreed, albeit less than enthusiastically. I had been quite happy avoiding church for the last few weeks.

By the time I finally got to Miranda's house, Sophia and Miranda were already sitting in the kitchen with hot drinks waiting for me. Sophia rolled her eyes and smirked at me as I came in the door, soaking wet and significantly later than agreed. I peeled off my jacket and sat down at the kitchen table, still feeling frustrated about my phone call from mum.

'Rough morning?' the (slightly) more compassionate Miranda asked, and passed me a mug of coffee.

I took a big sip, and sighed. 'I slept in, missed the bus, had to wait in the rain, and then mum rang to tell me she needs me to come to church again. And I haven't had coffee yet.'

'Oh.' Miranda scrunched her nose. 'Maybe keep drinking your coffee?'

I nodded and listened to them chatting away, giving me a chance to let the caffeine kick in.

'Feeling better?' Miranda refilled my mug.

I took a deep breath and let my frustration go. 'Much. Thanks.'

'So, Michael showed me this text he got the other day from Nick.' Sophia scanned my face as though she was looking for something. 'It was a picture of you and Nick smiling and eating popcorn in what I think must have been your living room, but with extra blankets. Nick had his arm around your shoulders, and all the text said was *new bff's*.' She raised her eyebrow at me. 'Care to share?'

I snorted. 'I think that friendship finished this morning after I snoozed my alarm a few too many times and woke him up. Still, three days is something, isn't it?'

'What friendship?' Miranda asked.

'That's what I would like to know, too,' Sophia said. 'Also: why am I hearing about this from Michael and not from you?'

'Oh, well, it's no big deal. We decided to try to do the Adult Thing, so buried the hatchet the other night. We're going to be friends from now on.' I tried to play it cool, even as nothing about this conversation, or about my new friendship with Nick, felt cool. When I thought about our friendship, I was reminded of being a six year old, staying with my grandparents in England for a week with Jack. They'd taken us to a circus where a giraffe ate my sunhat. Part of me had been delighted that I'd been so close to a giraffe, the other part had been terrified he was going to take a chunk out of my hair next. I couldn't stop watching as the giraffe's blue tongue kept moving the hat around his mouth. Unable to move, all I could think was that the giraffe was about to eat me.

I felt that same terrified delight when thinking about being friends with Nick. I was delighted that he seemed to like hanging out with me.

And terrified that my heart would get broken.

Miranda and Sophia both looked at me as though they couldn't quite believe what I was saying. I could see how they'd be confused, considering I had spent the last six years avoiding Nick.

'*Not a big deal,* my foot,' Sophia burst out. 'You guys have been fighting for six years, and then one night, entirely out of nowhere, you decide to be friends again? What do you mean *it's no big deal?*'

Looking at my coffee, I ran my finger around the rim. 'I guess we decided we are both adults and it's time to start acting like it?'

'Wow.' Miranda scanned my face thoughtfully. 'And how's that working out?'

I looked up and shrugged. 'It's going well. I think it's a better deal for me than for him, really. He cooks for us both and built a fort in the living room, and I don't have to think of pranks to keep him on his toes all the time.' I grinned. 'Then again, he doesn't have to deal with being pranked all the time, so maybe it's a win-win?'

Miranda smiled. 'I'm glad, after all these years, your feud is over. Maybe now things will be less awkward when we all get together.'

Sophia snorted and looked knowingly at Miranda. 'Yeah, with Jack back, it's nice to know at least Nick and Jules are going to play nice.'

'Oh come on.' Miranda rolled her eyes. 'Jack and I are fine. No problems there. I vote we talk about the social enterprise instead.'

'Me too.' I nodded, relieved not to have to talk more about Nick and excited about the possibilities the social enterprise presented, even as I was dying to ask Miranda about Jack.

'Cowards.' Sophia shook her head. 'Fine. Mir, did you make a plan for us?'

'Sure.' She got her tablet off the kitchen counter and found the spreadsheet she was working from. 'I was thinking we could go over my list, and then we can talk about what needs to be done next and who should do what.'

'Sounds good.'

'So the way I see it, we need to sign the papers to register as a social enterprise. Then we need to look at our funding and budgets again, and we should talk about adding people to the board. Then there are things like branding and logos. And maybe we could talk about the website, Sophia?'

Sophia nodded and Miranda continued, 'We should talk more about PR and social media. We also need to look at distribution of the cups we give away for free, or the charity side of the enterprise. Is that all good?'

'Right. Sure, makes sense.' Sophia nodded.

'I'm sure there are things I've missed, but I think that gives us a good starting point,' Miranda continued. 'So, have you had time to read the forms and documents we need to send in to register?'

'Yep, they looked good to me,' I said with a smile and pulled out the envelope with the papers I'd signed. I was so thankful Miranda knew what she was doing with all this, as I would have had no idea.

'I'm happy, too.'

We all signed the papers, and Miranda put them to one side to be sent in later.

'I've been thinking about board members, and also about start up costs,' Sophia said. 'Michael, Jack and Nick all seem to want in on this, and they have money to put in. What do you guys think about that?'

'I don't know.' I bit my lip as I thought about it. 'I feel like we need their money, but I'm not sure I want to give them any power in return. I might be friends with Nick now, but I still don't know that I want him interfering. Could we hold off on inviting them onto the board for now?'

'We could, but we do need money coming from somewhere,' Sophia said. 'I'm thinking it's worth talking to them about it, at least, and I would be happy to do that.'

'I'd like to know why they all want to invest.' Miranda looked up from her notes. 'It's not like they'll be making any money.'

Sophia nodded. 'I asked Michael, and he says they all have their reasons and none of them wants to share right now – which I agree is suspect.' She held her hands up. 'But I also think we shouldn't look a gift horse in the mouth. You know?'

'Yeah, ok maybe talk with them about the money and what they would want in return.' I was still unsure and felt like this particular gift horse maybe should be asked to open its mouth. 'Although, knowing Nick and Jack, I'm pretty convinced they will want to be part of the board. What other options do we have when it comes to funding?'

'Any investor we would ask would want input in how the money is spent. But we could try doing some fundraisers, seeing as it is a social enterprise?' Sophia looked at us. 'Like, I was thinking we could do the Loony Dook this year if you guys are both up for it?' She was referring to the longstanding Edinburgh tradition of going for a dip in the sea on Hogmanay, New Years Day.

I shivered at the thought.

'That's a great idea!' Miranda was always up for things like that. If it sounded adventurous and challenging, she'd jump into it with both feet. Me, not so much. Sure, I was up for some adventure once in a while, but going for a dip in the North Sea in January didn't feel like my kind of thing. At all. 'We could get people to sponsor us and come along and watch. And we could record it all and do a social media campaign around it and stuff.'

'I hear you guys, and I'll do it if I have to, but...' I wasn't convinced of this idea.

'Oh don't be a wuss. It'll be fun!' Miranda smiled, her eyes twinkling.

'Yeah, but also cold.' I shook my head but relented. 'Fine. If it will help us get going, then I guess I'm in.'

Sophia smiled. 'That's the thing: it won't yield much money, but it will hopefully give us some publicity, and that might mean more sales. I think it's worth doing, at least from a PR point of view. Funding-wise we are mainly looking for investors. And we need to look at what each of us can put in ourselves, as well.'

'Yes, looking at the budget, we do need to see quite a bit of money up front.'

Sophia showed us some mock ups she'd made of logos we could use, and we decided on one. Whilst Miranda made more tea, Sophia added the logo to the website. The website was starting to look great. We discussed what we needed to add, and I went home with a long list of things to write for it.

Miranda looked at her list again. 'Jules, have you had any further contact with Mrs Mwangi in Kenya?'

'Yes.' I shared the content of Mrs Mwangi's email and said, 'I've been working with Grace, and we've put together the content for a leaflet to go with the seminar which all girls that get a cup goes through. In the seminar they give some woman's health education and talk about periods in a helpful way. A big reason for why there is a problem in the first place is that periods are shameful and misunderstood. So doing short seminars helps combat the shame.'

'That sounds good.' Sophia nodded thoughtfully. 'I can do the graphic design for the leaflets if you want?'

'That would be great! And as we grow, it would be good to look at areas of the world where women are particularly affected by this. So anywhere where there generally is poverty, but I'm also thinking we could do something for women in refugee camps and that kind of thing in the future.'

'I have a friend working with women's health issues in South Africa who has said she would be interested in partnering with us, too,' Sophia said.

'Cool.' I shrugged and smiled. 'Obviously there is no lack in need but it's good to have a plan for what we're doing beyond the project in Kenya. We should evaluate regularly and look at what we learn in Kenya and how we can grow from there.'

'Sure.' Miranda nodded and looked up from her notes. 'Will you work on dates and costs for a first trip to Kenya, and also put together a document with some criteria for future partners, so we know how to prioritise as we grow?'

'Yeah, no problem.' I made a note on my phone. 'Will we have lunch on Sunday next week and catch each other up with where we've got to?'

Sophia smiled at the thought of food. 'Great idea.'

I smirked. 'I thought you might think so.'

Miranda started clearing the table and putting out a salad and sandwich makings for lunch. 'Last weekend of September is coming up. Are we doing sunrise on Arthur's Seat this year?'

Arthur's Seat is the mountain Edinburgh is built around and, ever since we were in our mid-teens, Miranda and I had climbed it to watch the sunrise on the last Saturday of September. Not that it was a big climb— it would maybe take an hour to go up— but at the top there is a great view of the city and the sea. Since our first year of uni, when we had met Sophia (who had moved up from England), she had joined our annual climb.

'Of course.' Sophia nodded decisively. 'It's tradition.'

'I'll bring the coffee and something to sit on,' I said, knowing I'd get terrible coffee otherwise.

'Will I cut some fruit up to bring then?' Miranda asked.

'Sure, and I'll bring some scones or croissants or something.' Sophia made a note in her phone.

Chapter 12

Julia

By the time we had finished lunch, it was past two o'clock, and the rain had stopped to let the sun out. I took the bus home and walked the long way home from the bus stop, enjoying the soft autumn sunshine on my face. I stopped at the Swedish café at the top of the Meadows to pick up some cinnamon rolls for Nick as a peace offering after waking him that morning. I found him in the kitchen, baking bread.

'Wow, that smells delicious.'

'Yeah, the first batch turned out nice.' He nodded toward a tray covered in a tea towel.

I struggled not to stare at him as he continued to knead and roll out the dough. He wore his hair in a man bun with a couple of strands escaping, and was wearing a gray short sleeved shirt and ripped jeans that looked entirely too good on him. The veins in his arms led up to his bulging biceps peeking out from under the shirt.

Tearing my eyes away from his arms, I went to lift the tea towel. 'What kind are they?'

'Those are rye, oat, and sunflower seed rolls. But I ran out of sunflower seeds, so I've put carrots in this one instead.'

'Sounds interesting. Have you tried them yet?'

'No, I've got to get these in the oven first. But you go ahead.'

'It's okay. I'll wait until you're done.' I put the tea towel back over the cooling rolls and looked at him rolling the dough into rolls which he placed on oven trays. Trying not to stare, I asked, 'Where did you learn to bake bread?'

He looked up and crooked a smile. 'My nanny taught me. Said it was a constructive way to get my frustration out.'

'I have so many questions right now.' I didn't know where to start. He had a nanny growing up? I shook my head. 'Does it work?'

He shrugged. 'Kind of. Want to have a go?'

'Nah, I'd rather watch you.'

He grinned, showing off the dimple in his left cheek, and the butterflies in my stomach took flight. I shook my head.

'I'm just about done. You can get some cheese and butter out of the fridge and put the kettle on if you want to be useful.'

I got the coffee cups out of the dish rack. 'I'm sorry my alarm woke you this morning. I bought I'm-sorry-cinnamon-rolls, but maybe I'll put them in the freezer for you now.'

He looked at me in surprise. 'You got me cinnamon rolls?'

'I got you I'm-sorry-cinnamon-rolls.'

'Forgiven. I love cinnamon rolls.' He smiled. 'My nanny used to make them for my birthday when I was a kid.'

'I thought they were a Swedish thing?'

'They are. She emigrated to America from Sweden. Still has the accent.'

I passed him his coffee and stole one of the buns from him. 'I didn't know that about you.'

His eyes found mine and his eyes twinkled as he said, 'Darling, there are many things you don't know about me.'

I rolled my eyes but smiled as I turned away to cover how my cheeks started to feel warm. If I was going to do the Friend Thing with him, I really needed to get hold of all the feelings.

Chapter 13

Nick

Despite my long week at work, I leapt up the stairs and opened the door to our flat. 'Hey Jewel, you in?'

'Don't call me that,' she sing-songed, but got up to meet me in the hallway.

I untied my work boots and stepped out of them as she hovered in the hall doorway. I looked at her and thought how nice it was to have someone to come home to. 'Hey, how do you feel about cats?' I bit my lip trying not to grin, but clearly failed if the wary look on Julia's face was anything to go by.

'Did you bring one home?' She raised her eyebrow at me, and hurried over as I pulled out the fluffiest little orange ball of fur. I held it up to her, and watched as her heart melted. The kitten looked like she had just woken up, still sleepy and a little annoyed, yet interested to see what was happening. Julia reached out a hand and scratched the soft fur behind her ear. 'Ah, what a precious little one,' she said in a gentle voice.

I had known Julia for nine years, and for most of that time, or at least a good chunk of that time, I had managed to stay at a distance from her. It had never been easy, and while she might have thought her little cutting comments would have put me off, I had enjoyed our sparring. Still, there had never been a point where I would have seriously considered starting a relationship with her. I wasn't going to play with her feelings, and a long-term relationship wasn't in the cards for me, so I had engaged in her little frenemy game, but never allowed things to go further.

Now, watching her with the kitten, I found myself reconsidering for the first time. I wondered what it would be like to be her man. The one she'd grow old with, have children with. The one she looked at like she looked at the kitten.

I was jealous of a kitten.

Reminding myself of all the reasons why starting a relationship with Julia was a terrible idea, I cleared my throat. 'I wasn't sure what you'd think, but this lady came over to the job site today with a couple of kittens and asked if anyone would take one.' I shrugged. 'There was a grey docile one and then this fiery one which scratched me when I went to stroke her. She reminded me of you, and I figured-'

'What? Are you saying I'm fiery and violent?'

Fiery and violent was the nice way of putting it. 'Yes. Yes I am.'

'I don't know what you're talking about,' she sniffed and picked the kitten up. 'Have you named her?'

'I figured whatever name I gave her would be ridiculed, so maybe we can find a name we both like-'

'Sure.' She went to sit down on the sofa with the cat. 'Did you say it's a girl?'

I nodded, and sat down in the armchair. I took off the wool socks I was wearing over the ends of my jeans and stretched out my legs. 'Yes, so I was thinking, her hair is orange, just like yours, so maybe we could call her Carrots?'

She glared at me and I fought to hide my smile. She was so easy to rile. 'One, we do not have orange hair, and two, we will not be naming her Carrots. You saying stupid things like that is exactly why it was no hardship to be angry with you for all these years.'

I bit the side of my cheek to stop myself from commenting. The anger she was referring to, though, had been more like flirting and less like anger. It had been fun and *safe*. Why I ever suggested we'd be real friends instead of continuing to engage in swapping cutting comments was beyond me. How was I meant to stay at a distance now?

She lifted the kitten up and looked her in the eye. 'Don't listen to the mean man over there. You've a lovely shade of strawberry blonde, darling.'

'Right. That's what I meant. Strawberry blonde. Of course,' I nodded. 'What's that you're eating?'

'Noodles and an egg.'

'Right. Looks yummy.' I wouldn't have touched her mushy noodles and hardboiled egg if you'd paid me. That egg was so hardboiled it had passed the green stage and was just gray.

'Yeah, I might have overcooked it all slightly. Still, it's food, isn't it?'

'Sure.' *Overcooked it slightly?* Understatement of the year. When Julia first moved in, I realised fairly soon her skills in the kitchen left much to be desired. She never spent much time cooking, and more often than not she had noodles or oatmeal for dinner. She had a frugal side, but much as she seemed convinced her diet was due to trying to save money, I was fairly certain there was more to it. A capable woman who could manage a classroom full of teenagers all day should have been able to cook better than that, especially when her mom was Karen.

'Well, we can't all be Jamie Olivers in the kitchen, can we,' she said and turned her attention back to the cat. 'Maybe we could name her something like Crookshanks.'

I scrunched my nose. 'Really? Who calls a cat Crookshanks?'

'Hermione in Harry Potter did.'

'Oh, so now we're wizards, are we?' I chuckled.

'Do you have a better suggestion?'

'Yes,' I said emphatically. 'Anything is better than Crookshanks. How about Pekoe?'

'What's that?' This naming business was going nowhere.

'Pekoe, like the tea. You know: *Orange Pekoe?*' How could she not know tea? She drank plenty of it.

'There you go with the orange again. Knock it off! Our hair is *strawberry blonde.*'

'No, that's what the tea is called. Orange Pekoe,' I snickered. 'Surely, you drink enough tea to know that?'

'I've never heard of Orange Pekoe before. I drink ordinary black tea in teabags.'

'Well in the States we call that kind of tea Orange Pekoe. But fine, you don't like it. So maybe Capsicum?' I bit my lip. 'That's what they call bell peppers in Australia.'

'Could we try less vegetables and more real names?'

'Ok, like what?'

She held the kitten up to the light to get a good look at her and said, 'Like Beatrix or Minerva.'

What was with the old woman names? 'How old do you think this cat is?' I snorted. 'Besides, this isn't the Middle Ages.'

She sniffed. 'I like those names. Have you never heard of Beatrix Potter, the author and illustrator?'

'And now you're going to tell me Minerva is the name of a character in some other riveting story you read as a child.'

She looked away as if to hide her eye roll. 'Minerva McGonagall is Harry Potter's teacher, but-'

'I knew it. Maybe let's stay away from references to Harry Potter, too?' I shook my head at her and yawned. 'If we're going for characters from the movies then I think Leia is a good contender.'

'Of course you do.'

'Why don't we table this discussion, and instead make a plan for this kitchen opening party we're having tomorrow? Maybe somebody has a good name we could steal.'

'Fine.'

I checked the fridge and pulled out ingredients. I was tired, but putting together chicken breast pieces in a balsamic sauce with cherry tomatoes over rice was no hardship. Julia's soggy noodles and overcooked egg sat abandoned on the coffee table. Perhaps her frugal diet was more to do with laziness than inability or even lack of finances.

'Jewel, there's enough here for you, too. Maybe give yourself a break and have some real food instead of that... slop?'

I could see her internal battle, and I was sure she would have refused my food a week ago – before we were friends – but now she sighed. 'Thanks, it looks lovely.'

She got up and regretfully put her noodles and egg in the compost while I got another plate out and dished her up some of my food. 'I hate binning food when there are so many people that don't have enough to eat.'

I bit my lip. 'I know technically that was food, once. But it doesn't look edible. Don't worry about it; nobody gets cooking right all the time.'

'I can cook food just fine.' She sniffed as though I had insulted her. I felt my forehead crease and gave her a doubtful look. 'The problem isn't that I don't know how to cook. It's that I don't have the patience for it. I get distracted and then things...'

'Burn.'

She sighed and nodded, her face a picture of sadness. 'Burn.'

'It's ok. You're good at other things.' I smiled when she rolled her eyes at me. 'Like, you're great with teenagers, and you have great ideas, and…'

'Yeah yeah, let's just eat.'

Chapter 14

Julia

After Nick cooked me dinner, we cleaned the flat together, and I went through a box I had packed up before going to Kenya and found some nice candles to decorate with. It struck me that, whilst it was just a couple of days since we had agreed to be friends, things felt more like we were an old couple cleaning the flat before the weekend. Thinking about how very natural it felt to throw a dinner party together made me uneasy to say the least. It felt inevitable that this *friendship* would end in heartbreak again, yet I felt unable to pull away and go back to being enemies. That scared me, so I decided not to think about it at all.

***

The next morning, Nick drove us to the supermarket to shop for groceries. Again, the feeling of being a couple was hard to ignore as we went through the shop loading the trolley together. Nick paid, and wouldn't take my offer of paying for half of it, which made it feel almost date-like. And that, too, was weird, as we were only grocery shopping – it wasn't as though we'd gone out for dinner or anything.

Walking past the flower stall on the way out, Nick pointed toward the flowers. 'What kind of flowers should we get?'

'Which do you like?' I said, trying to avoid the awkwardness.

'Considering I'm colour blind, I think it would be better if you pick, don't you?' His mouth curved up in the right corner as he raised his eyebrow.

I rolled my eyes and picked a bunch of deep pink roses and some baby's breath, thinking they'd make a nice arrangement.

'No lilies to go with the roses?' Nick asked.

I shivered. 'No, I can't stand the smell of lilies.'

'Oh?'

Without thinking I said, 'Yes. When my sister died people brought over lilies, and now that smell just reminds me of death.'

'Huh.' Nick got his wallet out to pay the lady for the flowers.

'No, you paid for everything else. I'll pay for these.'

He just shook his head and took the flowers up to the cashier. If it had felt like a date when he paid for the groceries, now it was worse. I couldn't remember a time when a guy had ever bought me flowers before.

'Nick, friends don't buy each other flowers,' I said when he came back to the trolley.

'Sure they do. Besides, we both get to enjoy these.' He took the trolley away from me and pushed it to the car as though there was nothing strange going on, so I shrugged it off and followed him.

We came home with ribs, corn on the cob, lots of fruit and vegetables for salads and a box of Nick's staple beer. Nick put the ribs in the oven to slowly cook for the afternoon, whilst I sorted out the flowers and set the table. Later, we were both in the kitchen sorting out the rest of the meal. I made a brownie to go in the oven once the ribs were done and started on some of the salads, whilst Nick kept an eye on the meat.

We spent the day telling stories of the last year, and maybe part of me imagined for a moment here and there what it would be like to be more than friends. I tried to quickly push those thoughts away, but eventually decided tomorrow would be soon enough to get back to reality.

I was chopping vegetables for a salad when Nick walked into the kitchen to check on the meat again.

'What's that song you keep humming?' he asked as he pulled barbeque sauce out of the fridge to put on the ribs.

I sighed. 'I keep getting these two songs we sang all the time in Kenya in my head. One is in Kiswahili and is all about how God is like no other, and the other is in English and is about how God is so faithful. Part of me loves the songs, because they remind me of Kenya. But I also hate them because when I think about God, I don't really think he's anything like as wonderful or exceptional as the songs make him out to be.' I waved my knife in the air as I talked. 'But I can't stop singing the stupid songs.'

'Oh yeah?'

'Yes. When I think of God, I'm not sure I love him much at all.'

'Oh, I know what you mean. I definitely don't love him either.'

'I mean, what's to love about him, really?' I went back to chopping the carrots for the salad. 'I know he died for me and everything, but I don't know what he expects in return? No matter what I do, it's never going to be good enough-'

'I don't think he wants to be repaid, though.' Nick was slathering the ribs in barbeque sauce and put one of the trays back in the oven to be grilled.

'Aye, technically I know that, but I think it's a load of rubbish.' I sighed. 'It seems to me he wants total obedience in return – for us to worship him and be prepared to do anything for him. In John it says that if you love Jesus you're to obey him.' I looked up at Nick. 'There are all kinds of things I wouldn't do, even if he told me to, so I guess I don't love him. And frankly, I'm not sure I want to worship a god that needs me to worship him. Especially when all I see around me is how messed up this world is. I don't think he's worthy of worship, you know?'

'Yeah, I hear you.' Nick snatched a carrot stick and leaned against the counter. 'I get angry just thinking about how people worship this god that is nothing more than a wrathful child abuser.'

'Still, I don't know what to do about it. I can't go through life not loving God, but also wanting to please him,' I said, mixing the carrots in with the potatoes and other vegetables and starting on the pickled gherkins. 'I'm so confused.' I turned toward Nick. 'Will you make the dressing for this potato salad?'

'Sure.' He went to get the ingredients out of the fridge and started mixing things for the dressing.

'Sometimes I wonder how things might be different if God was nothing like how I think. Like, what if he really didn't want to be repaid, and if he only had our best interests in mind when he asks for our obedience,' I said as I mixed the gherkins into the salad. 'What if God didn't send Jesus to the cross to be tortured, you know?'

Nick raised his eyebrow at me. 'You're talking about the garden of Eden, before sin entered the picture. And if it wasn't for sin, then maybe God would be ok, but God basically chose to deal with sin by killing his son. And that's where the whole concept fails in my opinion.'

I nodded, finished mixing the salad and started setting the table. We kept working in silence, both of us lost in our own thoughts, until we were just about finished and the doorbell rang.

Sophia and Miranda came in together. Sophia passed me a bottle of wine and gave me a hug. 'Gosh, something smells nice,' she said as she walked past me toward the kitchen. 'What's that you're cooking, Nick?'

'Hey, it might be me that's cooking,' I said.

Miranda gave me a dry look. 'You wish. If you were cooking we'd be eating noodles tonight. And there is no chance noodles can ever smell as good as that, whatever it is.' She pointed to the kitchen and gave me a hug.

'Yeah yeah.' I rolled my eyes. 'I did chop the veg and make the brownie though.'

'Good, good. There's hope for you still.' She smiled and pointed to the table as we walked into the living room. 'Nice flowers.'

'Nick had me pick them out.'

'He's buying you flowers now?' Miranda said quietly, her eyes wide.

'I know, I thought it was weird too, but he seems to think it's normal so, whatever.' I shrugged.

Miranda gave me a sceptical look but said, 'They're great flowers in any case.' She spotted the hand carved wooden salad bowl and tongs on the table. 'Wow, did you get those in Kenya?'

'Aye, they were a farewell gift from the school, to remember them by. Aren't they just gorgeous?' The bowl had a carved landscape with animals like giraffes, lions, zebras and so on along the outside of the bowl, and the tongs had two twinned stems with carved elephants at the top.

'No kidding.'

'They gave me them and two bags of Kenyan coffee.' I smiled. 'The coffee's gone now, though.'

'Yeah, I bet.' Walking into the kitchen, she said, 'Nick.'

'Miranda.' He leaned in to kiss her cheek absentmindedly as he kept listening to Sophia go on about what she liked about the kitchen.

As absentminded as those cheek kisses were, it didn't stop the wave of jealousy that came over me as I watched them. Embarrassed and confused, I turned away to get some glasses out of the cupboard. 'Who wants a drink?'

'Ah, and is this a new addition to the family?'

I felt my cheeks go hot as I turned to give Miranda a glare to make her stop with the awkward comments. She was scooping up the cat.

'I brought her home from work last night.' Nick smiled.

'Gosh, she's cute, but she likes to scratch, doesn't she?'

With his eyes sparkling Nick said, 'Reminded me of Jewel.'

Feeling all kinds of awkward, I sneered. 'Yeah, yeah, very funny.'

'What's her name?' Sophia asked.

'We haven't decided. Jewel hates all my suggestions, and I can't in good conscience name anyone Minerva or Beatrix, even if it is a cat, so her suggestions are out too.' Nick got the ribs out of the oven, spreading the smell of perfect looking ribs around the kitchen.

'Wow, that smells good,' Sophia said with a sigh. 'Bet you wish you weren't vegetarian now Mir, eh?'

Miranda smiled. 'Nah, that's alright. I'm sure they're lovely, but I'm sure I'll have plenty to eat.'

'If you have any suggestions that are not old lady names, we'd love to hear them,' Nick said as he got a knife out to start to separate the ribs. 'I was thinking earlier, Jewel – what do you think about Ginger?'

'No, that's an awful name. I'm not much of a cat person, but you can't call her Ginger.' Sophia shook her head.

'I know.' I grimaced. 'Honestly Nick, you are terrible at coming up with names.'

'I think you mean terrific, don't you?' He wiggled his eyebrows at me.

I sighed as I poked his shoulder. 'Aye, terrifically bad.'

101

Chapter 15

Julia

A few minutes later, Jack and Michael had arrived too. Nick was still cutting the ribs up as I got the corn-on-the-cob out of the microwave and set it on the table still in the husks.

'What do you guys think of the new kitchen?' I asked Michael and Jack, who were watching Nick and the ribs whilst sipping their beers.

Michael looked up. 'I like it,' he said and turned around. 'I think you've used the space well. Did you get rid of all the blue tack?'

Nick grinned. 'Yeah, there was enough blue tack in here to fill a tennis ball. It was everywhere. The drawers were all tacked together. It was just a matter of time before they would have fallen apart. Every piece of trim was stuck down with blue tack, and the door only closed because of the blue tack on the lock.' He shrugged. 'It's all gone now, though.'

Michael shook his head. 'These people and their blue tack, eh.'

'Hey, don't knock it. Blue tack and duct tape are what holds this country together,' Sophia said with a smile, giving Michael's arm a light push. He rolled his eyes at her and sipped his beer.

Nick shook his head. 'Well, this kitchen is now blue tack free. Also, all the things now live in their appropriate place.'

I straightened and looked at him, raising my eyebrows in question. 'As opposed to?'

He winked at me. 'As opposed to what it was like before, when you could never guess where you'd find a strainer or a glass.'

'What?' I snorted. 'Are you calling me disorganised?'

'Yes. Definitely.' He nodded decisively and grinned at me. I smiled back, because he was right. The kitchen had been an utter mess before. 'Anyway, let's eat.' He set the dish of ribs on the table.

The dining table was one of those skinny tables that folded down on both sides to make a small table to fit just one person or a couple of plants. Now, though, we had both sides up; with a nice table cloth, candles and flowers, it looked lovely. We all fit round it, with Nick and I sitting in the middle opposite each other.

Loading up our plates with ribs and salads, we stuffed our faces.

'Ah, this reminds me of being home in Canada,' Michael groaned. 'So good.'

'Oh, yeah?' I asked.

'Yeah, barbecued ribs and potato salad with corn on the cob, with a cold beer in the sun after a day at the beach. Can't get better than that.'

Nick put his head back. 'Yes, I think the food is what I miss the most about America too.'

'Really? Don't you miss your family and friends?' I asked.

He shook his head. 'Nah, my friends have moved on by now, and there's hardly any family to miss.'

'What about you, Michael? What do you miss about Canada?'

'I miss my family quite a bit.'

'Is it quite big, then?'

'Just my sister and parents, but we have a lot of cousins that we're close with.'

Nick said, 'I'll tell you what else I miss. The sunshine.'

'Ah, yes.' Michael looked at the rest of us. 'The sun is a big, yellow, hot thing that shines bright in the sky…'

'Oh, shut up.' Sophia rolled her eyes. 'Jules, would you shove him for me?'

'Hey…' Michael protested.

'Done.' I smiled. 'And for the record, I was surprised at how sunny it's been here since I came home from Kenya.'

'Except for the last two weeks,' Miranda muttered.

'Yes, I sure haven't seen much of it since coming back from Hong Kong,' Jack said.

'What's the cat called?' Michael changed the subject, stroking her back as she made herself comfortable in his lap.

'It doesn't have a name yet,' I said, still trying to eat more.

'She looks like Maple Syrup.' He held her up and set her down. 'Sweet little thing.'

I looked at Nick. 'I could go with Maple.'

'Me too.' He nodded, his grin making me all gooey inside. 'Maple the Fierce.'

And so the cat had a name.

When we couldn't eat anymore, we cleared the table, loaded the new dishwasher(!!), and Nick and Sophia got a game of chess going at the table.

'Let's have the brownie later; I need to lie on the floor a little first, I think,' I said, feeling rather full. Miranda brought over a throw and a cushion to lie on, and stretched out on the floor next to me with a sigh. Michael and Jack sprawled out on the couch and armchair with a beer each.

'Wine, anyone?' Sophia asked, and poured us some whilst Nick made his first chess move.

I looked at Miranda, who was scratching the nail varnish off her nails. 'Your nails look like they belong to a hobo. Let me go get some remover and we'll sort them out.' She shrugged, so I got up and got my nail stuff out. I put down a hand towel and started removing the old varnish.

'So, how's your cup project coming along?' asked Jack. 'Ready for investors yet?'

'Yes, we are.' Sophia gave a decisive nod. 'Miranda is adjusting the budget and we need to sort out the funding. Keen to invest, are you?'

He shrugged. 'I think you guys have a good idea and I think you'll need people around you to help with things like money, networks, publicity and things like that. At least initially. Don't you?'

'For sure. I think we're a little apprehensive because we feel that if we take people's money, then they will want to have a say as to how it is spent,' Sophia said distractedly as she moved something on the chess board. 'Check.'

Nick smirked and countered.

'Crap, I didn't see that coming. Right, let me think.' Sophia turned her focus back to the chess board.

'I think you girls should ask us guys to be part of your board.' Michael took a sip of his beer. 'Between us, we've got money, contacts and skills that could come in handy.'

'We know you guys could be helpful. I think we're just a little hesitant, as we're still only starting this project,' I said, and looked at Miranda's nails where I was finished removing the old nail varnish. 'Ok, now go wash your hands.'

'You can start up with just the three of you, of course, and between you I'm sure you have a lot of the skills. I don't really have much money to invest, but I was thinking I'd be happy to make you a promotional video if you want?' Michael said.

'Aw Michael, that's nice.' I blew him a kiss. He had always been the kind of guy to go out of his way to help others. 'I'm sure Sophia has ideas about that.'

'Yes, actually. I've been thinking we need something that both explains how the cup works, and also how they could be a solution for so many women. Selling the vision as well as the product.'

'I think we could start working on a script for it,' Michael said.

'Maybe you and Sophia could work on that, seeing as you guys live together?'

'Sorry, I'm not paying attention! I need to beat Nick here,' Sophia said and looked up from the chess board. 'What are you signing me up for now?'

'She's saying we should work on a script for a video together, seeing as we live together.'

'Sure, that works.' Sophia nodded distractedly.

I looked at Miranda as she sat back down. 'Which colour do you want now?' She picked a deep gray and held her hands out as I shook the bottle and started painting her nails.

'In the meantime,' Jack said. 'I think you should consider inviting us onto the board.'

Miranda rolled her eyes. 'Yeah yeah.'

'Where are you going to source the cups from?' Jack asked.

'None of your business,' Miranda muttered under her breath, but I think only I could hear her. She let out a sigh and said, 'I've got a couple of suppliers that have given me offers in China.'

'Oh yeah, what part of China?'

'Wouldn't you like to know,' she mouthed but answered Jack in a polite tone. 'One is in Guangzhou.'

'Are you going to go out for a visit?' Jack said.

'Aye, I'm thinking I'd like to go out and look at the options. And I want to see the factory.'

'If you need anything out there, I'm happy to come with you. I need to handle a few things in Hong Kong anyway in the next few weeks.'

'As if.' Miranda breathed through her teeth. Looking up at Jack she gave a polite smile and said, 'Thanks, I think I'll be fine.'

'I'm sure you will, love.' He rolled his eyes. 'I'm just saying I could help.'

'Beer, anyone?' I blurted to steer the conversation in a different direction. 'Or does anyone want a brownie?'

Miranda gave me a grateful smile and started fanning the hand I had finished painting the nails on. 'I'll have a top up of wine please.'

I filled up people's glasses and put the kettle on in preparation for dessert later.

'Check,' said Nick, and Sophia sighed and shook her head. 'Where is your funding coming from?'

Sophia moved her chess piece. 'We have a little money saved up, but you're right, we do need quite a bit more backing to get us going properly.'

'If you're doing it as a social enterprise, I reckon you should be looking for gifts, but also for loans,' said Nick. 'Check again. I'd be happy to put in both. And I'd be happy to help with whatever else you might need, too.'

'I want to say you're kind, but right now I'm a little annoyed with you. You've just ruined my plan.' Sophia pouted as she looked at the chess board. 'Or maybe... ok, no, that's fine. New plan.'

'Yeah, I can put money in too,' said Jack, earning him a glare from Miranda.

As the evening went on, we sat around, eating brownie with ice cream and peanuts. We talked about everything from our social enterprise, to Jack telling stories from Hong Kong, to Nick telling stories from the job sites he'd been on in the last year. Nick told a particularly gross one about being shot in the knuckle with a nail gun and ending up in hospital with blood poisoning, which started the injury stories off, and soon we were hearing all kinds of gruesome stories. It was late by the time they all left.

Nick looked at me once the door closed. Everything about this day had made me feel like we were an item, and I didn't want the evening to end. I knew he just wanted to be friends, and I promised myself I would stop pretending we were an actual couple tomorrow.

'Clean up tonight or tomorrow?'

'Tonight,' I said, trying to tell myself I was too busy tomorrow to handle the clean up then, even as I knew that I just wanted an excuse to hang out with Nick some more.

We straightened the living room and went to tidy the kitchen. I unloaded the dishwasher and filled it again, as Nick cleared the table and wiped down the counters. The kitchen was lovely, but small, and we were in each other's space a lot while working. He would stretch over me to put something away, or lean across me as he reached for something. I had goose bumps, and I was one hundred percent aware of him being so close. He bumped into me a couple of times, and at one point, I swear I thought he was about to kiss me, but he stepped away making some joke about how it was a shame he couldn't have extended the kitchen when he was renovating it. When things were put back to rights, we declared the kitchen properly open for business and called it a night.

I struggled to sleep that night, my skin still humming after cleaning the kitchen. I twisted and turned as I tried to make sense of this new friendship we were having and my feelings around it all.

Chapter 16

Julia

I had felt bad for not going to church since I came back from Kenya, but I didn't look forward to the guilt I knew would overwhelm me once I was there. To get rid of some of the anxiety, I ate the rest of the leftover brownie for breakfast before I set off. Nick was just getting up as I was leaving, looking much too good in his pyjama bottoms. I struggled not to stare at his chest. I knew he worked in construction, but did he have to go flaunting his muscles? I tried to remember that we were just friends, but failed dreadfully.

'You're going to church then?' He said, taking in the very appropriate dress I was wearing for church.

'Uh-huh.' I struggled to get proper thoughts to form into words. 'Why are you not wearing clothes?'

He smirked. 'Oh, am I distracting you?'

I quickly turned away, hiding my blushing face behind my hair as I put my shoes on. 'Whatever, I'm leaving. Bye.' I stumbled through the door, running down the stairs before I stopped to take a deep breath to get my heart rate to slow.

Being at church wasn't as bad as I'd expected. It was nice to see people and to catch up. Before the service started, I spoke to the new youth leader, Jessie, who asked if I was interested in helping out with the youth camp she was planning for the following summer. She was low on volunteers, so I felt bad and told her to count me in. Youth had always been my thing – that's why I'd become a high school teacher, after all.

The hour long service passed quickly compared to the day long services I had become used to in Kenya, and still it felt longer. It puzzled me that church in Edinburgh, where people seemed so wealthy and had so much to be thankful for, was so dull. In Kenya, where people were so poor, it had been such a time of celebration.

After the service, I helped mum serve teas and coffees. It seemed everybody wanted to speak to me and, whilst I enjoyed catching up, I came away feeling like they weren't all that interested in me or my experience in Kenya. Instead, when they found out I was only working part time at the high school, they quickly recruited me to do half a day a week in the church charity shop. The lady who organised the church visits to the old people's homes signed me up to be part of their singing group. I also agreed to join one of the church cleaning teams. Throughout these conversations I found it almost impossible to say no – all of their different initiatives and programs seemed so worthwhile. Still, I wasn't sure how on earth I was going to be able to fit everything in with teaching and with things about to kick off with the social enterprise.

After church, I met up for lunch with Sophia and Miranda at our favourite place in Bruntsfield, not very far from my flat.

'Gosh, this is a good burger,' Sophia said.

'I wish I had your metabolism.' I looked from her burger to my chicken salad. Her burger looked amazing. 'Still, this salad *is* nice too.'

'Uh-huh.' Sophia gave it a doubtful look. 'Oh, can I have the bacon in your salad?'

'No way, you greedy gorb. It's the bacon and avocado that make this salad,' I said over the food in my mouth.

'How can you want more meat after the rib fest last night?' Miranda had ordered some pancakes.

'Those were some awesome ribs last night.' Sophia wore a dreamy look.

'I know. Nick and I are having the leftovers for dinner tonight.'

Miranda glanced at Sophia before clearing her throat and asking, 'So what's going on with Nick and you?'

'What do you mean? There's nothing to say.'

Miranda raised her eyebrow at me. 'There's that cat he bought you...'

'A cat's for life, not just for Christmas,' Sophia helpfully chimed in.

Miranda nodded and continued, 'And then he bought you flowers?'

'He said they weren't a big deal, though. And friends give each other flowers, right?'

Sophia rolled her eyes at me. 'Has Michael ever bought you flowers?'

I thought about it. 'Yes, he has, actually. I mean, they were the I'm-sorry-you're-going-through-a-hard-time kind of flowers, and a long time ago.' I could tell Sophia was surprised by that. I shrugged. 'Michael's sweet like that.'

'Yes, Michael is, but Nick isn't,' said Miranda.

I sighed as I debated what to tell them, but decided honesty would be the best way forward, considering our history and how we were about to go into business together. 'Yeah, ok.' I took a deep breath. 'I know I said it wasn't a big deal that we're friends now, and all that, but I might have lied?'

Sophia and Miranda shared a knowing look.

'You don't say?' Sophia said dryly.

'You guys know that when I first got to know Nick, I had the biggest crush on him. For two years, he was all I could think of, and I was pretty sure there was nobody that could ever measure up to him.' Miranda and Sophia both nodded. 'So early on in our first year of uni, I had psyched myself up to think I had a chance with him, but soon realised that was never going to happen. We had a very awkward afternoon in October that year, and it was glaringly obvious that he didn't see me as anything other than Jack's little sister. I was pretty heartbroken and spent the next month crying. That's when Michael bought me flowers, by the way.' I looked at Sophia.

'Aw, that was sweet of him.' Sophia smiled. 'And whilst I hadn't heard about the flowers before, I did know the rest of it. It was pretty obvious you had a major crush on Nick back then, and you did talk slash cry to us about it when you realised he wasn't into you.'

'Uh-huh,' Miranda said. 'I reckon what happened was you decided you couldn't keep going like that, and so, if he couldn't be your boyfriend, you couldn't be his friend. So he became your enemy instead.'

I blushed. 'Well, that was how it started. But as time went on, I really started to dislike him for real.' I sighed. 'In any case, when

I came home to Edinburgh to find him living in my flat, all I wanted was for him to move out. But then a few weeks ago, I came home to the living room having been converted into a fort, and we had a long chat about how it might be time to grow up and put our feud behind us. So we decided to be friends. The problem is, though…'

'You started to fall for him again,' Miranda said in a matter of fact tone.

I closed my eyes and nodded slowly. 'Aye.'

'So what does that mean exactly?'

'Do you know how hard it is to be friends with somebody that looks like him?' I pulled my fingers through my hair in frustration. 'I come home to him fixing something in the kitchen wearing a pair of jeans and a tight shirt, or— like this morning— his pyjama bottoms. And nothing else. *Also*, it turns out he's actually a really nice guy, and he's smart and interesting.'

'You don't have to go falling in love with him just because he looks good,' Sophia said.

I rolled my eyes. 'If I could control it, I would. I just don't seem to be able to. I'm not sure what to do. I know he's not interested in anything other than being friends. So I'm thinking I just need to break it all off and ask him to move out. I don't think I can handle being friends with him.'

'Aw, Jules. Does it really have to be an all or nothing thing? I've been *married* to Michael for four years now,' Sophia said, using her fingers to make quotation marks in the air. 'And I know he's going to be asking for a divorce in the next few months, once he's got indefinite leave to remain in the UK, and that will suck, but I'm thankful I got to be with him for the time I have.'

'Sophia, the only reason you don't have a proper marriage to Michael is because you haven't had the guts to talk to him about it.' Miranda shook her head at Sophia, then looked at me intently and squeezed my arm across the table. 'I think you are right to break it off, Jules. If you know it's not going to ever go anywhere, you are better off breaking things off now than later. The longer it goes on for, the more it will hurt when you finally get there. Believe me.'

'Gah! Miranda!' Sophia shook her head. 'You can't throw all men out with Jack's dirty bathwater!'

Miranda looked away. 'That's not what I'm doing. Still though, broken hearts are not fun.'

'I know.' I sighed.

'Let's talk about something else,' Sophia said.

'Great idea.' Miranda nodded. 'Did either of you go to church today?'

'I went.' I put my hand up. 'It was my first time back since before I left. Has it always been like that?'

'Like what?'

'I got signed up to help lead the youth camp in the summer, work in the charity shop one morning every week, sing in the singing group that visits the old people's homes once a month, and clean the church every three weeks.'

Sophia looked at me, bewildered. 'Why did you sign yourself up to all that?'

'Well, I love youth, so that was a no-brainer. And I like clothes, and I love the idea of recycling and making sustainable affordable clothing options, so that was fairly straight forward, too. I like to sing, and I really feel for all those old people that never get visited, so I couldn't say no to that. And I figured if I'm going to use the church, I ought to be part of cleaning it.'

'What about Sunday school? Did you not get signed up for that?' Sophia said drily.

'No, Mum signed me up to that a few weeks ago, but I think I'm only on the emergency call list, so I might not have to do it.'

'Why do you do this to yourself?' Sophia gave me an exasperated look.

I put my hands up and said with conviction, 'Because the kids should have a good program!'

'But how is it your job to make all that happen? And how are you going to manage that with your schedule?' They looked at me as though I was some kind of mystery to solve. 'You already seem pretty stretched with how much you've been filling in for other teachers at school.'

I shrugged. 'I'm going to have to make time, aren't I?'

'Yeah, when you figure out how to do that, let me know, would you?' Miranda snorted. 'I could use an extra few hours in my week.'

I rolled my eyes at her, shaking my head. 'I know. But if I don't do these things, then who will?'

'Who knows? Who cares?' Sophia waved her hands in the air. 'Honestly, you can't be the saviour of all these people.'

'That may be, but somebody needs to do something.'

'There will always be people or projects that need help, but you need to decide what your priorities are. And right now, I want to know if you are just playing at this Project Cup thing, or if that's really something that you want to give a proper go. Because if you want to go for it, you won't have time to volunteer all your time to your mum's church projects.'

Miranda nodded. 'It sounds harsh, but Soph is right. I think Project Cup could be something amazing, but I'm only prepared to go for it if we're all prioritising it above all other projects.'

'Otherwise it's a waste of time.' Sophie looked at me.

'Ok, ok. I hear you guys. Fine. I'll tell them I spoke too soon.' I twirled my glass of water, the ice clinking around. I wasn't sure I could wriggle out of any of the things I'd signed up for, but I made a mental note to not bring it up again. What they didn't know wouldn't hurt them, right? I'd just work extra hard and they wouldn't find out. 'I was thinking about the youth camp, though. What do you guys think about starting some youth summer trips where we could bring the youth out to somewhere like Kenya to maybe learn about the issues people are facing in places like that?'

Sophia pursed her lips in thought. 'That's an interesting idea for further down the line, but I think we need to get things up and running before we can be thinking about things like that.'

Miranda nodded. 'You have some great ideas, Jules, and keep them coming, but that one is definitely not for right now.' She smiled as I rolled my eyes.

'You ok?' Miranda asked as the coffee we'd ordered arrived.

I nodded, put on a smile and said, 'Yeah, I'll be fine. Just a lot to process.'

She squeezed my hand. 'Do you still want to talk about Project Cup?'

I bit my lip, decided I needed something to take my mind off all the drama anyway, and nodded. So we pulled out our notebooks and switched gears.

'How did you get on this week, Jules?' Miranda asked.

'I looked up what it would cost to do three weeks in Kenya in January.' I slid the paper with all the numbers across the table to Miranda.

'Great, I'll add that in to the budget.' Miranda nodded and pulled up her budget sheet, and then looked up at us. 'I've looked at tickets to China, as well.'

'When do you want to go?'

'The sooner the better, right?' Sophia said.

'Yes, I was thinking October. I looked at some tickets.' She pulled up a different document on her laptop. 'I'd like to go ahead and book fairly soon as the prices keep rising. But then we need to decide what we're doing about funding this.' She looked at me and Sophia. 'I'd like to think we'll be able to take a salary at some point, but that won't be anytime soon. First we'll need to make some significant sales. We won't have sales for a few months, and I think we probably need to expect to not be able to take salaries for the first year at least.'

'Right.' Sophia and I nodded.

'We need to look at how we front all these initial costs like tickets to China and Kenya, promotional stuff and all that, not to mention the initial order of cups.' She gave an awkward smile. 'So I'll pay for my trip to China.'

'Really?' Sophia frowned.

'Yeah, I always wanted to go to China, and here's a great excuse.' Miranda shrugged.

After talking finances for a while we decided that, even with the savings we each had to put in, we would need to get a loan or some form of investment, as well.

'I think we need to talk with Jack and Nick again,' Sophia said. 'Nick would give us some kind of investment just to spite his dad, and Jack would at least loan us some money. They've said as much.'

I put my head in my hands and groaned. 'You guys, I hear what you're saying, but do you see how awkward it is for me to go home and effectively cut Nick out of my life today and then turn around to ask him to invest in my social enterprise?' I dragged my hands through my hair. 'And as far as investments go, it's a terrible one. We're basically asking him to give us money to spend on menstrual products! At best, he could get the money back by selling his share in the social enterprise, but he will never make any money off his investment. What guy would do that?'

Sophia shook her head, 'Yes, I know it sounds ridiculous, and you're right in that we need to offer him equity in the company, but you underestimate how much he disdains his money. Have you ever asked him about his dad?' I shook my head, and she continued, 'You should do that. It might explain a lot.'

'I get the awkwardness,' Miranda said. 'I don't want Jack involved either. We could offer them equity for money, but retain at least 60% of the company. That way they won't have a say in anything, anyway.'

'You'll have to see them at board meetings, but we don't have to have them very often, and we would write up an understanding where they would be silent partners,' Sophia said. 'Let me talk to them.'

'What do you think about asking Michael to do some promotional videos and we would pay him with equity? That way they would all be in on it,' I asked.

'That's not a bad idea.' Miranda nodded.

'Sure, I'll check with him too, then. Will you send me the budget in the next couple of days, Mir? As soon as you've adjusted it based on our decisions today? Then I can show it to them, and it will give me a clear idea as to how much I'm asking them for.'

'Yep.' Miranda made a note. 'Great. So is that everything for today?'

I nodded but Sophia shook her head. 'I wanted to run an idea by you guys, if that's ok.'

'Ideas are always welcome here,' I answered with a grin, and Miranda rolled her eyes and smiled.

'I have a work friend who has done some work for a company that has been sharing a market stall at the Christmas Market with two other companies for the last few years. They've worked out a schedule, and alternate the stall every week. That way each company only has to pay a third of the price for the stall, and they only have to cover the stall a third of the time, but they all get to take advantage of the Christmas Market shoppers.'

'Huh,' I said. 'That's a great idea!' The Edinburgh Christmas Market was an annual festival which attracted thousands of tourists from all over Europe and transformed the centre of Edinburgh in the weeks leading up to and after Christmas.

'Yes, I thought so too,' Sophia continued. 'So, this year, one of the companies has decided to pull out of the arrangement and, they're looking for someone to cover their dates. What do you guys think?'

'Do you have the figures?' Miranda asked.

'Of course.' Sophia smirked, pulling out a piece of paper with all the details for us to look over. We chatted for a while, and decided we would go for it.

'Yay!' Sophia did a quick clap with her hands and gave us a wide grin. 'This is so exciting!'

I laughed. 'I know!'

Miranda raised her almost empty glass of water. 'Cheers to going all in!'

I raised my glass of water and Sophia her cup of tea. 'Cheers!'

Chapter 17

Julia

As I left the restaurant to go home, I smiled in anticipation of seeing Nick again before remembering that I now had to unfriend him. I spent the walk home wrapped up in thinking about how to go about ending our friendship, how I could avoid going back on my promises to help out with things at church without Miranda and Sophia finding out, and Project Cup. By the time I was home I was an anxious mess.

I didn't know how to tell Nick to get lost, when what I really wanted was to keep going and hope everything would work out in the end. Still, I knew from experience that would leave me broken.

'Coffee. I need coffee,' I muttered as I kicked off my shoes and made my way to the kitchen, passing Nick in the living room on the way.

'Hey,' he said. 'How's it going?'

'Fine.'

'Right.' His expression clearly saying he didn't believe me. He didn't push, though. 'I was thinking, now that I'm done with the kitchen, I'm going to start on the bathroom. So I need you to move all your stuff out of there.'

'Sure, fine.' I said, his words not even registering as I filled the kettle and put it on, filling a cafetiere with coffee powder and grabbing a bag of crisps out of the cupboard as I waited. After the lunch I'd just had I wasn't hungry at all, but the anxiety needed to be fed.

Nick sauntered into the kitchen and leaned against the counter. 'Are you going to tell me what's going on?'

'Do you want coffee?' I asked as I stuffed my mouth with crisps.

'Ok.'

I reached to get him a cup, and he got the milk out of the fridge. I filled the cafetiere and waited quietly for it to brew, even as I felt like I was about to explode with anxiety. Nick raised his eyebrow as he waited me out, and as I plunged the coffee I couldn't help but blurt out, 'Look Nick, I'm sorry, but I can't do the friends thing with you.'

He sighed and gave me a patient smile. 'What do you mean?'

'I mean that here we are being friends and flat mates, and on one hand the last couple of weeks have been great. I've enjoyed not being angry at you all the time...' I stopped, trying to work out how to say the rest.

'And I've enjoyed not having salt in my coffee in the mornings,' he said, not missing a beat. He looked at me pointedly as I bit my lip, trying not to smile.

'I bet.'

'So what's the problem?'

I poured the coffee and decided to just 'rip the plaster off,' and took a deep breath. 'The problem is, and always has been, that I don't want to be your friend.'

'Why not? I'm good friendship material.' He looked puzzled. 'I cook, renovate things, pick up after myself – what's wrong with me?'

'There's plenty wrong with you, you numpty. That's not the problem. The problem is I want to be more than friends with you. And I know you don't see me that way.'

'You do?' He frowned.

I took a deep breath and looked at him. 'Of course. I've always known. Well, ever since that time when I was in my first year of uni, when Michael and I went over to see you and you hardly spoke to me and just wanted to play xbox games.'

'What?' Nick's frown grew deeper.

I sighed. 'Remember that time when Michael and I came over and you told me to have some grapes and then ignored me and played computer games with Michael for the rest of the evening?'

Nick snorted. 'What? So I played computer games, and from that you take that I don't like you?'

'Yes!'

Nick shook his head, a smile tugging at his lips. 'Jewel...'

'Look, I get it. You see me as Jack's little sister, and you probably always will. You wouldn't date a girl like me. You date nice, well put together girls, like lawyers or who work in banking.

Girls that wear heels and suits and that have nice, glossy and straight hair. Not a quirky, frizzy-haired girl who looks drunk when wearing heels, and who loves teenagers, and coffee, and has millions of strange ideas, and can't cook.'

I looked at him carefully, his blank face not giving away any of his thoughts. It struck me that he would be great at poker.

'I know all that,' I continued. 'But when I'm with you, I still end up wishing that things might be different.'

'Keep going.' Nick took a sip of his drink.

I shook my head and figured I didn't have anything to lose at this point. I steeled myself and kept going. 'I wish you'll wake up one morning and want to be with me the way I want to be with you. I start pretending that we are a real couple, not just friends. And I know if this continues, I'll end up a heartbroken mess again.'

'Again?'

'Yes! Again.' I gave a dry laugh. 'Why do you think we've been fighting all these years?'

He smirked. 'I didn't realise you were a *heartbroken mess.*'

'Gah!' I pushed my hands through my hair and pursed my lips. 'Anyway… One day you'll find one of those nice, composed girls you like, and she'll stick. You'll end up marrying and having a family with her. And if I'm your friend, I'm meant to be there in the background to cheer you on. I'm supposed to be happy for you and make friends with her, when in reality I would be shattered and I'd want to scratch her eyes out and buy a dog just so he would chew her fancy heels.' I sighed, finally coming to the end of my words.

'Wow.' He bit the inside of his cheek as if to keep from smiling. 'I told you you're just like Maple.'

Ignoring his last comment, I looked him in the eye and said, 'So. As nice as these last few weeks have been, I can't be your friend. It hurts too much.' I looked away as I started feeling the embarrassment that was now flooding me after blurting everything out without filter.

'Huh,' he said, causing me to look back at him. His mouth pulled up on the left side as he raised his eyebrow. 'That sounds like an ultimatum.'

'What? No!' I gave my head a violent shake. 'I'm not giving an ultimatum. I'm informing you that we can't be friends, so you need to move out of here.'

'It sounds to me as though you're saying you can either be my girlfriend or you can not be in my life at all.'

Startled, I cleared my throat. 'But being your girlfriend isn't an option, so…'

'Why not?'

I tilted my head and spoke slowly, as if speaking to someone of lower intelligence. 'Because you don't like me that way.'

He slowly raised one of his eyebrows. 'Says who?'

My eyes widened and my hands went to my hair again. I was starting to feel exasperated with him. 'Listen, we've known each other for nine years now, and in the beginning I didn't exactly try to cover up that I had a crush on you. You just ignored me. When I came over with Michael in my first year of uni, you made it pretty clear that you weren't, and never would be, interested in me.'

'Yeah, you said that. But what does that mean?'

'Argh,' I groaned. 'I mean, I showed up looking as much as I could like somebody you would normally date, and you didn't even look at me. You offered me some grapes and put the xbox on. You were clearly not interested.'

'Oh, I remember now.' He sighed. 'Are you talking about that time when Michael rang and said you guys were on your way and that I should put out some snacks or something? So I ran to the corner store and picked up some crackers, brie and corn chips…'

'And grapes.' I inserted. 'You offered me grapes.'

'Right. And grapes. I put it all on a tray and told myself to play things cool just as you guys buzzed to be let in.' He moved some hair out of his face and put it behind his ear. 'I knew you had a crush on me, but I couldn't get involved with you then. You were Jack's sister, and he'd told me from the start that you were off limits. So I played it cool, and I figured that was all ok. It's not like I brushed you off or anything!'

'What? You wouldn't even look at me! You acted entirely bored and then spent the rest of the time ignoring me and playing X-box with Michael!'

He looked away. 'Yeah, well Michael told me afterwards that I'd been a bit aloof. Look, it wasn't easy. I wanted to be with you but I couldn't. So I needed you as close as I could, but without it going anywhere. Michael told me you were pretty broken up about things, so I bought some flowers for him to give to you...'

'*You* bought those flowers?' I said, stunned. 'I thought they were from Michael.'

'Yeah. He agreed not to tell you they were from me.' He shrugged again. 'Anyway, then I didn't see you for a couple of weeks. The next time I saw you, you told me you didn't hate me, but if I was ever on life-support, you would happily unplug me to charge your phone, or some other insult like it. Delivered with a too-sugary smile of course.' He shook his head and grinned at me. 'You always had the most terrible insults.'

I smirked. 'Yeah, I might have Googled 'clever insults' so as to always have one ready for you.'

'Of course you did.' He sighed. 'At first I was just stunned, but when I left that night I couldn't stop laughing. And I figured if you couldn't be my girlfriend, at least I was the only one in your life that you had an awkward frenemy relationship with. So I started playing along, and it stuck.'

My eyebrows were approaching my hairline. 'And it stuck,' I repeated.

He looked at me as if I was being slow. 'Yeah, it stuck.' His mouth curved into half a smile and he kept going. 'It worked fine for what? Six years? Then you left for Kenya and I was going crazy with how much I missed you. So I spoke to your dad and moved in just a month after you left. Everything here reminded me of you. Even the way you had "organised" the kitchen.' He made air-quotes with his hands and gestured to the kitchen. 'Man, the kitchen drove me crazy, but I couldn't change it for the longest time, because at least it reminded me of you. Then you were about to come home, and I figured it was time to sort it out.'

'Right.' I rolled my eyes at him and muttered, 'Except I still don't know anyone else that would renovate someone else's kitchen for free.'

He kept going. 'And then you were back. Just as testy as you always were and, to begin with, I couldn't wait to hear what barb would come out of your mouth next. But the more I was around you, I figured it was time we moved on. We were kids when this all started, but we're adults for real now. I figured I'd get you to warm up to the idea by being my friend first.' He nodded and smiled. 'Sort of worked.'

'*Sort of worked?*' I stared at him. 'I feel so patronised. Couldn't you have spoken to me about all this instead?'

'You mean like you did?' He said pointedly.

'I didn't have a plan for how I was going to lure you into a relationship.' I looked away. 'I still don't understand why you didn't just talk to Jack in the first place.'

'Yeah, looking back, maybe I should have. I wasn't as smart back then, maybe? And maybe I wasn't ready for a relationship. And I didn't want him to kill me or anything.'

I snorted. 'Like he could kill anyone.'

'Yeah whatever. Jewel, my point is…' He took my hand in his and looked me in the eye. Any annoyance I had been feeling toward him forgotten as my heart went crazy in my chest. Now all I could feel was his eyes studying me and the skin where he was touching me was on fire.

'Yes?'

'Being my girlfriend is an option I think you should consider.' His eyes didn't leave mine as his other hand went to tuck my hair behind my ear.

'Oh yeah?' I breathed, my mind having gone blank.

His mouth quirked up. 'Yeah.'

'I need some water,' I blurted, pulling away to fill a glass at the sink. I took a long sip, my thoughts rushing back as I started to be able to breathe again. Was he for real? I turned toward him again, feeling my cheeks go hot as I saw him grin at me. 'How do you expect me to be able to think when you look at me like that?'

'I don't think you need any more time to think.'

I put my water down and looked at him. 'I think… you might be right.'

I watched as he came toward me, slowly, his piercing green eyes locked on mine, as though he was trying not to scare me off.

As if that would have been possible.

The air sparkled with anticipation. Not quite able to believe what was happening, I took a step toward him. He stopped a few inches away from me and ran his hands up my cheeks. His eyes dipped to my mouth and I felt my arms find their way to his waist. I held my breath as I felt his gentle, strong hands cup my face.

I closed my eyes as he moved in to brush his soft lips against mine. He felt warm and strong and safe and I never wanted to leave.

Too soon he pulled back. He searched my face as if to get a reading of what I was thinking. When he was sure I wasn't about to bolt, he said, 'I take it you're not going to make me move out then.'

I smiled. 'Again.'

Rising to my toes, I ran a hand up his chest and to his face. The scruff of his beard brushed against my fingers as they went to his neck to bring his mouth to mine again.

This time he tilted his face to the side as his lips explored mine. He retreated a little, just to come back and nip at my bottom lip. His tongue darted over the bite as if to soothe it. His hands cradled my head, fingers massaging my scalp as he deepened the kiss. He tasted of cinnamon, and I wasn't sure if my lips tingled because I was *kissing Nick*, or because of the cinnamon.

I felt my chest expand, and I'm sure I moaned.

I had kissed guys before. Of course I had. Like, there was the guy I'd dated for two years in uni before I found out he was also seeing about five other girls at the same time. And a couple of others after that.

This was different, though.

It felt like I was being kissed for the first time, the memory of the others paling into insignificance as his lips moved across mine.

Pulling back, I took a moment to catch my breath. One side of his mouth pulled up and he pulled me in for a hug, his face burrowing into the hair at my neck. The few and far between hugs we had shared in the past had been quick and awkward, and still his cologne smelled familiar.

'I can't believe this is really happening.' I sighed. 'It's going to take me a little while to get used to this not just being a dream I'll wake up from.'

He kissed my forehead and looked down at me. 'You don't think you've had nine years to get used to the idea of us?'

Smiling, I rubbed my cheek against his chest. 'No. I spent the last seven years convinced this would never, in a million years, happen.'

He dipped his head to mine, and I tilted upward to meet him. His lips drifted across my cheek, placing soft kisses along the way.

'I love your freckles.'

I pulled back, shaking my head to clear it. 'You what?'

'I said I love your freckles. They remind me of the summertime. How the sun shines on you and you're all I can see.'

I rolled my eyes at him. 'Yeah right.'

He shook his head at me, but didn't press. Instead his lips found mine again, his fingers playing with my hair, each tug causing my scalp to tingle. He kissed me for a good long while, scrambling my thoughts until I felt dizzy.

Or maybe that was caused by a lack of oxygen.

I took a deep breath, savouring the smell of his cologne as he lifted me onto the kitchen counter.

'Do you know how many times I've thought of doing this?' he murmured between kisses.

He only pulled back when his phone chimed on the counter. Looking down at my face, he sighed, 'I'm meant to be playing squash with your brother this afternoon.'

'Um…' I pulled away so I could form coherent thoughts. 'That's ok. I've got to mark book reports, so it's probably for the best.' My mouth was still tingling as he reached for his phone. 'Is he downstairs now?'

'Yeah.' He kissed me again, quickly this time. 'I better go before he comes up.'

'Good luck.'

'Oh, I'll beat him, no worries,' he said with a confident grin.

'It might be an idea to let him win this time to help him come to terms with us being together?'

He rolled his eyes. 'As if.' Then he gave me a stern look and said, 'Don't go anywhere. We're picking this right back up when I get home.'

I smiled. I was right where I wanted to be – no need to go anywhere.

He was whistling as the door closed behind him and I turned back to the now stone cold coffee on the counter. My smile stretched from ear to ear as I waited for the coffee to warm up in the microwave.

I picked up the kitten that was leaning against my leg. 'You saw all that Maple, didn't you? I'm not just making it up, right?' I rolled my eyes at myself and sighed. 'How am I supposed to concentrate on book reports now?'

I got my coffee and spent the next two hours on the couch in the living room, the kitten cosied up next to me. I tried my best to focus, but mostly I stared out the window with a cheesy grin on my face.

Chapter 18

Nick

All logical thought had fled my mind as I was wrapped up in the whirlwind that was Julia. We had fought our feelings for each other for so long and now that we'd let go, I didn't want to leave.

The force of the feelings was overwhelming, though, and I knew we both needed some space to process the way our relationship had shifted. So instead of cancelling squash with Jack, I left Julia with a kiss, grabbing my phone before running down the stairs.

'I was starting to think you weren't coming,' Jack said as I got into his car.

I grinned. 'Yeah, me too.' I wasn't sure how to tell him about Julia and me, but I wasn't going to keep our relationship a secret. 'So…'

Jack turned to me as he waited at a red light. He bit his lip as he studied my face. 'Julia and you finally decided to go for it, huh?'

I shook my head but couldn't stop my grin. 'Something like that, yes.'

He slapped my shoulder. 'About time, man.'

I took a deep breath as I realised he wasn't upset. 'How did you know?'

'Just a hunch. Or it might have been the text Julia sent two minutes ago saying "be kind to Nick". I figured she'd only say that because she'd been so mean to you she was worried she might've broken you…' He shrugged. 'And then your face gave you away. Not seen you smile like that much since…' He thought about it. 'Ever.'

I caught sight of my face in the side mirror. Yes, that smile would have been a giveaway. 'So, you ok with this?'

'Couldn't wish for more.' He nodded. 'I don't want to hear any details, though.'

Even as I felt relief at Jack's reaction, I had a niggling feeling that it was all too easy. Jack knew me better than most, and I knew he shouldn't be happy his sister was involved with me. He should be warning me off, reminding me of how I'd always said long-term relationships weren't my thing, and questioning where I was going with all this. Had I changed my mind? Was I suddenly thinking I could give a long-term relationship a go after all? Or was I just playing around with Julia?

Not sure about the answers to any of those questions, I focused on getting my attention on the squash game.

***

Jack didn't stand a chance against me on the squash court that day. All the thoughts as to whether Julia and I were right to start a relationship fell to the wayside as I hit the ball.

'Bit off your game, huh?' I said, after I'd won three straight games.

Jack grinned. 'Yeah, maybe it's been a while since I played squash. Out of practice.'

'Uh-huh, about six years?'

'Something like that.'

'Well, I'll be happy to keep beating you until you get back into it.'

'I'm sure you are.' He snorted. 'Shouldn't be long before I'm back to where I used to be though.'

I grinned. 'Well, in any case, I've got to get back home to your sister.'

He shook his head but instead of giving me a glare, like he should have, he smiled. 'Yeah, and that's about as much as I want to hear about that.'

Maybe he believed Julia had changed my mind about relationships, and maybe he was right. Maybe I could see myself in a long-term relationship with her after all.

***

Walking up the steps to the apartment, I decided getting involved with Julia didn't have to automatically come with a lifetime plan. We could see where things went and take it easy. Right?

Right?

I took off my shoes in the hallway, feeling good about my decision, and stepped into the living room where she sat.

Her wild hair was covering part of her face as she sat curled up on the couch. She was asleep with the cat curled up next to her and her books scattered all over the coffee table.

I knew then, coming home to her would never be a hardship. She was home for me, and if I got to come home to her for the rest of my life, I'd be a lucky guy.

Careful not to wake her, I covered her in a blanket and kissed the top of her head before going for a shower, as I promised myself to do everything I could to be the man she deserved.

***

When I came back, Julia was awake again and back at work with her school books.

'What did Jack say?' she asked.

'He's fine,' I said with a shrug. 'He hasn't played in a few years, but I couldn't let him win. He'll be sore tomorrow.' I kissed her cheek, breathing her in before going to the kitchen.

'Do you want a beer?' I asked, my head in the fridge as she came into the kitchen.

'Yeah, thanks.' She came up behind me and I turned to her and kissed the crook of her neck.

'How's it going?' I closed the fridge and she rose onto her toes to peck me on the cheek.

'Not bad.' She smiled. 'Do you want me to warm the ribs, or how do you want to eat them?'

'I'll sort it out.' I smirked. 'We wouldn't want to burn them, would we?'

She pushed at my arm and did her best not to smile. 'I think I could warm ribs without burning them.'

I raised my eyebrows at her. '*You think*, being key words there. Let's not take any risks.'

'Yeah, yeah.' She rolled her eyes at me and went back to the couch.

I sorted out the leftovers and passed her a plate before sitting down next to her on the couch.

'This is the messiest meal ever, but it's so good.' She sighed between ribs.

'I know.' It really was good.

Everything was good. I had Julia and ribs. What more could I wish for?

'So… I had lunch with Soph and Mir after church, and Soph said I should ask you about your dad.'

I straightened. It was as though she had thrown a stone through the window, shattering glass everywhere. 'What about my dad?'

'Exactly. What about your dad?'

I stopped chewing and looked at her over my rib. I didn't want to talk about my dad with her. Not with anyone. I looked away. 'I don't know what you're talking about.'

She raised her eyebrows and pursed her lips. 'Sure you don't.'

Things had been so good just a minute ago. Why would we ruin it all with talking about my dad? 'Look, I don't have much good to say about him. So let's talk about something else, ok?'

She looked at me before deciding to drop it. 'Fine.'

'Great.' Thankful she didn't insist, I went back to my ribs and kept eating. 'So… Do you still have work to do tonight, or do you want to watch a movie with me?'

'I've got more work, but I guess I can do it in here and watch a film at the same time.' She seemed hesitant at first but picked something to watch and spent the evening curled up next to me. Her books were spread out on the coffee table and the movie was on in the background, but no assignment was marked that evening. And I wouldn't be able to tell you what movie we watched.

All I had eyes for was my wild Jewel.

Her eyes sparkled up at me, as though she knew some secret she couldn't wait to share with me. Her hair was soft between my fingers as I held her close and placed gentle kisses over her face.

How had we waited nine years to do this?

Chapter 19

Julia

I checked my phone when I went to bed that night, and saw the notification that Sophia had sent a message on the thread.

Sophia: Did you talk to Nick?

Me: Yes. Didn't go how I expected it to though.

Sophia: …

Me: I think we decided to be more than friends…?

Sophia: You think??

Me: Yes

Miranda entered the conversation: Are you for real??

Me: Aye

Miranda: Are you sure this is what you want?

Me: Only for the last nine years.

Miranda: Well then I'm thrilled for you!

Sophia: Me too!! I want all the details!

Me: Going to sleep now. I'll tell you when we go up Arthur's Seat.

Sophia: That's A WHOLE WEEK away!

I chuckled. We all had full-on work schedules over the next week, so we wouldn't see each other until our Arthur's Seat climb.

Me: I know!! Maybe I'll ring you guys, but I need to sleep now. Good night xx

***

Over the next week we fell into a routine. Nick started dropping me off at school on his way to work, and when we came home I watched him cook dinner. Once in a while he would allow me to chop something, but on the whole, he did the cooking. I can't say I missed eating pot noodles, porridge, or a can of tuna and a boiled egg for dinner, and he was happy to cook.

I spent evenings marking assignments, lesson planning, emailing Mrs Mwangi and Grace about the visit in January, meeting with Jessie about the youth work, coming up with a better system for the church charity shop, practicing singing with the church singing group, visiting old people's homes and cleaning the church.

Nick soon told me I had taken on more than I could chew, but I insisted I had it all covered. He would roll his eyes at me, but didn't push. Instead he would sit me down on the couch, hand me a pillow to curl over and give my tense back a massage. I couldn't bear the thought of dropping any of my commitments, even though I would've much rather spent my evenings with Nick.

Once in a while, I came home to little surprise gifts that he'd bought me. The first couple of gifts were nice.

No that's not true. All the gifts were nice.

Still, him buying me gifts started feeling awkward fairly soon.

If he'd bought me flowers once and left it at that, it might have been fine, but it never seemed to stop. Two sets of big flower arrangements were delivered, one at home and one at school. He came home with a coffee mug, some expensive smelly candles and two pairs of gloves.

I knew he had money, but surely he had better things to spend the money on? I was feeling increasingly uncomfortable with the idea of him spending his money on me, especially as the gifts became increasingly expensive.

***

On the last Saturday of September, I got up at 5 am and got myself ready to go up Arthur's Seat. It was still dark when I met up with Miranda and Sophia at the bottom of the steps by the Duddingston Loch car park. There weren't many things that I would've gotten up this early for on a Saturday, but watching the sun rise with Soph and Mir on Arthur's Seat was special. Being in Kenya, I'd missed it the previous year, and I remembered the last couple of times before that, it had rained and still it had been amazing. Today, though, the weather forecast showed a big round sun.

'Fancy meeting you here,' Sophia said around a yawn as I arrived.

I smiled. 'Is Mir here yet?'

'I am.' Miranda's voice came from under the trees by the bottom of the steps. 'You girls ready for this?'

'Are we seriously running up the steps?' I asked.

Miranda frowned at me. 'Of course we are. It's tradition. We can walk once we're on the other side of the road.'

I groaned. 'Right, well, we better get started then.'

'We have an hour until the sun is meant to rise,' Sophia said as we started running up the stairs.

Though I'd lost some weight in Kenya, I quickly realised that skinny did not equal fit. I watched Miranda and Sophia jog up the steps, barely breaking a sweat, as I huffed and puffed up the stairs, my legs aching in places I had forgotten existed.

'It's too early in the day to be running up hills.' I panted when I got to the top of the steps. 'I think I might die.' I lay down on the pavement on Queen's Drive, the road that circled Arthur's Seat about a third of the way up the hill.

Miranda smiled, and I might have wanted to kill her, just for a brief moment, as she said, 'Ach, it's good for you. I do those steps three times a week as part of my 10K run.' She didn't sound winded at all.

'Yeah, well, we can't all be fitness freaks. Who has time for running when there's ice cream to be eaten?' My heart was still beating like crazy, but it was getting easier to breathe.

Sophia laughed. 'No kidding. Are you ready to go again? We can walk the rest of the way now.'

'Thank goodness.' I sighed and put my hands out for Sophia to help me up.

Miranda rubbed my arms as I stood up. 'Want me to carry your bag?'

'No, I'm alright now.' I sighed and started walking up the hill again. It was slowly getting a little lighter, but it was still hard to see where we were going. 'It's a good job I didn't bring the champagne I was looking at last night at the shop.'

Miranda laughed. 'Champagne would have been a great idea!'

'I figured we could've made a toast to our new social enterprise.'

Miranda peered at me and smiled. 'You know, if you had brought champagne I would totally have been fine to walk up those steps.'

'What happened to "of course we run, it's tradition"?' I said, imitating her voice and she laughed.

'Meh, who cares about tradition if there's champagne?'

'I guess I know for next time.' I was definitely making a note of that one.

'How was being home?' Miranda asked Sophia. Sophia had been to see her parents in the Lake District for a couple of days during the week.

'This is home,' Sophia said. 'But if you're asking what it was like to see my parents, I'd have to say it was just as miserable as always.'

'Aw Soph.' I reached out to squeeze her arm. 'That sucks.'

'Yeah, well it's nothing new.' She rolled her eyes. 'Mum is a total doormat and Dad is mean to her. I've asked her so many times why she stays with him, but she says she made a commitment for life when she married him.'

'It doesn't sound healthy at all,' Miranda said with a frown.

Sophia laughed. 'No, you can call it many things, but *healthy* isn't one of them.'

'I can see what she means about wanting to be true to her commitment to marriage,' I said. 'It seems today people are so quick to throw away relationships that could be fixed. It's like we're too lazy to put the work in.'

'Yes, but this isn't like that.' Sophia shook her head. 'My dad is autocratic and abusive. He has no respect for women in general and definitely no respect for her. She does everything and he just sits there waiting for her to serve him. And nothing is ever good enough for him. It's always been like that. I don't think he would know how to boil an egg for himself; she's just always done it for him.'

'That does sound pretty awful.'

'Having seen them my whole life, I'm pretty convinced I never want to get married.'

I glanced at Miranda who gave me a knowing smile. 'You already are married, Sophia.'

She looked away. 'Sure, but that's different. It's just a legal thing. You know that.'

We got to the top just as the sun rose. Taking in the beauty of the view of the city and the sea, we got our cell phones out and took some selfies.

'Gosh, I love coming up here.' I took a deep breath of the fresh morning air.

Miranda nodded. 'I know. We don't do this often enough.'

'That sun rising is about the most beautiful thing you'll ever see, but it's too cold to stay up here,' Sophia said, jumping down from the boulder on the top and hopping up and down to keep warm.

We were fortunate to be out on a clear morning, but, even with the sun coming out in its beautiful glow, the air was chilly. So, we climbed down from the peak and found our usual picnic stone where we spread out our blanket. Sitting down, we dug into the feast of fruit, croissants, pain au chocolats, coffee, and the pancakes Sophia had made, sprinkled with icing sugar and lemon and rolled up.

'This feels so decadent,' I said as I bit into a strawberry.

'Goodness, yes.' Miranda sighed. 'Wouldn't take long to get used to, though.'

'Ok, Jules, we've waited a lifetime here.' Sophia raised her eyebrows at me as she took a pancake roll. 'Tell us what happened with Nick.'

'Right.' I smiled dreamily. 'Yeah, so we're a thing.'

'Mhm.' Sophia nodded. 'We gathered. So what happened?'

'Well, I went home and told him we couldn't be friends any longer because I wanted more.' I rolled my eyes. 'I told him everything, even how I wanted to get a dog just so he would chew the shoes of whatever girl he eventually married-'

Miranda snorted. 'Did you really say that?'

'Oh yes.' I nodded. 'So I finally got to the end of it all, and am waiting for him to say, *"yes sure, I'll start looking for somewhere else to live"*, or something, but he didn't. Instead he told me he'd been waiting me out and wanted me to be his girlfriend.'

'Really?' Sophia said, putting a hand to her chest.

'Yeah, he told me he'd always been interested in me, which I'm not sure I believe, but I figured I'm not going to pass up the opportunity.' I shrugged. 'So we've been hanging out a lot these last couple of weeks.'

'Aw, that's so nice.' Miranda smiled.

'Yeah, it has been nice. He's a good guy, Nick is.'

'Why don't you believe him when he says he's been interested in you for years?' Sophia asked.

'It's not like he hasn't had the opportunity to talk to me about it, for one.' I held a finger up. 'And for two, it's not like it's stopped him from seeing about a thousand other girls in the meantime…'

'Hold on, though,' Sophia said. 'Didn't you say that you've had a crush on him since he first started coming around? And haven't you had loads of opportunities to do something about it?'

'And you've seen a few guys yourself in the last nine years, haven't you?' Miranda jumped in.

'Yeah, but that's different.'

'Why? Just because the guys you went out with turned out to be idiots?' Sophia asked.

Miranda nodded. 'I think you should give him some more credit. If he says he's been interested for a long time, then I would believe him.'

'Maybe.' I shook my head. 'It's been a while since I've been in a relationship like this, but is it normal for the guy to be buying gifts all the time?'

'What do you mean "all the time"?' Sophia asked.

'Well, we've been a thing for a week and he's bought me flowers twice, a couple of those expensive candles, a coffee mug, and he got me new gloves the other day.' I sighed. 'I know he's just being kind, but I'm starting to feel overwhelmed by it all. Like, what does he want in return?'

Sophia and Miranda looked at each other. 'Are you joking?'

I shook my head. 'No!'

'Aw, Jules.' Miranda rolled her eyes at me. 'Next time just say *thank you*. If he's got the money to spend, why shouldn't he spend it on you?'

I shrugged. 'It just seems so wasteful.'

'If that's your biggest problem, I think you guys will be fine.'

I nodded and the conversation went somewhere else. Still, in my mind I couldn't let go of the niggly feeling of awkwardness around all the gifts and, as we walked down the hill, I resolved to speak to Nick about it when I saw him next.

Chapter 20

Julia

I spent the afternoon snoozing on the couch and woke when Nick came home. Sitting down at the end of the couch, he put my feet in his lap. 'How was the sunrise?'

'Gorgeous.' I sat up and got my phone out. 'Here have a look.' I passed him the phone and he started swiping through the pictures. He laughed when he came across some of the group selfies we'd taken but kept on swiping. Holding up the phone, he showed me a picture of me which Sophia had taken. I was sitting on the picnic blanket with my coffee, looking toward the sea.

'I like this one.' He smiled and took the phone back, swiping across the screen.

'What are you doing?'

'Just sending it to myself.'

Charmed, I smiled and leaned back with a yawn. 'How was your day?'

'Alright,' he said, putting the phone down. 'I had to run some errands in town, so I got you something.'

Suddenly wide awake, I sat up, taking my feet off Nick's lap and folding them underneath me. 'You really don't need to buy me presents all the time Nick.'

'I know, but I found this necklace I thought you'd like. It'd look great around your neck, so I thought: why not?' He shrugged and passed me a box from one of the high street jewellers.

The sense of dread as I opened the box made my stomach clench. Picking up the gorgeous gold pendant necklace, my mind went crazy as I thought about how much it must have cost. 'Nick, this is too much.' My mouth felt dry and I was starting to feel nauseous.

'Oh come on, it's not a big deal,' he said, giving me what I'm sure he thought was an encouraging smile. 'Put it on.'

I held up the necklace to the light and couldn't get past the thought of how much it had cost. Hating the thought of him spending money on me, I said, 'Look Nick, I'm sorry, but I can't take it. You should take it back to the shop.'

'What do you mean *take it back to the shop*? No, it's yours! Don't be silly.' He got up off the couch, putting distance between us.

'I'm not the one being silly here. This obviously cost loads of money, and I don't think you should be spending that kind of money on gifts for me.'

'What, so I'm just allowed to get you cheap stuff?' He looked at me as though I'd grown another head.

I rolled my eyes and sighed. 'Maybe hold off on buying any more gifts for a while. It makes me feel like you're trying to buy me or something.' Even as the words came out of my mouth I knew they weren't the real reason for why I didn't like him giving me gifts. Still, I didn't even want to think about the real reason, never mind talk about it.

From watching his face, though, I could see that I probably should have made something else up if I was going to make something up. He looked hurt.

Glaring at me, he said evenly, 'I'm not into buying people, Julia.'

I looked away as I felt how my face went red. I felt nauseous, my hands were clammy, and my heart was beating out of my chest. This was not how I wanted this conversation to go. 'I'm sorry, I didn't mean that. I don't mean to be ungrateful…'

'So what did you mean?'

'I meant that all these gifts make me feel uncomfortable.' I gestured to the flowers on the table and the necklace on the couch. 'I know you have money, but I don't like it when you spend it on *me*.'

'Why not?'

'I don't *know*!' I wasn't shouting, but it was close.

He looked at me in silence, trying to figure me out. 'I think you do know.'

I looked away. 'Fine. Maybe I don't want you to spend your money on me because I did nothing to deserve it. And I feel like all these gifts puts some kind of expectation on me, but I don't know what the expectation is, so I feel like I will never be able to meet it. I will fail. And I don't want to constantly be a failure at everything.'

I looked at him again. He shook his head. 'Why do you think my gifts come with strings attached?'

I tilted my head and frowned at him. 'That's how the world works, Nicholas.'

'Don't look at me as though *I'm* the one being weird here.' He pulled his hands through his hair as he looked at me, eyes wide in frustration. 'That's *not* how the world works.'

'Of course it is.' I shrugged. 'So you buy me a gift, and I'm thinking, *I did nothing to deserve this, what is he expecting of me now?*'

'You might not have done anything to deserve it. Maybe I want to give you gifts to show you that I care for you as a person, regardless of what you have or haven't done.'

My laughter sounded hollow. 'So you get me a birthday card on my birthday. You don't shower me with gifts every day! How am I ever supposed to live up to all those expectations?'

He bit his lip as he stared at me in silence for a long time. I thought I had finally got through to him when he said, 'I think you know this isn't about strings or expectations for me, and I think *that's* what freaks you out. You don't believe you're worthy of being given things just because.'

I felt my cheeks go warm and turned my face away from him. Feeling restless, I stood up and started folding the blanket.

'Think what you like, just stop it with the presents.'

'Message received,' he said as he reached for and pocketed the box with the necklace.

'Great.' My smile felt awkward.

He nodded, but didn't look at me.

We spent the evening awkwardly dancing around each other, avoiding stepping into each other's space as much as we could. Nick went for a long run, and I took the opportunity to go to bed before he got home to avoid any more awkwardness.

It took me a long time to fall asleep that night. I put it down to my long afternoon nap, and the fact that I was still feeing worked up about the necklace and all the things Nick had said. I went over our conversation over and over again. Was he right? Did I feel uncomfortable because I felt unworthy?

***

I must have passed out from exhaustion at some point though because, the next thing I knew, I woke up, my heart in my throat with a nightmare that had been a recurring one for the past sixteen years. I looked at my phone.

03.43am.

Too fraught to go back to sleep, I got up to have a cup of tea. I was as quiet as I could be, but the sound of the kettle boiling must have woken Nick, who came into the kitchen dressed in his pyjama bottoms and a soft gray t-shirt. He tucked his hair behind his ears as he blinked at the kitchen light.

'What are we doing up?' He yawned. His arms stretched over his head, causing his t-shirt to ride up and I felt my mouth go dry at the sight of his abs.

I swallowed. 'Nothing.' Turned away, I focussed my attention on pouring the water into my cup rather than looking at him. He might be a good distraction from the nightmare, but I was still feeling conflicted after our earlier conversation.

'What time is it?'

'Almost four. You should go back to bed.'

'Yeah, is that what you're doing?'

'I'm going to have a cup of tea first.'

I glanced at him and found him studying me. 'I'll have one, too.'

'Do you even like tea?'

'Sure, why not?'

'How do you take it?'

'I don't know.' He shrugged. 'Surprise me.'

I gave him a dry look, but made his drink.

Nick sat down in the armchair with a sigh as I curled up on the sofa, wrapped in a blanket. Rubbing his eyes, he sipped his tea. 'Jewel, what's wrong, darling? Tell me.'

Not sure what to say but comforted by his gentle voice, I leaned my head back and closed my eyes.

'You might be right when you say I have a problem with guilt and unworthiness.' I sighed.

'Oh yeah?' I felt his eyes on me and waited for him to start bugging me about being right, but he must have either been too tired, or realised now wasn't the time.

'Yeah.' I sipped my tea and looked away.

'Tell me about the dream,' he said, causing me to look at him again.

'Dream?' I avoided.

'Yeah, you were screaming.'

I felt my cheeks grow hot. 'Sorry. I didn't mean to wake you.'

'Tell me.'

And sitting there with my tea, I told him what I had never told anyone before. I closed my eyes and thought back to the dream, quietly sharing it with him as the tears started falling down my face for the first time.

Chapter 21

Julia

It was a familiar dream, a dream I had dreamt many times. I had known, even as the dream started, that I should wake myself up, but I felt so wrapped up in all the feelings that waking up had seemed impossible.

In the dream, I was nine and with my family on holiday in the west highlands. It was summertime and one of those idyllic holidays where we stayed in a little cottage at the foot of one of the mountains. I had always loved the highlands, and even as a nine year old I recognised how beautiful it was. We spent the days visiting the nearby villages, going for hikes in the mountains and making forts, and the evenings drinking hot chocolate and roasting marshmallows over the fire in the fireplace. At the time, Dad always had ideas about fun things to do, and Mum would follow along with his craziness.

Jack was eleven and hadn't quite hit the awkward puberty stage yet, so was still fun to be around. And Josie was four and so excited to be on holiday in the highlands with lots of places to explore. I had brought along a couple of my favourite books, but I didn't spend much time reading during the week as we were busy doing lots of fun things instead.

I liked this part of the dream, and felt myself wanting to dwell there for as long as I could, stretching it out into far off memories that seemed so real, it was like I was there.

One night, Dad convinced us that in order to really experience the outdoors, we needed to take our sleeping bags with us up the mountain to sleep under the stars. It was a warm, still night and Mum and Dad took us to a loch to go for a quick evening dip before we hiked up the mountain to a sheltered place. We rolled out sleeping mats and sat in our sleeping bags, sipping hot chocolate whilst Dad told stories of some long ago battles that had happened in Scotland. The longer we sat there, the darker it got and the more the midges found us. It wasn't long before we started being eaten alive by them.

As it was the height of summer, we knew the sun wouldn't set until late in the night, and it was nowhere near dark when Mum told us it was time to brush our teeth and lie down to sleep. We got ourselves ready, and soon the five of us were lying there waiting to fall asleep. I remember burrowing into the sleeping bag as much as I could— only my nose sticking out so I could breath, to avoid the midges. It was most uncomfortable and I couldn't see myself falling asleep any time soon. Still, we all knew Dad had made his mind up and complaining about it would help not at all.

We lay there desperately trying to get comfortable for about twenty minutes until Dad sat up and blurted, 'I cannot stand these midges, darling!' He looked at Mum, ran his hands through his hair and shook his head to get the midges off as she gave him a kind smile. 'New plan: let's sleep in our beds in the cottage tonight instead.'

We all drew a sigh of relief, and quickly packed all our things up so we could go home and get some midge-free sleep.

Up until this point in the dream, I felt happy, thankful even, to have such memories to delve into. Still, the dream didn't stop there, and as much as I wanted to wake up, I knew I had to stay and finish the dream out.

The house we were staying in was a stone's throw away from a sealoch. There was a little stream that came off the mountain that ran through the garden, and Mum kept telling us to be careful by the stream.

Five days into our week's holiday, Mum asked me to take Josie for a walk on the mountain with Jack to give our parents time to get dinner ready. We had been going for walks there all week, so we knew where to go. The sun was shining, so the midges were under control and it was nice and warm.

I took Josie's hand as we crossed the road to start going up into the woods. 'Let's play a game,' I said.

Jumping in her little hiking boots, Josie pulled at her trousers which kept inching down and said, 'Yes!'

'Jack, what do you think? How about hide and seek?'

'Ok, you girls hide and I'll find you. Stay in this section though; don't cross the next road,' Jack said, referring to the logging road about a hundred or so meters up the hill. Josie and I ran into the woods together, as fast as Josie's four-year-old legs could run. We found a big rock and hid behind it as we listened to Jack finish counting in the distance.

'Ready or not, here I come!'

Josie looked at me, her eyes twinkling, and couldn't quite keep the giggle in as she said, 'Let's jump out and scare him when he gets here!'

I laughed, pulling her in for a hug. There were pieces of moss and leaves stuck to her strawberry blond curls and she looked like a golden but dirty little angel with her big smile. 'Sure.'

Soon we heard Jack come closer. I looked at her and whispered, 'One, two-'

'Surprise!' Josie jumped out from behind the stone before I got to three. She always had been impatient, and never could keep a secret.

Jack snorted as I stood up. 'Found you!'

I rolled my eyes at him. 'Yeah yeah...'

'Did we scare you Jack?' Josie said, jumping up and down with excitement.

'Yeah, on the inside I jumped on one leg, I was so frightened,' he said with a smirk. Despite being eleven, and having some rather bratty moments at times, Jack had a sweet spot for Josie.

She looked delighted. 'Our turn to count!'

We counted whilst Jack hid, and so the game went on until we eventually got bored and decided to go back to the cottage. Jack ran ahead whilst Josie and I looked to see if we could find any ripe raspberries on the way down. There was one final raspberry bush by the side of the stream, and I stopped to see if there were any last ones on the bush whilst Josie ran ahead of me with a 'You can't catch me!' and a giggle. I looked up and started to run after her as she neared the road.

I hated this part of the dream. I hated most of all that, even though it was a dream, I seemed to have no power at all to change anything in the situation. I was entirely powerless and wrapped up in the events as they continued to play out as though it was seventeen years ago and I was frozen into the memory.

151

It all happened so quickly, yet, for me, it was as though time slowed down. As I ran after her, I saw her step out of the woods and onto the logging road, just as a big timber lorry came round the bend in the road.

I screamed as loud as I could, but nothing could have stopped the lorry, which seemed to pull Josie under instead of passing her. I ran forward, but didn't know what to do, so I waved my arms at the driver as he tried to keep driving. He must have heard or seen me, as he soon stepped out of the lorry to see what had happened and why his lorry seemed to be stuck.

Mum and Dad must have heard me scream, and soon came running out of the cottage and up to the road to see was going on. In the distance, I remember overhearing a neighbour ringing for an ambulance. I was just frozen there. I ran towards Josie, who was lying under the lorry, but didn't know what to do. I stopped and my scream died as I watched mum get Josie out, hugging her as she realised she was already dead.

That's when the dream ended. As it always did.

I sipped my drink, my tears making the tea taste salty.

'Aw, Jewel.' Nick moved from the armchair and sat down next to me and started rubbing my back as he let me cry. And despite the awkward feeling of him watching me cry, I didn't feel embarrassed at my tears. I was too wrapped up in feeling the pain of the memory which had never been acknowledged before. I turned toward him and he leaned back, pulling me with him to let me rest my face on his chest as he stroked my hair.

When my sobbing eventually quietened down, I said, 'The rest of that night happened as though in a fog. I remember that the ambulance came and took Josie away. We followed in a taxi. I remember watching as soft tears trailed down my Mum's cheeks and how Jack shook from crying so violently. Dad sat there calmly, trying to comfort Mum and Jack. I remember thinking that surely this was all a bad dream and I would wake up soon enough.' I snorted. 'I wish.'

Nick ran his hand through my hair, bunching it up at my neck. 'Jewel.'

'When we got to the hospital, we were told there wasn't anything that could have been done to save Josie; she'd died instantly, and they said she hadn't suffered. We got to see her as she lay in a hospital room with two candles burning on the table beside her bed. She was so still, which was a stark contrast to how she never had been able to sit still for anything, but she didn't look dead at all. Someone had taken her shoes off, and that's the only thing that reminded me that she wouldn't be coming home with us. That, and the two candles which were burning on the bedside table.'

'Aw darling,' Nick whispered as I sighed.

'My parents had big meltdowns after it happened. Nobody was the same after that summer. I felt like I didn't just lose Josie, but I lost my whole family that day. Then again, that's better than what I deserved.' I straightened and swiped the tears off my face. 'I still can't believe I let my sister die there. What kind of a monster am I?'

Nick sighed. 'You seem to have come to a few interesting conclusions about all this.'

I straightened and wiped at my cheeks. 'I was meant to be taking care of Josie and watching over her, and that's when she died. Obviously I'm to blame.'

'You were only nine.'

'So? I was old enough to take care of her. I should have done a better job.'

Nick rolled his eyes at me. 'How did you deal with it all?'

'I guess I shut down and tried to be strong for people around me. It was the only way I could handle it.' I sipped my tea and thought about it. 'I think partly I couldn't cope with all the emotions I was feeling, and partly I felt so responsible for Josie dying that I felt I had to keep things together to make the rest of the family be able to cope. I was on autopilot for days — no, weeks— after that day.' I laughed, and winced at how forced it sounded.

'Did you cry?'

'I would force out a tear or two when the situation called for it, but I never felt it. I felt nothing. Only guilt. Tonight is the first time I've ever really cried about it at all. I've never felt as though I have the right to cry. Eventually, I guess days became weeks and weeks became months, and a few years later our family had found a way of living on without Josie.'

'Wow.'

'Yeah, it was pretty awful.' I sighed. 'There you go, though. That's where all that guilt you keep saying I carry around with me comes from.'

He raised his eyebrow and gave me a dry look. 'Yeah, I can see that. It wasn't your fault though. You know that, right?'

'Yeah, people keep telling me that.' I shrugged. 'It doesn't make a difference though. At the end of the day, I was responsible for Josie, and I let it happen.'

He frowned. 'What could you have done?'

'I could have held her hand, so she wouldn't run off. I could have kept my eyes on her and seen what was going on so I could have stopped her. There are a million things I could've done differently.'

He looked at me in disbelief and pushed his hands through his hair to get it out of his face. 'You're being ridiculous. You were nine. Are you meant to carry around all that guilt for the rest of your life?'

I cleared my throat. 'Nick. My negligence caused my sister to die. I can't ever make up for that, no matter how many lifetimes I live. My parents lost their daughter. Because of me.'

Nick shook his head. 'But...'

'No, you don't understand. I can't tell you how much I have wished that I could have died in her place, but even wishing that makes me feel guilty. I don't deserve to be in heaven.'

'But isn't that the point? None of us deserve heaven, but it's God's gift to us, and there's nothing we can do to deserve it.'

'Now you're evangelising me? Really Nick?'

He shrugged and looked away. 'Well, at some point you've got to forgive yourself and move on. You can't carry this guilt around forever, or it will kill you.'

I snorted. 'Thank you. I appreciate that you care about me, but I don't think you have any idea what you're talking about.' I sipped my tea, and set the cup on the coffee table. The tea was lukewarm now.

Again he pulled his hands through his hair in exasperation and bit his lip as he looked at me. 'That may be. Still, it would seem to me as though everyone deserves the chance to find happiness in life, even you. But you won't even consider it as an option. It makes me wonder…' He stopped himself and looked away as if to gather himself.

'What?'

He took a deep breath. 'Nothing. It doesn't matter. We should get some sleep before it's time to get up again.' He stroked his hand down my back. 'Listen, I'm sorry about your sister.'

His eyes, which had been filled with frustration only a moment ago, were now gentle and kind as they looked at me. He tucked some of my hair behind my ear, and I suddenly felt self-conscious. My cry earlier hadn't exactly been the gentle, discrete kind and I was quite certain my face was all blotchy now. His shirt was still wet.

'Thanks for letting me cry all over you.' I looked away to cover my embarrassment.

He smiled. 'Any time.' He pulled me in for a hug and pressed a kiss to my forehead. 'Come here. I'll tuck you in.' He took my hand and directed me back to my bedroom. He held up my duvet for me to crawl in under and proceeded to tuck the duvet tightly around me. Pressing a kiss to my forehead he said, 'Night night.'

I nodded, my eyes already closed, and drifted off into a peaceful sleep as he left the room.

Chapter 22

Julia

I woke a few hours later when my alarm rang, feeling rested despite the hours I'd been up in the night. I thought back on our conversation as I stretched in bed before getting up. Nothing had changed in my perception of what had happened that day so many years ago. For the first time ever, though, I had shared the pain of it with someone else.

It puzzled me that, rather than feeling embarrassed at how I'd shared it all with Nick last night, I actually felt lighter.

A little less alone.

Huh.

I smiled as I got up that morning, not even feeling bad about going to church.

I had hoped Nick would come with me to church that morning, but he was already gone when I came in the kitchen. He had left me a note on the kitchen counter.

Couldn't sleep, so gone for a run. See you later. N

Instead, I went to church on my own, and managed to escape before I was signed up to do anything more. Feeling like I was winning at life, I walked with a skip in my step toward the little Greek lunch place in the Old Town where I was meeting Sophia and Miranda for lunch. Arriving a few minutes before them, I got a coffee and pulled my phone out to go over the notes from our last meeting. Sophia texted to say she was running late, but Miranda showed up right on time. I got up and gave her a hug as she came in the door.

'You alright?' I asked as she sat down.

'Not bad.' She smiled. 'I booked my tickets for Hong Kong, so I'm going on Saturday for three weeks.'

'Yay! What did they say at work?'

'It was fine. I have most of my annual leave still to take, so it wasn't a problem.'

'Great. So what's this I hear about Jack going as well?'

Miranda rolled her eyes. 'Aye. He says he has to go anyway, so he waited to book his tickets until he knew what dates I was going. I didn't even tell him. Sophia the traitor told him.'

'Ouch.' I frowned. 'She was probably just trying to be... kind?'

'Nah, he blackmailed her. She asked him to come onboard as an investor and he said he'd do it on the condition that she told him the dates I would be in Hong Kong, and that I stay with him when I'm there.'

I looked at her. 'Well, that's awkward.'

'Aye, no kidding.' She sighed. 'Speak of the devil.'

We watched as Sophia narrowly avoided crashing into an older man as she hurried towards us. 'Sorry I'm late. I left late. Sorry.'

Miranda gave her a disapproving look as I got up to give her a hug.

'What?'

'That is the worst excuse ever. No wonder you're late if you left late.'

'Yeah, yeah, ok sorry.' She chuckled to herself, but gave Miranda her best serious face. 'I'm sorry. Did you guys order yet?'

'Not yet.' We ordered our falafel wraps, and Miranda and Sophia took out their note pads and tablets as we waited for the food to arrive.

'Right.' Sophia got down to business. 'So I spoke to Jack, Nick and Michael, and they are all happy to come on board with funding and promotion.'

Miranda sneered. 'At a price of course.'

Sophia sighed and dropped her pen on the table. 'Are you going to be passive aggressive this whole meeting, or can we have it out and be done, do you think?' Her eyebrows grazed her hairline as she waited Miranda out.

Miranda scowled at her. 'If I wanted a trip to Asia with Jack, I'd have gone a long time ago. Like, for instance, when he asked me to marry him and move out there with him six years ago...'

Sophia rolled her eyes. 'Oh come on! You totally *wanted* to go with him! The only reason you didn't was because your mum was so sick. So don't give me that.'

Miranda bit her lip, studying Sophia through narrowed eyes.

'Listen, I don't want to hurt you; I know that year was the most horrific year of your life, and I'm sorry about that.' Sophia reached out to put her hand over Miranda's, her eyes sad. 'I can't pretend that you didn't want to go, though. You did.'

Miranda looked away. 'Yes. I did. But that ship has sailed, and going down memory lane with Jack for three weeks is not going to be helpful to my mental health.'

'What if this is the ship coming back for you? Maybe you should give it a chance?' I said hopefully.

She glared at me. 'Yes, because *heartbroken* is my favourite state to be in, and I can't wait for that to happen all over again.'

'Right.' Sophia rolled her eyes. 'At this point the plans are that you will travel to Hong Kong with Jack, and stay at his flat there. And when you go to China, he'll go with you. So whatever does or doesn't happen between the two of you is up to you. But those are the plans.'

'Great.' Miranda sighed. 'So he's booked his tickets already?'

'Yes, he's booked on the same flights as you,' Sophia confirmed with a nod. 'I'm sorry, you know. Jack was pretty clear about his terms, though and he wouldn't budge no matter what I offered instead. So there we are.'

'So did Michael and Nick have terms as well?' I asked as the food arrived. Two halves of a falafel wrap over a green salad with a side of hummus. My mouth was about to have a party.

'No, they were both pretty eager to get involved. But Nick did say he was interested in going with you to Kenya, if you're up for that, Julia?'

I smiled at the idea and nodded. 'That would be fine.'

'If you give me your notes, I'll work on writing up some contracts for all of us, so we have it in writing,' Miranda said.

'Really? Do we need contracts?' I asked. 'I mean, we've known the guys for years.'

'It's not to make things awkward, rather, the opposite. It's a way to protect our relationships. So I'll write up a contract for all of us to sign, with our different commitments laid out from the start. This way everyone knows what we're all agreeing to.'

I rolled my eyes but nodded. 'Ok, sure.'

'We don't come here often enough. This is so good.' Sophia sighed over her food. 'So we might have to do some fundraising later on but for now, with Jack and Nick coming on board, we should have our start up costs covered.'

'Great,' Miranda said. 'I'll adjust the budget.'

Sophia took a sip of her water. 'I've got a few ideas about fundraising, as well. But I think we should talk about your trip first. Am I right in thinking that you're going to visit two different companies and their factories and, based on what they can offer, put in an order?'

Miranda nodded. 'Well, there's no point in dragging this out. We're pretty clear on what we want, so it would be good if I can go ahead and put the order in. That way we could have them by mid-November so we could start selling them. I feel we need to get this going now; what do you think?' She looked at us.

'Sure.' I nodded. 'I'm sure you'll get us a good deal, and I don't feel I need to input on the decision there, unless you feel unsure.'

'Same.' Sophia frowned. 'I think it's important you feel like everything is above board with this, though. I don't want us to contribute to problems with low wages, or even environmental issues in China just because we want cheap period cups.'

'I know. That's the whole point with why I'm going.' Miranda agreed. 'I've found a company in England that might be able to produce the cups otherwise, but they are much more expensive. I think we should try China first.'

'Great.' Sophia checked her list. 'Seeing as the budget balances now, have you looked at tickets to Kenya in January, Jules?'

'Yes.' I pulled out a piece of paper. 'I spoke to Mrs Mwangi and Grace, and they say I can visit for the first two weeks of school in January. They start back on the 7th, so I was thinking we'd leave on the 5th and stay for three weeks. That way, I'll have time to help give all the high school girls period cups and do seminars with all of them. And I'll try to work with Grace to see if there's an organisation in Kenya we could partner with on a long term basis to distribute period cups and do training.'

We talked about dates and budgets for a while. Miranda had been busy, and things all seemed to be in order.

'If you let me know all the bank details, I'll make sure to pass them on to Jack, Michael and Nick so they can deposit the money they're putting in quickly. That way you can pay for the cups.'

'We're cutting things pretty close here, aren't we?' I frowned as I looked at my calendar for the next few weeks.

'Yes, but I think we should be fine.' Miranda didn't seem stressed and, as she dealt with these types of things all the time in her job, I figured we'd be alright. She looked at Sophia. 'Is the website work going ok?'

'Julia's got a few things still to write, but we should be live in the next couple of weeks.'

'Do you know how to make it like an online shop?' I asked.

'Do I know how…' Sophia muttered and rolled her eyes. 'Of course I know how!'

Laughing, I held my hands up. 'Sorry!'

'Ok, well, you guys work on that this month then,' Miranda said. 'If you want any input you can email me.'

'Sure.'

'Is that all for today?' Miranda raised her eyebrows questioningly and Sophia and I nodded. 'Great!'

Chapter 23

Julia

On the way home I swung by the Swedish café and picked up some cinnamon rolls to share with Nick. I still felt lighter with the relief of having at last shared the story of how Josie died. I whistled as I ran up the stairs of the apartment building, and opened the door.

'Honey, I'm home!' I sing-songed.

'Hey,' Nick said from the bathroom where I found him packing all our bathroom things into two big boxes.

'Hey, what's going on here?'

'I thought I'd get started on sorting things out in here. I'm going to rip everything out of the bathroom next weekend so we can get moving on the renovation.'

I scrunched my nose as I anticipated having no bathroom for the time of the renovation, but didn't say anything. Holding up the bag with the cinnamon rolls I said, 'Take a break?'

The left side of his mouth pulled up and he nodded. 'It'll take me five minutes to finish this up. Do you want to make coffee?'

As I was in the kitchen, he came up behind me, dropping a kiss at my neck as I was waiting for the coffee to brew.

'Did you have a good run this morning?' I asked.

He shrugged. 'It was alright. I couldn't sleep, so I ran to Arthur's Seat and walked up the hill. I sat there waiting for the sun to come out, but it took too long, so I decided to go to the beach instead. Thanks,' he said as I handed him his coffee.

I shook my head at him. 'Sounds long.'

'Yeah, it was long.' He shrugged. 'But it was nice. I watched the morning start down there and had a coffee at the Beach House cafe when it opened.'

'Nice. Did you run back too?'

He frowned at me. 'Of course.'

'Of course you did,' I said dryly and sipped my coffee. 'I met with Mir and Sophia this afternoon to talk about our Project

163

Cup. Sophia said you want to come with me to Kenya in January?'

Nick gave me a crooked grin. 'Yeah. Is that ok?'

'Uh-huh, that would be fine.' I nodded and bit my lip in thought.

'What?'

'I don't know, I suppose I'm wondering why you're up for funding our social enterprise? Period cups doesn't seem like the kind of product you would normally invest in, is all.'

He pulled out a cinnamon roll and took a bite, considering his words before saying, 'Is this more of our conversation from yesterday about the gifts? 'Cause I'm not sure I can handle...'

'No... Well, I'm going to assume that you're not investing in Project Cup as a gift to me.' I hesitated, looking up at him. 'Right?'

'Right.' He nodded decisively.

'Although after yesterday you would say that, wouldn't you?'

His eyes twinkled. 'Maybe.'

I sighed and went to pinch his bicep.

'Hey, none of that.' He smiled as he stepped away to set his coffee down. Turning serious, he leaned against the counter, folded his arms across his chest and looked at me. 'Nah, you don't need to worry. I want to invest because it would drive my dad crazy if he knew that's what I'm using his money for.'

I frowned. 'And that's a good thing?'

'Yeah, that's a good thing.' He snickered to himself and took another bite before saying, 'Look, my Dad is not a nice person. He's a sadistic horrible excuse for a human being.'

In all my years of knowing Nick, I had never heard him speak of anyone with such venom in his voice. 'Wow, those are some strong words.'

'Yeah. I wish I could say I was overreacting, but...'

'What did he do?'

He looked away, his jaw set as he said, 'I don't really want to go into it.'

'Ok.' I let the subject drop, even as I felt disappointed that he didn't want to share, considering I'd told him all about Josie's death last night. Still, he looked so raw I couldn't push. Instead I

164

set my cup down and went to put my arms around him. 'That's ok.'

He took a deep breath, rested his chin on top of my head, and pulled me closer. 'You smell nice.'

I smiled. 'Thank you. You smell nice too.' Those were the truest words I'd spoken all day. If I could bottle his scent I'd make a killing.

'Anyway, it's my money now and it is pretty damn satisfying to spend it on something that helps people. So there you go.'

I nodded. 'Jack has also put money in, and he had a few conditions.'

'Did he?' Nick gave a surprised chuckle. 'I guess I shouldn't be surprised.'

'Uh-huh.' I nodded and looked up at him. 'Did you have any conditions?'

He lifted an eyebrow and shook his head. 'Nah, I don't have any conditions. But I would really like to go to Kenya with you in January. If you're ok with that. I'd like to meet the people you keep talking about, and stuff.'

'Yeah?' I smiled up at him.

'Yeah.' He shrugged and looked away as though embarrassed.

Suddenly giddy, I laughed. 'Then we should book our tickets this week.'

***

We booked our tickets on the Tuesday night. We both felt excitement and anticipation about the trip, but for me it was more. I felt like the trip signified a solidifying of our relationship. It felt like by booking the trip we were saying that our relationship was more than just a fling – the trip signified us being in the relationship for the long-term. That made me feel all giddy, and I struggled to sleep that night.

***

The following Saturday, Miranda and Jack left for Hong Kong. I was sitting with Maple the cat and my coffee in the morning when my phone chimed.

Mir: How important is your brother to you? You won't mind if he never comes home again, would you? Xx

Me: Nah, he's not that important. Do what you have to do xx

165

Mir: Great, coz I'm already feeling my patience wearing thin, and we're not even in the air yet. Gosh, why did I agree to this?

I noticed her lack of kisses at the end of her text, a clear sign she was agitated.

Soph: Think of the money. You'll be fine! Enjoy yourself and if things start back up with Jack, what's the harm, amiright? Xx

Mir: Sure, it's only my heart that's at stake... Also, that sounds like you're pimping me out!

I snorted, my coffee almost coming out my nose, causing Maple to jump out of my lap. I grabbed a tissue as Nick came in the room. 'You ok?'

I coughed and nodded. 'Mir and Jack are just at the airport leaving now.'

'Great!' He smirked, getting his own coffee.

He was still barefoot in a pair of jeans and a tight white t-shirt. The phone chimed again and I pulled my eyes away from him and back to the conversation I had going on.

Soph: Stop! I'm not pimping you out – all I'm saying is you could take the opportunity to have a fling with him

Me: So long as I don't have to hear the details! Xx

Mir: Got to go, they're boarding our flight now. X

Me: Have a good trip! Xx

Soph: Have fun xx

'Hey, would you be up for a surprise mystery road trip?'

'Do you have somewhere in mind?' I asked.

'Yeah.' He bit the inside of his cheek and nodded.

'But you don't want to tell me?'

'Nah.' He shook his head. 'Do you trust me?'

I narrowed my eyes. 'That doesn't sound fun…'

'Maybe not, but I think it would be nice to get out of the city.' He shrugged.

I pulled my hands through my hair. 'Give me half an hour to get ready.'

***

After sharing about how Josie had died the previous weekend, I felt more connected to him than ever. Still, I didn't like not knowing where he was taking me. I had a feeling I wasn't going to like it. Trying my best not to ask about our destination, I sat on my hands as Nick drove out to the city bypass.

'Where are we going?'

'You'll see,' Nick replied, his eyes steady on the road. 'Music?'

I nodded and got my phone out to find a playlist to plug into the car. He beat me to it though, picked the Black Keys and turned up the volume.

'Hey...' I turned the music down.

He raised his eyebrow and smiled at me, turning the music back up again. 'Driver gets to pick.'

'How far is it?' I asked, still trying to figure out where we were going.

'Far.' He glanced at me. 'You've got time for a nap if you want.'

I sighed and looked out the window. The clouds hung low over the Pentland hills as we drove past them in the rain. I pulled out my phone again and pulled up Instagram, but there was nothing to keep my attention.

'What are we doing in Glasgow?'

He rolled his eyes at me. 'We're not going to Glasgow. Look, I'm not going to tell you where we're going, so settle in and relax a bit.'

I grimaced, but made myself comfortable, closed my eyes and let the car rock me to sleep.

Chapter 24

Julia

I woke up as we were coming off the motorway and going north of Glasgow. The road was windy with lots of roundabouts, and I fought a wave of nausea. I sat up straighter, took a deep breath and tried to focus my attention on the road and scenery.

'Feel better, sleepy head?'

I ignored him in favour of trying to stabilise my stomach. I wished I'd had something to eat other than a banana with my sip of coffee that morning.

'Where are we going?' I tried again.

He sighed. 'I'll let you know in half an hour.'

We were going up the side of Loch Lomond. The scenery was beautiful, but I felt a big rock of dread forming in my stomach, causing the nausea to get worse. Just north of Loch Lomond lay Arrochar where my sister had died that awful summer seventeen years ago. I hadn't been back since, but I had a feeling that's where Nick was taking us.

'You're going to want to pull over so I can be sick outside instead of your dashboard.'

He glanced at me. 'Really?'

'Your car, your choice,' I said, keeping my eyes on the road.

'Hold on two minutes and I'll pull in at Luss.'

I fought to keep my stomach under control until the car was stopped in the car park. I rushed out the door, wearing only socks on my feet, and just made it to a tree nearby before emptying the contents of my stomach on the ground. I stood up unsteadily and held on to the tree to find my balance again. I took a deep breath and fought to keep the tears out of my eyes. I didn't want Nick to see me like this.

I wiped my face with my hands when I heard him come up behind me.

'You ok?' he asked, handing me a bottle of water.

I nodded and took a sip. 'Thank you.'

'Put your shoes on and let's go for a little walk to give your stomach a chance to settle.' He handed me my shoes and I pulled them on over my damp socks.

We walked through the quaint village in silence until we got down to the dock overlooking the loch where we leaned against the railing as we took in the beauty of it all. It wasn't raining anymore and the clouds were higher now, so we could see most of Ben Lomond across the loch. The mountain was painted in greens, with the trees just starting to change into vivid orange and red. There were a couple of boats on the mostly still lake. It was beautiful. The air was clear and I filled my lungs with it.

Nick turned toward me and studied my face. 'You know where we're going, don't you?'

I nodded and looked at him. 'I don't understand *why* we're going there, but I know *where* we're going, yes.'

He looked at me for what felt like eternity before saying, 'I'm sorry.' He cleared his throat. 'I shouldn't have taken you here without you knowing.'

'Uh-huh. It would have been nice to be able to make a decision for myself.'

'We can go back if you want.' He stepped closer and took my hand in his, a question in his eyes.

Everything in me wanted to go back. Still, I felt bad for him. He'd obviously wanted to do something nice for me and not realised how sore a spot this was for me. 'No, it's ok. You've driven all this way…'

He shook his head. 'Look, I made a mistake; I don't mind going back. Don't tell me what you think I want to hear, just because you feel bad for me. This isn't about me, it's about you. And if this is too much, then let's go back.'

I looked at him. 'But you think I need to deal with my shit.'

He bit his cheek, but nodded. 'If you ever want to be able to enjoy life again, I think you need to leave the past behind you. You deserve happiness and joy, but it's like you're stuck in a prison of guilt. But it's got to be your choice. I can see that now.'

I nodded. 'Ok.'

We stayed on the dock until my stomach rumbled. 'I might need to eat something before we keep going.'

Nick smiled. 'I've got a picnic in the car, but we can stop at the petrol station to pick something up if you want.'

We got some crisps and I picked up a bunch of flowers before getting back in the car and driving the last fifteen minutes up to Arrochar. I was silent as he found a place to park. Nick opened the boot of the car and took out rain jackets, rain trousers and walking boots for both of us and we pulled them on. I grabbed the flowers and Nick put on a backpack before closing the boot. My legs shook with dread as I looked at the mountain. Why had I agreed to this?

Nick came up beside me and I let him pull me in for a hug. I breathed him in and felt him place a soft kiss at the top of my head. His arms around me felt right. We stood there for several minutes and when he let me go, I felt like maybe I could do this.

'It'll be ok,' he said and patted my arm.

I nodded and plastered on a smile, which must have looked as fake as it felt as Nick's lips pulled up on one side and he reached out for my hand. I gently squeezed his hand, and we set off.

***

Arrochar lay at the end of a sealoch, Loch Long, and the tide was out. The seaweed and mussels lay spread out across the beach and the seagulls cried out as they flew low, looking for food. Across the road from the loch lay the village, at the foot of the mountain, Ben Arthur. It had been summer last time I was there, seventeen years ago, and the mountains had shone in their green hues in the sun. Now it was autumn, and a bit cloudy. The leaves were turning, and what had been green was now yellow, orange, red and deep dark green. The forest looked like it was on fire.

'How do you want to do this?' Nick asked. 'Do you want to tell me about it?'

I cleared my throat. 'I told you how it happened, right?'

'Yeah. Do you want to show me where?'

I nodded. 'Ok.'

We walked past a big white house and I stopped when we reached the bend in the road. 'We were staying in that white house just there.' I pointed.

Nick nodded. 'Nice spot for a house.'

171

'Yeah, and there's that little garden and the stream. I remember the garden as being bigger, but I guess I was smaller.' I smiled as memories flooded me. 'There is where Josie died.' I pointed to the bend, a couple of meters away from where we were standing.

I pulled the plastic wrap off the flowers and laid them by the side of the road. I knew Josie wasn't there to see them, and I wasn't sure why I had wanted to bring flowers, but it felt right. It felt like in bringing the flowers I acknowledged all she had been to me. They weren't payment for letting her die, but a little way to acknowledge who she had been to me.

'Part of me wishes I had a bigger, more vibrant bunch of flowers, and the other part of me feels like there are so many other things I should spend my money on instead.'

Nick ignored me. 'Tell me about her.'

I took the hand he offered and we started walking up the mountain along the stream. 'Josie was like a little beam of sunshine. She was full of ideas, and it was like she was bursting with energy.' I told him some stories, one story leading to another and uncovering memories I hadn't thought of for years. We kept walking up, joining a path up the mountain that took us up above the tree line.

'Gosh, it's been a long time since I've thought about her.' Nick smiled at me, and we stood there in silence, my eyes locked with his for a few moments. I felt my cheeks heat and pulled my eyes from his to look at the scenery. 'I love this view.'

Nick turned and looked out over the loch. 'Yeah, it's stunning.'

The rain that had been so heavy in Edinburgh was nowhere in sight here. Still, it was getting colder the further up we went.

'Have you been to the top before?'

I shook my head. 'Do you want to go all the way up today?'

'Sure.' He shrugged. 'I've got the picnic, and the weather looks like it will hold, so why not?'

We walked up mostly in silence, stopping once in a while to point out something or to give each other a hand at trickier places. When we finally got to the top, Nick pulled out a blanket to sit on and we leaned against a big rock as we had tuna sandwiches at the top of Ben Arthur with coffee out of a thermos.

'This is nice.' I took a deep breath, filling my lungs with the crisp mountain air.

'You sound surprised.' Nick gave me a smug look and kissed my cheek.

'Yeah, it's not what I would have planned, but it turned out ok.'

Nick cleared his throat and turned his face toward the view. 'Well, don't speak to soon.'

'What do you mean?'

'Well…' He glanced at me as though nervous.

'Oh, you've clearly got something to say, so just say it.'

'You know I care about you, right?'

'Right…' I looked at him. 'You're starting to scare me now, Nicholas.'

He tucked some of my hair behind my ear, and looked me in the eyes. 'It's just that I've been thinking about what happened with Josie, and I know people have told you that it wasn't your fault.'

I nodded. 'Yes.'

'And it wasn't.' He studied my face now and I concentrated on keeping my features relaxed to not let on the turmoil I was feeling inside. 'But you still seem to think it was your fault.'

'Uh-huh.' I picked up some little rocks to turn over in my hands and look at, so I wouldn't have to look at him.

He waited until I looked up at him again. 'Have you ever thought that you could forgive yourself, instead of carrying all that guilt around?'

I sat up, startled as though he'd slapped me in the face and narrowed my eyes at him.

'I mean, you seem to believe that God can forgive anyone anything, right?' He didn't wait for me to answer and kept going. 'I know you did nothing wrong, but what if you had? What if instead of the accident, you had taken out a gun and killed her? Could God have forgiven you then?'

'I suppose…'

173

'So if God has forgiven you, then isn't it kind of arrogant to not forgive yourself? I mean, if the God who created the universe forgives you, but you still don't think you should be forgiven, aren't you in a sense…' He stopped.

'What?' I struggled to process what he was saying, still stuck on him thinking I was arrogant.

'Well, aren't you then saying that your opinion about whether you should be forgiven or not is more important, more informed, more *right* than God's opinion about it?' He looked away and paused, and then at me again, his eyes determined. 'I think that's got to be the height of arrogance.'

I looked away and muttered, 'Well don't hold back or anything.'

He sighed. 'You know I don't mean to hurt you, Jewel. It's just. I just wish…'

I tried to remember that he cared about me, but all I felt was raw. As though someone had grated my heart on a cheese grater and left it for the birds to feed on.

'I'm sorry.' His eyes were sad as they looked at me. 'Again.'

I nodded and looked away to hide the tears that were threatening. I struggled to swallow over the lump that was forming in my throat. We sat in an awkward silence for a few minutes and when I had my voice under control again I said, 'I think it's time we went home.'

Nick went to speak, but thought better of it and nodded. We packed the picnic and blanket into Nick's backpack and started scrambling our way down the mountain. When we hit the tree line, the clouds had lowered over the mountain, seemingly out of nowhere, and we were caught in the rain. We picked up our speed, and walked as fast as we could down the mountain and to the car. There, we shrugged out of our wet and muddy rain clothes and walking boots and sat in the car. Nick turned the heating up and we were soon back on the road driving toward Edinburgh again.

We spent the next three hours mostly in silence as Nick drove us home. Awkward didn't even begin to cover what I was feeling. I avoided looking at him, unsure of what he might see if I gave him my eyes, so I focussed on the road and the scenery.

I felt broken. And worse, I felt like he knew I was broken.

I kept coming back to his words at the top of Ben Arthur. Could I forgive myself for letting Josie die? Was I being *arrogant* if I didn't? I couldn't make heads or tails of what had happened between Nick and me on the mountain. I couldn't help but feel like kicking myself for letting my guard down around him, and decided the only way forward was to forget about it.

I'd managed not to think too much about Josie's death for the last fifteen years, so putting this day out of my mind shouldn't be too hard.

I shook my head and tried to think about lessons I had coming up instead.

When we got home, we both sat there in silence for a moment, neither of us knowing quite how to move forward, before Nick cleared his throat. 'Look, I'm sorry.'

I felt bad for him and held my hand up. 'No worries, Nick. It's ok.' I reached for his face, rubbed my hand along his scruffy cheek and kissed him gently.

'I didn't mean to hurt you, I just...'

'Listen, it's ok.' I smiled at him. 'Let's just pretend it didn't happen. Everything is fine. Let's have popcorn and watch a film tonight.'

He frowned, and I got the feeling he wasn't quite on board with that strategy, but he nodded. 'Ok.'

Chapter 25

Julia

I didn't sleep well that night, and got up early to find Nick already up and dressed. He handed me a cup of coffee as he said, 'I'm going to start ripping the bathroom out today, so you might want to have a shower and all that first.'

'Ok.' I sipped my coffee and pushed my hair out of my face. 'Do you need any help?'

'Nah, I should be fine with the demo, but if you want, you can come with me to get paint and things. I'll do that first.'

I thought for half a second about the assignments I had to mark, the lesson plans I had to make for the week ahead, and all the website copy I still had to write.

I smiled at Nick as he leaned against the counter. 'I'm in.' I got up to give him a kiss before turning to go have my shower.

We spent the best part of the Sunday picking out paint and buying a bathroom suite. Despite the awkwardness of our trip to Arrochar the day before, I was keen to spend time with Nick. He, on the other hand, kept our conversation on a surface level, continuously coming back to the bathroom. I started to feel like he was pulling away. He did it in such a nice way, I told myself I was just being paranoid, but I did feel weird about it all. Still, I decided not to take it personally, and thought he was probably just distracted with his bathroom project.

The bathroom suite would be delivered a couple of days later, but we brought the paint home anyway. Nick spent the rest of the day pulling the bathroom apart and putting the old bathroom suite in a skip he'd rented that had been delivered to the street the day before.

A couple of days later, I came home from work to find Nick packing a suitcase.

'Hey, what's going on?' I asked as I put my heavy school totes down on the couch.

He dragged his hands through his hair, looking around the room as if to see what else to put in the bag. 'I got a phone call to say my old nanny's in hospital.'

'Oh? What's happened?' I still wasn't sure what he meant when he said nanny. Was he talking about his Grandma or had he really had a nanny?

Nick shook his head as if to clear it and looked at me. 'She had a stroke. I've got to go to see her.'

'Oh no! I'm sorry.' I handed him a hair tie for his hair and watched as he pulled his hair into a man bun. 'What can I do?'

I stepped closer and ran my hands along his strong arm, stopping him from going back to his suitcase. He pulled me in and wrapped his arms around me, holding me close against his chest. I felt him take a deep breath.

'It's going to be ok,' I said, stroking his back. 'Have you got your tickets booked?'

'Yes, I leave early tomorrow morning.'

'Good. How's the packing going?'

'I don't know. I think I got everything.' He tried pulling away, but I held on to him and he relaxed against me again. 'Passport, tickets, toothbrush and a couple of changes of clothes, right?'

'Right. It sounds like you're all set.'

We spent the evening in a pub, Nick with his usual American lager and me with a big glass of red wine and a plate of chunky chips. I tried to ask about his nanny, but Nick didn't want to talk about her at all, and spent the evening distractedly checking his phone. After what seemed like a lifetime of awkwardness, he said he needed an early night so he could be at the airport by four am. I tried to hold his hand on the way home, but he wouldn't let me, pushing his hands into his pockets as we hurried home in the cold rain.

Once home, he just wanted to get ready for bed, so I pulled him in for a long hug, my hands sliding up his arms to hook round his neck and pull his face down. His hair tickled my face, so I tucked it behind his ears, the scruff on his face a stark contrast to the softness of his hair. His eyes were full of pain as he held my gaze, and I wondered how close he was with this grandmother slash nanny I had never heard about until now. I realised then that despite knowing Nick for nine years, there were a lot of things about him I didn't know at all.

'I'm going to miss you,' I whispered.

'Yeah, me too.' His voice was gruff as he held me and gently touched his lips to my face. He trailed soft kisses along my cheek, until he reached my ear where he nuzzled his face into my neck and stopped to take a deep breath. His beard tickled my neck, so I turned my face to press my lips to his.

Any thoughts I'd had fled as he then proceeded to give me the most thorough kiss I had ever had, taking his time to taste, nip, suck and lick my lips. There was no room to think. Instead my body was overtaken by feelings over which I felt utterly out of control.

I would happily have kept going, but he pulled away. We had decided from the start that we would take things slow, and he was too honourable to go any further yet. My face was flushed, my heart beating like crazy and I wished I wasn't such a good girl. I saw desire in his eyes, and I hoped he would kiss me like that again, but he sighed and pressed a chaste kiss to the top of my head before stepping away.

'Good night.'

I took a deep breath to calm down and bit my lip to hide my smile. 'Yeah, good night.' I shrugged, playing it off as though that kiss hadn't just turned my world upside down, and concentrated on getting ready for bed. It took me a long time to fall asleep that night, my mind replaying the kiss over and over again.

He didn't wake me when he left, but left a (rather short) note on the coffee table.

Will text when I get there. N

The following morning I had a notification on my phone.

Nick: Landed. Trip ok. At hospital. Switching phone off.

I replied even though I doubted he would still be awake, as it would have been 1am in Chicago.

Me: Great. Hope you're ok! How's your nanny doing? Will be praying for you. Miss you xxx

It was true that I missed him. There wasn't much time to think with things being so busy with my commitments at church, teaching and hanging out with Sophia to work on building the website for Project Cup. But I did miss his straight forward opinions and crooked smirks.

Also his kisses.

I missed being wrapped in his strong arms and thoroughly kissed. A lot.

And then there was the issue of the bathroom. His trip to America couldn't have come at a worse time from that perspective. Apart from the toilet, Nick had ripped everything else out before he left, and it was now all in the skip on the street behind the house. A couple of days after he left, the new bathroom suite was delivered, and I had the delivery guys stand it in the living room as the pieces wouldn't fit in the bathroom with their packaging.

It was chaos.

I told myself it would only be a few more days before he would be back and could sort it out again. I could put up with having showers at the gym for a few days. It might, in fact, be a good incentive to go to the gym a bit more regularly.

Another thing in a state of chaos was my mind. Ever since going up Ben Arthur with Nick, I struggled to get to sleep. I went over and over our conversation at the top of the mountain but, no matter how many times I went over it, I was unable to get past the bit where Nick had called me arrogant. Was I really arrogant?

And once I finally fell asleep I dreamed about Josie and the accident, but I also had nightmares about being in situations where I did everything I could think of to save people from dying, but nothing I did was good enough and they all died. I would wake up, heart pounding, and spend the next few hours talking myself out of the anxiety the dreams had induced.

Then, the night before he was due to come back, he sent me another text.

Nick: Had to delay my flight back. Got to stay longer to sort some things out. Will be in touch.

Me: No worries - hope you get everything sorted and that your nanny is ok! The bathroom suite arrived. It's waiting for you to put it in when you get back ;) Missing you xxx

***

Standing in front of the mirror the following morning, it was clear I had stretched the no shower period for as far as it would go – my hair was streaky and I smelled – and the poor sleep made my face look swollen. I washed as best as I could in the kitchen sink, applied deodorant and concealer to the bags under my eyes, spraying my hair full of dry shampoo and pulling it up in a messy top knot. Thankfully, I only had a couple of lessons to do before I could go see Sophia and Michael after work and use their shower.

'I thought Nick was coming home today?' Sophia said once we were on the couch with big cups of tea.

'So did I, but he had to delay his flight so he could sort some things out.'

'That sucks.'

'Yes.' I sighed. 'Can I shower here tonight?'

'Of course. Why?'

I explained the bathroom situation and Sophia rolled her eyes. 'Men, eh. Of course you can use our shower.'

I had a long shower and got changed into a pair of sweat pants and an oversized light green jumper I'd found at the church charity shop. Feeling clean for the first time in days, I left my hair to air dry as I sat on the couch. Sophia poured me a big glass of red wine and handed me a few slices of pizza from the oven. I let out a deep, long sigh and felt my shoulders relax.

Chapter 26

Julia

We got Skype set up and called Miranda. It was late at night there, but she seemed wide awake and happy. We chatted for a while about her time in Hong Kong and China before talking about Project Cup.

'Did I tell you I got the stall for the Christmas Market sorted?' Sophia asked as she took the last slice of pizza off her plate.

'Oh, yeah?' Miranda said. 'What do we need to do to get ready for it?'

'I guess we should talk about that. Julia and I can make a list?'

'Great.'

Sophia and Miranda chatted for a while about logistics and I sat back with my wine. I was starting to feel like I'd been up for way too long.

'Do you think I have a Messiah complex?' The words slipped out before I could censor myself when there was a gap in the conversation.

'What?' Sophia frowned.

'Never mind, it's nothing.'

'I don't know, it sounds like an interesting question.' Miranda took a sip of her tea. 'I've been thinking about it quite a bit in view of us starting this social enterprise.'

'You have?'

'Yeah. I think any time there are obvious power imbalances where one party is charitable to another which is less powerful, it's worth asking questions.' She shrugged. 'Colonialism has not been particularly helpful in the long run.'

'Huh.' I frowned. 'But colonialism is to do with a more powerful party exploiting a weaker area or people, and we're not exploiting anyone.'

'I guess it depends on how we look at it. If we are the powerful party, and we get something out of our working with these projects in places where people have less power, then you

183

could argue that it falls under colonialism. Particularly if whatever we get out of it comes at a cost to the weaker party.'

'So are you saying we're doing more bad than good by starting *Project Cup*?' Sophia asked.

'Nah, I don't think so, not in the way we're doing it. But it would be easy to do a lot of damage if we did things differently.' She shrugged. 'If, for instance, instead of partnering with organisations that are already out there, we came in and told them we wanted to sort out their problems so we would give their girls period cups on the condition that we first got to educate them for an hour.'

I flinched. 'Isn't that what we're doing though?'

'No! That's exactly what we're not doing.' Miranda frowned and shook her head. 'We're partnering with a school that have identified a problem and they've found a solution which they are pursuing. Part of that solution is that they are educating the girls on women's health issues. All we're doing is supporting them, mainly financially, in what they already are doing. If we were pressuring them to do something they didn't want to do, or exploiting their stories and making them seem weaker than they are in order to make us seem stronger, or if we were giving the girls an impression that they are somehow dependent on us, then there would be a problem. But we're coming along side a project that is working, and telling stories of hope to inspire others to get involved. The girls are learning they can be powerful if they apply themselves to their education, made possible by the cups that the school is giving them.'

'Huh.' I bit my lip as I thought about it.

'This is why it's so important that we are conscientious about how we source the cups. It's not ok for us to contribute to making people in China poorer because we want a bigger profit margin, even though our profits are going toward making life better for others.'

'No, I entirely agree with you there.' Sophia nodded sharply.

'So, do we have a Messiah complex?' Miranda shrugged. 'I don't know, but I think we want to keep checking that what we're doing is actually making a difference in a good way, and that we're not exploiting anyone.'

184

I nodded. I hadn't thought much about colonialism since being at university. 'Ok, but that's not actually what I meant, though.'

'No?'

'No.' I took another sip of my wine, wondering if I really wanted to go down this rabbit trail, but decided I was getting nowhere churning it over and over in my head. Maybe it would help to talk about it. 'I was asking about the Messiah complex because Nick keeps saying that I seem to need to save the world. He thinks I'm some kind of a do-gooder trying to appease my conscience.'

Sophia scrunched her nose. 'Oh.'

'Yeah, and I don't know what to make of it.'

She went to speak but seemed to think better of it.

'Go on.'

'I'm not saying he's right, but I have wondered why you're always taking so many things on. I know you told me and Miranda that you would step away from doing all those things at church, but I'm pretty sure you're still doing them.' She bit her lip. 'Why?'

'I told you, they asked and I couldn't turn them down.'

'And why can't you turn them down, again?'

I frowned and held my hands up. 'If I don't do all those things, then who will?'

Sophia held her hands up as if to say *I rest my case.*

Miranda winced. 'I hate to say this, but it sounds as though Nick might have a point.'

I sighed. 'Yeah, I was afraid of that.'

'You know it's ok to say no to things, right?'

I snorted. 'Of course I know.' Except, it never felt ok.

Sophia gave me a dry look. 'So you only say yes because you absolutely want to volunteer at the church charity shop and teach Sunday school and clean the church and whatever other things you've signed up for?'

I rolled my eyes. 'Ok fine. I hear you. So maybe I have a Messiah complex.'

She shrugged. 'Yeah, probably. Still, now that you know, you can work on it, right?'

I took a deep breath. 'Yeah.'

'I know you don't like talking about Josie,' Miranda said gently. 'But I wonder if maybe you feel so responsible because of what happened to her.'

I rolled my eyes. 'Yeah, that's what Nick said.'

'You told him about her?' Miranda's eyebrows went up.

'Yeah.' I pulled my fingers through my still damp hair and wound it into a bun at the top of my head. 'And then he took me to Arrochar, and we went up the mountain and talked about it.'

'Really?' Miranda sat closer to the screen, looking intrigued.

Sophia frowned. She knew Josie had died when I was little, but didn't know much else. It wasn't something I liked talking about, and she had respected that.

'Yeah. So I'm not sure what to think about it all.'

Sophia reached for my arm and said, 'It's ok. You don't need to have it all figured out.'

I bit the inside of my cheek. 'Yeah.' Pushing the feelings around my sister's death aside for all these years had worked to help me get through life, but maybe it was time to start dealing with it all.

We talked a little more before Miranda said, 'Look, it's almost three am here and I need to get up in four hours, so…'

We wrapped up the call, and then Sophia and I spent some time making the list for the Christmas stall, which ended up being rather long. It felt overwhelming and exciting, not to mention the slight worry over how we were making big plans without having any product to sell yet. Still, we would get nowhere without a plan, so plan we did. We also worked on the website. Sophia uploaded the texts I sent her, added some pictures and made it look great.

Between not sleeping the previous night and that glass of wine, my mind soon started to feel sluggish. I yawned and stretched out. 'I love this layout, Soph.'

'Sure. I'm done for tonight, though.' Sophia smiled and started closing the laptop down. 'Have you heard much from Nick?'

'He's terrible at texting, so all I've had is two short messages.'

Sophia frowned. 'That's weird, I'm sure he texts Michael loads.'

My eyebrows shot up. 'Really?'

'Hey, Michael?' Sophia raised her voice.

'I'm right here; don't shout at me.' Michael's steady voice came from the kitchen and Sophia rolled her eyes.

'Have you heard from Nick?'

Michael sauntered in to the living room and sat down on the couch. 'Sure, all the time! It sounds like things are pretty intense for him. It sounds like it's been quite an ordeal to get his nanny all sorted out, eh?' Michael looked at me, as if I was in the know and would agree.

All sluggishness gone, I straightened and sat up. 'What? I've heard nothing from him at all. All I get is two sterile texts without even a kiss at the end!'

Michael gave me an embarrassed look. 'Uh… He's pretty focussed on being out there right now.'

Sophia reached out and squeezed my hand. 'I wouldn't read into it, hon.'

'What else has he said?'

'Ahh…' Michael looked away. 'Just that he's working on getting his nanny into an assisted living home and stuff.'

'Right. Fair enough.' I bit my lip, wondering how I was to interpret all this.

Michael took a sip on his beer and sighed. 'Look, Nick's story is his to tell, but his nanny means a lot to him. She took care of him from when he was three until he went to high school, and I think she was the only stable person in his life when he was growing up. You know how his dad's an asshole, right?'

'Sure.' I cleared my throat and nodded as I felt my cheeks go red. I did know Nick didn't like his dad, but he'd never told me why. I was embarrassed knowing I was supposed to be his girlfriend but everyone else knew more about him than I did. 'I didn't know he had a nanny. I thought he meant his grandma.'

Michael's mouth pulled up on one side in an almost-smile. 'No, his granny's dead. The nanny's probably the reason he's as sane as he is.' Michael gave me a long look and shook his head. 'Nick's had a rough life. I know he's got all the money, but money doesn't buy everything.' He sighed. 'He'll tell you when he's ready.'

187

I didn't have it in me to go home that night, and didn't have school the following day, so I stayed over. I shared Sophia's double bed with her, which I had done many times before, and I normally slept well there. This time, though, despite being tired, I lay awake thinking.

Why was Nick being so distant with me? And, not for the first time, I wondered what his story was and why he was so reluctant to share it with me.

I thought back over the last couple of weeks before he left. The argument we'd had about the gifts, the night time conversation when I had told him about Josie, and our trip to Arrochar came to mind. I went over each conversation again and again trying to pick out where our communication had broken down, but got nowhere. I thought we had ended both those conversations more connected?

Chapter 27

Julia

The next week, school was on half-term break, and I spent most of the week working at the church charity shop. As Sophia had managed to book us in for the stall time share at the Christmas Market from the end of November, I now *had* to give up some of the other volunteer projects I had agreed to. I had spoken to Paul, the manager at the charity shop and we decided I would work there for the full five days of my half-term break, before giving up working there entirely. Part of me was happy to be on my way to being free of that commitment, but the other part of me just felt guilty.

About everything.

I felt terrible for not following through on my commitment. Leaving Paul in the lurch with Christmas season coming up bordered on being unkind – he was overworked already. He told me he understood, but I knew it would mean more work for him.

At the same time, I felt bad for agreeing to spend my whole half-term holiday overhauling the shop. I could have spent that time doing all kinds of things to prepare for the Christmas market instead. Why did I let my fears around what other people thought about me dictate how I was to spend my time? Did I have no boundaries at all?

On top of all that, I still felt a lot of anxiety around my relationship with Nick. He hadn't texted since the day when he'd told me he'd delayed coming home, and, as I didn't want to seem desperate, I hadn't texted him either. I didn't know what to make of the situation at all. So I spent the week sorting clothes and feeling miserable.

Writing the last bits of copy for the website helped distract me, as did going through my photos from Kenya to try to find pictures to use on social media.

On the last Saturday of October, Miranda and Jack came home. Sophia and I went over to Miranda's the following day to catch up. Miranda was still in her pyjamas when she opened the front door to let us in. The time away seemed to have done her good. She was looking nicely tanned and less stressed than she had when she'd left.

'Hey,' she said around a yawn. 'Gosh it's cold out there. Come on in quick.'

We took our bags of food into the kitchen as Miranda went for a quick shower. I put the kettle on and made tea and coffee as Sophia started pulling food out of the bags we'd brought.

'She looks like she had a good time away with your brother.' Sophia wiggled her eyebrows at me suggestively as she got a mixing bowl and a frying pan out of the cupboards.

I couldn't help but smile. 'It would make Mum's year if they got back together again. And I've always thought Miranda would make the best sister-in-law...' Sophia cleared her throat loudly and gave me a pointed look. I smothered a laugh. 'Yeah, you would make a great sister-in-law too, but you've already married someone else...'

'Still, I wouldn't want to be considered second to anyone.' Sophia put her nose in the air as she tried to hide her grin.

I rolled my eyes but pulled her in for a hug. 'Second best? Anyone that considers you second best is an idiot.' I started setting the table. 'Does Michael have sisters?'

Sophia chopped some vegetables up, adding them to the bowl. 'Yes, two sisters and a brother. I haven't met them though, other than a quick hello on Skype once.'

'Do they know about you guys being married?'

Sophia shrugged her shoulders. 'I don't think so. It's not a real marriage though, so there's no reason for them to know. I never told my parents either.'

'Never told your parents what?' Miranda asked as she came into the kitchen dressed in sweats and a big knit jumper, her dark hair still wet from the shower.

Sophia looked up and smirked. 'About my pretend marriage to Michael. But never mind about that, I want all the juicy details of your time away with Jack.'

'Oh stop.' Miranda rolled her eyes. 'It wasn't like that, and you know it.'

'I've noticed you're both back without either of you having killed the other. That's got to mean something, right?' Sophia tried to hide her smile.

'Wrong. Soon after he came back, we decided to put our past behind us and just be friends. So that's what we did.' Miranda shrugged her shoulders and got the bread out of the toaster.

Sophia bit the side of her mouth and gave me a dry look. We had both seen Miranda and Jack together the first time around, and both found it hard to believe they'd be able to do just friends now.

'Great.'

'Yeah, it was nice. We spent a week in Hong Kong so Jack could finish up his work, and he showed me the sights. Then Jack came with me to mainland China and we sorted out getting the order for the period cups.'

'I know. I saw some of the pictures already.' Sophia nodded with a smile and put the frying pan with the frittata on the table. 'Ok, I think we're ready to eat.'

'This looks amazing, Soph.' I sighed.

'I know.' She smirked and sat down. 'Dig in.'

We had our frittatas with toast and a fruit salad Sophia had brought with our coffee and tea. It was nice to have Miranda back again.

'This is delicious,' Miranda said, and I nodded in agreement. 'So how did you guys get on with the website?'

'I think we're getting there now,' Sophia said. 'I'll show you after we've eaten. We also made the arrangements for the market stall. I've made a sign which I need both of you to look at before I order it.'

'The website looks amazing,' I said. 'Sophia's done a brilliant job of the design for it. I think we should be able to take it online once you've seen it today.'

'I'm more interested in hearing about the cups.' Sophia smiled. 'You bought some, didn't you? Will they get here before the market starts?'

Miranda nodded. 'Sure. I visited the two companies and talked with them about quotes and quality and design, and all that, and also about workers' conditions and their environmental policies.

The company I decided to go with charges a little more, but I liked the ethos for how they run things. I think I got us a reasonable deal, at least to start with. I bought two designs in two sizes to begin with. So that's two thousand five hundred cups that should be arriving in the next few days.'

'Really? That sounds so quick!' I said.

'Aye, I paid a little extra to make sure to get them here before the market starts.' She shrugged. 'Besides, I got it all sorted in the first week, so they've had about two weeks already. They should be shipped by now.'

'Wow! That's awesome.' Sophia sing-songed.

'Huh,' I said. 'What will we do with them if we can't sell them?' I was starting to feel a bit of panic at the thought of having bought so many.

Sophia smiled and shook her head in my direction. 'Don't worry Jules. Of course we'll be able to sell them. Now, tell us about the designs Mir.'

'Sure.' She got up and reached into a bag on the kitchen counter, pulling four period cups out and putting them on the table. 'I brought these samples back.'

'Perfect!' I clapped my hands in excitement as I looked at them. 'These will be great!'

Sophia got her camera out and took some pictures of them for the shop part of the website.

'They'll come here in one big box on a pallet, so we'll need to repackage them all. We could order some little bags to put them in or something.'

'I was actually thinking about that, and I know of a company that would give us a good deal,' Sophia said. 'Shall I look into that?'

'That'd be great. Thank you,' I said and Miranda nodded. 'Where will we store all these cups?'

'What do you think about using my garage for now?' Miranda asked.

'Are you sure you're ok with that?' I asked.

Miranda shrugged. 'I've got the space, so we might as well use it.' And so it was decided.

We spent the rest of the day looking over the website, talking about the Christmas market and making rotas for when each of us would man the stall, and so on. By the end of it, we had a comprehensive plan for the next couple of months with spreadsheets and lists in a shared online storage folder that we all had access to.

I also had a headache.

Up until this point, we had done a lot of planning and preparations for the enterprise to be set up. And still, it felt like we were playing a (very elaborate) game, with nothing about it feeling very real.

Now though, we had *two thousand five hundred* period cups on their way. And when I thought about those two and a half thousand cups, I felt both excited and completely panicked.

What had I gotten us into?

Chapter 28

Nick

Coming home after being away was normally a relief.

Not this time.

This time, my back and shoulders were stiff and no matter how I tried, I couldn't get comfortable during the flight. I tried watching a couple of movies on the in-flight entertainment system, but nothing held my attention. I kept asking myself how I'd gotten myself into this mess.

For *nine years* I'd been able to stay away from Julia. And then, over a matter of *weeks*, I had somehow ended up convincing myself that maybe we could have a relationship after all.

But now I was more convinced than I ever had been, that Julia and I would never be a good fit.

She was *it* for me. She just wasn't for *me*.

As much as I had buried my head in the sand and pretended we were just seeing where things were going, if I was honest, I knew Julia and I were in a long-term relationship. She thought we were on the journey towards getting married and having a family. But that was not going to happen.

Long-term relationships were *not* for me.

My time in Chicago had been a much needed reality check, and now I had to sort out the consequences of my burying my head in the sand with Julia.

I'd gone to see Nanny Mary straight from the airport, and from then on, my time had been busy. After catching up with her, I got started on a long list of things to sort out her care. She didn't have insurance, and wasn't able to pay for her hospital bill, never mind the follow-up care she needed. She'd been out of options when her friend, Mrs. Jones, had called me.

Mrs Jones told me Nanny Mary's husband had died of cancer a few years earlier and left her close to bankruptcy with the medical bills. They didn't have children, so she had nothing, and nobody to take care of her. At one point when her husband was alive, they'd asked my Dad for a loan and he'd refused, despite the fact she'd been on his payroll for fifteen years, and he more than had the means to help. It didn't surprise me. That was my Dad. He didn't see any reason why he should have to pay for other people's health care just because he had more money than they did.

While I didn't have the type of money Dad did, my parents had set up a trust fund for me when I was first adopted. I got access to the money when I turned eighteen, which is how I was able to move to Scotland and go to university there. After leaving the rest of the money in the account for the following few years, I had recently used some of it to invest into Project Cup. Dad would have a heart attack if he knew I'd spent his money on "charity", but I saw it as the only right way to spend it. Dad had been doing fishy deals for as long I could remember, so using some of his earnings to make the world a better place was the least I could do. Still, there was plenty of money left in the trust fund, so I paid Nanny Mary's hospital bill and spent the next few weeks making sure she'd be taken care of.

I hadn't meant to see Dad at all, but then, the last afternoon before I was due to go home, I bumped into him at the bank. I had made all the arrangements for Nanny Mary and was planning to have a nice steak dinner before catching the plane the following morning. I was leaving the bank as he entered the building, and we were both looking at our phones instead of at where we were going.

'Sorry,' I muttered, and would have kept walking had he not cleared his throat. I looked up and recognised him. We looked nothing alike.

Never had.

I shook my head to clear it. 'Oh, hi. George.'

'Nicholas.' He nodded, his eyes cold as he looked at me. 'Long time no see.'

I cleared my throat and wondered whether to smile. How does one appropriately greet their estranged adoptive father? I wasn't sure what the protocol was, so I gave what I thought of as my car salesman smile. 'Yeah. How've you been?'

'Fine, fine. I got married last month.'

'No way.' Ever since mum died, there had been a steady stream of women around him, but he'd never spoken of them.

He nodded again. 'Yeah. Michelle is… nice. You'd like her.'

'Oh yeah?'

'Yeah. And she's pregnant.'

'Oh, wow.'

'Yeah, so…'

'Wow, well that's…' I cleared my throat again, keeping the smile in place as I nodded. 'Good for you.'

He frowned. 'I suppose so.'

'Well, I've got to get going here, but good luck, I guess.'

'Yeah. See you around.'

I nodded and left without looking back. I went back to the hotel I was staying at, put on gym clothes and spent the rest of the day in the gym. I had plenty of feelings to work out.

Thinking about our awkward interaction at the bank, I wondered if he had smiled at all, but I couldn't recall. My own smile had been fake of course, and I wondered why I bothered to put on a show for him.

To say I'd been surprised when he told me he had remarried was an understatement. Mum had been the light of his world, and when she died, something in him died, too, and he changed. He went from being caring and kind, to distant and harsh. He threw himself into making money, and saw women as a means to an end.

Dad had gone from being a man who would do anything for his wife, to a cold abuser who took his pain out on his child.

I wondered if he'd fallen in love with this Michelle lady, or if he was getting married because that was what was expected in his circles. And I thought of that poor baby, which would likely grow up with parents that were only together for show, and who really couldn't care less when nobody was watching. I hoped they'd at least get the poor kid a good nanny.

I disliked George as a person, but, having lived with him for 18 years, I did understand him. He was a victim of having loved and lost his wife. I used to hate him for it, but since meeting Julia, I had started to understand him better. It was all too easy to fall in love and be entirely wrapped up in the person. At least if the person was anything like Julia. And then, if the person died, I couldn't see how I would ever recover.

So I'd had to forgive my dad. Because, while I looked nothing like him and we didn't share DNA, I knew there was a strong chance I'd end up like him.

I shuddered. I would do everything in my power not to become like him. I would have to make sure not to fall in love.

Ever.

And while I was a strong guy, able to protect myself from emotions like love, I knew Julia deserved better. She deserved somebody that would love her beyond everything else.

It just couldn't be me.

By the time I got to the conclusion that I would have to break up with her, I had run ten miles, worked the weights and was pounding away at a boxing bag. I stopped hitting the boxing bag and sank down to the floor, head in my hands. I focussed on taking deep breaths of air until I felt able to leave.

Drained to the bone, I picked myself up, spent the night in bed trying to think of other ways forward – it was a pointless exercise and I knew it – before jumping in the taxi to the airport.

Despite feeling exhausted, I couldn't sleep on the flight. By the time we landed, I had picked the skin off my cuticles, causing a few of them to bleed. I forced myself to take a few deep breaths, and got through customs without problems. Getting a taxi from the airport, I stopped on the way to buy some moving boxes before I went home.

Julia hadn't lived there for long, but everywhere I looked there were signs of her. Candles on the coffee table, sticky notes with reminders scattered on different surfaces, nice blankets and cushions on the couches, art on the walls. The place even smelled like her.

Everything in me wanted to stay and pretend everything was fine. Still, the longer I left breaking up with her, the more it would hurt. So I got my boxes out and got to work.

Chapter 29

Julia

The next time I got a text from Nick, it was to tell me he was coming home.

Nick: Booked my flight back to Edinburgh. Landing on Thursday

Again, the shortness of it concerned me, but I decided to ignore it and replied.

Me: Can't wait to see you! Xxx

That Thursday, I was so excited I couldn't think of anything other than Nick finally being home. I got through teaching my three lessons at school, but I doubt anyone learned anything as I was all over the place and couldn't concentrate. I hurried home and was out of breath and warm by the time I finally got through the door. I dropped my school tote bags in the entryway and called out, 'Are you home?'

'In here,' Nick replied.

I might have squealed as I bounced over to his bedroom, where I stopped in the doorway, my stomach full of butterflies. He sat, head in hands, on the bed, with a half full moving box beside him.

'Hi!' I beamed at him. 'You're home!'

His hands dropped and he looked up at me, his eyes... sad?

'Is your nanny ok?' Why did he look *sad*?

'Yeah.' He pulled his hands over his face and stood up abruptly. His hair was still wet from a recent shower and hung in loose curls just touching his fitted gray t-shirt. Just seeing his arms made me ache for a hug but, instead of coming toward me, he turned to his chest of drawers to scoop up a bunch of t-shirts. I watched as he dropped them in the box and went back to open the next drawer, careful not to look at me or say anything else.

It was all starting to feel very awkward. Wasn't he happy to see me?

'So…' I said slowly and waited until he looked up.

He gave me a... *bored* look, raising his eyebrow expectantly. 'Yeah?'

Back when we used to fight, he used to give me the same look, designed to make me feel like a nuisance, something I used to be accustomed to back then. Now though, I thought things had changed? Embarrassment flooded me and I concentrated on not letting it show on my cheeks. My efforts were futile, my cheeks felt like they were on fire. 'So, how was your trip?' I said tentatively but upbeat, still pretending nothing had changed.

'Look, I'm going to stay at Michael and Sophia's for a while.' His eyes were on the box as he dumped some jumpers in.

Unsure of what was happening, I frowned and asked, 'I don't understand. What do you mean?'

He threw a sock in the box and sighed heavily as he sat back down on the bed and ran his fingers through his hair. 'You know, I really thought I could do this.'

'What?'

'This.' He pointed at the two of us. 'You and me. The thing is, I'm not cut out for relationships, and you're never going to let yourself be happy.' He looked away and I felt all happiness and anticipation drain away. All I had left was a dead weight in my stomach.

I swallowed. 'What do you mean you're *not cut out for relationships?*'

'Look, it doesn't matter. This was a mistake, and the point is I'm ending this before it gets away from us and it's too late.' He got up again, his face set, and started to put things in the box again. 'I'll be at Michael's until I can find somewhere else. I'll be coming in to fix the bathroom.' He looked up at me. 'You can stay for as long as you need. I'm not kicking you out or anything.'

'You... What?' I shook myself to try to clear the fog my mind was in.

He took a deep breath and held on to the box, which was now overflowing. 'The flat. I bought it off your dad a year ago.'

'*What?*' I said in a high pitched voice I didn't recognise as my own. My mind was spinning from how everything was going so differently to what I had expected. How had I read the situation so wrong? 'Why am I only now hearing about this?'

Nick bit his lip and looked away as he decided what to say. 'I moved in just after you left for Kenya, and I asked your parents not to tell you about it. Then I started thinking about all the renovations I wanted to do, so I spoke to your dad about it. When he didn't want to invest the money, I told him I would buy the flat from him. He agreed, so I bought it just before Christmas last year.'

I flinched. This was all news to me. 'Why didn't you tell me?'

'It was back when we had our enemy thing going on, and I thought it would be a funny way to get back at you for something. But then we got together, and I didn't know how to tell you. And the longer I didn't say anything, the worse it got, so I just kept quiet.'

I still felt confused and betrayed and my throat was constricted, making swallowing impossible. 'Why are you moving out if you own the flat?'

His hard eyes met mine. 'Because it was your home first, and you're free to stay for as long as you need to.'

'But…' The reality that I had been sponging off him for months now dawned on me, and I felt horrified at the thought. 'I haven't paid you rent!'

He shrugged and turned away for some more things to put in his box. 'Doesn't matter. It's not like I need the money. And if you did pay rent you would have to work more hours at the school, which would be a waste of your time in view of the enterprise you guys are setting up.'

'So you've been *taking care of me*?' I asked, my voice rising. The patronising *Neanderthal*!

He sighed. 'If that's how you see it.'

'What, because I can't take care of myself?' I asked, eyebrows raised. 'Well, I'm sorry you felt you had to take care of stupid, irresponsible little Julia.'

He straightened and turned, looking me in the eye. His eyes were determined— no, fierce— as he said, 'I don't think you're stupid or irresponsible. I think you have no boundaries and you're a guilt-ridden mess. I was trying to give you a break so you could focus on getting your enterprise started, as your dad had just sold your flat out from under you.'

203

'Tell me how you really feel, why don't you?' I rolled my eyes as I turned to leave. 'I'll be out by tonight.'

As I left the room Nick sighed. 'Wait.'

I stopped but didn't turn toward him. I didn't think I would ever be able to face him again.

Ever.

'I'm sorry. I shouldn't have said that…'

'No worries. It's all cool.' I said dismissively and walked to my bedroom where I got my backpack and suitcase out of the closet and started to pack things randomly.

By now my eyes were leaking and no matter how many times I would swipe at my face, the tears just kept falling. I kept as silent as I could as I packed my bags with a frantic energy until I heard the front door shut.

Maple came in my bedroom and leaned against my legs. I sat down on the bed, my suitcase full beside me, picked up Maple and rang Miranda. Swiping the tears away again, I took a deep breath and ordered myself to calm down. She answered on the fourth ring.

'Mir, I'm going to need some help.'

'Anything,' she said, no questions asked, and I felt overwhelmed with how thankful I was to have a friend like her. 'Oh darling,' she said as she heard my breath hitch.

'Can I stay with you for a while?'

'Of course! Where are you? I'll come get you.'

'At the flat.' I swiped at my face again.

'I'll be there in twenty minutes. Don't do anything drastic. Whatever is going on obviously sucks, but we'll get through it together.'

'Ok.' I stared at the phone after she'd hung up before setting the cat down. 'I'll have to leave you here, Maples,' I said in as steady a voice as I could manage as I went back to packing. 'I'll be in to check on you when I get the rest of my things.'

Talking to the cat helped, and soon I'd filled the backpack as well. Miranda was there a couple of minutes later. Together we put my bags in the car and left before Nick came back.

After we'd unloaded my things in her spare bedroom, Miranda made me a big cup of tea and sat me down on her couch. She passed me a box of tissues. 'Tell me what happened.'

The tears started again as the whole story spilled out of me. When I got to the part about Nick owning the flat, Miranda seemed surprised. 'Wait, what?'

I took another tissue and wiped at my face as I sighed. 'Yeah. He said he bought it just before Christmas last year.'

We heard the front door open and Miranda stood up. 'Hold on. Hello?'

Jack pulled the zipper of his jacket down as he walked in the living room. 'Hey.' He gave Miranda a flirty smile and she rolled her eyes. 'Oh, hey, Jules.' He nodded at me, saw the used tissues lying all over the sofa and frowned. 'What happened?'

'Do you want him to leave? I can get him to go if you want.' I detected both concern for me and hopefulness that Miranda might have a reason to put Jack out of her house.

'Nah, it's ok.' I shook my head at her and looked at Jack. 'Nick came back from America and broke up with me.'

Jack ran his hands through his hair and down his face. 'Are you sure?'

'Pretty sure.' I gave him a dry look. 'He told me he wasn't cut out for relationships and he wanted to end it before it was too late.'

Jack shook his head in disbelief. 'The little idiot!' he muttered, then groaned, 'Ah, no! Now I have to go kick his arse.'

'Wimp.' Miranda snorted.

'Seriously? Have you seen his arms?' Jack looked at her.

'I'm sure a strong guy like you can take him.' Miranda's voice dripped with sugary sarcasm.

'Of course.' Jack ignored her sarcasm and gave her another flirty smile before turning serious. 'Still, I was hoping he'd straightened himself out and wasn't going to make a pig's ear out of it when he finally pulled his finger out and started dating my sister.'

'Needless to say, you were wrong,' Miranda said.

'I'm still here, you guys.'

Miranda's eyes went from flirty to concerned as she turned to at me and put a hand on my arm. 'Yes, so why didn't anyone tell us that he bought the flat?'

'I don't kn-'

'He didn't tell you?' Jack interrupted.

'You knew?! And didn't tell me?' I felt my cheeks go red as I fought to keep the humiliation out of them.

'Yeah.' Jack shrugged. 'He told me not to say anything because he wanted to surprise you or something.'

'Uh-huh, and what a surprise it was.'

Jack zipped up his jacket and pulled out his phone. 'I'll see you later,' he said as he walked toward the door. 'Michael? Uh-huh, yeah it's Jack.'

The front door slammed shut and Miranda and I looked at each other. 'Boys.' She shook her head. 'You know you can stay here for as long as you want, right?'

I tried to give her a smile, but it felt more like a grimace. 'Thank you. I think I'm going to need to sleep a bit before I can make any decisions about what to do about getting a new place.'

Miranda made up my bed, and that evening we drank wine and watched Grease like we used to when we were teenagers. Despite feeling rubbish, John Travolta in his tight shirts and flirty eyes pulled me in. I pulled a sickie the next day and spent the weekend in bed.

Chapter 30

Julia

A week after I'd left the flat and moved in with Miranda, the cups arrived, and, as it turns out, two and a half thousand cups are an awful lot of cups. I signed for the pallets when they arrived, and put them in Miranda's garage as we had arranged. Eager to see what they were like, I opened one of the packages and saw there were about a hundred cups in each box, all randomly lying on top of each other.

I sent a quick text to Miranda and Sophia

Me: The cups arrived! Had a little thought: Soph, how did you get on with finding out about options for packaging?

Soph: Are they all there?

Me: Haven't counted. Should I?

Mir: Def count them. I looked at the budget again: there's no more money to spend after the promo and stand have been paid for.

Me: Anyone want to come help me count to 2500?

Soph: Wish I could. In a meeting all afternoon. Will come over tonight x

Miranda didn't answer but showed up with pizzas to put in the oven after work so we didn't have to sort out cooking. We spent the evening counting cups – they were all there – and talking about our options for packaging. In the end, we decided to use the masses of material I had bought in Kenya and had planned to sew into sheets for people for Christmas. The material happened to fit nicely with the colours of our logo, so we would use it to sew little bags to package each cup in. It would be more work than we had expected, but was the best option from a financial perspective.

We decided to set up a production line in Miranda's living room, so Miranda pulled out her sewing machine and I went over to my parent's house to borrow mum's. As I still hadn't been back to the flat since I'd left it a week earlier, I knew I would need to go and pick up the rest of my things, the material for the period cup pouches included. I didn't want to do that when Nick would be around though, so decided to leave it until the next morning, and sent Nick a text to let him know.

I wrote and deleted the text without sending it about twenty times before Miranda wrote it for me and sent it:

Me: I will collect the rest of my things in the morning. Hope that's ok

It wasn't long before I received a text back:

Nick: Sure. I'll be at work

The next morning I had a big cup of tea before jumping in the shower and then spent the best part of an hour procrastinating before taking the bus to Nick's flat. Jack had promised he would come and pick me up; I just had to ring him to tell him when to show up, but there would be a lot of packing to be done first.

The flat looked much like it had when I had left, except the new bathroom suite, which used to be boxed up in the living room, was now unpacked and still sitting in the living room. It surprised me that Nick hadn't sorted out the bathroom yet, and I wondered what he did about showers. Still, everything else seemed much the same.

Maple came up to wind herself through my legs. I picked her up and sat down on the living room couch, exhausted at the thought of moving all my things out of the flat.

'I think you've grown, love.' I sighed and Maple snuggled close. 'Ah darling, I missed you, too.'

I spent the morning sorting out the rest of the things in my bedroom. A lot of things were still in boxes, not unpacked yet after I had packed them to make room for someone else to live in the flat whilst I was in Kenya. I got everything out of the cupboard and reorganised it all, deciding what to put in my parents' garage, what to take to a charity shop, and what I wanted to keep.

At lunchtime I looked in the fridge and found a lunch box with Nick's homemade curry leftovers. 'Finders keepers.' I smirked at Maple and put the contents of the box on a plate and into the microwave.

I inhaled the curry, not allowing myself to stop to dwell on how much I missed Nick's cooking, then made a pot of coffee and went to find the packed up moving boxes we had in the closet in the hallway. The kitchen would be next.

I found my box of noodles and cans of soup, and packed my favourite cups. Most of the things in the kitchen were mine, but I felt bad taking them, as I didn't need them when staying at Miranda's anyway. After debating the situation with Maple for a while, I sent Nick a text.

Me: Do you want me to leave you any dishes in the kitchen?

Nick: No. Take whatever's yours

His text came within a minute of me sending mine, and I went from feeling guilty to feeling hurt. I might have broken a couple of the dishes as I packed them somewhat angrily.

I texted Jack to let him know he would need to rent a van and packed box after box until all my things were packed. Jack arrived as I was folding the last of my blankets in the living room. We were carrying things out of the flat and into the van when Nick showed up.

Still wearing his work boots over his knitted socks with his slacks tucked in and a high-vis jacket, he looked tired.

Tired, but so very handsome.

His hair was pulled back into a neat bun at the back of his head, but his beard was longer and scruffier than I had seen it for a long time. He stopped to talk to Jack, and nodded to me as I carried a box down to the van. When I came back up, he picked up a couple of boxes and helped us load the rest into the van.

If I'd had any hopes that he would have looked at me and changed his mind, they were thoroughly shattered. Instead he avoided eye contact as much as possible and did his best to get us out as quickly as he could. Apart from Jack having a chat with Nick, we didn't say much, just went up and down the stairs, from the flat to the van with boxes. Thankfully, it didn't take long.

'I think this is the last of it.' Jack put the box in the van and closed the door. He shook Nick's hand. 'Hey, man, thanks for helping out.'

'Yeah, thanks.' I climbed into the front seat.

'No worries. I'll see you guys around.' Nick gave an awkward wave as we drove off.

We got to the lights at the end of the street and Jack looked at me. 'You ok?'

'Uh-huh.' I nodded and turned away. The whole day had been emotional. It was an end of not just me and Nick, but also of the time I had lived in the flat. Packing up all my things had brought home how much I was going to miss the place. I sighed. 'Onward and upward, right?'

Jack winced at the fake positivity in my voice, but nodded. 'Aye.'

Late that evening, Jack showed up at Miranda's after spending the evening with Nick and Michael. 'Jules?' he hollered from the hallway. He was holding a box, which was making scratchy noises.

'Uh-huh?'

'Nick said you forgot this.' He handed me the box and I lifted the lid. Maple screeched as she jumped out, looking decidedly dishevelled, her hair standing on end.

'Oh, darling.' I soothed and picked her up. 'You didn't like the box, did you.'

'Great. Good night.' Jack nodded and shut the door.

'But…' I started. I had left Maple at the flat in part because she wasn't exactly mine. I mean, she was mine, but she was Nick's too. As he'd picked her out and brought her home, I had felt I couldn't take her. Also, she reminded me of Nick and I figured having her around would make it harder to move on.

Moving on was already proving to be hard enough.

Now here she was, though, clinging to me with all her might, and Jack had already gone.

I sighed. 'You can stay tonight, but then you have to go back to Nick. You are his cat, after all.' I said in a gentle voice and stroked her as I carried her to my bedroom.

Maple slept in my bed that night, a cosy but painful reminder that Nick was further away now than he had been when he was in America. He would never be mine to snuggle up with again.

I convinced Miranda to take Maple back to Nick's the next morning. I gave her a tearful goodbye, packed her into the box much against her will, and Miranda took her away.

211

Needing to get out, I put on my winter coat and went for a long walk down to the beach at Portobello to clear my head. The beach was quiet that morning. The sea lay calm, the tide was out, and the clouds were high in the air. I sat down in the sand and watched the water as I wondered how to deal with everything.

The loss of Nick, the flat, and Maple brought back all the thoughts that were stirred up by the trip to Arrochar. How could I forgive myself for letting my sister die? How could anyone forgive me for that?

Thinking of our day in Arrochar, I remembered Nick saying, 'If God has forgiven you, then isn't it kind of arrogant to not forgive yourself?'

If God has forgiven you.

Did I believe he had?

Yes.

Tears started running down my face as I realised I had chosen to live under my own judgement, rather than in God's forgiveness. For the first time in over a year, I opened my mouth to talk to God. I'd spoken about him a lot over the last year, but it was a long time since I had last spoken to him. I hadn't felt like I had much to say to him. Now, though, I could see that, in my arrogance, I had disqualified God from being God and decided I was more qualified to be God than he was.

'I'm sorry,' I whispered as my tears kept falling. 'I'm so sorry. I have been so arrogant and full of pride, thinking too highly of myself, even as I deceived myself into thinking I was worthless. But I do know I am not qualified to make these judgements and, as you have forgiven me, I forgive myself for my part in letting Josie die. Only you are God.'

As I sat there on the beach, I experienced an overwhelming feeling of being loved and free. In my mind's eye, I saw how I was being wrapped up in a big embrace and held close on God's lap. And I knew that, right there and then, something massive had changed in me. I no longer needed to live in guilt and shame, but was free. The song I'd picked up in Kenya came back to me and I sang *hakuna mungo kama wewe* – there is no god like you. This time it didn't feel trite, but true and right.

I walked back home, a lightness to my step. Passing Miranda's house, I knocked on the door to my parent's house instead. I went on in and found Mum in the kitchen with her knitting and a cup of tea. I made myself a cup of coffee and sat down opposite her.

'Can I have a look at the photo albums?'

Mum smiled and put down her knitting. 'Of course!' I went to get the albums out and she gave me a gentle smile when she saw which ones I had got out. 'It's been a while since I looked at those pictures.'

'Yes, me too.' I hadn't looked at them for fifteen years. It had been too painful. Now, though, I felt it was time. 'Will you tell me about her?'

Mum squeezed my arm. 'I'd love to.'

As we looked through the pictures of Josie, Mum and I both cried, and laughed, and rolled our eyes as we remembered her. Stories I had forgotten came back to me, and I realised I hadn't been able to grieve Josie's death because I had been so wrapped up in guilt. Now that the guilt was gone, though, I felt the pain of the loss. As painful as it was, it was also lovely to, for the first time since the accident, be able to remember my sister – not just the accident. I had been so focussed on her death that I had forgotten so much of her life.

When I left Mum's house I still felt raw and vulnerable, but I had a sense that everything had changed in me.

Chapter 31

Julia

The next few weeks, I spent every free hour sewing little drawstring bags for the period cups. My back ached from hunching over the sewing machine, but I was thankful to have the time to think. I had a lot to think about as I was working out what forgiving myself and letting God be God actually meant. I wanted to work out how to live in God's forgiveness, and what it meant to belong to him fully. I found that my instinct was still to feel guilty and unworthy, or to say yes even when I wanted to say no, or to cut corners when spending money on myself because I felt unworthy. Still, I was committed to working it out, and for me that started in my head.

It also kept me from obsessing over what had happened with Nick.

Jack seemed to spend a lot of time on Miranda's couch, which made for nice company. We caught up on what we'd been up to during the years he'd lived in Hong Kong, and whilst everything in me wanted to ask about Nick, I never did.

Instead, I spent plenty of time obsessing as I tossed and turned at night. The more I thought about it, the less I understood why he had broken up with me. Part of me was hoping he would come round after a few days and realise he had made a mistake, but, as the days stretched into weeks, that became less and less likely.

Then, one evening, Miranda and I were pulling drawstrings through the cuffs of the little bags as Jack was drinking a beer on the couch and watching the football. Miranda cleared her throat. 'So, it's been a long time since I saw Nick.' She gave Jack's foot a kick to get his attention.

'What's that?' he said, looking up from the TV.

'*Nick*.' Miranda gave him a pointed look. 'It's been a long time since I've seen him. How's he doing?'

Jack glanced at me and I quickly looked away. Part of me didn't want to hear about Nick at all, but the other part was desperate for any news of how he was doing.

'Yeah.' Jack cleared his throat and I got the impression Miranda and Jack had talked about having this conversation in front of me. 'He's not doing so good.'

'Oh?' Miranda asked, feigning surprise. 'Is he having second thoughts about the breakup then?'

If I hadn't been dying to know what Jack was about to say, I would have laughed at how stilted their conversation was.

'He doesn't want to talk about it, so how am I supposed to know?' Jack sighed and looked me in the eye. 'Look, I went over there to beat him up a bit when I found out he'd broken up with you, Jules, but I couldn't do it.'

Miranda smirked at him. 'Ah, maybe if you spend some more time in the gym, you might be able to take him later?'

'Very funny.' Jack gave her a dry look and turned back to me. 'I got there and he looked like someone had run over his dog. So Michael and I have been taking turns with helping him sort out the bathroom in the flat. He looks like he hasn't slept much in the last few weeks.'

'So what do you think it going on?' Miranda pressed when I stayed silent.

'I don't know. I'm not his psychologist.' Jack took a sip of his beer and shrugged. 'All I know is that he's got a pretty terrible dad, and I expect he would have seen him when he was in the States. Might've messed him up some.'

It felt both better and worse to know Nick wasn't happy. Better, because I couldn't think of anything worse than to be forgotten quickly by him, as though I was just a blip on his radar. Worse, because now I had all kinds of other questions, and maybe I felt a little sorry for him. Still, it felt like a terrible waste that he would break up with me so we could both be miserable.

That night I slept better. Maybe I was comforted knowing Nick was hurting too, or maybe I was just exhausted from all the sleepless nights.

***

216

On the Saturday morning, a week before our first week at the Christmas Market, we had our first board meeting. After Nick broke up with me, I worried about him being part of the board for Project Cup, so I tried to pull a sickie for that first board meeting. Miranda saw right through my 'terrible headache' and rolled her eyes at me.

'I thought you had a stronger spine than that,' she said, using her best disappointed voice.

Embarrassed, I sighed and was thankful I still had plenty of time to get ready. I dressed quickly in my best skinny jeans and a light grey sweater and put on some make up. I left my hair down, but brought a hair tie just in case it got too out of control. Miranda gave me a smile of approval as we got into Jack's car, which settled my nerves at least temporarily.

Sophia and Michael hosted the meeting over breakfast in their flat. I have no idea what we ate, as I was rather preoccupied with avoiding Nick. We had agreed that Miranda would be our chairman as she was best at keeping us from going down rabbit trails. I volunteered to take the meeting minutes so I could look at my computer screen rather than have to face people.

We spent time talking about the process so far and what we were hoping to accomplish at the Christmas Market. Then Sophia talked about our internet presence before Miranda brought up money.

'Did you all see the budgets I sent out the other day?'

Jack sat up straighter and pulled out his copy of the budget. 'Yes, I saw them and I've got a couple of questions.'

'Right.' Miranda rolled her eyes at him as though it was no surprise to her that he's been the one to raise a question.

'If you don't hit the targets you've got during the Christmas Market – and, let's be real, it's not exactly the most Christmassy product that has ever been sold at that market, so…' He held his hands up and shrugged. 'How then are you going to raise the money you need to see come in before the Kenya trip?'

Miranda smirked at him and looked at Sophia who smiled. 'Good question. I was thinking we could do a sponsored Loony Dook at Hogmanay?'

I groaned and shivered just thinking about it. It had been years since I was crazy enough to join in with the traditional swim in the sea on New Year's Day. Most people that did it were blue from the cold, wind and rain *before* they'd gone into the sea, never mind *after*.

'Great idea! I'll do it,' Jack said.

Miranda rolled her eyes. 'Who's going to pay you to do it, though? You've done it every year you've been home since you were about eight.'

'Yeah, that's a good point.' Sophia nodded. 'In order for it to work, it's got to be someone that wouldn't do it unless they got paid, you know?'

'Fair enough. I'll just join whoever does it then.'

'Me too,' Nick said, and high fived Jack.

Michael grinned. 'I'll do it too.'

'None of you will bring in any money.' Sophia said and pursed her lips in thought. 'I think us girls should draw sticks to see who has to join the guys. Obviously we all have to help raise the money.'

Miranda and I nodded so Sophia pulled out a box of matches. She took out two sticks, cut one in half and handed the three sticks in different sizes to Michael. He held them for us girls to draw a stick each. 'The longest stick gets to do it.'

We each pulled a stick and Sophia drew the longest and lost. Or won, if you counted getting hypothermia a prize.

I breathed a sigh of relief as I noted this in the minutes. We spent a few minutes sorting out a date after Christmas for our next meeting, and when we were done, Sophia offered more hot drinks and we all stayed for a while longer as I failed to think of an excuse to leave early.

'How are you getting on with refitting the bathroom, Nick?' Miranda asked.

Nick shook his head and groaned. 'What a nightmare that has been. They sent me a bathtub with the wrong feet, so I had to send the feet back, but then they sent another set which also didn't fit, so then I had to send the bathtub back. Finally last weekend I got it all sorted.'

218

'Yeah, Jack was saying you were having trouble.' She nodded. 'Glad it's sorted now, though.'

I'd known nothing of this. Jack may have told Miranda about it, but nobody had told me. It struck me then how out of the loop I was. And how out of the loop I had been throughout my whole relationship with Nick. *I* may have told him things about me that I had told nobody else, but *he* had told me next to nothing about himself. I knew him no better now than I had before we'd gotten involved with each other. I'd been too busy spilling my guts to him to realise it wasn't being reciprocated.

Had I not asked the right questions of him? Or why had he felt unable to share and be vulnerable with me?

I knew then that, once I got over Nick, I would require more in any new relationship I entered. Being vulnerable would have to go both ways.

Chapter 32

Julia

It was the last week of November when we got our first week at the Christmas Market stall. Miranda and I met up with Sophia by the stall at six am. It was just as dark and cold as one might expect six am in November to be, but at least it wasn't raining.

The company that had used the stall the previous week had cleared it out the previous night, so it didn't take long to get everything set up in the little wooden cabin stall. We knew period cups weren't the most Christmassy thing, so we weren't expecting to sell many as presents. Instead we had a dual focus of selling the cups and engaging people to see that they could be part of a solution to help young women stay in education as a way to get out of poverty in places like Kenya. Apart from our 'buy one, give one' campaign, we also had an option for people to donate money toward projects like the one in Kenya. We had leaflets and sign up forms for our newsletter – all of it pointing toward our website where people could get more information.

Once it started to get light outside, I went to pick up hot drinks for us all to warm up. By the time I got back, the stall was ready and open for business. It looked great, and I felt proud to see what we'd achieved. I might have been *feeling* like I was entirely out of my depth, but our stall *looked* professional and as though we knew what we were doing. That was mostly down to Sophia's marketing skills and Miranda's business knowledge.

'This looks amazing.' I passed Miranda her green tea. 'I'm so thankful we're doing this together. I'd be lost on my own.'

'Yeah, it looks good!' She nodded. 'Now all we need is some customers.'

Sophia took her hot chocolate and took a sip. 'Right, customers.' Setting her drink down, she said, 'I think it would be good to go over some hooks and sales pitches before it gets busy.'

Miranda scrunched her face. 'Really?'

Sophia elbowed her arm and grinned. 'Yes, really. You'll thank me later.'

'Uh-huh.' Miranda nodded, unconvinced.

'Probably wouldn't hurt,' I said. 'We do have the most out-of-place product in this whole market…'

'Yes, so we're going to have to be a bit savvy in how we go about getting people to buy them.'

'Fair point.' Miranda reluctantly agreed. 'What's your idea?'

'Maybe we could role play a few different scenarios so we can figure out how to handle different types of customers?'

'Oh, I love a bit of acting,' I said in my best posh English accent.

Sophia rolled her eyes. She gave us a few scenarios and we spent the next half hour role playing.

Soon enough, the market started getting busy, and we found that when one of us was on the outside of the stall talking to potential customers, we were able to pull in quite a few people to have a look. By lunchtime we'd made our first sale, and three people had donated a few pounds toward the cups for the Kenyan girls. It wasn't much, but it was something.

And that something felt good.

The first sale I made on my own was to a girl in her mid-twenties. We spent some time talking about the cup and how it works before I said, 'And in buying a cup for yourself, you contribute toward giving cups to young women in places like Kenya, where girls can't afford sanitary products.'

She frowned. 'So what do they use if they can't afford sanitary products?'

'They'll wrap up cloth or use toilet paper. Some use chicken feathers or goats' skin or even mud.' I watched as her face scrunched up in disgust and nodded. 'I know. Gross, right? Just imagine the amount of infection and leakage. So the girls don't tend to come to school during that time of the month, which of course means that they miss a lot, and eventually can't keep up.'

'Wow, I had no idea. That's terrible!' She waved her hands about in frustration. 'It's always the women that suffer worst in poverty. Gah... the injustice!'

'I know! So, the period cups are making a difference for teenage school girls in that they can use them and not miss school. They can keep up with school so they don't have to drop out, which means they can get proper jobs when they finish school.'

'Really? Does that work?'

'Yes. We're working with a high school in Kenya who have tried it and it works. The girls stop skipping school when they have their periods. Out of the 30 girls they trialled only a couple of girls didn't end up using them. One of the girls I spoke to told me she had missed school so much last year that her dad had said that if she wasn't going to be able to pass her classes in school, he would arrange for her to get a job in Nairobi through a friend of his.'

'Doesn't sound like a good situation.'

'No, it really isn't. There are no good jobs for fourteen year old girls.' I shook my head. 'Anyway, because she used her period cup, she was able to be in school much more, and was able to pass all of her classes.' Sarah had been one of the girls we had worried about the entire year. She had been falling behind from the start of the year, and whilst we had offered extra help, she wasn't able to keep up in her classes. 'She told me her dad had agreed to let her stay in school for at least another year.'

'Wow, so *that's* great!'

'No kidding! I almost cried when she told me.' I bit my lip. 'So, our company is about helping schools or organisations fund period cups so more girls can stay in school.' I told the girl and her friend what their options were, and they both ended up buying cups and giving extra toward the cup projects.

Who said period cups didn't fit in a Christmas Market?

We were overwhelmed by how much feedback we got. The period cups were either received very positively or with disgust – much like Marmite. Some people loved the idea and were easy to sell to, whilst others seemed about ready to vomit just thinking about period cups. Still, each week we were at the stall, we sold more cups than we had the previous week, and it wasn't long before Miranda told us we had sold enough to cover the cost of the cups we'd bought. We still had a bit to go before we had covered the cost of the stall and advertising, but in the week leading up to Christmas, we would have been in the black had it not been for the flights to Hong Kong Miranda had bought and my flights to Kenya.

In the alternate weeks when we didn't have the stall, Sophia started an advertising campaign on social media which started driving traffic to our website, and soon we were selling cups there too.

We weren't overwhelmed by orders, but they started trickling in, a little at a time.

It felt great. All our hard work was starting to pay off and I started feeling excited about the trip to Kenya. In view of Nick's and my breakup, I was now assuming I would be taking the trip to Kenya alone, and I was thankful to be able to get away from everything after Christmas.

***

When I got a break from working at school and at the market stall, I went Christmas shopping. I'd bought most of my gifts in Kenya already – beautiful carved salad tongs, sugar bowls and things like that – but there were a few things, like Secret Santa gifts for work, I still had to buy. Since I had forgiven myself and started working on living in God's forgiveness rather than under my own condemnation, I had started to feel as though there were a few things I needed to change about how I lived.

When I had judged myself, I had lived under guilt and shame, never feeling worthy of anything. Every blessing I had, I couldn't enjoy because the guilt would swamp me. So when Nick had given me gifts when we were dating, or when anyone would give me a compliment, I made things awkward because I couldn't handle the feelings of guilt. Or when it was time to eat, I would only buy the cheapest foods, whether I liked them or not, because I didn't want to spend money on myself. Instead I gave money away to people or projects I felt were more worthy, or, more recently, I spent it on Project Cup.

Now, though, I was starting to understand that God hadn't only forgiven me, but Jesus had died to show me how much he valued me. And if God thought I was valuable, then I must agree.

I wasn't about to go disagreeing with God again.

Still, after living in guilt and shame for fifteen years I had programmed myself to be awkward, or eat porridge and a tin of tuna for dinner, or to feel generally unworthy, and I had found it was a hard lifestyle to break. I had put up a reminder on the bathroom mirror at Miranda's, and had little notes scattered around the house, but I still found myself struggling to remember that I was loved and worthy.

So when I came across a perfume called Amour in a department store on Princes Street, it called out to me. I stopped to smell it and fell in love.

Up until that point, I would never have considered splurging on a new perfume for me. Instead I would buy cheap body sprays at the supermarket to keep from smelling bad. But now, I felt it was right to buy something to remind me that I was loved, loved, loved by God.

So I did.

And in defiance of the twinge of guilt I felt when I handed my card to the cashier and paid the extortionate amount of money the perfume cost, I squirted some on my neck and wrists.

From then on, I started every day with putting on my new perfume, and every day I would smile and remember that God loved *me*.

***

We packed up our market stall late on Christmas Eve, as the other company would have the stall from Christmas Day until the second of January. Then we would have it back for the last few days of the market. This suited us well, as it meant we had a few days to recharge and to change our marketing strategy from being about Christmas to being more centred on starting a new year.

It also meant we had Christmas off to spend with family. As I had been in Kenya the previous Christmas, I was looking forward to celebrating with family this year. Of course, in our house, *family* also included Miranda, Sophia, Michael and Nick. And, whilst I was looking forward to Christmas dinner and other traditions, I wasn't exactly thrilled about Nick being there. But he was still part of the family, even though he didn't want to be *my* family, so I would have to suck it up.

225

Since our breakup, things had been awkward, not just for us but for everyone, and I was starting to feel pressure to push past the awkward and adjust to being friends. It was tempting to go back to being mean to him, but, whilst that might have been fine when I was nineteen, I was twenty six now and felt I should *try* acting like an adult. Maybe if I could learn to be his friend, I could learn to get over him?

Chapter 33

Julia

Jack was turning the Christmas music up as Miranda and I walked through the door. We were both wearing the ugliest Christmas jumpers, which Mum insisted on buying us all every year. She spent hours going through the charity shops after Christmas to find new Christmas jumpers for the following year.

'Oh, good morning, girls,' Mum said, her hands deep in the turkey as she tilted her cheek toward us to be kissed.

Michael stood by the stove frying things for the stuffing, and Mum had Sophia baking the birthday cake for Jesus – Mum's idea. The only person not there yet was Nick.

'Morning,' I yawned and leaned in to kiss Mum's cheek.

'Happy Christmas,' Miranda said cheerfully.

'Oh good, the little elves are here,' Jack said with a twinkle in his eye as Mum got Miranda chopping vegetables next to him as he peeled potatoes.

'What do you want me to do?' I asked Mum.

'I've got the perfect job for you, dear. Would you set the table?'

Jack chuckled. 'That's because she doesn't want to take any risks with Christmas dinner this year.'

I rewarded him with a dry look.

'Now, now, Jack,' Mum said as she finished rubbing the turkey with oil and herbs. 'Be nice to your sister.'

I went to get cutlery out of the drawer. 'Uh-huh, that's fine. I don't mind setting the table.'

'Ho ho ho.' Dad came into the kitchen wearing a Santa hat. His eyes smiled over his glasses as he watched us work. 'Who wants a coffee?' He took orders and went about making drinks all wrong until I took over and got him to sit down.

'Did you give Becky her Christmas p-i-g-s e-a-r yet?' Mum asked.

'Not yet. We've just been for a w-a-l-k in the p-a-r-k.'

228

I was in the dining room setting the table when Nick arrived. Hearing him say, 'Merry Christmas,' in his soft accent sent my heart into my throat, and I took a deep breath before going back into the kitchen for the plates. He was admiring my mum's turkey, which was just on its way into the oven.

'Nick.' I gave him a nod.

He looked up and my heart felt as though he had stabbed me. 'Jewel,' he replied. I looked away and hurried to get the plates out of the cupboard, feeling his eyes on me the whole time.

Back in the safety of the dining room, I set the stack of plates on the table and turned to look out the window as I took a deep breath. It hurt to hear him call me Jewel as though it meant nothing, when just a few months earlier it had been a term of endearment for me.

Someone cleared their throat behind me and I quickly wiped at my face to remove any trace of emotion before I turned to continue setting the table. 'Yes?' I looked up and saw Nick standing there watching me.

'I…' He went quiet and I raised my eyebrow.

'You what?'

'Look, Jewel…'

'*Please* stop calling me that,' I said in a pained voice.

He nodded and cleared his throat again. 'Sorry. Look, I can leave if this isn't working for you.'

If my heart wasn't broken before (it was), it broke then. It was one thing for a relationship to not work out between Nick and me, but I wasn't going to come between him and the rest of our friends. I didn't know a lot about Nick's family or home life before he came to the UK, but I knew his parents had never been interested in him and that he'd grown up lonely. And I knew he thought of my family as his family.

I couldn't ask him to leave on Christmas.

I shook my head at him. 'No, it's ok. We're adults, right?'

He gave a sharp nod and smiled. 'So they say.'

I gave him a weak smile back. 'If you're looking for a job, you can go hunt down a couple of chairs so we can all sit round the table.'

***

229

When we'd finished dinner and the dishes were done, Nick and Sophia got the chess board out. Jack looked at me. 'Backgammon?'

I smiled and topped up my wine. 'Ready to lose?'

Jack laughed. 'When's the last time you beat me? When you were eight?'

'Your memory obviously needs refreshing,' I said, and sat down.

'We should play Settlers later,' said Sophia.

Michael groaned. 'Really? Must we ruin every holiday with these board games?'

Sophia gave him a disdainful look, then smiled at Nick, who gave her a broad grin. 'Yes, we must.'

'Ach, Michael, what are you on about? Why don't you like board games?' Miranda looked up from her phone.

'Board games are for bored people. And only boring people get bored, amiright?' Michael shrugged.

'No, you aren't right.' Sophia rolled her eyes. 'Honestly, I think there's something wrong with you... Did your mother drop you on your head when you were little or something?'

Michael smirked. 'Nah, but forced family game nights every week will do that to you.'

'Are we all going to the midnight service tonight?' Mum asked as she sat down with her cup of tea.

'Sure,' said Miranda.

'Really?' Nick groaned.

'Oh come on, son, it would do you some good to go to church once in a while.' Mum smiled.

Nick gave her a weak smile before looking away and rolling his eyes. 'Mhm.'

Becky butted Mum's knee and she looked at Dad. 'Want to go for a Christmas walk with me and Becky?'

'Always.' Dad smiled and cracked a nut as he got up.

Once they'd left, Miranda asked, 'You're not into church, Nick?'

He sighed and moved a chess piece across the board. 'Nah, I'm not much into worshipping a child abuser with power issues, you know?'

'Wait, what?' Miranda looked up from her phone.

'Yeah, isn't that what church comes down to? God is mad at us for not keeping the law he made impossible to keep, and he demands a sacrifice to be appeased. So Jesus, God's son, comes to take our punishment and all God's wrath upon himself in our place, so we can be free and go to heaven. There, we get to spend eternity worshipping a god who makes his own son die a most horrific death.' He smirked and said in a scathing voice, 'Woop-woop.'

Miranda snorted. 'Well, when you put it that way...'

Sophia sighed. 'Honestly Nick, is that what you think the Christian message is?' She gave him an incredulous look, and for once I was thankful to have a friend who had thought through her beliefs, even if it did mean she sometimes drove me crazy with her endless theological obsessions, which she frequently had tried to engage me in. She moved a chess piece. 'Check.'

Nick shrugged. 'Isn't it, though?' He made a move.

Sophia looked at him as though he was crazy. 'No!'

Nick smirked. 'No, you don't like my move, or no, you don't think that's what Christianity is all about?'

Sophia cleared her throat as she pondered her next move. 'Both.'

'Well, that's not entirely fair, Soph,' Michael said. 'There are lots of people that would say that *is* the Christian message. It's just, there are other ways of looking at it too.'

Sophia rolled her eyes and made her move. 'Fine, there are lots of different ways of thinking about it, and here's another way of looking at it.' She raised her eyebrows at Michael as if to say, *Better? Are you happy now?* Michael nodded and put his beer to his lips to hide his smile. Sophia continued, 'The Christian message is about a God who is love. Everything he does, every thought he has is full of love. God isn't capable of child abuse, because there is no room for abuse in love. And God doesn't forgive us because Jesus died on the cross as a sacrifice in our place, God forgives us because that is who he is. Think about the story of the prodigal son who returns to his father after squandering all his money and living a debauched lifestyle. When the son comes back, the father runs toward him, hugs him, gives him presents and throws him a party. He doesn't demand a sacrifice.'

Nick nodded, and moved again. 'Ok, but then what do you think the cross is all about? Why did Jesus die?'

I swallowed. 'I always thought Jesus died on the cross to buy us free from the devil. I thought the devil owns us because we sinned and so Jesus had to come and buy us back. Right?'

Looking round the room, it appeared as though most people agreed with me.

Michael cleared his throat and set down his beer. 'I think the cross needs to be put into context of the rest of Jesus' life, where he showed us an alternative way of living. He showed us how leadership is about servanthood, and he visited with the undesirables of the day, like tax collectors and prostitutes, and made room for people to interact with him without shame. He performed miracles and talked about a new world order where the peacekeepers and the meek are blessed. He showed us how to care for the poor and how to treat strangers…'

'Yeah, yeah, and on it goes until we get to the cross,' Sophia cut in. 'So Jesus spent his life disempowering sin and death, and then he dies on the cross and makes it clear that death has no power anymore. He takes captivity captive and makes a spectacle of evil.'

'So, don't you think it's like in the Lion the Witch and the Wardrobe, where Aslan takes Edmund's place and is killed to pay off the evil white witch?' I asked.

Miranda snorted, 'C.S. Lewis?'

'Hey, don't knock C.S. Lewis; he's brilliant.' Michael gently elbowed Miranda with a smirk. 'But no, I don't think that's what happened on the cross.' He took a quick sip of his beer and continued, 'I think the cross isn't about payment, but about disarmament of evil. And Jesus is not a sacrifice in order to appease God, but more like God feeling the consequences of the sin he is forgiving. It's like a *manifestation* of his forgiveness instead of his *means* of forgiveness.'

I set my tea down and took the dice Jack handed me. It was my turn to roll. A four and a two. Distractedly I made a move whilst Miranda asked, 'Long discussion for what purpose? It doesn't really matter what you believe the cross is about, so long as you are clear on where you stand with God.'

Jack rolled his eyes and muttered, 'She would say that, wouldn't she?'

'What?' Miranda looked at him.

'Huh? What? I didn't say anything,' he said and gave her his best innocent look. 'Did I?'

'I think you're right and wrong, Miranda,' Sophia said, chess game long forgotten. 'At the end of the day, if you know you belong to God, he's not going to hit you over the head because you have some wonky beliefs.' She smiled. 'He's good that way. But where you're wrong is where our ideas have consequences. What we believe influences how we live our lives. Like if Nick here believes God is a child abuser, he is likely to end up hating God and wanting nothing to do with him. And that would be a shame, when a different perspective might have him loving God with everything he is. That could have massive consequences in how he lives his life, right?'

'Yeah ok, I get it.' Nick stood up, abandoning the chess game. 'I'm going for some fresh air.'

'Anyone for another drink?' Miranda took orders as Jack's and my attention went back to our backgammon game.

'Did I say too much?' Sophia asked with a frown as she put away the chess pieces.

Michael shrugged and rolled his eyes. 'Maybe the last bit about how he's miserable because his beliefs are wonky might have hurt some, considering where he's at right now.'

'I think it's a good thing you laid into him, Soph. He needs somebody to challenge his way of thinking.' I paused. 'I think we all do.'

'Should I go check on him?'

'I'll go.' I stood up. 'Jack's winning this game anyway.'

'You sure?' Jack raised his eyebrows at me.

I shrugged. 'Call it a win and we can rematch later.'

'That's not what I meant...'

'I know. It's fine.' I took my glass, put on a coat and winter boots, and stepped outside onto the porch, where Nick was sitting with his beer. He had his woollen winter jacket on, and the collar was straightened to cover his neck. I felt his eyes follow me as I got a chair and sat down.

'You ok?' I asked, reminding myself to keep things friendly.

He gave a short nod. The silence stretched out as I sipped my wine.

I knew I had no way of helping him sort through his thoughts, and our relationship now was undefined, at best. We hadn't had a proper conversation since the day he broke up with me. I had let go of any hopes I had carried of us getting back together. The past few months had showed me his mind was made up. As sad as I was about that (very), I now had a choice as to how to move forward. Before, when I was secretly in love with him for all those years, I had chosen to be his enemy in the hope that he would notice me as someone more than Jack's little sister. Now, though, I felt being mean to him would allow me to keep being in love with him. So I had to find another way of relating to him. Ignoring him wouldn't work, as he was like a son to my parents, on the board of our social enterprise and part of my group of friends. He was everywhere I looked.

If I wanted to get over him, I would have to learn to be his friend. Perhaps not his best friend,—that might be too painful—but a friend nonetheless.

I sighed and put down my wine. 'This is awkward.'

He raised his eyebrows as if to say it was awkward because I was invading his space. I ignored him and continued, 'I've decided the way to get rid of the awkwardness between us is to be friends.'

'Yeah?' He gave me a sceptical look.

'Yeah.' I cleared my throat. 'It's not fair on everyone else to keep going like this. I think you're mostly a good guy and I can use a good guy friend, you know?'

He set his beer down, 'Ahh…'

'And you don't need to worry about me still carrying a torch or anything. I know we're not getting back together.'

He looked at me and held my gaze, my eyes steady even as everything in me wanted to look away.

'Okay,' he said carefully.

I reached my hand out. 'Hi, I'm Julia, how's it going?'

He raised his eyebrow at me and studied me. When I thought he wasn't going to take my hand, he reached out and shook it slowly as he tilted his chin at me. 'Nick.'

I smiled. 'Nice to meet you.'

He rolled his eyes, but his lips pulled up on the left side, revealing the dimple in his cheek.

'Yeah, so seeing as we're friends now, I was wondering what you're thinking about what Sophia said.'

He gave a dry chuckle. 'I thought you might have a motive.'

I smiled. 'Uh-huh.'

He looked away then shrugged. 'Sure, she has some interesting ideas.'

'Yeah, I was wondering more about what you think about what she said at the end. About how what we believe effects how we live our lives. Do you think you might be missing out?'

'Look, Julia.' He gave me a determined look as he enunciated my name carefully. 'If you're hoping I'll have a come to Jesus moment here with you right now, you're going to be disappointed.'

I snorted. 'I just thought…'

'No, you know what, listen: I'm happy to be your friend, but you've got to respect my boundaries. And I don't want to talk about this.'

I flinched. 'Fine. Sorry, I didn't realise it's such a sensitive issue.' I stood up to leave.

'Instead of pushing me on my issues and beliefs, maybe you should focus on sorting out your own,' he said in a hard voice as I walked back to the door stiffly.

'Sure thing. Sorry I brought it up.' Closing the door behind me I took a deep breath. I shrugged out of my coat and took my boots off as I debated whether to go back to Miranda's and eat my feelings or stay and pretend everything was fine. In the end I decided to stay. It was Christmas, after all.

As Jack and I played another game of backgammon, Nick texted Jack to say he'd left, and I breathed a sigh of relief even as a traitorous part of me wondered if he was ok.

The rest of us had Christmas cake and went to the midnight service with Mum and Dad. And despite everything going on with Nick, it felt good to be home for Christmas.

Chapter 34

Nick

Apart from going to board meetings, I made sure I stayed away from Julia. It was the only way to stay sane. Seeing her was too painful.

Still, I had made the right decision, and now there was no going back.

Whenever we had board meetings, I found myself trying to joke around with everybody, pretending that everything was fine. All while on the inside, my soul was rotting away and I wasn't sure I would ever be fine again.

Ever.

Although at first things had been a bit awkward with Jack, I still hung out with him and Michael. I saw more of Michael, as Jack spent most of his time with Miranda trying to get her to go out with him. When Jack left for Asia six years ago, he broke off their engagement and, though he seemed to have come home having had a change of heart, Miranda now seemed determined not to go back to being his girlfriend. Jack kept saying he felt like she was hiding something – perhaps Miranda and I had more in common than I'd thought and she too had a good reason for not being in a relationship with one of the Reids. Still, Jack seemed hopeful, and I hoped they would be able to work it out.

Michael was more available, and I saw him at the gym a fair bit. He wasn't much for small talk, so I could hang out with him without having to pretend everything was fine. Still, when he talked, he was real and honest, so I tried to avoid getting into situations where we might end up in real conversation. For the most part, I was successful.

Until I wasn't.

Just before Christmas, us guys went to catch the football game at a pub in Cowgate. It was a good game and our team won. On the way home, Michael asked me what I was doing for Christmas.

I shrugged. Mrs Reid had, as she usually did, sent a group text with the plans for Christmas weeks ago. I hadn't replied. Julia would be there, and I was sure I was the last person she wanted to have Christmas with.

'He's coming to our house for Christmas, like always,' Jack said, as if it was a done deal.

I frowned at him. 'I don't think so, man.'

'Why not? You always have Christmas at ours.'

'Yeah, I think it's best if I stay away this time, though.'

'You little chicken shit…' Jack shook his head. Michael cleared his throat, but Jack kept going. 'I'm running out of patience with this drama. Honestly, how long is this going to go on for?'

'Look, it is awkward enough the rest of the times we're all together, I don't want to impose at Christmas.'

'No, you look…'

Michael slapped his chest and gave him a look. He glared back at him. Michael raised his eyebrows, and Jack stepped down.

'So I take it from all this silent communication you're doing that you've been talking about me.'

'Yeah, well…' Jack started. Michael cleared his throat again and Jack threw him a glare and continued, 'Yes, we have. This is ridiculous. You're coming to Christmas and that's that.'

I sighed. 'Julia's your sister. You ought to have her back.'

'Yeah, she's my sister. And you're my brother.' He shrugged. 'And no brother of mine is spending Christmas on his own. Don't make me pick sides.'

I took a deep breath of the December night air. It was like I could breathe again. For a couple of months I had felt like I had lost *everybody* in breaking things off with Julia. Jack had seemed ok with me, but I knew he had to pick Julia's side. Considering Jack and his family were more family to me than my Dad had ever been, that had sucked.

So to hear Jack call me his brother… I looked him in the eye and nodded. 'I'll be there.'

He slapped my back and rolled his eyes. 'Course you will.'

I snorted. 'Besides, I wouldn't miss your mom's turkey.'

'Ah, the gravy…' Michael sighed. 'We should stop for some chips. I'm hungry now.'

And so I went to the family Christmas.

I couldn't remember ever celebrating Christmas growing up, although I knew from pictures that we used to celebrate before mom died. There was a picture of mom and me at Christmas when I was three. She was pregnant then, and she was smiling at me as I was holding up my Christmas stocking to the camera. But I couldn't remember any of it. And after she died, we never celebrated *anything*, never mind Christmas.

So yeah, Christmas this year was awkward, and it all ended badly, but it was also Christmas, with food, and weird games and presents and the required theological and political conversations.

Then, a couple of days later, Jack, Michael and I were at the pub again. We'd been talking about the Loony Dook we were doing at Hogmanay, when Jack said, 'So, Nick…'

Michael rolled his eyes and I knew what was coming. I cleared my throat.

'Michael and I think…'

'Hey, don't pull me into this!' Michael held his hands up.

'Fine.' Jack shot him a glare. '*I* think it's time we talk about why you broke up with Jules.'

I sighed. 'Do you really though?'

It was my turn to be glared at.

'Fine. What do you want to know?'

'Well it seems a strange coincidence that you broke up with her after you came back from being in America. Makes me wonder what happened there.'

I shrugged.

'Did you see your dad?'

Taking a sip of my beer, I looked away and answered. 'Yeah, just briefly at the end.'

'And…'

'Turns out he got remarried.'

'Yeah?'

'Yeah, and he's got a baby on the way.'

'What?' Jack set his drink back down. 'Really?'

I snorted. 'Uh-huh.'

'That's… unexpected.' Michael bit the inside of his cheeks and narrowed his eyes as he looked at me.

'Yeah, a bit.' I shrugged again. 'It's his life, though, so…'

'Still, his life has been a big influence on your life for a long time.' Michael sipped his beer. 'The other night, when Sophia was going on about our views of God…'

I sighed. 'Can we talk about something else?'

Jack nodded. 'Are you going to tell us why you broke up with Jules, or would you like us to guess?'

I used to appreciate Jack's directness. Not so much now, though. Now, I wished he would direct it somewhere other than me.

'Look, you and I know your sister deserves someone that will marry her and be there for her. She wants children, and she'll be a great mom one day. But I can't be her husband, and I can't be a dad to her children. It's just not in me.'

'What?' Jack seemed outraged. 'Then what were you doing with her in the first place?'

'Look, I told you, you should have been concerned back then.' I held my hands up.

'There was nothing to be concerned about!'

I took a long sip of my drink. Was there *any* chance of getting out of this conversation?

Michael frowned. 'I think there's more to the story. We saw you with Jules back then, and you weren't that far off from proposing.'

I snorted. As if. 'Yeah, I was wrapped up in her and it might have seemed the next step would've been to propose, but I would never do that to your sister.' I looked at Jack. 'You've got to understand that.'

'Understand what?'

'I can't be that man for her.' I shook my head. 'And I'd rather break it off now, before…'

Michael looked up from peeling the label off his beer. 'Before what?'

'Before…' I looked away and took a deep breath. 'She realises she picked a guy that's incapable of loving her and any potential children the way she or they deserve to be loved. I can't do that to her.'

'What do you mean incapable of loving her? Anyone can see you love her.' Jack shook his head.

241

'You don't get it.' I took a deep breath. 'Jewel is the kind of girl that a guy can get entirely swept up in. She's wild and strong and she's full of life. If that happened to me, I would never be able to come back from it. And I've seen how destructive that can be.'

'What?' Jack frowned at me. 'Are you talking about your dad now?'

I pulled my hand through my hair and tucked it behind my ear as I leaned back. 'Sure. He was all wrapped up in mom, and since she died he's been a shell of himself. A mean, twisted shell that was incapable of kindness.' Sitting back up I gave Jack a determined look. 'And I will not become like him.'

Michael bit the inside of his lip as he studied me, his eyes narrow. 'Is that all?'

I went to nod as Jack said, 'Nah, there's more. You're afraid of not being good enough for her.'

I closed my eyes. Jack was closer to the truth than I could admit. 'In any case, I think we can all agree we want what's best for Julia.'

'Uh-huh.' Jack nodded. 'And it sounds like you need to grow a set.'

I rolled my eyes. 'That's a bit rich coming from you, don't you think?'

Jack snorted. 'Yeah, I messed up with Miranda back then. I spent years drifting, trying to find some form of purpose in Hong Kong, before I realised I was going about things all wrong. So here I am. And I don't know how long I get to live, but I know the time I have is not going to be wasted because I was too scared of rejection.'

I took a controlled breath and said through gritted teeth, 'That's good for you, but I think it's fair to say our circumstances are a bit different. Don't you think?'

Jack looked away as though disappointed. I leaned back in my seat and took another sip, finishing my pint. Jack stood up, collecting our glasses. 'I've got to take a leak. And I'll get the next round.'

242

With Jack gone, Michael looked at me. 'Look, I don't want to poke a sore spot, but have you thought any more about what Sophia was saying the other night?'

'Yes, actually.' When I left the Reid's house on Christmas day, I had opted to walk home to clear my head, rather than take the bus. 'I like what you said about Jesus dying not as a payment to appease God, but as a manifestation of his forgiveness.'

'Yeah?'

'Yeah.' I nodded. 'It means God isn't some vicious, angry being that demands a sacrifice.'

Michael smiled and nodded. 'Yeah. I like that too.'

'And I think Sophia is right in that our views of God influence how we live our lives.'

Michael bit his lip. 'So, if you don't think God's a mean twisted being, incapable of kindness…'

I lifted an eyebrow. 'Putting words in my mouth now, Michael.'

'Yeah,' He laughed. 'Don't you think it's interesting how similar your view of God and your view of your dad are though?'

'Yeah. You may have a point there.'

He shrugged. 'Have you ever wondered what it might be like if God wasn't anything like your dad? If God was kind?' His eyes were determined even as he seemed relaxed in his chair. '*Really* kind.'

I frowned. 'No.'

Michael drank his beer silently for a while before saying, 'Maybe you should.'

Jack came back, and we ended up talking about other things, but Michael's words stayed with me. I hadn't wanted anything to do with God since I had believed him to be mean. But what if God really was kind and truly loving? Would I want to know him then?

243

Chapter 35

Julia

On Boxing Day morning I woke up early, and decided to go over to talk to Mum and Dad about Nick. A few months earlier, I hadn't been able to bring up with them the issue of them selling the flat to Nick without telling me, because I hadn't wanted them to feel uncomfortable. But since then, I had come to new conclusions about myself.

One of the conclusions I had reached was that if God had gone to the lengths of dying in order to show me how much he cares about me and how valuable he thinks I am, then I ought to treat myself with respect. Treating myself with respect meant a lot of things, but, as an example, I had decided I didn't have to absorb all uncomfortable feelings for other people in order to be worthy of existing.

Mum and Dad were having breakfast when I walked in, so I got a cup of coffee and sat down with them. Not quite sure how to bring the whole situation up with them, I said, 'Christmas was nice, wasn't it?'

Dad nodded. 'Uh-huh.'

I gave a stiff smile and looked out the window. 'Shame about the weather, eh?'

Mum put down her tea. 'It's nice to see you dear, but what brings you over at this time of the day?'

Mentally rolling my eyes at myself, I took a deep breath and blurted out, 'Mum, why didn't you tell me you guys sold the flat to Nick?' There, I'd said it.

Mum frowned. 'Didn't we?'

I tilted my head at her. Was she being serious? 'No! I found out when he broke up with me. He told me I could keep staying in his flat until I found somewhere else.'

Dad frowned and shook his head. 'Nick talked to me about it when he bought the flat. It was part of our agreement that you could stay for as long as you wanted.'

245

'And that was a nice, albeit rather inappropriate, thought.' I took a deep breath. 'Still, why would you make arrangements like that for me without telling me?'

'You know we only care about you, Julia.' Mum reached for my hand. 'And our Nick is a bit confused just now, but I'm sure he never wanted you to be hurt.'

I tried to smile at her as I gritted my teeth. 'Yeah, I know, but next time it would be nice if you could talk to me before making deals behind my back.' I looked at Dad.

He bit the inside of his cheek. 'Noted.' He cleared his throat before saying, 'I'm sorry you had to find out when he broke up with you.'

Dad apologising to me put a needle in my balloon of frustration, and I felt the fight go out of me. 'Yeah, it was shit, but I'm ok now.'

Mum sipped her tea. 'I think this is the first time you have come to us with something that's bothered you like this since Josie died.'

I cleared my throat. 'Yeah, well, I didn't want you to feel bad or anything. I felt like I'd already broken your lives enough by not keeping Josie safe…'

Mum grabbed my arm. 'Julia…'

I gave her a weak smile. 'It's ok. I don't think that way anymore.'

Chapter 36

Julia

A few evenings later we had another board meeting, this time at Miranda's. Miranda and I had made a big pot of vegan chilli, which we served up in the kitchen before taking our bowls into the living room. Nick arrived late, and Miranda got up to get him some food.

His eyes found mine as he sat down with his bowl on the couch across from me. I looked away and avoided his eyes, unsure of what to think of how he kept looking at me. After Christmas, I wasn't sure where we stood, and I wasn't sure how to bridge the awkwardness.

And that evening he hardly spoke to me at all. Apart from confirming that he had got the time off work and that he was looking forward to going to Kenya with me the following week. Which, considering he had broken up with me months earlier, seemed like pretty big news.

'What?' I squeaked and my eyebrows disappeared into my hairline. I had been sure he would pull out of the trip.

'Yeah, is everything all set for the trip?' he asked. 'Is there anything you need help with sorting out?'

I cleared my throat, trying to find my calm even as my stomach was reeling. 'No, it's fine. I've got it all covered.'

Conversation moved on, and I closed my eyes and took a deep breath. I was thankful Michael had offered to take notes, as most of the rest of the meeting was a blur to me, my mind preoccupied with feelings and panicked thoughts. Now I would have to spend the next few days rearranging the trip to include him after all. Was there no justice at all in this world?

Miranda elbowed me gently as we came to the end of the meeting.

'What?' I asked.

'Are there any last things to discuss?' She asked again.

I swallowed as I scrambled for something to contribute. 'Sure… is everything set for the Loony Dook at Hogmanay, Sophia?'

She gave me a weird look and said, 'Yeah, we just went over all that. Are you ok?'

Crap! I nodded sharply. 'Of course. Sorry.'

Sophia cleared her throat. 'I just wanted to mention about how we start our last few days of the Christmas Market on the second of January,' Sophia said. 'I was thinking we need to capitalise on the New Year's resolution idea now. Start the new year off healthier and more environmentally conscious by getting the period cup, but also give a less fortunate woman somewhere in the world the same chance.'

'Good thinking,' I nodded, trying to clear my head to focus on Sophia. 'Do we have all our days covered now?'

Miranda pulled up her rota and looked it over. 'All except the last two days. I asked your mum to fill in a couple of times, and Sophia and I are able to cover the other days when you're not around. But we're going to have to close up a couple days early.'

'Ok, sure.' It was a shame we weren't able to cover all the days, but I didn't feel bad about it. There would be other Christmas Markets. I did feel pretty bad about going to Kenya with Nick, though.

Or maybe 'bad' was the wrong word. In any case, I was confused.

As I rearranged the itinerary to include Nick over the next few days, I struggled to decide what to feel about it all. In the end, I decided this would be an opportunity to become friends with him, and that I should make the most out of any friendly feelings I had towards him. I determined that the trip to Kenya would be my way to get out of being in love with Nick and into a nice friendship with him instead. Much like the one I had with Michael.

That was possible. *Right?*

***

There were a lot of people at the beach when we got there on New Year's Day, so we spent a long time looking for a place to park. In the end, we caught someone leaving and were able to snag a parking space fairly close to the beach, which we were thankful for, considering everything we had to carry. I hadn't been to the beach since that morning when God and I had had our talk about forgiveness, and as I looked out at the ocean I wondered why.

It was beautiful.

I took a deep breath of fresh sea air and let my mind clear as I looked out at the sea. It was a cold and blustery day with big clouds covering the sky, and the water was choppy from the wind. Still, it filled me with peace inside. I wrapped my scarf tighter round my neck to ward off the chill and was thankful to be bundled up in a thick woolly sweater under my winter coat.

'You up for this?' Miranda asked Sophia as we walked along the prom and onto the beach.

'Sure.' She gave a strained smile. 'Nobody ever died of hypothermia, right?'

Miranda rolled her eyes at her. 'You're not going to die. Besides, the guys do this every year and they're still alive, aren't they?'

'Yes, that does make me feel much better. And warmer,' Sophia said dryly.

'Just think of how much money you've raised.' I grinned at her. 'Rather you than me, though!'

'Yeah, somehow three hundred and fifty four pounds and thirty five pence doesn't quite seem worth freezing my behind off for. You know?'

'That's why we're here, though.' I shook my collection box and scrambled the pennies we'd put in to have something to shake.

The beach was full of people doing dooks or watching their crazy friends, so we found a spot on the beach and took our coats off to show the Project Cup t-shirts we were wearing over our thick jumpers. Handing out flyers and talking to people, we did our best to raise both money and awareness for our cause. And people did give, which made Sophia feel a little better.

The guys soon found us. They had run to the beach and didn't seem at all affected by the cold weather. Running up to us, Jack held up his hand to high-five Sophia, and she gave a fake smile and a most unenthusiastic 'Yay' as she high-fived him back.

He gave her a hug and rubbed her hair until her smile widened and she groaned, 'You stink! Get off me, you Neanderthal.'

Jack chuckled and let her go. 'You ready?'

'I don't know that I'll ever be ready for this,' Sophia muttered. 'Why doesn't anyone ever tell me when my ideas are awful?'

'Let's do this!' said Nick and Michael gave an uncharacteristic 'Yeah!' as they started peeling their clothes off. Soon the guys were down to their board shorts and Sophia stood shivering in her Project Cup t-shirt and yoga pants.

'You all set?' Miranda asked and got her camera ready, snapping pictures of Sophia and the guys, who were posing as though it was the height of summer and twenty five degrees, rather than New Years' Day and freezing cold.

'Sure, let's just get it over with.' Sophia gave her best smile, as Nick said, 'Ready, Set, Go!'

Off they ran down the beach and into the waves, the water splashing all over. Miranda followed closely with the camera. Sophia squealed and the guys cheered and threw themselves into the water. Nick, Michael and Jack took a few strokes and swam out as Sophia quickly stood back up and started running towards us. She was shivering, her lips blue as I wrapped her in a towel and rubbed her arms. 'Yay! You did it!'

She gave me the biggest grin, relief all over her face as she shivered into the towel. 'Yay!'

I bent to pick up her clothes to hand to her, and that's when I was caught by big, wet arms lifting me from behind. I turned my face to confirm what my body already knew, and saw Nick grinning at me. Jack grabbed my legs and pulled off my boots.

'What the…' I shook my head, wriggling to try to get down but they held on tight as they ran me down to the water. 'Put me down!'

'Just a sec.' Nick laughed as they threw me in.

My whole body tensed as it landed, the cold water flooding my body. I pushed my head above water and drew a deep breath, only to have a wave overtake me and give me a lung-full of seawater. Ordering my feet to start working, I stood up, coughing frantically to clear my lungs. I took a sharp breath that felt like knives were stabbing my chest as I ran onto the beach as fast as my little legs would carry me. My wet clothes clung to me, and I tried to wring them out as I ran.

Nick laughed merrily as he watched me, his towel wrapped around his hips, somehow not looking cold in the slightest.

'You!' I shouted and pointed at him.

'Here.' Miranda cut in and wrapped a towel around me, doing her best to keep a straight face. Jack chuckled, watching me as I clung to the towel.

'Traitor.' I sneered at him and grabbed at my hair to wring it out.

Nick laughed. 'Oh, come on Jewel, it's just a bit of fun.'

'You are so dead.'

'Ooh, I'm so scared,' he said in a high pitched voice.

'You should be, you sick person…'

'Let's get you into some clothes and you can kill him later.' Miranda held my towel as Sophia helped me out of my wet clothes and change into Miranda's jumper and my winter coat.

Later, after Sophia and I had both showered and put our warmest woollies on, we curled up on Miranda's couch with blankets, whilst Miranda poured us big cups of tea.

'Do you think we'll ever feel warm again?' Sophia asked, teeth still chattering.

Miranda smiled and shook the collection boxes. 'You made quite a bit of money though.'

'Great, did you count it up?' Sophia asked.

'Yes, we're almost at a point now where we're not going to need to ask anyone for any more loans. For now at least.'

Sophia set her tea down. 'I'm thinking maybe we could do a sponsored run in the spring. What do you think?'

Miranda nodded and looked at me. 'You're awfully quiet. Are you ok?'

I sighed. 'Yes, I'm ok, and it's great we're doing ok with the budget, and I'm happy to do a sponsored run in the spring, maybe round Arthur's Seat? But I'm also *so* not ok.' I set down my tea. 'What the heck was Nick *thinking*? We hardly speak to each other for *months*, then we decide to be friends, then he tells me to mind my own business and backs off completely for *days*, and then he throws me in the sea *midwinter*. I'm so confused! And we're going to *Kenya* in just a few days.'

Sophia shook her head at me. 'Maybe you need to have a little chit-chat with him.'

'Or maybe I could just kill him!'

'Uh-huh. That'd work too, I'm sure.' Miranda rolled her eyes. 'Are you all set for the trip now, though?'

I nodded. 'Aye, it's all arranged.'

'That's great. Are Nick and you travelling together or are you going to check in separately?'

'I wish.' I sighed. 'No, when we bought the tickets we arranged to check in together. That way I can check in one of my bags in his name.'

'I've been thinking, if we keep selling like we have been over the last few weeks, we're going to need to partner with other schools or organisations as well as the school in Mombasa.' Miranda said.

'That's a good point. I'll send Mrs Mwangi an email and see if she can connect me with somebody that can help.'

'So…' Sophia drew the word out and looked at Miranda. 'Have you made any decisions about Angus from the bank?'

'Angus from the bank?' I raised my eyebrows. 'How come I live with you, but this is the first I hear of Angus from the bank?'

Miranda cleared her throat and blushed. 'I think I've decided to go out with him.'

'Oh, yeah?' Sophia grinned widely.

'Yeah, I think so. I mean, I can give it a go.' She shrugged. 'It's not like I'm agreeing to marry him by going out for dinner once, right?'

'Right.' Sophia nodded. 'Absolutely.'

'Wow, it's been a while since you dated anyone.' I reached out to stroke her arm. 'How do you feel about it?'

Miranda sipped her tea. 'I guess I'm nervous? He's a good guy, you know.'

'Yes.' Sophia nodded. 'And, most importantly, hot.'

Miranda blushed again. 'Yes, well, there's that.'

'If this is the Angus I think it is, yes, he *is* hot.' I smiled. 'It's nice that you're dating again.'

Miranda sighed. 'I decided it's a new year, and it's time to move into a new phase.'

'Not a minute too soon,' Sophia said. 'I can't remember the last time you had a date.'

Whilst Miranda had dated a little over the years, nobody had stuck. There hadn't been a serious boyfriend in her life since Jack.

'Uh-huh, it's been a while.'

'Probably more like a year,' Sophia said.

'Something like that. I think I decided to take a break after that guy Edward left me with the bill in the restaurant after following a girl he used to date. I never heard from him again. Honestly, men are such…'

'But now here you are,' I cut in with a smile. 'About to date Angus. And he's a good guy.'

'I think we need alcohol,' Sophia said. 'To toast the New Year and your date, and also to warm me up. I'm still cold from the sea.'

So we had wine and cheese and crackers for dinner, and went to bed early. The next morning we went into town to set up our stall for the last few days of the market. We sold cups and gave out flyers until it felt like there wasn't a person in Edinburgh that hadn't heard about Project Cup.

Chapter 37

Nick

I had spent the days after the night in the pub turning the idea of being on speaking terms with God over and over in my mind. I decided I might have been too hasty in deciding God was mean and, if nothing else, it was worth taking a closer look at the evidence on either side of the argument.

And in taking a closer look, I realised I had been wrong about a lot of things.

As much as I had once accused Julia of being arrogant in judging God's judgements as not good enough, I now could see that I had been just as arrogant in how I had labelled God an abusive and mean being. Now when I thought about it, I realised it had been easier for me to be angry at God and write him off as harsh and unloving, than it was to search his true nature out. I saw now that knowing God for who he really was meant I would have to confront my own pain.

I'd gone for several long runs in the cold winter rain, speaking with God as I worked out all the thoughts going round in my head. During one of those runs, I found myself asking for God's forgiveness for my arrogance, and asking for him to reveal himself me. I hadn't even finished speaking before the Bible verse Karen and John had on their kitchen wall came to mind: *Ask and it will be given to you; seek and you will find; knock and the door will be opened to you.*

When I got home, I got a big glass of water and dusted off my Bible. Not sure where to start, I opened it randomly and started reading in Revelations where I came across this verse: *Here I am! I stand at the door and knock. If anyone hears my voice and opens the door, I will come in and eat with that person, and they with me.*

As I read that verse, I found myself smiling. It seemed God and I were both knocking on doors, and we both wanted to know each other. I put the Bible aside and went for my shower with a new sense of hope. I knew I'd have to confront pain and work out difficult stuff, and confronting pain was not something

I liked doing. But maybe I could do it together with the God I was starting to realise was loving and kind.

As I started reorganising my understanding of the world on the basis that God was not horribly evil, but actually good and kind, I found myself facing my feelings around my relationship with my Dad. Michael had been right – my understanding of who God was had largely been based on my relationship with my Dad.

I had spent so many years trying to avoid Dad— it had seemed every encounter with him growing up had been painful. But now that I was pursuing a new understanding of God, I would have to do the same with my relationship with my Dad. I had hated him for how he had treated me, but now as I looked closer, I could see he had been acting out of his own pain. In my hurt and anger, I had painted him all black and left no room to see him as a real person.

But as I stepped back and looked closer, I could see that there were reasons for why he'd turned out the way he had. Acting out of his own pain was not an excuse for anything he'd done, but it did help me have empathy for him in a way I hadn't been able to before. And with the empathy came a willingness to forgive. How he had treated me would never be ok, but I didn't want to live in a place of judging him any longer.

I wasn't sure if I'd end up sending it, but I had started writing him a letter. Not to make him feel bad, but to invite him to have relationship with me again. Whatever that might look like.

I went for a run with Michael the next day and told him all about it. He let me talk his ear off until, at around five miles, I had no more words left. Then he looked at me and said, 'So, remind me why you broke up with Julia again?'

I shook my head. 'I don't even know now.' I did know, though. In releasing forgiveness toward my Dad, I now found myself in the awkward position of understanding that I had broken up with Julia because I was afraid.

He smirked. 'Might be worth working that out.'
***

Every time I saw Julia I was reminded of how I'd lost her, and I struggled to remember why I'd been so stupid as to break

257

things off. After the break up, I had decided I wouldn't go with her to Kenya – it would be too awkward for both of us to spend so much time together so soon after breaking up. We needed time to adjust and work out how to be friends instead.

But after all the revelations I'd had in the days after Christmas, I went to the board meeting and saw her again.

She was every bit as beautiful as I remembered.

And it was every bit as awkward as usual.

I did my best not to speak to her, so as not to say something stupid, even as I felt drawn to her like a moth to a flame. Instead, I did what I usually did and tried to have a laugh with everybody. Still, it felt stilted and I found myself staring at her when she wasn't looking.

Her hair was wild as it cascaded down her shoulders, and she looked… well. She was radiant – full of life and light. She'd always been wild and vibrant, but that day she looked even more so.

On the spur of the moment, I decided the awkwardness would have to go. We needed an intervention, and Kenya would be as good a time as any to sort us out. So I asked if we were all set for the trip.

It was clear she hadn't been expecting that, but she didn't seem upset about it, so I breathed a sigh of relief and prayed it would be ok.

By the time New Years Day, or Hogmanay as they call it in Scotland, and the Loony Dook came around, I had decided I'd been an idiot to break up with her. I wasn't going to let fear control my life any more. Instead, somehow, I would get her back.

So I dunked her in the sea.

Sure, it might not have been romantic, but it did say everything I wanted to say. And, after the previous seven years of fighting each other in order to cover our feelings, I was pretty sure she knew what her dunking meant. Then again, if her somewhat frustrated reaction was anything to go by, it might not have been the right move.

Still, I packed my bags with a grin on my face as I prepared to deal with the wild-haired, angry bee that was Julia.

***

I had gotten to the airport in plenty of time, excited about the trip and about seeing Julia again. After looking for her and not finding her, I got into the check-in line and pulled my phone out to text her. I got no reply, so kept my place in the line, unsure of what to do.

It wasn't until I got to the front of the line that I started second guessing myself for real. Up until then, I had been fairly sure she would show up. But then, there I stood and it would be my turn next. *Had I entirely miscalculated this?*

I knew she wasn't over the moon about me coming with her to Kenya, especially after I'd dunked her in the sea. Still, I hadn't expected her to pull out of the trip altogether.

I stepped aside and let the couple behind me go ahead of me. Still no Julia.

Biting the inside of my cheek, I debated what to do, but in the end I decided I would keep waiting.

There were only five more people in the line still behind me when I finally saw her.

Suitcases trailing awkwardly behind her, she walked as fast as she could. Her hair was wet and clung to her face, messily flowing down her shoulders as she tried to work out where she was going. Her eyes found mine and time slowed down.

Her breath hitched, and I watched as the relief in her eyes gave way to annoyance.

Wild-haired, angry bee was right.

And that gave me a little bit of hope. At least she wasn't indifferent to me.

'Shut up,' she said and handed me two of her bags. 'Here, hold these.'

I took the bags as she dug out her passport and ticket. 'Ready?'

'I was born ready.' She rolled her eyes as we shuffled our things up to the check-in desk. We put our bags on the conveyor belt to be tagged. My one backpack had several kilos to spare, whereas Julia's three bags all weighed just under the upper limit. She huffed at me, but at least we didn't have to repack her bags.

The check-in clerk asked us all the questions and then went on to allocate our seats. Julia did her best to smooth her now-drying-and-getting-wilder-by-the-minute hair, and smiled hopefully at the clerk. 'Don't worry about seating us together. We'll be quite happy sitting wherever.'

'No, that's ok. Here.' The lady gave us her warmest smile and handed me our boarding cards. 'Have a great trip!'

Julia sighed as she looked at our seat numbers. We were seated next to each other on all three of our flights. 'Great, thanks.'

I shook my head and thanked the lady with a smile. Didn't hurt to be friendly.

We went through security and got to our gate just as they started boarding.

'Do you want the window or the middle seat?' I asked, again trying to be friendly, as we walked down the aisle to our seats.

'Window.'

'Go on then.'

Julia got herself settled into her seat and watched as I folded myself into the middle seat. My legs touched the seat in front of me and my shoulders just fit under the headrest. I'd just gotten comfortable when a generously proportioned woman in her fifties sat down next to me. I sighed when I thought about how I'd now be stuck in the middle seat for the next seven hours until we landed in Doha, Qatar. Maybe I needed to dial back the friendliness some.

I watched as Julia pulled her hair to the top of her head and twisted it into a knot.

'I've got a spare, if you're out.' I pulled a hair tie off my wrist and held it out to her.

She huffed, but accepted it and tied her hair back. 'Thanks.'

The security notices started and I listened as I watched Julia ignore them in favour of getting a travel blanket out. She pulled up her legs and leaned against the wall, snuggling into the blanket as our plane took off.

'You warmed up yet?' I figured her accepting the hair tie was a sign it was safe to talk.

She raised her eyebrow at me as if to say she was unimpressed. 'Are you going to talk the whole way to Doha, or can I leave my headphones in my carry-on?'

I rolled my eyes. 'Look, Julia, I don't want to fight with you. I'm sorry about the Loony Dook, ok?'

She sighed. 'Are you?'

'Kind of.' I winced at her glare. 'You've got to admit it was pretty funny, though.'

She rolled her eyes. 'Yeah, fine. Now, I haven't slept all night, so if you want to stop fighting, I suggest leaving me be for a few hours to let me sleep.'

I gave her my most understanding smile and watched as she promptly fell asleep.

By the time she woke up, I had watched a made-for-TV movie that threatened to kill whatever brain cells I still had, and they were serving dinner. Seeing the signs of travel sickness on her face, I unscrewed the cap off my water bottle before handing it to her. 'Here, you should drink something.'

She took the bottle and sipped it slowly.

'And you should eat something, too. It'll help you not be sick. We wouldn't want a repeat of our trip to Arrochar.'

'So bossy,' she muttered and closed her eyes as we waited to be served.

I put our trays down, and soon there was a nice meal of honey-glazed chicken over rice with steamed vegetables in front of me. As far as airplane food went, it looked great. 'Eat and you'll feel better.'

Julia sighed, but picked up her fork and started on the rice. It seemed to stay down, and then we both had a glass of red wine to finish it off. The wine seemed to go straight to Julia's head, which might be why she ended up agreeing to play two lies and a truth with me.

'I'll go first.' I bit the inside of my cheek as I studied her face before saying, 'Why are you mad at me?'

'I…'

'And remember,' I cut in and held up a finger. 'One of your answers must be the truth.'

'Fine. Let me think.' She huffed and looked away. 'Ok, first answer.' She put a hand to her chest and raised her eyebrows to give the air of faked innocence. 'I'm not mad at you at all!'

'Right.' I snorted and studied her face closely. She thought I thought she was lying. She was clearly telling the truth though. 'Keep going.'

'Second answer. I'm mad because you threw me in the sea mid-winter the other day.' There was no way she was still mad at me for that. We'd both done much worse to each other back in the day. Whenever we were anywhere near water we had always tried to accidentally get the other wet. As juvenile as that was, it was part of what we did.

I bit my cheek. 'Keep going.'

'Third answer.' She shrugged and tried to look blasé. 'I'm mad at you because that's what we do, isn't it? I wind you up, you wind me up and we hate each other.'

'You make it too easy.' I smirked.

Julia sat up straighter. 'How is that easy?!'

I shrugged. 'Your first answer is the truth and the other ones are lies.'

She raised her eyebrow in question. 'Oh?'

'Yeah, your second answer might have been true if I'd asked you on New Year's Day.' He laughed at the memory. 'You looked mighty pissed then. But once you warmed up, you realised you were just surprised, and maybe a little annoyed with yourself for not seeing that you had it coming.'

'Wow, you think you know me so well.' She rolled her eyes.

She was right. I did know her well.

'And your third answer might have been true before, but even then I'm not sure it was ever the truth, you know. I don't think we ever hated each other, you know?' I smiled at her and watched the confusion take over her face. 'It was all just a game to get the other person to notice us.'

She blushed and took a sip of water. Trying to pretend everything was fine, she gave a strangled laugh. 'Uh-huh, keep going.'

I leaned in to study her face and felt my smile slip as a pang of awareness shot down my spine. Leaning closer, my eyes drifted across her face, down to her lips. Her face was tilted up toward me and her breath hitched as I almost gave in to the urge to lower my lips the two inches to kiss her then. Instead, I met her eyes again. Her eyes were open, and I saw vulnerability there instead of frustration. I knew she would have let me kiss her.

She would have enjoyed it.

But we had too much to talk about before we might be able to get there again.

I pulled back and sighed. 'So the truth is your first answer. But I know that, not because of my amazing deductive reasoning skills, but because I know you.'

She tensed and narrowed her eyes, her anger flaring up as she raised her finger at me. 'That was always our problem. You think you know everything about me, and who knows, you might. But I know virtually *nothing* about you.'

She was right. Back when we had been dating, I didn't want to tell her too much about me because I was sure she would realise how unsuited I was for her. But now, I no longer wanted to hide anything from her. I wanted her to know me. The real me. I nodded and pursed my lips. 'So go ahead, it's your turn.'

She huffed but sat back and studied me. I had nothing to hide. She lifted her chin in challenge. 'Ok. Tell me why you can't stand your dad.'

That was my Jewel. Going straight for my weak spot.

I smiled at her as I thought of where to begin.

Chapter 38

Julia

I watched as Nick leaned back in his seat, biting the inside of his cheek as he closed his eyes. When he didn't say anything, I tensed up. I worried I might have overstepped a boundary and wondered how I could get out of this awkward conversation without ruining our whole trip. I also felt a weight in my stomach, which I think might have been sadness. Why didn't he want to let me know him?

'Ok, here we go.' Nick interrupted my jumbled thoughts and I felt myself relax a bit. 'Answer number one: My Mom and Dad met at a bar in Chicago. Mom was from Edinburgh and was in the US for a month in the summer after finishing university. I guess they fell in love pretty quick, and they arranged for Mom to come back to Chicago to live out there. Dad's about ten years older than Mom, and was already working in banking and making a lot of money, so they got married after just a few months. She was working at the bank as well until she found out she was pregnant. She was thrilled; they both were. But then, just over halfway through the pregnancy, they found out there was something wrong, and a few days later she miscarried. The doctors told her not to try again as she would be unlikely to be able to carry a pregnancy to term and it would put her own life in danger. She was devastated. Dad told her he didn't want her to risk her life, but if she was set on having kids, they could adopt, and eventually she agreed. So they adopted me. I'm told my biological mother was fifteen when she had me. She didn't want to have an abortion, but didn't want to keep the baby either, so she gave me up for adoption.' Nick took a sip of his beer.

I waited, convinced his answer number one was a lie. This was a good story, but surely I would have known a long time ago if Nick was adopted, right? *Right?*

'Mom was happy and that made Dad happy, and we were all a happy family for a while. Until I was about three. That's when Mom found out she was pregnant again.' He rubbed the scruff on his face and looked at me. 'She knew Dad would've had her get rid of the baby, so she kept it a secret for as long as she could. She went for a scan and everything was fine, so she decided to tell Dad. He went ballistic, but somehow she convinced him to calm down. He hired a nanny to take care of me so Mom could rest. And, by some miracle, Mom carried the pregnancy to term. But then, there were big complications in labour and somehow both the baby and my Mom died. Dad took it pretty hard, as you would perhaps expect. He didn't like being at home and seeing reminders of her everywhere, so he engrossed himself in work and in women. I still had Nanny Mary, so I was taken care of, and for the next few years I rarely saw him. He switched off from me entirely, and whenever he saw me he would turn away. I spent those years knowing that my Dad hated me. I never went hungry and I always had what I needed, and I am grateful to him for that. But he was my Dad, and he wanted nothing to do with me at all. If it wasn't for Nanny Mary, I'm not sure what would have happened to me. So, answer number one is that I hate my Dad because when I needed him, he wasn't there for me.' He smiled and raised his eyebrow as if to say *what do you think?*

In all honesty I wasn't sure exactly what to think. My heart ached for the adopted little boy whose mummy had died and whose daddy had abandoned him, but I was still pretty sure he wasn't adopted. So answer number one had to be a lie. 'Right, keep going,' I urged him on.

His smile transformed into a grin that told me he knew I was hooked, and I fought a blush as I slapped at his arm. He chuckled, rubbing his arm pointedly. 'Answer number two: When I was maybe eight, I started feeling like I wanted to know my Dad. I wanted him to be proud of me and for him to know me. I understood that we would never be one of those happy families again, but at least we didn't have to be strangers. So I tried to get his attention in all kinds of ways. I tried being good and successful at school and sports, and, when that didn't work, I started getting into trouble at school. I guess I figured any attention would be better than none at all, right? That didn't work either. So I started pranking him at home. I did some pretty light things, like short sheeting his bed and that kind of thing. But then one night he came home and I guess it was all just too much. I was in bed already, and he came in and woke me up. He shouted at me. I'd never seen anyone so mad before. I was terrified, so I wet the bed. And that's when things got really scary. He dragged me out of the bed, shaking me and yelling at me about how he hated me and about how I was such a dumb little shit. I cried, and then he hit me.' Nick glanced at me. 'I'll spare you the details, but it wasn't pretty. He left my face alone, and he made it clear I was to tell nobody about it, or he'd put me back up for adoption. At that point, I almost hoped he would. But then, I had Nanny Mary and it would have been awful to have to leave her. So I decided I would stop the pranks and try to keep to myself instead. But it was like I'd unleashed a river. For the next few years it didn't seem to matter what I did, whenever Dad wanted someone to punch, I was it. So answer number two is that I hate my Dad because I spent years of my childhood as his punching bag.'

Nick's eyes had clouded with sadness as he had been speaking and now he tilted his head at me in question. I got a sense that, although it seemed he was asking if I thought he was telling the truth or a lie, he was wondering whether I was judging him. It confused me to think he worried I would judge him for telling me he was hit by his Dad as a child.

I didn't know what to think. This story just kept getting worse. Was he making all this up to see how long he could string me along? Or was this really where he came from? A rock of dread had started to form in my stomach and I hesitated before saying, 'Ok, keep going.'

Nick looked at me, as if searching my face for something before he continued in a low voice. 'Answer number three: By the time I was in high school, most of the abuse had stopped. He would still do things to hurt me, but not physically anymore. He sacked Nanny Mary, so from then on I took care of myself, but she kept checking in on me, and I decided to stick high school out and wait until I was eighteen when I could access the money in my trust fund. He wouldn't leave me any money for groceries, so I got a paper round to pay for food. If he saw I had money he would make me pay him for things. He said I was paying him back for taking care of me for so long.'

'How old were you?' I interrupted, horrified at his Dad's behaviour.

Nick bit the inside of his cheek and tilted his head to the side in thought. 'Maybe fourteen?' He shrugged. 'I always liked maths and science, and did well at school. At this point, Dad had done really well for himself at the bank, and I started realising that not all his dealings were entirely above board. I think money became everything to him, and it didn't seem to matter who he had to hurt in order to make more of it.'

Nick stopped talking to listen to an announcement over the speaker system. We were going through turbulence and were asked to return to our seats and fasten our seat belts. Nick rolled his eyes, but fastened the cap on his water bottle so it wouldn't spill before he continued. 'When I was eighteen, I got access to the first bit of the trust fund my parents set up for me before my Mom died. They'd set it up with a big chunk of money when they adopted me, and then when Mom died, her life insurance money went into it as well. I felt bad spending the trust money on me, but I decided I would go to Scotland and see where Mom came from, and spend a few years here. I had the right to a British passport, so things were straight forward enough. I ended up at the university in Edinburgh and never felt the urge to go back, so I stayed.'

'Do you ever miss America?'

He frowned. 'Sure, there are things I miss, like food and the weather. I miss a few people as well, but on the whole I feel like Scotland is more home to me now than America is.' He shrugged and went on. 'Then, in early October, a friend of Nanny Mary called to say she'd had a stroke and was in hospital. I went out to see her and to see what I could do to help out. When I was there, I found out her husband had died of cancer a couple years earlier, and she was close to bankruptcy with the medical bills. And she had no children to take care of her. When her husband was going through treatment for the cancer, they asked my Dad for a loan, but he didn't feel inclined to help. Anyway, I sorted things out for her and she's now getting assistance at home. So, answer number three is that I hate my Dad because he consistently has used his money to hurt people.'

He stopped talking and turned to look at me. I struggled to get a read of his face. It was carefully blank. I didn't know what to think. Part of me still didn't think he was telling the truth. I felt like I would have known some of it, considering he'd been part of my group of friends for the best part of ten years. Still, it didn't sound as though he'd made any of his story up, and the thought of it all being true made me feel sick. If it *was* true, maybe he felt a measure of shame about his background, and maybe that's why he hadn't told me before.

I frowned and rubbed my forehead as I thought about it. My eyes narrowed as I kept studying his face. Had this confident, smart, kind man really had to go through all that?

'Are you going to guess?' His lip was hitched up on the side and he gave me an expectant look.

I answered with an absentminded nod. 'Uh-huh.'

If the story was true, Nick's Dad was a horrid, horrid person. Compassion rose within me for the child Nick had been. I could see his Dad struggling with life after his wife died, but what kind of a man takes it out on his child like that?

I tucked a bit of hair that had fallen out of the knot I'd tied it in to tame it earlier behind my ear, and cleared my throat. 'I can't pick one. I'm going to have to say you're cheating, and all the answers you've given are true.'

Nick reached for the hand I was using to gesture and held on to it. He threaded his fingers through mine and used his thumb to stroke the back of my hand. My hand tingled, and when he looked at me my breath hitched. His lip turned up on one side and my stomach clenched. 'You're wrong.' He paused for effect. 'None of the answers I gave is true.'

I blinked in surprise as relief flooded me. But I also felt betrayed that he'd spent the last half hour toying with my emotions when I thought he was finally willing to let me get to know him. I pulled at my hand, needing him to stop touching me. 'What? That's cheating! You made up this heart-wrenching story just to mess with me?'

269

'It's cheating when I do it, but not when you do it? Sounds like double standards to me.' He smirked and let go of my hand. 'None of the answers are true. Not in the way you think, at least. All of what I told you is true, but none of it is the reason I hate my Dad.' He sighed. 'Answer number four is that I don't actually hate my Dad.'

I studied his face. 'What?' If all of what he'd told me was true, I was pretty sure I hated his Dad. 'You have every right to hate him if that's how he treated you.'

His face was arranged in a neutral way, but his eyes filled with sadness. 'I know, and for many years I did hate him. I've had quite a bit of counselling since I moved to Scotland, and that's helped some. But then, a few of days ago, Jack, Michael and I went out for drinks. We ended up talking about our conversation at Christmas, about what the Cross is all about again, and they were like two dogs with a bone.' He swivelled his plastic beer cup and looked into it before taking a sip. 'I've been thinking a lot, and I've come to a place where I know I have to separate what my experience with my Dad has been like, from the other decisions and beliefs I have about God, and life, and the world. And in order to do that, I have to spend my time working out how to not come at things from a position of hating my Dad, but from a position of being able to consider lots of different ways of looking at things. Like for instance, Jack pointed out that my reasons for breaking up with you might not all be entirely thought through.'

If anyone had asked me what I thought Nick and I might talk about during our flight to Qatar, I would never in a million years have guessed this. I was stunned. 'No?' I croaked. I winced when it came out sounding like a frog. I quickly cleared my throat and this time it came out sounding much more normal 'No?'

Nick smirked. 'Well, I had a few reasons for breaking up with you,'

'None of which you communicated to me.' I wasn't bitter at all. Not. At. All.

He gave me a wry look. 'Yeah, sorry about that. I'm not sure you would have got it, though. And I had reasons, but, looking back, Jack was right, it wasn't very thought through. A big part of why I broke up with you was that I'd just been painfully reminded of what a crap relationship I have with my Dad. The last day I was home, I ran into Dad randomly at the bank. I hadn't seen him in years, and it was… odd, seeing him again. He told me he'd gotten remarried and they had a baby on the way, and it shook me up, thinking of that poor kid. I guess it reminded me of where I came from and why I don't have relationships.' He paused, as if to consider his next words carefully. Then he looked me in the eye and said in a gentle voice, 'You should have somebody in your life who loves you more than anything, someone who doesn't hold himself back to protect his own heart, but is willing to throw himself in with everything. And if you were to die, he should be strong enough to pick up the pieces of his heart and still be a good man.' He shrugged and put his hands up, showing me his palms. 'Look, I don't share genes with my Dad, but my relationship with him is the only father-son relationship I have experienced and, I'm ashamed to say, I'm not sure I would do any better than him if I was in the same position. That's why I can't hate him anymore. I mean, I *could* hate him, but then I'd have to hate myself too.'

I took a deep breath and let it out slowly as I thought about his words. 'I'm so confused right now.'

He chuckled. 'Yeah, welcome to my life.' Shaking his head, he continued, 'So there I was, in the pub with Jack and Michael, and I started realising that maybe I could experience a different type of father-son relationship. You know: if God isn't a child abuser like my Dad was, but if he really is kind and loving, and if I spend time getting to know him, then maybe I could have a different understanding to draw from. And that got me thinking that maybe it is still possible for me to be that person for you.'

I put a hand against my belly to stop the sudden burst of butterflies, not wanting to get my hopes up. My heart lurched. 'What do you mean?' I said hesitantly.

He took my hand in his, studying our joined hands. My hand tingled, despite my mentally telling myself to be calm. He looked up, his eyes gentle as he held my gaze. 'There were a few other reasons for why I broke up with you, and maybe we can talk about them later. But what I mean is that I would like to be friends with you for a bit, while I take some time to re-evaluate my life. I need some time to allow for a different way of thinking to marinate in my mind. I want to see if my life could be different if I operate from the perspective of God being good, and if I change the way I relate to him. I'd like to see if maybe that would allow me to become that guy for you. And I think I'm asking if you would be willing to wait for me?'

Stunned, I took a deep breath. And then I took another.

A horrible thought struck me and I tensed. My eyes narrowed as I studied Nick. 'Are you doing all this for me?'

He gave me a look as if to say he was unimpressed, even as his lips curving up into a charming smile. 'Not everything is about you, Jewel.'

I rolled my eyes and slapped at his arm. 'Are you sure about that?' I said cheekily.

'Yeah, you're special, and I hope you'll wait for me to figure things out, but I need to do this for me. I don't want to be stuck in this place for the rest of my life. I want to discover what life could be like if God and I were on speaking terms. You know?'

I nodded slowly and felt my shoulders relax. Also, I felt my heart flip over in my chest. 'Yeah, I know.'

'So can we be friends now?'

'Uh-huh.' I nodded and stuck my hand out to shake his. 'Friends.'

Nick shook my hand and grinned. 'Great. We should have another drink to celebrate before we talk about the other reasons why I broke up with you.'

Chapter 39

Julia

'Did you get any vaccinations before coming to Kenya?' I asked Nick.

We were sitting in the departures lounge in Doha, waiting for our connecting flight to Nairobi. We'd been through the tax free shop, picked up a newspaper and some cashews and tried on all the perfumes. Now we were sitting in the waiting area smelling... lovely, drinking coffee and doing our best to stay awake.

'Yeah,' he said through a yawn and rubbed his face. 'I got a couple, and they gave me malaria pills as well.'

'Have you had any side effects from them?'

After the long conversation about Nick's Dad on the airplane, Nick had gone to get some wine for me and a bottle of beer for him. We'd toasted our friendship and smiled over the rims of our glasses as we drank. I felt a sense of relief that Nick had been willing to share his story with me, and I knew I was one of very few people he'd ever told. I also felt hope, and whilst I knew we were just starting our friendship, all the butterflies I had tried to banish before had somehow escaped and were making themselves known in my stomach again. He only had to look at me, and I felt it to my toes.

Still, there were still loose ends that needed to be tied up and that made me feel unsettled and antsy. 'So did you want to talk about the other reasons why you broke up with me?' I'd asked.

He studied me and smirked. 'Yeah, but I'm not sure it's a good idea to talk about it here. Maybe we should just enjoy being friends for a while.'

I sighed, both with relief and a smidge of irritability. Relief, because I wasn't sure we'd be able to discuss the break up and keep our new friendship. Irritability, because loose ends.

His smirk widened into a grin and he patted my knee. 'There'll be plenty of time to hash it all out later.'

'Uh-huh, that's what I'm worried about,' I said under my breath. 'Fine, perhaps it's best if we build a stronger bridge before you attempt to drive a lorry across it.'

'In my professional opinion as an engineer, I think that's a great idea.'

So we didn't talk about the break up. Instead we watched a film together and ate airplane snacks.

The flight was soon over and we landed in Doha after midnight. I enjoyed the feeling of stepping off the aircraft and into the warm night air, even though I only got to enjoy it for a couple of minutes before being herded into the terminal building where we were now sitting talking about malaria pills.

Nick shook his head. 'Nah, no side effects.'

'Good for you.' I smiled as I pulled my hair tie out and started braiding my hair to get it out of my face. 'I get some vivid dreams the night after I take them, but otherwise I don't get any either.'

The chairs in the terminal building had armrests which made it impossible to sleep comfortably. We tried playing cards, but were too tired to concentrate. It felt like the night went on forever before we were finally able to board our morning flight to Nairobi. By the time we were in the air, I was asleep and, despite not having much space and being uncomfortable, Nick slept for most of the journey too.

When we landed in Nairobi we both felt discombobulated, sticky and sore. Also, despite knowing we still had a few more hours to travel to get to Mombasa, I was elated to be back in Kenya. After going through the passport control, we went to pick up our luggage. I was giddy and bouncing with excitement as I stood watch over the luggage trolley whilst Nick stood by the conveyor belt collecting the bags and bringing them to me. When we finally had them all he looked at me with a crooked smile, probably wondering what on earth he'd gotten himself into.

I found a mirror and caught a glimpse of a messy redhead with a crazy smile on her face. I laughed out loud and said, 'You could have told me my hair's a mess.'

Nick looked at me and shrugged. 'I like it like that. It's more you than when you've got it done all neat. It's wild and free.'

'That's just a nice way of saying I look crazy.' I rolled my eyes but gave up on trying to tame my hair, deeming it a lost cause.

'Ready?'

'I was born ready,' I said, this time without a hint of sarcasm in my voice. Nick laughed and started pushing the trolley toward the "nothing to declare" exit.

Excited to be in Kenya again, I'd forgotten to mention to Nick how the arrivals hall would be full of people shouting to get our attention. Offering anything from a taxi ride to safaris or hotel rooms, the noise was overwhelming.

Nick looked at me in question and I said, 'Yeah, this bit tends to be a little intense. We'll leave the trolley here, but we carry the luggage ourselves. I don't want anything to get lost.'

Nick looked for where we could leave the trolley, and already a man tried to take a bag from him. I smiled at the man and declined his offer of help as kindly as I could, and put on my back pack. 'Are you ok with those bags?' I asked as I put my carry-on across my chest to balance the weight out.

Nick gave me a look as if to say he was offended I would doubt his ability to handle the luggage. 'Of course.'

'Great. Let's go.' I steered him through the crowd, out of the arrivals hall, and through a dry field. On the other side of the street lay the building for domestic flights.

We were able to get seats on the next flight to Mombasa, and spent the next three hours waiting.

'Why is everyone dressed as though it's cold?' Nick asked. I looked around and noticed people were dressed in suits or long-sleeved dresses, as though they hadn't got the memo that it was *hot*.

I shrugged. 'I know. I'm sweating like a pig here. You get used to it, though.'

Flying across Kenya is an experience. The journey takes less than an hour, and, if you were quick, you might have time to go to the toilet between the seat belt sign going off after takeoff and it going on again for landing. Though you wouldn't want to miss any bit of the scenery out the window. I let Nick sit by the window, as he hadn't made the trip before, and we spent the trip looking out.

I used to think Africa was either jungle or desert, and had expected Kenya to be dry, with yellows and browns colouring the wide expanses of savannah, perhaps with the odd tree thrown in for a dash of colour. But Kenya is mostly green. Lots of different greens, and, you notice when you fly, there's a surprising amount of clouds. When we were about halfway there, I reached across Nick to point out Mount Kilimanjaro peeking up above the clouds in the distance.

'Can you see it?' I asked, and I looked at Nick, who nodded and looked back at me with a slow smile. 'It's the highest mountain in Africa.' My voice was awkward as I only then realised how close we were.

'Is that so?' he said and ran his hand along my face to tuck some hair behind my ear, paying no attention to the mountain. Everywhere he touched tingled as though electrified, and my breath hitched. He'd tried on a couple of perfumes at the airport in Doha, but underneath them, I could still smell him.

I sat up straight and cleared my throat, doing my best to remember that we were only friends even as I knew we were headed for more. We weren't there yet, though, and I wanted to honour Nick's request to allow him time to work things through in his head. It might also be good for me to have some time to continue to allow my realisation that I wasn't God, and that I was forgiven, to solidify in my heart before storming into this relationship. This time I wanted our relationship to have the best possible foundation when we eventually did decide to go for it.

Until then, friendship.

I snuck a glance at him and he gave me a crooked smile as if he felt the same things as I was. He gave a sharp nod. 'Friends.'

'Friendship is nice.' My smile was strained and I sounded unconvinced even to my own ears. I winced.

Nick chuckled and turned back to the window where Mount Kilimanjaro was still visible. 'Looks like a cool mountain, in any case.'

***

We landed in Mombasa in the early evening, and by then there were only a few taxi drivers around still hoping for customers. I was able to get some Kenyan Shillings out of the cash machine and spoke to one of the taxi drivers to agree on a price. We drove out to the coast and stood waiting in line for the Likoni ferry to take us out to Likoni for about an hour, since it seemed *everyone* in Mombasa was trying to catch the ferry out to Likoni. We had our windows down and the smells brought back all kinds of memories from my time in Kenya. I felt myself relax as I started to feel like I was coming home. As we waited, we watched the people around us. Some waved at us, others pointed and shouted at us, but it was all friendly. I liked that about Kenya: everyone seemed friendly.

'When I first came to Mombasa, I arrived on a Friday night,' I said. 'It was all very overwhelming, and I didn't know what to expect, so I felt quite nervous. The house keeper at the school, Lily showed me to my room and got me some dinner, which I picked at. I wasn't used to eating ugali with everything yet, and my stomach felt a bit unsettled after all the travelling.'

'Oh, I read about ugali. It's a maize porridge, right?'

'Yeah, that's right. It's a staple food, and it's fairly bland, so it goes with everything. If you don't serve it, people don't feel as though you've fed them.' I snickered as I thought about it. 'Term hadn't started yet and the school was quiet; the only people around were the other five live in teachers. They were in their mid-twenties to mid-thirties and had already eaten. When I arrived, they were playing a game of cards at a different table. They all looked at me, but none of them spoke or introduced themselves or invited me to join in. I thought that was because I had just arrived, but throughout the rest of the weekend, *nobody* spoke to me. I was sure everybody hated me, and I was still getting used to the food and having showers out of buckets. I missed home like crazy. I kept hearing them have fun together, but nobody ever engaged with me.' I frowned as I thought about it. I had been confused and a little devastated to realise I would spend the year being shunned by everyone. I remembered feeling like I had made the wrong decision to come to Kenya, and what was I doing committing for a whole year?

Nick raised an eyebrow at me. 'Are you going somewhere with that, or is that the end of that delightful story?'

I swatted his shoulder lightly and just about managed to keep a straight face. Just. 'Then a few weeks later, I found this book in the staff library. The school has teachers from the UK and Australia on exchange programs on a regular basis, so I guess someone had left the book behind when they'd gone home. It was great and explained how different cultures work differently. I had assumed the other teachers weren't interested in getting to know me, when *they* were assuming I didn't *want* to know them because I didn't go over to introduce myself and join in.' I gave an embarrassed laugh. 'I made so many cultural mistakes.'

Nick laughed. 'Isn't it funny how cultures can be so different? When I first came to Scotland…'

'You stood out like a sore thumb!'

Nick sighed and gave me a pointed look. 'And you wouldn't let me forget it.'

'I know. I wasn't very nice to you.' I grimaced to try to hide my smile. 'Sorry about that.'

Nick snorted. 'As if you're the slightest bit sorry.'

'You weren't exactly very nice yourself.' I watched as he chuckled. I had always liked his chuckle, even back in the day when he used to chuckle whenever he got a burn in. It was soft and delighted and made me feel like he was having a secret joke that I might or might not be in on. It would bother me to no end that not only did he have one up on me, but I would feel his chuckle as a ripple in my stomach and all the butterflies would come alive.

'Yeah. Sorry about that.' He smirked at me. 'Had you been to anywhere else in Africa before coming to Kenya?'

I felt a sudden need to reach out to stroke a strand of his hair that was misbehaving. Stopping myself just in time, I tucked my hands under my legs instead. 'No. I went to see Jack in Hong Kong once, but other than that I hadn't done much travelling.'

'I've never been to Africa before but, from what I've seen of Kenya so far, it's amazing.'

'I know. After I understood the culture a bit better, I soon fell into a routine and fell in love with Kenya. Jeremy, one of the other teachers gave me a quick tour of the area where he pointed out the doctor's practice, the grocery store and the best place to

buy Coke; all the most important places, you know.' I smiled.
'And I started going to the market to buy green oranges, eggs,
carrots, peanuts and other random things that tasted better than
any of the kinds I'd had back in Edinburgh. I got to know the
Coke vendor on the corner of the street, and I found I wasn't as
scared of the two rats that seemed to live under the wardrobe in
my bedroom as I would have expected.'

'Huh, how about that.'

'Yeah… I didn't make friends with the rats or anything, but I
got used to it, you know?'

'Sure. I'm not that big a fan of rats myself.' He nodded and
looked through the windows at the people around us. 'I wonder
why everybody is walking so slowly. Nobody looks like they're in
a hurry.'

'Just wait a couple of days and you'll be moving at the same
speed. The heat and humidity takes it out of you.'

'What does *mzungo* mean?' Nick said, referring to the way
people kept shouting *mzungo* at us.

'It just means white person. It's not racist, so they're not trying
to insult us. They're just pointing out that we're white.'

Nick winked at me. 'Well, you're pretty pale in any case.'

I socked his arm but grinned at him. 'You're pretty pale
yourself. Hopefully we'll have a tan when we go back.'

When we finally arrived at the school, it was just after 6pm,
and the sun was getting ready to set. The few people that were
around had eaten already, and John, one of the school caretakers,
showed us to our rooms and sorted us out with some ugali, and a
bean stew, which we quickly ate before zipping ourselves into our
mosquito nets and going to bed, exhausted beyond belief.

The next morning, I woke with the sun— just after 6am— as
the town started coming alive again. I 'showered,' using water in a
bucket, and slathered on sunscreen before braiding my hair,
hoping to keep the heat and humidity from making it stick to my
face. Feeling much better, I put on a little mascara and decided I
would need to get some sun. Nick had been right when he said I
was pale. I dressed in a knee length black skirt which buttoned
from waist to hem, and tucked in a sleeveless loose pale pink

shirt. I slid my feet into a pair of flats and went in search of something to eat.

Nick was already having breakfast on the balcony outside our rooms when I got there. He was looking relaxed, wearing a nicely fitted shirt with a pair of sun glasses hanging from the top and a pair of shorts. His hair was damp and pulled back in a bun, and he gave a smile that made my heart speed up when he saw me. 'There's no coffee.'

I grimaced. 'Crap! I forgot I normally have to buy my own coffee here. Is there tea though?'

'Depends,' he said, and I frowned in question. 'There's a pot which has tea leaves, warm water, powdered milk and a bunch of dead ants in it over there.'

I laughed despite not having had caffeine yet, and poured myself some tea, doing my best to strain out the ants and tea leaves. 'We'll have to go to the store today and pick up some coffee.' I took a sip and hoped it would kick-start my brain.

I had a bowl of fruit with my tea and we ate in silence. Nick read the paper, and I watched the sea and listened to the crickets and the sounds of the city awakening. In the distance, to our left, we could see people lined up in wait for the ferry which shuttled people back and forward to the mainland. It was already starting to get hot.

'You sleep alright? Get a shower?' I asked.

Nick looked up from the paper he was reading. 'Yeah, not bad. I've never had a bucket shower before, so I'm not sure I'm much cleaner, but it was nice to wash up a bit.'

Doing my best not to think of him in a shower, I forced a laugh, which sounded more like a croak. 'Bucket showers take a while to get used to, but you still smell nice.' I paused as Nick smirked and I realised I'd made it sound as though I'd tried to smell him. I blushed and waved at his head. 'You seem to have gotten your hair washed, anyway.'

Nick grinned and I could see how he debated making me squirm, but decided against it. Instead, he folded the paper and put it aside, before looking at me again. 'What's on the agenda today?'

Chapter 40

Julia

The head teacher at the high school, Mrs Mwangi, was a strong lady who wore her head high and had a reputation of taking no prisoners. She was just a little on the heavy side, and tended to wear bold colours. At first glance, she was an intimidating figure, but once you got to know her, you would find a soft heart that seemed able to embrace people in a way I hadn't seen many be able to do.

'It's so good to see you again, Mrs Mwangi.' I wore big smile as I went to shake her hand.

She ignored my hand, and, in a rather uncharacteristic way, went in for a hug instead. Surprised, I took a moment to respond, but squeezed back just as she pulled away. 'It's lovely to see you, too. How have you been?' She searched my face and then said without apology, 'You look pale.'

I laughed. 'Yes, we don't get as much sun in Scotland. It's nice to be back in the sun and warmth.' I turned towards Nick. 'This is Nick. He's on our board of directors.'

Mrs Mwangi shook his hand. 'How do you do?'

'It's a pleasure to meet you, Mrs Mwangi, and thank you for letting me tag along with Julia.'

Mrs Mwangi smiled, and her eyes twinkled as she looked between Nick and me. 'Of course. Have you ever been to Kenya before?'

Nick shook his head.

'Then you must spend a few days, maybe at the end of your stay, exploring the country.'

'I was thinking we might stay a couple of days closer to Nairobi— maybe see some animals,' I said.

'Yes, I will give you the contact details for a friend that runs a guest house. She will be happy to host you.' Mrs Mwangi nodded in decision and then turned to me. 'Now, have you had a chance to see Grace and talk about the cups since you arrived?'

I hid a smile at how straight to the point she was. 'Not yet. I was hoping you might help me with a couple of things, Mrs Mwangi. I have brought five hundred booklets, so there should be enough for every girl in the school to get one.' I reached into my handbag and got some papers out. 'I've made them so they complement the workshops Grace and I have talked about. And just to give you an idea as to what the seminar involves, here's a booklet for you.'

Mrs Mwangi took the booklets and started to leaf through them.

'The workshop includes an overview of female reproductive health and menstrual hygiene. Then we'll talk a little about sex and STDs, and about the cup.' I waved my hands in the air as I talked. 'How to use it, how to clean it, that sort of thing.'

Mrs Mwangi nodded. 'How long will the workshop take?'

'Grace and I think we should allow about two hours. We could probably deliver the content in forty minutes, but it would be good for it to be as interactive as possible and to allow time for questions and to have some discussion.'

'Yes, that sounds good. I will speak to Grace, too, and then we will allocate time for you both to deliver the workshops for all the girls, and give out the cups. You will thank your business partners for the money toward buying all the cups when you go home.'

I smiled and nodded. 'We're just happy we get to be part of what you guys are doing here. Actually, I wanted to ask you what the best way to make cups available to more girls in Mombasa and Kenya in general might be. Are there some good charities or other schools you could suggest for us to partner with?'

Mrs Mwangi made a note and said, 'Leave it with me and I will make some enquiries.' She looked up. 'Now, I think it would be good for you and Grace to give the seminar to all the teachers this week, before the youth start back again on Thursday.'

'I'm sure we could do that.' I paused and bit the inside of my lip as I thought about how best to phrase my question. 'Are they... I mean, do they know what it's all about?'

'No, all they know is that you're here for a visit. But I will speak first and they will listen to you both, don't worry.'

'It's just, when I was last here and the topic came up with some of the teachers, they found it difficult to talk about. I think it's really important that this becomes a time of demystifying all this, rather than making it even more shameful for the girls, you know?'

'Yes, I know.' Mrs Mwangi smiled. 'But we have some data which you will find will help you with the other teachers.'

'Oh yeah?'

'Yes, it's a small sample group, but normally we have about a fifty percent dropout rate for girls, and over fifty percent of the girls would miss a couple or more days every month because of their periods…'

'Is it really that bad?' Nick cut in. 'I know Julia says so, but is it really?'

'Well, I think the data speaks for itself.' Mrs Mwangi looked at Nick. 'About a year ago, we gave one year of girls a cup each, and in that year only two girls dropped out this year. And attendance is up, now only about five percent out of the sixty girls in that year will regularly miss days because of their periods. We've also noticed their academic performance has improved significantly.'

Nick gave me a sideways smile. 'Wow. That's impressive!'

Mrs Mwangi gave him a somewhat patronising look. 'Yes.' She turned to me and continued, 'So I think we'll talk about that a little to begin with, and if anyone has a problem they will be welcome to come and see me.'

'That's great,' I said. 'Thank you.'

'And we'll take the opportunity to educate the boys as well. Separately from the girls, but still. Maybe at the same time?'

I glanced at Nick, feeling unsure of what she meant. 'Sounds like a good idea. What do you have in mind?'

'Mr Muema and Mr Okoth will do some workshops with the boys. I was thinking you would be willing to help with this, Nick, seeing as you're here? Mr Muema is our biology teacher, and Mr Okoth, our PE teacher. I'm sure they would be thankful for some help. What do you think?'

Nick cleared his throat. 'I'm not sure I have much to offer there, but…'

'Oh I'm sure you'll be fine. Mr Muema and Mr Okoth have a good plan, so I'll let them fill you in.' Mrs Mwangi waved away his concerns. 'Great. I will let them know.'

Nick nodded and then sat in silence as Mrs Mwangi and I spoke for some time about our website and social media and whether it was ok to take photos of the students (it was), what had happened at the school since I had left, and went over our schedule for the next ten days.

'Julia, it is great to have you with us again.' Mrs Mwangi stood up to usher us out of her office. 'Maybe take the rest of the day to prepare for the next few weeks, and indeed, to show Nick around. You can speak to the teachers in our conference tomorrow morning.' She turned to Nick. 'I hope you have a nice stay with us.'

He nodded politely and didn't say anything until we were back on the balcony in the staff accommodation building.

'She's…' He paused in search for the right words.

'I know. She can be a bit…' I couldn't find the right word either, so I gave a shrug and an awkward smile. 'But she's got a heart of gold and she works so hard to deliver the best education experience for the youth at this school. She's amazing.'

'Oh, I'm sure she's… great.' Nick gave a weak smile. 'So you'll give me a crash course in how to teach high school kids, right?'

I smiled. 'Yeah, let's talk about it later. Let's take a walk into town to buy coffee. Bring some money in a concealed sort of way.' Nick scrunched his forehead in question and I continued, 'You don't want to be a target for pick pockets.'

'Ah…' Nick nodded.

***

A trip into town was an adventure every time. In the year I lived in Likoni, I never got used to it, and I was excited to get to show it all to Nick. It was just over a mile to go from the school compound to the ferry, and most of the time I would walk there. To walk a mile might take me twenty minutes in Scotland, but in Kenya it could easily take an hour. It's so hot, you make sure your arms are held away from your body so as not to get stuck in the sweat you're producing at a rate that shouldn't be legal. You set off thinking you want to make sure you get the pace right, preserving your energy for what you know is coming, but also getting enough airflow under your arms so as to cool off a little. Cooling off from the airflow is a nice thought, but it doesn't work, and you soon slow your pace down to that of a snail.

As we walked, Nick took photos. 'Isn't it interesting how there are these amazing mansions with massive walls with broken glass and barbed wire at the top, and next door there's a tin shack where the door is really a curtain?' He shook his head. 'Blows my mind.'

'Aye, the stark contrast between rich and poor feels quite overwhelming at times. It's so in-your-face.'

'No kidding.' Nick nodded and smirked at me. 'I bet your guilt was out of control living here.'

I looked away, an embarrassed smile on my face. 'Pretty much.'

He shook his head at me, and reached out to tug on my braid. 'I get it, you know.'

'You can't touch me when we're in public,' I said, taking a step away, in part to distract him, but also because I didn't want rumours going around about me at the school.

Nick raised his eyebrows in surprise. 'Why not?'

'It's not seen as proper here, and it could get me in trouble at the school.'

'Oh.'

'Yeah.' I sent him teasing smile. 'So keep your sweaty hands to yourself.'

He held his hands up and took a step away, a cheeky smile on his face. 'So, how much further?'

'Not that far.'

It took us another twenty minutes to get to the ferry, because we had to make a stop to buy drinks. Nick got a bottle of water to rehydrate, but I couldn't resist getting a coke as I still hadn't had any coffee and my head was starting to feel sore. The coke felt delightful, cooling me off a little as it slid down my throat.

At the ferry terminal, we waited in the scorching sun for what felt like an hour, but was probably only ten minutes. The longer we stood there, the less space we had, as hundreds of people packed in behind us, and started pushing. After the cars had driven on, the gates for the pedestrians were opened and we ran with everyone else, pushing to get as far onto the ferry as possible. When the ferry left the dock there were people in every space.

'Wow, that's… something.' Nick looked bewildered as he turned to look behind him. 'We're packed on here like sardines.'

I snickered. 'I don't think health and safety is a thing here.'

'No kidding.' Nick snorted and raised his chin to point toward the cars. 'Just look at that van with the roof box missing.'

'Which one do you mean?'

'The van that has about a carload of things on top of the roof – without a box for it.' Nick shook his head in disbelief and I laughed. 'It's just strapped on with some flimsy rope.'

'That's a *matatu*. We're taking one to get to the shop once we're on the other side of the sound.'

Nick bit his lip as he thought about it. 'Wait, is that like *Hakuna Matata*?'

I laughed at him. 'You like the Lion King?'

'What? Yes, I guess, as a child, the fatherless feelings in me connected with Simba.' He snorted and rolled his eyes. '*Hakuna Matata* is Kiswahili though, isn't it?'

'Yes, it is. *Hakuna* means *there's no* and *matata* means *worries*, like the song says. *Matata* and *matatu* are different though. We're going in a *matatu*, which is a minivan transport. It's like a bus.'

Nick nodded, and I hid a smile. *Matatus* were the craziest kinds of buses.

Chapter 41

Julia

Nick had worn a bemused smile for the whole matatu journey, apart from at a couple of points when we almost hit motorbikes and the driver hit the brakes hard. Traffic in Mombasa was different from in Scotland. In Mombasa, people honk their horns as a greeting, to make sure other vehicles are aware of them, or just to show frustration. Apart from the eleven passengers (two more than there were seats in the vehicle), there were also four hens. We then went through the supermarket to pick up things like coffee and, when our bellies started screaming at us, we had lunch at a little air conditioned coffee shop, which was where we were sitting now.

'Jewel, did you ever think any more about the trip we took to Arrochar?' Nick started after we'd been eating in silence for a while.

Our trip to Arrochar felt like an age ago. I picked at my salad and fries as I thought about what to say. Part of me still felt he had been out of line that day. The other, stronger part though, was thankful somebody had dared say something.

I took a sip of water and cleared my throat. 'Yes. Well I've thought a lot about what you said on the mountain.' I looked away and croaked out, 'And I've decided you were mostly… right.'

'Huh? What did you say?' Nick turned his ear to me and looked at me attentively.

I huffed and looked at him. 'You were right.'

'Can't wait to hear this,' Nick sing-songed under his breath as his lips curved up and his eyes twinkled. He looked like a rooster in a hen house.

'You're not going to get to hear anything unless you wipe that arrogant smirk off your face,' I sing-songed back.

Nick's smirk widened and his head fell back as he laughed. 'Sorry, it's just nice to hear, you know?'

I rolled my eyes but softened. 'It took me a while to admit, but I guess I was pretty arrogant to think my opinion of whether I was worthy of being forgiven was more important than God's.'

Nick bit the inside of his cheek and leaned back as he listened. 'What changed your mind?'

I took a deep breath as I thought about it. 'I was tired of living under the guilt and unworthiness,' I said, slowly. 'Now I think back to what it was like, and I felt mousy all the time.'

'You're not a mouse though.' Nick shook his head slowly and I sensed he felt proud of me.

I bit my lip to hide my smile from taking over my face as I shook my head in agreement. 'I'm not a mouse.' The more I thought about it, the more preposterous an idea it seemed, and from deep in my belly, and quite unexpectedly, a laugh bubbled out. Less of a laugh and more of a giggle, it surprised me. I put a hand over my mouth as if to contain it and met Nick's crinkled and twinkly eyes across the table. His eyes held a gentle pride and relief as they recognised the absurdity of the lie I had lived under. He reached for my hand and pulled it away from my face, holding onto it on the table as I let my laughter free.

I giggled, not quite knowing why, for quite some time— Nick beaming at me across the table the whole time. Afterwards, I was thankful to have been sitting in a secluded coffee shop as such an outburst would have seemed strange to most people, but at the time I couldn't have cared less. As the giggles transformed into tears and then into a sense of anger or determination, Nick kept hold of my hand. He stroked his thumb across the back of my hand, but otherwise only his eyes changed, and joined with the pride and relief was empathy and kindness. It was as if he had longed for me to experience the sense of relief and freedom I was now feeling, and nothing could have made him happier.

When my weird outburst subsided he let go of my hand, and sat back. His eyes sharpened. 'So you decided I was right... then what?'

I took a couple of deep breaths, thinking things through before I spoke. 'I spoke to God about it and I explained how my way of doing things wasn't working. So I apologised for being... arrogant, and then decided to do things his way instead.'

'Uh-huh.' Nick nodded as if it all made sense. 'That all sounds great, but what does it mean?'

'I…'

'Jewel, you've spent your life around Christians and you know all the right words to say. I'm not interested in hearing them, though. I want to know how this is going to change your actual life.'

'Hard ass,' I said, putting on my best American accent.

He wouldn't let me off the hook that easily and raised an eyebrow. 'Well?'

'It means I'm trying to learn to say no to things so I can say yes to myself, not because I deserve things, but because God cares about me, so I will too.'

'What do you mean you don't deserve things?'

'I don't. Quite obviously I'm not deserving of much. What did I do to deserve to grow up in Scotland rather than in a tin shack in Kenya? Nothing. I don't get good things because I deserve them.' I paused to take a breath. 'Might sound harsh, but it's the truth. I don't *deserve* forgiveness, it's just *given* to me. And in living in that forgiveness, I get to enjoy life instead of feeling shameful and unworthy.'

'Sounds like a good deal.' Nick gave me a crooked smile.

I shrugged. 'Yes, I'd say so.'

'So what have you been enjoying lately, that you wouldn't have enjoyed before?'

'All kinds of things. I bought a perfume, I've made an effort to eat better— like now, I didn't order the cheapest thing on the menu, but I ordered something I wanted to eat— and whenever I feel guilty or full of shame, I try to focus on what I'm thankful for. I know it all seems like small things, but…'

'No, I think that's huge!'

I looked at him, seeing the depth of his sincerity on his face. 'Thank you.'

***

That evening, I left Nick to get acquainted with Mr Muema and Mr Okoth, or Jeremy and Joshua, who he was going to help with the workshops for the guys. They seemed to connect easily enough, and I went to spend the evening catching up with Grace.

It was wonderful to see her again. Over big cups of tea, I told her about Nick, she told me about the guy she'd started seeing, and filled me in on all the school gossip. We also spent some time looking over the booklet I'd brought, and we went over what we wanted to say to the teachers the following day.

When Mrs Mwangi had invited me to be part of the Women's Issues group, I had soon learnt there was still a lot of stigma around women's health issues in Kenya. When Grace and I had first suggested giving the high school girls period cups, there were embarrassed looks even in our group.

For me, who had grown up in Scotland, where fighting for equality with men on health issues meant campaigning for the tampon tax to be scrapped, periods were just part of life. In Scotland, periods impact our lives, but people are not afraid or ashamed to talk about it. At least for the most part.

In Kenya though, things were different.

Grace, who taught biology at the school, came from a good background. She'd done well at school and her family had paid for her to go to university. And still, she found it difficult to talk about periods.

Grace was amazing, though, and when I would have given up and decided people's shame was all too much, she wouldn't let me. The injustice she felt around the girls dropping out of school for something as simple as not being able to afford sanitary products fuelled her determination not to let the shame win. She got our Women's Issues group working, and soon enough, with Mrs Mwangi's backing, we started campaigns to convince the rest of the teachers. And the parents. And then the girls.

And in her defiance of the shame, we started to be able to get through to people, which is how we were able to give the girls of one class period cups the previous year. Still, we knew a lot of the teacher struggled with shame around speaking about periods, so we wanted to be well prepared for our workshop with them the next day.

We came up with a good plan and, though I was exhausted when I finally got to bed that night, I was looking forward to the next day even as I did feel a little nervous.

***

Nick was eating his breakfast on the balcony when I came out. My stomach was unsettled, probably due to nerves, and wouldn't allow me to eat anything, but I sighed when I saw Nick had made me a cup of coffee. 'I might keep you around if you're going to make me coffee in the mornings,' I said as I sat down.

Nick looked up and gave me a crooked smile. 'How did you sleep?'

'Not great. The coffee is helping, though.' I took another sip. 'I'll be fine after the meeting with the teachers.'

The side of Nick's mouth pulled up. 'When have you ever struggled with teaching? It'll be a walk in the park.'

I would have laughed if I wasn't still waking up. His confidence in me was refreshing and gave me a bigger buzz than the coffee did. 'Uh-huh. We'll see.'

'How was your evening? Did Jeremy and Joshua give you an idea as to how you can help?'

He nodded. 'Not sure how helpful I'll be, but I'm up for helping.' Seeming relaxed enough about the whole thing, he leaned back and let me drink my coffee in silence as we watched the sea.

When Nick and I got to the teachers' meeting room, they had already been meeting for an hour. Grace had saved us seats, so we sat down as Mrs Mwangi wrapped up what she was saying. Then she said, 'Now, for the next part of this morning, I need you all to leave the room, and when you come back in you need to leave any feelings of shame at the door. This will be a shame-free zone for the rest of the morning.'

People gave each other questioning looks, but started to leave the room. Teachers I hadn't caught up with yet came up to say hi and I introduced them to Nick. Most people assumed we were together, and after a few too many knowing looks when I emphasised that we were friends, I gave up correcting them. I focussed on keeping my cheeks from going red, and when I stole a glance at Nick, he seemed amused by it all. At least it served as a good distraction from being nervous about the seminar.

When everybody was seated again, Mrs Mwangi stood up. 'I'm sure you are wondering why I said you need to leave shame at the door for this seminar.' People nodded. 'It is because now we will spend the rest of the morning talking about something that I know there can be some shame around. We will talk about menstruation and how it impacts our young girls.' Now people started fidgeting and looking away. Some took out pens and started doodling distractedly, and, despite most of the people in the room being black, you could tell the majority of them were blushing. 'Some of you have seen Julia Reid is here visiting us. Last year, she was part of the Women's Issues group here at the school, and after leaving Kenya, she went home to set up a business in Scotland where they sell period cups like the ones we gave out to the year threes last year. They use the profits to help schools like ours be able to give high school girls free period cups to help them stay in school.'

When Mrs Mwangi went on to share the outcome of giving the year three girls period cups the previous year, people started to relax a little, and when she invited Grace and me to come up, the atmosphere was one of interest rather than embarrassment. In our seminar, we went over what we would be teaching the girls. We passed round a couple of cups so everyone got the chance to see one, and we spent time in discussion groups. By the end of it, everyone was engaged and talking freely, their initial embarrassment forgotten.

The issue of how to handle any difficult questions or protesting parents was discussed in a couple of the groups, and at one point Mrs Mwangi stood up and said she'd be sending out a letter to the parents, and to direct any questions or concerns to her.

'See?' Nick said as we left them to their meeting. 'Cake walk.'

I let out a relieved laugh. 'Now we just need to do the same with all the four years of high school girls at this school and years seven and eight at the primary school.'

Nick had been sitting at the back of the room to begin with, but as the teachers had started warming up, he'd taken some pictures. As the internet was being slow, we spent the afternoon sending them to Sophia to use on the website and in social media.

The first seminar Grace and I did was with a group of fourteen-year-olds in their first year of high school. We had put the chairs in a circle and made sure to greet each person as they sat down. They were girls with such potential, and they were all beautiful, despite the awkwardness that came with puberty. We had a similar outline to the seminar we'd done with the teachers, and took time to talk about how to prevent pregnancy, how STDs were spread, as well as explaining the basics of the menstrual cycle. As the girls warmed up to us and started sharing, Grace and I listened to the girls talk about their beliefs and experiences. After hearing story after story, each stranger than the previous one, I soon started to think nothing else could shock me. Then a new story would come out and top it. I had known girls were using newspapers, chicken feathers, soil or other such things to soak up the blood when on a period, but I was surprised to hear, for example, how some girls thought pregnancies could be prevented by drinking a coke before having sex.

'Today we would like to give each of you a gift. In fact, you may call it a bribe.' I laughed a little. The girls didn't laugh. They looked like they didn't know what to think. Grace rolled her eyes at me, and I knew she thought I was being overly dramatic. I took out the cups, which came in nice little cotton pouches, and started handing them out. 'You can go ahead and open them.'

I waited for everybody to open their pouches and take their cups out before I held one up. 'Has anyone seen one of these before?' Everyone shook their heads. 'Any guesses as to what it is?'

'It looks like a bell,' one of the girls said.

'Or a hat?' one girl quipped and put it on her head. I smiled as the girls laughed.

'Ok, fine, we'll tell you,' Grace said when they ran out of ideas. 'This is a period cup. It's something you use instead of pads when you have your period. I'll explain how it works in just a minute, but first I want to explain why I have given you one each.' The looks on the girls' faces ranged from confused, to embarrassed, to just blank.

'We know some of you girls tend to stay at home from school whenever you have your period. And I get it, I really do. If you haven't got pads and you're leaking, going to school doesn't work very well. But the problem is that when you miss school, you fall behind, and eventually girls fall behind so much they can't catch up, and that's when they decide to drop out instead. The thing is, though, if you want to get a good job, then you need to stay in school and get good grades.'

The girls were making a sport out of avoiding our eyes and shifted in their seats as though they were getting increasingly uncomfortable. 'So here's a solution to the problem.' Grace held up the cup. 'Your cup is reusable and will last you about ten years. I will give you a cup on this one condition: you need to agree to use it and to stay in school.'

None of the girls said anything. I guessed if the option was chicken feathers, mud or rolled up old clothes, then the cup was definitely a step up. We explained how the cup was used and how to take care of it. Then we spent some time in discussion groups and Grace and I answered questions.

When the workshop was over and the girls had left, I held out my hand to give Grace a high five. 'What do you think? Did we get through to them?'

She gave me a big smile and nodded. 'Only time will tell, but I think they heard us.'

Chapter 42

Julia

A few days later, Nick and I had peanuts and oranges on the balcony in the evening, comparing our experiences. It was dark save for the candle we had lit on the table, and all around us we heard the crickets, bats and the sea in the distance. I sat curled up in a wicker sofa with Nick next to me, his legs stretched out across the balcony. It was still warm, so I had put on a light jumper as there was a slight breeze coming off the sea, but had tied my hair up into a knot to let the breeze cool my neck. Nick wore a moss green t-shirt with a vague print across it, which showed off the veins in his arms.

Nick told me his talks with the boys had gone mostly well. 'We never had to use the games we had planned in case it all fell flat and nobody was interested.'

I snorted. 'Fancy that: the teenage boys were interested in talking about girls and sex.'

Nick rolled his eyes and smiled. 'Yes, I guess I should've remembered girls and sex are some of the only things teenage boys care about.'

'So, are you considering changing careers now?'

Nick laughed out loud at the thought. 'Nah, I think I'll leave teaching to you; you're great at it. I enjoy hanging out with teenagers, but teaching is too much pressure.'

We listened to the bats and I looked toward the sea, where you could still see the smooth waves roll in toward the shore. Nick was leaning back in his chair, eyes closed he appeared close to sleep. Looking at him, I wanted to reach out and touch his face. To lean in and sniff his neck and feel his strong arms close around me.

I sighed and distracted myself by turning to look at the sea instead. Shelling a couple of peanuts, I thought about the things Nick had told me on the airplane about his life. I had made a point not to bring it up again as I didn't want to rock the boat, but I still had questions.

Lots of questions.

I wondered if I would ruin everything by asking.

'I can hear you thinking, Jewel, what's going on?'

I gave an embarrassed laugh and said the first thing that came into my head. 'Were you really adopted?'

Nick turned his face to look at me and opened his eyes in surprise. 'You don't believe me?'

'No, I mean, *yes!*' I scrambled. 'Yes, I believe you. It's just you've never said anything about it and I would've thought…'

'What?'

'I guess it would be a big deal to be adopted?'

He shrugged. 'I guess it was. I don't know. It's not like I remember anything about that. I think the adoption thing was one of the few good things that happened in my childhood. At least until Mom died.'

He closed his eyes again, and, as he seemed relaxed enough, I kept going. 'Have you ever tried to find your birth mother?'

'Nah.' He shook his head. 'I always thought I was the problem. You know, if I had been better, then Dad wouldn't have acted the way he did. I was a curse to him. And I expected that would be the same to whoever I was around. I didn't want to be a burden to yet another person, and I figured her life would be hard enough without me, you know? Besides, she'd already given me away once.'

I looked at him, and everything in me wanted to cry. I couldn't imagine how awful things must have been for him. I cleared my throat but couldn't seem to get any words out.

'It wasn't until I came to Scotland and started hanging out with Jack and Michael that things changed.' Nick sat up straighter and shrugged. 'I didn't have to buy stuff for them to want to be my friends; they just *liked* to hang out with me. And then Jack took me home to your family, and your mom and dad always treated me like I was theirs.' He gave me a crooked smile that made my heart speed up. 'And then there was you.'

'I was *horrible* to you!' For the first time, I felt terrible at how I had treated him. All those years of me being mean to him must have been awful for him.

He bit the inside of his cheek as if to keep from laughing. 'Yes, do you want to apologise now?' His eyes held a challenge I couldn't decipher.

I rolled my lips between my teeth as I thought about it. I should have wanted to apologise but, as I thought of all the reasons for why I'd acted like I had, I couldn't bring myself to do it. Slowly, I shook my head. 'No.'

He smirked. 'You sure?'

'Yes, I'm sure,' I said, more determined now. 'It was my best option. I was never going to be able to be your friend. So I could be your friend's awkward little sister who had the most obvious crush on you and followed you around everywhere, or *maybe* I could have avoided being around you and been civil whenever I had to, *or* I could be around you and be mean but still have some dignity.'

His smirk was now a gentle chuckle. 'That's some great logic.'

I took a sip of water and avoided looking at him, turning instead toward the sea. 'I'm sorry if I hurt you though.'

'Yeah?'

I glanced at him. 'Yeah.'

'Don't worry about it.' He grinned cheekily. 'I knew what you were doing the whole time.'

I slapped at his shoulder as a blush rose on my cheeks. 'Sure you did.'

'It was the first time I had ever experienced someone being mean to me in an attempt to cover that they really cared. Up until then my dad was just mean. He didn't give a shit about me. But it was always clear that you cared.'

'It was?'

He nodded. 'Yeah. You'd say things like, *I don't exactly hate you but, if you were on fire and I had water, I'd drink it…*' he imitated a high pitched Scottish accent.

'Hey, you were pretty bad yourself with things like *I don't have the time nor crayons to explain this to you.*' I put on a deep voice and American accent. 'Or, *what do you want to do if you grow up?*'

He smirked but otherwise ignored me and continued, 'But you'd eye flirt with me like crazy, and you were always in my

301

space. And you'd do kind things for me when you didn't think I noticed.'

Still embarrassed, I rolled my eyes.

'I think it was healing to be around you. Your family loved me and they taught me I wasn't a burden. But when they might have smothered me, you taught me not all barbs were a sign of hate.' He sighed and shrugged. 'And I might have been crazy about you, too.'

'Then why didn't you *say* something?' My hands were waving in exasperation.

'There was Jack…'

'That's bull. He would've been fine with it and you know it.'

He gave an embarrassed chuckled. 'Yeah, I know. Jack was an excuse. The real reason was that I didn't think I could ever be in a relationship with anyone without poisoning them. I didn't want to turn into my dad, and I didn't want to turn you into my dad.'

'How would you have done that?'

'I would have poisoned you and become a burden to you just like I had to my dad. And I was terrified I would love you in the same way my dad loved my mom, and if you died and left me with a baby, I would be to the baby like my dad was to me. I couldn't cope with that as a possibility. I decided when I was maybe twelve that I was never going to have children, and I always knew you would want them. You'd make a great mother. But no child should have me as their father.'

I thought about it, watching the waves as the silence stretched between us. 'What changed to make you want a relationship with me after all?'

'I always wanted to be with you, and when you gave me your ultimatum…'

'It wasn't an ultimatum! It was self-preservation.' I pulled my hands through my hair in exasperation.

He shrugged. 'Whatever it was, it meant I could only be in your life if I was your boyfriend. And the alternative was inconceivable to me then.'

I took a deep breath and pulled my fingers through my hair, causing it to come loose of the knot. I let it fall out, gathering it to one side to tame it somewhat. 'Then we dated for a few weeks

302

and you went back to Chicago and came home and broke it all off. Why?'

'In America, I ran into my dad, and remembered who I was and all the reasons for why we wouldn't work in the long term, and I decided that pulling the band aid off sooner rather than later would hurt less.' He put his hands out as if to say he was laying all his cards on the table. 'Look, I'm not proud of it. I should have been more open with you from the start, but I had all these beliefs that I couldn't work around.'

'Uh-huh,' I said, motioning for him to keep going.

'I think differently now.' Biting the inside of his cheek, he leaned back in his chair and stared out at the sea. We sat in silence for a while, letting the sea soothe us, before he went on. 'Having this new understanding of God changes things for me. If God is kind and loving, then I can trust him to be there for me even if I was to lose you.' He glanced at me. 'I'm not going to turn into my dad.'

I looked at him as if to say of course you're not, you little shit.

He snorted. 'Well, give me a break. I'm still working things out in my head, but the more I think of God as loving and kind, it feels like it fits, you know?'

I nodded. I felt the same way.

'I know I want to be with you. And when we get together, I'm not going to be the one to back away again.' He pinned me with his eyes. I shivered as the anticipation ran through me. He looked away and said, almost to himself, 'And maybe one day, I think I *would* like to find my birth mother.'

I sighed. 'I think that might be a good idea. There's no rush, but she might want to know you, too.'

He nodded. We sat quietly for some time. The longer we sat there, the more I noticed the mosquitoes, and soon they became unbearable.

'I'm getting eaten alive here. I'm going to have to go inside.' I stood up. 'I appreciate you talking things through with me. I feel like I'm starting to know you.'

His expression was sincere as he stood up and reached out to touch my hand. 'I want you to know me.' Pulling me toward him, he leaned in and kissed my cheek. I walked into him and wrapped my arms around his neck as he wrapped his around my waist. I felt him take a deep breath as I snuggled into his chest, feeling oddly comforted, and we stood there just hugging until he kissed the top of my head. 'Thank you.'

I pulled away and nodded. 'Are you coming too?'

He shook his head and sat back down. 'I think I'll stay for a little while. I like watching the ocean.'

Chapter 43

Julia

The following morning, Nick wasn't on the balcony when I came out to have breakfast. I thought he might want a sleep-in, so had my coffee in peace, but as my mind woke up more, I realised something was wrong. It was too hot to enjoy a long lie, and Nick was always on the balcony before me. I came to the conclusion he either felt embarrassed about the things he'd told me the previous evening, or he was ill.

I made him a cup of coffee and went to knock on his door. When he didn't answer, I felt the handle and, as it wasn't locked, let myself in. 'Nick?'

'Yeah?' He groaned and tried to sit up in bed. Some strands of his hair stuck to his sweaty face and he ran his hands across it to get the hair out of the way. He was wearing a t-shirt, and his blanket was wrapped tightly around him like a cocoon. No wonder he was sweating. It was still early, but already it was in the mid twenties.

'Are you alright?'

'Yeah, fine.' He laid back down again. 'It's really cold though; aren't you cold?'

I frowned. 'No. Are you feeling unwell otherwise?'

'Head's sore, but I've got some pills I can take.' He sighed. 'I had some wacky dreams, so haven't slept much.'

'I got you some coffee anyway.' I put his cup down next to the bed.

'Thanks.' His eyes closed again.

'I've got to go get ready for my seminar. Will you be ok here?' His lethargy made me wonder if there was something seriously wrong with him. He'd seemed fine last night, but to see him like this was worrisome. 'Do you need me to get you anything?'

'Yeah, I'm ok.' He sounded exhausted.

'Maybe try to get some sleep. Do you have a water bottle handy? You need to drink enough water.'

He didn't open his eyes but pointed to the side of the bed where there were two unopened bottles.

'Great.' I didn't want to leave him, but had to go. 'I'll check on you at lunchtime.'

I left and went to speak to Jeremy and Joshua to let them know Nick was ill so they would have to do their workshops without him. They glanced at each other in concern and frowned at me when I told them about Nick's symptoms.

'Do you think he can stand up?' Jeremy asked.

'I thi-'

'I think you need to take him to the doctor,' said Joshua.

'You don't think he's just got a fever?'

'I think it's malaria, and in that case he needs treatment straight away.' Jeremy gave a sharp nod. 'I almost died from malaria once. It is a very serious disease.'

'He's been taking his anti-malarials, though.' I frowned. What was the point of taking preventative medicine if they didn't prevent you from getting the disease?

'He needs to see a doctor,' Joshua said, his voice firm.

'Ok, well I can take him at lunchtime.'

'You should take him now. I will see if I can get two pikipikis. He can't walk all that way.'

'But my seminar...' I said as Joshua left to sort out the pikipikis, or motorbike taxis.

'I'll speak to Grace,' Jeremy said kindly. 'She can either do your seminar herself or we can rearrange.'

I started to feel rather anxious then. I knew malaria was life threatening, but I had thought our anti-malarials would take care of it. And how was it possible that, when I had lived in Kenya for a year and hadn't got it, Nick picked it up after being there for ten days?

Still, I went back to see him and found him still on the bed in the heap I'd left him in. He lifted his head as I came in. 'Is it lunchtime already?'

I gave him a weak smile. 'No, honey. I spoke to Jeremy and Joshua about you missing the seminar today, and they say we need to get you to the doctor.'

I got him to put on a pair of shorts, a clean t-shirt and, at his insistence, a hoodie. I took one of his bottles of water and reached for his arm. 'Are you steady?' I asked as he swayed.

'Yeah.'

He didn't look steady, but I got him outside and up to the main road where Joshua was waiting with the pikipikis and drivers. Joshua helped me get Nick onto the back of one of the motorbikes, and I climbed onto the other as the drivers started them up. I felt the wind pull my hair out of the braid as we rode at what felt like breakneck speed, but didn't care that my hair was going to look like a lion's mane by the time I got to the clinic. I held on to the pikipiki for dear life, and was thankful for the breeze. Concerned for Nick, I kept looking behind me to see that he was ok. The air, or maybe it was the way his driver seemed to have no concern for safety, seemed to have woken him up a little, and he was clutching on to the bike. It was a bumpy ride with all the potholes in the road.

There were only a few people in the waiting room when we arrived at the clinic. We went to the desk to ask for an appointment, and found Jeremy had called ahead. We didn't have to wait long before a nurse called us. She was wearing blue scrubs and had a no nonsense attitude.

'And what can I do for you?' The nurse asked as we sat down. No smile.

'Nick here isn't feeling well.' I leant forward as Nick slumped back in his chair. 'He has a fever and a headache, and he's been having strange dreams, so our friend Jeremy thinks he might have malaria.'

The nurse gave us a bored look and went to get a blood test kit out of a drawer. I looked away as she took Nick's arm and drew his blood. 'It probably is malaria, but the doctor will need to look at the blood. I will give it to him, and you can meet with him in an hour.'

We sat in the waiting room for the next hour, Nick's head resting on my shoulder for most of the time. I kept trying to get him to drink, but he wasn't interested, waving the bottle away when I offered it to him.

Doctor Okongo was a short man with glasses, and he wore a lab coat over his shirt. He gestured for us to sit down, so we sat in the chairs in front of his desk as he took his glasses off.

'You have malaria.' He shrugged and waved with his left hand. 'Most people here have had it. But as you are not from here you don't have much resistance. I can give you either pills or you will have to get injections. The pill would be fine if you were living here, but the injections will have a stronger effect in killing the malaria.'

'Are you saying you think he should have the injections?' I asked.

Doctor Okongo nodded. 'Yes.'

'Ok.' Nick nodded. I think at this point he would have agreed to anything, just to be allowed to go back to his bed.

'The nurse will sort you out. Then, you will need to come back every day for an injection for a total of five days.'

'That's fine.'

'There were loads of mosquitos out last night. That's probably what got you.' I frowned at Nick, who was sweating and taking off his hoodie.

'No, no. It takes a week from the time you get the bite until you get symptoms. How long have you been here for?' Doctor Okongo asked.

'Ten days.'

'So he will have gotten it one of the first days he was here.'

I rolled my eyes at Nick as we returned to the waiting room. 'I can't take you anywhere without you picking up dangerous diseases...'

That got a weak laugh out of him and I persuaded him to drink some water.

When we finally got to see the nurse again it was almost lunchtime. We walked into the exam room and she looked at me. 'You can sit there.'

She pulled out the biggest needle I had ever seen and waved it at Nick. 'I will give you this injection on your left buttock. Tomorrow we will switch sides.'

'Ahh...' I watched as the blood left Nick's face. 'Maybe I should just get the pills the doctor talked about?'

'Don't be a chicken, Nicholas.' I grinned at him in challenge. There would have been no way I would ever have let anyone come close to my buttocks with a needle that size.

Nick rolled his eyes but went with the nurse to get the injection. A few minutes later we were outside with strict instructions to come back the next day.

'Can you walk back or should I get us some pikipikis?'

'I can't go on a pikipiki. My butt is sore. Did you see that needle?' He looked as if he couldn't quite believe it himself.

'I saw,' I said as a shiver ran through my body. 'My mum used to give us an ice cream after we'd had injections when I was little. Would you like an ice cream?' I smiled and reached for his arm giving him a patronising pat.

He glared at me. 'I have to go back and do it all over again tomorrow.'

I scrunched my nose at the thought. 'I know.'

Still, we stopped at a shop and I got ice creams for both of us and a couple of bottles of water. We had missed lunch at the school and had a long walk in front of us, considering Nick was walking at a snail's pace.

Over the next few days I would take Nick breakfast in bed and a bucket of water to wash with before going to do a seminar with a group of girls. The first few days Grace and I had given the seminar and cups out to groups of girls I hadn't taught before, but now I got to see the groups I had taught English to the previous year. It was great to see them all again and to hear how they were doing.

After lunch, Nick and I would walk to the clinic for his injection. He told me his butt was a big bruise, all black and blue, after the injections, even though they alternated which side they gave it to him on. He could take a pikipiki neither there nor back, so it made for a long and sweaty outing. When we got home he would spend the rest of the day lying in bed on the least sore side.

I would go and have dinner and catch up with the other teachers before spending the rest of the evening in his room telling him about my day. After four days, he was still very weak but much more alert. He still didn't want food, but I kept him well supplied with water, fruit and peanuts to snack on.

'How's it going, sicko?' I asked as I came in that evening.

He was sitting up awkwardly in his bed, the mosquito net closed around him, reading a book. 'Apart from a sore butt, I'm not bad.'

The sore butt gave the situation levity in my opinion. I knew malaria was no laughing matter, and a couple of days ago I had been quite worried about him, but a sore butt? Funny. 'Oh yeah?'

He gave me a bored look. 'Yeah.'

'I'm sorry it hurts.' I almost, almost was able to hide my amusement.

His eyebrow lifted as if to say *don't even bother*. 'Tell me about your day.'

'No, tell me about your sore butt,' I said, grinning.

The side of his mouth started to pull upward, but not enough to call it a smile. He tried to hide it with a yawn and stretched. 'I'm getting tired of being the butt of every joke around here.'

I laughed. 'I guess it's my way of coping with you having a life threatening disease.'

His eyes softened. 'I'm sick of being sick.'

'I know.' I reached out to stroke his arm. 'That's a sign you're feeling better.'

'Uh-huh.' He rolled his eyes at me and sighed. 'Tell me about your day.'

'As we did the last workshop yesterday, I had a meeting with Grace and Mrs. Mwangi this morning to talk about how our social enterprise can partner with other schools and organisations to help fund free cups for more teenage girls. Grace agreed to be our rep here in Mombasa, and Mrs Mwangi gave me a couple of charities that are already working with women's issues and that might be willing to partner with us.'

'That's awesome.' His eyes lit up. 'Have you contacted them already?'

'Aye, there were two charities that seemed more interesting, so I rang them and will meet with some of their people in the next couple of days. Mrs Mwangi knows them well and I've done some research on them, too. They seem like very good and transparent organisations. One of them is an international Christian Missions organisation that does assemblies at the school regularly, and the other is an international charity with a focus on women's health.'

Nick smiled. 'That's impressive!'

'We haven't met with them yet, but it sounds promising. We'll see.' I shrugged, but I felt hopeful.

Chapter 44

Julia

The next day, Grace, Mrs. Mwangi, and I met with the representative of the Christian Missions organisation. Their Mombasa team leader, Gloria— a Kenyan lady with braided hair— and her Australian co-worker, Maria, came to the school midmorning. The five of us met in the shade of a tree outside.

I asked them about the organisation they worked for, and was impressed with how none of them were paid by the organisation. Instead they lived off gifts, mostly from families and friends who believed in what they were doing and wanted to support them. They had lots of full time staff all over the world and offered internships with training and placements. They did everything from working with refugees, to working with Bible literacy projects, to after school clubs, to runway models during fashion week, and so on. In Mombasa they had a team that acted like chaplains to lots of different high schools, and regularly spoke at assemblies and took RE lessons.

'One of the downsides with our organisation, from your perspective, will be that we are so decentralised,' Gloria said. 'Our structure is based on relationship and not on hierarchy, which we think is great, but it means that even if we in Mombasa would love to partner with you in giving period cups to girls that need them, we can't guarantee that any other team in the world would.'

'Oh, that would be a shame.' I frowned.

'We do have relationship with lots of other teams that work in similar situations around the world, also in schools, but I'm thinking it might be a good solution for people in refugee type situations as well. And we would be happy to share about the period cups with them so they can partner as well. If they want to. But we don't have a hierarchical structure that could make a decision about this and then all teams fall in line. If you see the difference?'

'Do you think they would be interested? I mean, I can't guarantee how many projects we'll be able to fund every year, but it would be good to have projects lined up.'

Maria smiled and nodded. 'Yes, for the most part, I think most teams would be very interested.'

'After working with the high school here, we have decided it's important that girls or women get to participate in a workshop about women's health issues before they get their period cup.' I handed Gloria and Maria a booklet each and they leafed through them. 'Is that going to be a problem in view of you being a Christian organisation?

'I don't see a problem with this,' Gloria said, and Maria shook her head in agreement. 'Our organisation is interdenominational, so there may be teams that are less happy to talk about these things than we are, but generally I think this is all fine.'

'I must say that I was hesitant at first,' Mrs. Mwangi cut in. 'But these cups have transformed the way our girls attend school. It's amazing what a girl that is empowered with some education can do.' She went on to share her data.

'I'll be leaving in a couple of days, but Grace here is amazing, and we've been working together with this project here.' I smiled at Grace and she rolled her eyes. 'Grace will continue to be our rep at the school here, and is open to training you in how we run our workshops.'

Gloria nodded and we arranged a time for their team to go through a workshop with Grace.

That afternoon I told Nick all about my meeting with Gloria and Maria on the way back from the clinic after he'd had his last injection. He seemed much steadier. Still, we walked slowly to cope with the heat and his sore butt.

Pride shone in his eyes when he looked at me as I told him we'd decided to go ahead and partner. A giggle escaped as I thought about how relieved I felt and how excited I was.

'How will you know if they do what they say they'll do?

'We talked some about that,' I said. 'I asked them about how their team finances work and I told them we'd work out some paperwork to make the partnership clear as far as expectations go. And, from a quality control perspective, Gloria has agreed to be our liaison and keep us informed. So things should be straight forward, I think.'

'I guess there's always the possibility…'

'I know there's risk involved, but I think it's slim. We've checked them out and Mrs Mwangi knows them well. Besides, we've got to take risks otherwise we'd never do anything.'

'I suppose so.' Nick gave me a crooked smile. 'Speaking of taking risks, sometimes they pay off.' He glanced at me. 'And sometimes taking the risk results in getting malaria.'

I raised my eyebrow at him. 'Oh, but I wasn't that much of a risk, was I?'

He his smile grew into a grin. 'Considering the amount of times you've threatened to poison my coffee, I think there was a bit of a risk involved.' His eyes sparkled. 'Particularly after I dunked you in the sea at Hogmanay.'

I slapped at his arm as we turned off the main road and onto the path down toward the school's back entrance. The path had the school wall on one side, and was lined with trees on the other side, making it more of an alley. 'I guess there was that.'

'And you weren't exactly thrilled with me for quite a while before that.'

'Are you saying I should be proud of you for taking the risk and coming to Kenya with me?' I wasn't convinced.

'Nah.' He shook his head, serious now. 'I would go anywhere to be with you. It wasn't a risk. It was all I could do. I couldn't miss seeing you here, working your magic.' He stopped. He took my hand in his and I forgot all about being appropriate in public. His eyes were gentle as he gazed at me. 'You're it for me.'

I couldn't speak as my heart was in my throat. I swallowed and smiled. 'Yeah?'

'Yeah.' He stepped closer and brought a hand to the back of my head, where he played with my hair as I looked up at him. His other hand was still holding mine. He brought his head down close to mine and my eyes fluttered closed as he pressed his lips to mine.

It wasn't more than a peck, but it made my skin tingle in anticipation of the many more kisses I saw in our future. The school bell rang and I jumped as though I'd done something I shouldn't have. I gave a flustered laugh.

He kept hold of my hand as he stepped away. 'I'm still sick and we're sweaty and I'm not going to touch you in public anymore, but...' Nick tugged on my hand to get me to look at him again. 'I don't want to drag this out anymore. I've had a lot of time to think these last few days. I'm on a journey with God, and so are you. It'll probably be a long journey. But I know that I want to be with you, and I will trust him to take care of us. Whatever happens.'

I smiled. 'Whatever happens.'

That evening we sat on the balcony with our water bottles and peanuts. We only had a couple more days in Mombasa before beginning our journey home. We sat close together, his arm around me as we watched the sea.

Who am I kidding— we didn't watch the sea. The sea was beautiful, I'm sure, but so were Nick's eyes.

And his lips.

His lips were amazing too.

***

A couple of days later we started our long journey back to Scotland. To break the journey up a bit, we had decided to spend a couple of days at the guest house which Mrs. Mwangi had recommended, outside Athi River. In order to see more of the countryside, we opted to take a matatu for the eight hour long ride rather than fly.

The matatu started out only half full, which we were thankful for. Whilst we had left all the period cups in Mombasa, we had picked up a few things to take home, so we had some luggage. But we picked up a few people along the way, and soon we were sitting squashed together in the back of the van with our bags in our laps. We were thankful to be able to see out through the side window, and it was mostly a beautiful journey. We left the humid coast and travelled through the bush, climbing fifteen hundred meters in elevation, before arriving at a much drier Athi River.

Athi River is a town close to Nairobi, but the guest house where we were staying lay just outside of the city. It had a compound surrounding it with a high fence to keep out the wild animals. It was dusty and dry, and so the vegetation was different. The trees had big, flat crowns that made them look more like clouds on sticks than like trees, and the twigs held sharp, inch long spikes. The bushes were much rougher and they too were spiky.

We arrived late in the afternoon and were oriented to the compound by Mrs. Miroyo, the owner. She told us whilst lions were uncommon, we might see wildebeest, giraffes, antelopes and all kinds of other animals, particularly in the early mornings if we ventured out. No lion had been sighted for some time, so we felt safe enough going out for a walk in the early morning, hoping to see a giraffe.

Nick, who was feeling much better, woke me with a knock on my door just as the sun was about to rise. I checked my phone. It was 6.30am. The air here was cooler in the mornings, so it was easier to sleep in, but Nick knocked again. 'Are you decent?'

I sighed and dropped my head back onto the pillow. 'Kind of.'

The door opened and he entered, holding a mug of coffee out to me. It smelled amazing. 'Get up! The giraffes are waiting for us!'

I groaned and reached for the cup, my hair standing on end in a mess.

He pulled the cup away. 'You can have it once you're up. Mrs. Miroyo said we can take the cups with us.'

'You're mean.'

He grinned as he left the room. 'You know it.'

I dressed quickly and tied my hair up in a bun on top of my head. I washed my face and brushed my teeth with some drinking water before going out to Nick. He was leaning against the wall next to the door drinking his coffee as he watched as the day started to dawn. It was still fairly dark as we set off. Nick had his camera ready and took pictures of every tree we saw, so it took us a while to get to the compound gates, by which time the coffee had kicked in and I was starting to feel a little more awake. It was much lighter, and we were starting to see rays of sunshine over the treetops.

Once out of the compound, I convinced Nick to put the camera away so we could walk down the road holding hands. He grabbed my hand and pulled me in for a hug. I wrapped my arms around his neck as he looked down at me and gave me the softest smile. 'I love you,' he said and watched as my smile grew. Our eyes held, each of us beaming maniacally at the other.

'I love you too.'

Nick threw his head back and laughed. He sounded amused and free and maybe a little relieved. 'Yeah?'

I nodded and pulled his head toward me, quickly licking my lips and tilting my chin up. The kiss was gentle to begin with, soft enough that all the details registered: the hot, wonderful feel of his lips, the taste of the mix of our tooth pastes and coffee, the way his beard rubbed against my cheek and upper lip, the strand of his hair that fell against my cheek and so on.

But then he nipped at my lip. I moaned and the kiss grew hungry. My eyes slid down over his chest as he covered my lips with his, and his hands slid up my back to cradle my head. He devoured my mouth, and I shivered, entirely wrapped up in him.

Pulling back, he grinned down at me again, before placing gentle kisses across my cheeks until he found my neck and started nuzzling it. His beard tickled and I let out a laugh. 'We should look for the giraffes.'

He stilled, his head still in my neck, and took a deep breath before nodding. He stood up and smiled. Tangling his fingers with mine, he started forward only to stop abruptly. In a low voice, but not without excitement, he said, 'There are five wildebeest up there!'

I looked and saw them grazing maybe fifty meters away. They didn't seem to have seen us. Nick and I stood still so as not to frighten them as we watched. After a minute or two, one of them raised his head as an antelope approached. Deciding the antelope was too high energy to be around, the wildebeests trotted off. The antelope jumped all over the place and had a little calf with her. The calf was just as excited, but a little more cautious as it followed its mother. They didn't see us until they were maybe twenty meters away, at which point they took a sharp turn to the right, almost hitting a tree full of yellow birds as they fled. The birds flew out of the tree, as though to check to see if everything was ok before resettling into the tree. It was magical.

Nick pulled me close and gave me a crooked smile as the birds settled and their chattering died back down. 'Marry me.'

I gasped, both ecstatic and confused. It was only a few weeks since we'd agreed we would try to be friends, and now here he was proposing to me. Everything in me wanted to say yes, but I didn't want us to rush into something too hastily either. 'Are you sure that's what you want?'

He gave a slow nod. 'I know you could think this is too fast, but I've known for years that the only person I ever would want to marry is you. Even back when I was planning on never marrying anyone, I wanted only you to be my wife.'

I nodded and smiled. 'Yes.'

'Yes?' He raised an eyebrow. 'Yes, what?'

I cleared my throat. 'Yes… please?' I said, not knowing what he was asking.

He laughed. 'You're saying yes?'

'Yes!' I shook my head at him as I rolled my eyes, my grin wide across my face. 'Honestly, we're going to have to work on our communication skills, though.'

'I don't have a proper ring for you here.' He grinned back at me. 'But I've got one in Scotland. I bought it months ago. I wasn't planning on proposing to you then, but when I saw it, I thought of you, and then I didn't want anyone else to have. So I bought it.' He shrugged, 'Now it seems I have a use for it. What do you think?'

I shrugged, acting nonchalantly even as my face couldn't contain the happiness that filled me. 'I suppose that's ok.'

'I do have this wine gum ring though.' He pulled a sweet bag out of the pocket in his shorts and got the last sweet out. A yellow wine gum ring.

'Aw, you're giving me your last sweet.'

Going down on one knee, he held my hand and put the ring on my finger. It was just a little too small, but he got it on before kissing the back of my hand. My eyes teared up as I held my hand up to look at it. 'Come up here and kiss me,' I said, a little embarrassed at all the feelings of overwhelmed happiness.

We didn't see any giraffes that morning. And we spent the rest of the day taking it easy and visiting a local market. At that point,

I took the ring off. 'I don't want the ring to be stolen when we're out,' I said with a twinkle in my eye.

Nick laughed. 'Are you going to eat it?'

'I don't know. Maybe I should keep it forever?' I bit my lip as I thought about it. 'Maybe if I paint it with nail polish it'll go hard so I can keep it?'

Nick shook his head at me, rolling his eyes. 'Eat it. I'll buy you another, and another. You don't ever have to worry about running out of rings.'

The following morning, as we left the guest house compound I felt a sense of sadness at leaving. I knew I'd be back at some point, even though I knew Grace would do a great job of being our liaison in East Africa. But until then, I would miss the sunshine, the people, the culture, and the beauty of Kenya. Nick squeezed my hand and gave me a smile that said he understood. Kenya had found her way into his heart too.

The taxi driver asked if we had seen any giraffes during our time in Athi River and I shook my head and glanced at Nick. 'No, but we've see antelopes and wildebeest and animals like that, so it's ok.'

Then, only a few minutes later, the driver turned the wheel sharply to avoid an antelope that had jumped out of a bush into the road. As he narrowly avoided hitting the antelope, I followed it with my eyes as it leapt out of the road and into the bushes on the right. Just a few meters further in on our right stood three giraffes.

They were glorious. Long necks and awkwardly graceful, they stood by the side of the road eating leaves from the tops of the prickly trees.

'Wait, can we stop the car?' I asked, and the driver slowed down to a stop. 'Look at the giraffes!'

Nick looked to where I was pointing and we both turned into the worst kind of tourists, snapping about three hundred pictures on our phones. The driver rolled his eyes at us and kept saying that we needed to get going if we didn't want to miss our flight. We ignored him and Nick caught my hand and pulled me in for a selfie with the giraffes in the background.

'This can be our engagement photo.' He shot me a sideways smile and I looked at him with stars in my eyes.

Who cared if we missed our flight? I was going to get to spend the rest of my life with this man.

THE END

Sign up to Emma Browne's newsletter so you don't miss out on all the news and sneak peeks for Miranda and Jack's book! www.eepurl.com/dmvk0H

Author Notes & Acknowledgements

Thank you for reading Julia and Nick's story. I am beyond honoured and rather baffled that anyone wants to read what I write – especially considering the weirdness levels. Whatever you thought of Cross My Heart, don't forget to leave a review – I'll read every one! And don't forget to sign up to my newsletter here: www.eepurl.com/dmvk0H

Thank you to Ernest for pushing me to think outside of the box and for challenging me not to settle. Thanks also for the names for the social enterprise. My favourite was Hakuna Matwatta. Thank you also for being patient with me, and for walking alongside me through the highs and lows of life. I love you.

Thank you to my girls. You both inspire me, and I'm so utterly blessed to be your mum.

Thank you Sylvia for reading as I wrote. Your initial encouragement inspired me to keep writing.

Thank you to Samuel, David, and MaryBeth for beta-reading.

Samuel: thank you for giving me new ways of looking at things and for challenging my thinking.

David: thank you for walking alongside me and continuously challenging me and championing me to know Jesus more – and thank you for reading my story over and over again!

MaryBeth: thank you for your honesty and kindness and for cooking for me and taking me under your wing all those years ago.

This story would not be what it is without all of your input.

Thank you to Mary for editing: thank you for being an inspiration to so many and for giving of yourself to champion young people to know Jesus more. Thank you for all the hours of editing and for continuously finding ways of encouraging me throughout the manuscript.

Thank you to Nicole for taking time to proofread the final draft for me. You're a joy to work with – as ever.

Thank you to Sister Cecilia and the other nuns at the Convent at Omberg. Thank you for praying for me and for letting me retreat at the convent.

Thank you to Youth With A Mission. You guys are amazing and I'm so thankful for the thirteen years I got to work with you all.

Thank you Jesus for showing me what love is.

Printed in Poland
by Amazon Fulfillment
Poland Sp. z o.o., Wrocław